DEADLY
INVESTMENT

Andres Kabel

DEADLY INVESTMENT

ISBN 978-0-6483068-1-8

CHAPTER 1

Guided by his lifelong mantra—data, analysis, conclusions—Peter Gentle began with the corpse.

It lay on a metal gurney, a sheet pulled back over the head. Stitching, jagged in parts, violated the torso. Peter swept black hair out of his eyes and leaned closer. The dead man's skin looked like pale concrete, and he repressed the urge to touch a knee, to check if it felt as cold as it appeared. The left shoulder was mottled as if bruised, but Peter couldn't be sure, and he glanced back at Mick Tusk standing near the door like a block of granite.

Come on, big guy, give me a hand here, Peter thought. This is your field, not mine.

But Mick's wraparound sunglasses never wavered. Peter momentarily cursed himself for bringing the hulk in as his partner.

How life could bewilder! Peter had only ever seen one other dead person, his grandfather, laid out in a suit with a carefully constructed smile on his face. Now here he stood, thirty-four years old, an unemployed actuary with a lifetime of solving theoretical financial problems, peering at the cadaver of a stranger. Accompanied by an ex-cop who pumped iron, espoused the virtues of tofu, and still listened to Led Zeppelin.

He suppressed a shudder. Mick had snuck them into the Victorian Institute of Forensic Medicine, and they stood in a pristine autopsy room with walls lined by stainless steel sinks and benches. Ever since the body had been wheeled in, Peter had gagged on a rank scent of compost bins and hospitals. Relentless fluorescent light eliminated all shadows.

"Enough of a sticky?" The orderly, a scrawny man with pitted skin, seemed to be enjoying himself.

Peter shook his head, flopping hair back into his eyes. "No, I need to see it all."

The orderly smirked, exposing yellow teeth. Peter sensed Mick moving forward to intervene, then the orderly whipped off the sheet with a flourish.

Peter reeled at the unholy face, pulverized flat by a force that had driven nose into flesh and exposed the left side of the face down to glistening bone. Sutures ran around the edge of the shaven skull. An empty eye socket hurled abuse, and the corpse's lips seemed to sneer. He tried to look away but bile rose up his throat. How the hell could anyone commit this… this atrocity? He clutched at the gurney, missed, and fell.

Rocklike arms caught him.

"Take it easy." Mick's voice held a note of gentleness.

Shaking, he looked up at Mick's broad face. He struggled upright. "Thanks."

The room was silent except for the distant clank of machinery. Peter stared at the travesty of a face for a moment longer, trying to catalogue the crime as if with a policeman's eyes.

The pounding in his chest wasn't simply horror, he knew; it was icy terror.

The orderly made to cover up the body but Mick stayed him with one silken movement.

"Wait," Mick said.

Peter watched Mick remove his sunglasses and train those steady blue eyes on the corpse. He saw no reaction at all in Mick's sculpted face. How could the big lug soak it up like that?

Mick nodded.

The orderly chuckled and tugged the sheet over the body. "Now we're even." He shuffled back through the double steel doors with the gurney.

"A mistake, arranging for you to view the body." Mick's deep voice purred. "Amateurs always find death a rude surprise."

Peter breathed heavily and wiped a sheen of sweat off his brow. "And how do you find death, big guy?"

"A corpse is just a corpse."

Peter surveyed his companion. His teenage memories, his only memories, of Mick Tusk were of a Slavic giant who attracted fights. Mick starred in the school football team, sat at the back of the class, and bewitched girls. In all respects the opposite to Peter, who never played sports, dominated the teachers, and found girls a problem. Mick didn't look much different now. Tall and broad-shouldered, with stubbly blonde hair, he matched Peter's image of a Russian bouncer.

"Very philosophical." Peter hurried through silent corridors out into the sunlight of an early autumn morning. "You know, some influential minds considered him a genius."

"Dead genius, dead moron, they're all dead," came the soft response behind him.

The Institute shared a sprawling, modernistic building with the Coroner's Court, on the southern edge of the Melbourne business district, nestled between the new glitz of Southbank and arterial feeders onto the freeways heading east and west. Peter smelled exhaust as he struggled to calm himself.

Across the street, Bishop paced by his Jaguar, barking into his mobile's lapel mic, looking cool despite the heavy pinstripe. With his dyed red hair and quick movements, he was like no lawyer Peter had ever met.

"You guys have fun?" Bishop's eyes, fierce and slightly almond-shaped, seemed to drill Peter.

He recalled the one-eyed face and his gorge rose. He felt as if he'd swum too far from shore and had no choice but to go on.

"Just another stiff," he said, dredging up slang from the Ed McBain he'd just read.

Mick's lips tightened. Bishop laughed, a shrill bark.

Through a gap in the apartments lining the street, Peter glimpsed the glistening black needles of the Rialto Towers. Just the tonic he needed. He jiggled his feet.

"Are you two in a union?" He grinned. "Come on, let's move it."

***

As befitted one of Melbourne's top legal firms, Calico & Leicester resided on the 50th to 52nd floors of the very same Rialto Towers, which rose skyward from Collins Street to dominate the western end of Melbourne's central business district. After alighting on the 50th floor, Bishop led them through a muted lobby lined with paintings, up wooden stairs to his corner office facing the bay. The room reeked of an aftershave Peter couldn't recognize. The lawyer slammed the door and hung his jacket on a wooden coat rack.

Peter had expected ostentation but the room felt ruthlessly functional. Floor-to-ceiling glass made up two of the walls, recessed in the corner like a reverse French window, and thin black venetian blinds had been lowered to ward off the morning sun. A bookcase jammed with neat files and books covered another wall. To Peter's astonishment, the remaining wall, a glass one looking out into the general workstation area, was covered in Dungeons & Dragons posters. A mahogany desk, bare except for a document precisely in the center and a large telephone console to one side, took up half the room. Behind it an exercise bike faced a computer console with one of those snazzy new flat screens Peter coveted. Fans whispered like faraway surf, and he could hear filing cabinets clattering outside.

Peter hunched down into a cushioned metal chair at the steel-legged glass table. His head buzzed.

Mick took a neighboring seat and removed his sunglasses. Peter almost sighed at him. Mick hadn't said a word in the Jaguar, and in his brown leather jacket, tee-shirt and jeans, back straight and eyes centered impassively on Bishop, the big man stood out as an interloper in the corporate world.

Bishop dragged the tall leather chair from his desk over to the table. He sat back, fingers locked over his black vest. Peter was accustomed to lawyers with plain faces and brand-name glasses. Bishop looked more like a graphic artist with his short frame, and his Eurasian face capped garishly by bright red curly hair. His narrow eyes studied Peter and a smile played on his full lips.

"Will you take the case?" Bishop's speech was an oddly alluring combination of a modulated British accent and the machine-gun delivery so typical of ambitious lawyers.

Peter drummed fingers on the tabletop. He'd already pondered Bishop's question. This venture was risky, well outside his training. But solving a crime seemed as much a matter of analytical intelligence, with which he was well endowed, as of experience. Mick's policing expertise should make the data collection easy. And there was no doubt Peter needed to earn some money. Fast.

He felt the familiar, breathless thrill of a difficult intellectual hunt.

"We'll take it," he said, jerking as Mick simultaneously snapped, "No."

Peter glared. Are you crazy, he wanted to shout, this is your ticket out of poverty.

Mick's still eyes met his for a long moment. Then Mick pursed his lips, scooped up his sunglasses, and walked over to stare out the window.

"The facts again, please, Mr. Bishop. For Mick." Peter surprised himself with a forceful voice. Questions were already whirring in his head, and he began to cross and uncross his legs compulsively.

"Kantor Keppel worked late in his office four nights ago," Bishop said. "The mainframe records show activity until 10:30 when he logged off. His body was found a couple of hours later in a stairwell by a security guard. The police say he died instantaneously—"

"There is no such thing as instantaneously," Peter said. "Everything takes some time."

He saw Mick shake his head.

Bishop ignored the interjection. "—they have no firm suspects, there were no clues left at the crime scene, and everyone seems keen to close this case."

"Except the widow," Peter said.

Bishop's eyes never left Peter's face. "Mrs. Keppel rings me hourly with mad accusations about the company, Keppel's colleagues, and the dog down the road. She's not in good mental shape, but she's rich and she's paying me to pay you."

Bishop seemed to come to a decision. He beamed at Peter and, quick as a terrier, leapt over to the desk and returned with the document.

"Sign here," the lawyer said.

"You're nuts," Mick said from the window, his voice close to a snarl. "Fucking nuts. We don't even have a private investigator's license."

"We'll get one."

The venetian blinds crackled as Mick rifled them. "This is murder, not some mathematical problem. You don't even know how far you're out of this league."

"Lucky I've got a homicide whiz like you," Peter said.

He signed without reading.

"Well done," Bishop said. He shook hands with them at the door. "Report daily, starting with this afternoon."

Outside, the aroma of cheap coffee set Peter's stomach rumbling. A secretary handed Bishop a thick manila folder, which he presented to Peter. "Copies of the case documents.

Don't ask how I obtained them."

"Why us, Mr. Bishop?" Peter said, breathing through his nose to quell ferocious glee. He refrained from looking at Mick. "Why pick us for this job?"

The lawyer's smile lit the corridor. "Kantor Keppel was the intellect behind Scientific Money. Geek-speak is the language there, and the police can't speak a word. Only an actuary can figure out what Scientific Money does, and you're the only actuary I know crazy enough to tackle something like this."

Mick turned from the elevator button. "Why the hell should the company have anything to do with it? Why not an angry mistress?"

"Believe me, Scientific Money has everything to do with this."

This is a game to him, Peter thought. "How do you know, Mr. Bishop?"

Bishop tapped his forehead. "You think I'd take on a murder case for a dipstick widow if I didn't know in my bones there's company shenanigans afoot? No, my egghead and beefcake, find the killer soon and you'll be richer, and I'll be richer and happier. Good luck."

In the packed elevator Peter and Mick stood side by side in silence, but when they burst through the revolving lobby doors into the street, Mick exploded.

"You lunatic!" he said. "How could you get us into this? You've no idea what you're doing. Absolutely clueless. Why do you think we'll do any better than the cops?"

Peter watched a tram rattle past.

"And with that bloody lawyer, too," Mick continued. "A

vulture, just like all of them."

Peter filled his lungs with air. Somehow the very atmosphere in Collins Street always smelled sweeter than anywhere else.

"Why, Gentle, why?" Mick said.

"Simple, big guy. It sounds fun to me, and if you don't earn a decent dollar soon you'll have to take Dana and the kids out begging. Stop whining and let's grab a cappuccino."

With hands in pockets, Peter headed up Collins Street, Mick grumbling behind him.

CHAPTER 2

"Can you fit us in, Hec?" Peter Gentle yelled over the hubbub that was Draconi's Bar & Grill.

Hector Fox raised his walrus face from conversation with a man wearing red stockbroker's suspenders. They both gawked at Mick, and Peter couldn't blame them. Standing with arms folded over his chest like a presidential bodyguard, the big man certainly didn't fit Draconi's typical customer profile.

Peter sighed. "Hec? Can we have one of the far booths? Pronto?"

"Let me see, Peter." Hector rushed off.

"For God's sake, big guy, off with the sunnies," Peter said.

Mick complied. His eyes were fierce from his street outburst. "How come the waiter knows you?"

"He should." Peter inhaled the aromas of bacon and coffee, licked his lips. "I'm one of his best customers. I used to come here every day when I lived in town. It's a great place. And he's no waiter. Hec used to be a judge, and when he retired, he bought this place and did it up."

He followed Mick's gaze around the room. Wooden chairs

squeaked on pine floorboards. The gleaming wooden bench of the central bar was covered with elbows of businessmen sipping midmorning coffees. Staff wearing white aprons over crimson outfits scurried around dozens of round wooden tables. Around the perimeter, suits filled rows of cushioned booths. Large globes, hanging from the vaulted ceilings, cast a diffuse light, so that objects farther than twenty meters away seemed to fade.

"Isn't it just wonderful?" Peter closed his eyes to soak up the blanket of voices, punctuated by the click of coffee grinders and the sibilant purr of cutlery being washed by Miguel at the bar. "It's open seven days a week, breakfast, lunch, and dinner. Hec lives up above."

"Not my style."

"What is your style? McCafe?"

Peter experienced a surge of memory as he spotted the crinkling in the corners of Mick's eyes that he recognized as amusement.

"Get stuffed," Mick said. "Actually, McDonald's is the go for us now. Where else for a three-year-old and a five-year-old? This place is too bloody wanky. I prefer pubs. Used to, anyway."

Hector materialized.

"This way, Peter m'boy," he said, steering Peter by the elbow.

Peter grinned at Harvey Jopling reading a newspaper at the bar. Harvey saw Mick and widened his eyes.

"Actually," Peter said, "we run a club here, called the Skulk Club. That's Harvey, he's the founder."

They slid into a booth with high-cushioned backs and Mick slapped the file on the rough wooden tabletop. Deeper in the cavernous restaurant the noise level didn't diminish, but individual sounds were more muffled.

"Bacon and eggs, Hec," Peter said, "and a short black."

All traces of nausea from the morgue had finally left him. He drummed trembling fingers against his legs, marveled at his own excitability. A mobile trilled in the next booth.

Hector cocked an eyebrow at Mick.

"Plain omelet, please," the deep voice growled. "Any herbal tea?"

Hector laughed, his jowls shaking. "That's a first. No, far too healthy for the Young Turks we get here."

"Decaf latte then."

Peter watched Hector rush off. He slumped back against the wall, lifted a leg up on the seat, and scrutinized his soon-to-be partner through narrowed eyes.

"Let's have it then," Peter said. "Clear the air."

He was beginning to recognize changes in Mick from the fifteen-year-old he'd known. Mick sat erect but relaxed, his body at ease with the surroundings, yet somehow poised for action. No doubt the years on the police force had bred that physical preparedness. The blue eyes were impassive, more guarded than Peter recalled. At school, twenty years ago, the football star had erupted at any provocation. As an adult, everything seemed under rigid control, but did that old temper simmer like slow-cooking soup?

Mick thrust his chin forward. "This whole thing is a crock of shit."

He raised thick fingers one by one.

"One: we don't have a private investigator's license and it'll take twelve months to get one, a full license. Two: you've no bloody experience at this. Three: I know you won't believe me, but this work can get dangerous. Four: the police won't help us at all, in fact they'll consider us bloody nuisances. And five…"

Watching Mick take a chest-expanding breath, Peter felt a rush of pleasure. Jesus, he thought, this will be fun.

Only serendipity could have brought them together again, and the gods, conspicuously absent from Peter's life for so long, had been smiling a week ago. Shopping at Chadstone, he'd been startled when a hard hand landed on his shoulder. He'd recognized Mick immediately. Mick had been almost desperately friendly, and over a beer Peter found out why. After a decade in the police force, Mick now drove cabs to support a young family.

"And five," Mick repeated, "I've been trying to keep away from cop-related work."

Peter winced as his fingers caught on a knot in his hair. "Why?"

Mick removed his jacket, revealing forearms knotted with muscles, and leaned his chin on his hands.

"I didn't leave the force." Mick's voice was almost a whisper. "They discharged me."

"You were laid off?"

"The bastards labeled me unfit. For psychological reasons. They called me too violent."

It was the wrong thing to do, but Peter laughed. "You? Too violent? Jesus, Mick, all I remember from school was that you were violent every other day."

Mick's broad shoulders relaxed. "You're right, I was a handful then. But that was just a phase—"

"A phase? I remember three years of it." Peter whooped with

laughter. Heads turned toward them.

"Yeah well, in fact that phase lasted a few more years." Miracle of miracles, Mick was grinning. "But I gave all that up when I joined the force."

"Then why the discharge?"

Callused fingers rubbed a cheek. "I became involved in some cases that obsessed me. And I solved them, but the methods were… well, I guess I did let the rough stuff get out of hand."

Peter didn't know what to say.

Mick gripped the edge of the table. "Get it? I'm trying to move away from that scene. And Dana wants that, too. A number of ex-cops have rung me and asked me to join their investigation or security ops. Told them all to shove it."

A waitress deposited coffee and food. Peter uncurled to lean over the mixture of rising aromas. He drummed fingers on the table in time with his racing pulse.

"Let me address your concerns." Did he sound too pompous? The Skulk Club members were forever ribbing him about his precise language. But for God's sake, he thought, English is meant to communicate, not obfuscate.

"One," he said, mimicking Mick's fingers, "as long as we apply for a license immediately, its absence shouldn't impede us. If asked, we just say a license is pending. Two: what you have to realize is that actuaries investigate situations, just like police detectives do. And I'm a quick study. So with your experience, why can't we make fantastic investigators?" His feet tapped on the floor. "Three: we won't do any of the dangerous stuff. As soon as we track down the murderer, we'll hand the matter over to the police. Four: I bet I can persuade the police that we'll be an asset to them if we all help each other."

Bacon crunched between Peter's teeth. "And five: we're not talking a permanent job here, just one short assignment."

"That's just words, Gentle," Mick said. "You've no idea of the bloody world we'd be entering. The world beyond… this." He waved a hand to encompass Draconi's.

"Maybe so. But listen, have you ever met anyone smarter than me?" Peter didn't wait for an answer, sensing the upper hand. "And you're the one who knows exactly what to do. Together we're bound to do a great job."

Outside, a siren wailed; inside, voices cascaded in a comfortable blur.

"Listen." Peter began to wave his hands around. "Think about the money. A hundred dollars a day just to do the job. And $80,000 if we succeed."

He pulled the contract out of his jacket pocket and pointed. "Look. Here. Don't you need that kind of money? Hey, your face says it all. Me, I need that money so badly, I'm going to do this with or without you."

"Yeah, but you're crazy."

Peter changed tack. "What about the body? Aren't you interested in bringing justice to the poor guy?"

"That's what the coppers are for."

"And if the police can't figure it out? Don't you want to give it a go?"

No response. Peter rocked his body tensely. "Okay then, just think of this as helping me out. Old school friends and all that."

"You were just as much a pain in the arse then."

One last go, Peter thought.

"Why not let's do it like this. Just give it one week and then we can both reassess. What do you say?"

"You haven't changed a bit," Mick said. "All bullshit and theory. Let me think about it over a piss."

The Herculean figure slipped from the booth. To ease his tension, Peter strolled outside to sip his coffee. The lane was as quiet as it would get. A Japanese tourist snapped shots of his polite wife. A couple of secretaries laughed over coffee in glasses. Frizzy clouds sat immobile in the blue sky.

Please, Peter thought. I need you, Mick.

***

A week earlier, sitting over potato chips and beer in the smoke-filled Matthew Flinders pub, Peter had explained to Mick that he considered fate to be distinctly unkind.

"I'm an actuary. Do you know what that is?"

"I've heard of it," Mick said.

"We're like mathematicians of insurance and investment. We work with demographics and probabilities and interest rates. It's a profession that only takes the best minds, like mine. We provide the intellectual glue that makes finance work. You know, it was voted the world's best profession last year."

"That so?" Muscles bulged through Mick's Nirvana T-shirt.

"Shut yer mouth, mole!"

Peter looked over at a huge red-faced man by the window. A beer gut hung over his belt and his arm tattoos were as wide as Peter's head. A woman shrank in front of him.

"I thought you wanted to be a mathematician," Mick said.

"You're right. And I went through university aiming for

that." Peter sipped his beer. "I always wanted to be famous. To have my name in a math history book, as a genius of the purest type. But then I found there were even brighter people around."

The man by the window kept spitting words at the woman. She had thin arms. Peter grimaced; even a hint of violence made him queasy. Mick didn't seem to notice.

"Anyway," Peter said, "I did the right thing and went into the corporate world. I've done all right. People say I'm the smartest actuary in Melbourne."

A minuscule smile softened Mick's face. "Now I remember. The modest one at school."

"Hey, I'm just repeating what others have said."

A man belched at the neighboring table.

"So what went wrong?" Mick said.

"I worked for Rock Mutual for five years and then was doing really well at a consulting firm. All my clients said I was invaluable. But the firm was merged, acquired really, and they moved most of the work to Sydney. I was laid off. I don't know about the police, but the private sector gives good severance packages, so the money was okay. The trouble is, most of the actuarial jobs are now in Sydney. I worked there last year on contract, but it's just not my kind of city. I've been working on and off, various projects, but I can't seem to get that permanent position. Did I tell you that I've started studying biotechnology to keep my mind occupied?"

He looked up for sympathy but Mick had gone. Peter saw he had somehow negotiated the tables full of people and now leaned over the couple by the window. Mick must have said something, for the man let go of the woman and reared upward, but a flat hand effortlessly held him down. Mick leaned down to whisper. The man slumped back.

"What did you say to him?" Peter asked when Mick returned.

"I don't like abusers." Nothing had altered in Mick's visage. "I told him I'd shove his face through the window. Only more forcefully."

Peter felt weak in his legs.

They shook hands and exchanged phone numbers, but Peter never expected to see Mick again. After all, they'd only been friends for a year, and twenty years ago at that.

Then the weird and wonderful call from Bishop yesterday afternoon, on a Tuesday going nowhere, had sent Peter's mind whirling.

"You attracted to money and a puzzle?" the lawyer had thrown at him. Peter had only ever met Bishop in crowded business meetings, so at first he was bewildered. Out of the mess of his thoughts, one idea had surfaced like a spuming whale. He had to have Mick Tusk by his side.

***

Back inside Draconi's, Mick's solemn face filled Peter with momentary dread.

"Okay," Mick said. "I'll give it three days. Just to get you going."

"Three days! Are you crazy or do you just act it? You know that's ridiculous."

Hector held a finger to his lips as he weaved past. Damn, Peter thought, must have got excited again.

"And what's more," Peter said, "none of this 'just to get you going' crap. While you're in, you're in. Come on, Mick, a week won't kill you."

A long pause.

"Fuck it," Mick said through clenched teeth. "Five days."

The first rule of negotiation is finding a win-win solution. "Five days, okay. But that's five days full on, twenty-four hours if necessary. Right?"

A single nod.

Peter pumped an arm into the air.

"Yes!" he yelled. "Now try stopping us."

A hush fell over the nearby tables and he saw Hector gaping.

Mick astounded him by clasping his raised hand with a brick-hard grip. Peter had to blink at the sudden surge behind his eyes.

"Let's hit it, big guy," he said. "Tusk and Gentle. Has a good ring to it, eh?"

Around them Draconi's settled back into its normal clamor.

Peter sat down and slapped the tabletop. "Step one. Data gathering."

Mick flicked through the pile of photocopied material. "This is the entire case file. How the hell did that freaky lawyer get hold of this?"

"Never mind how. Let's zip through it. It's 9:30 now. Why don't we work flat out until 10:30 and then reward ourselves with another coffee?"

"What? Your tenth?"

"Some of us have brains to stimulate."

"You wish." Mick handed over a neat pile of pages. "I'll take the crime scene and autopsy reports. You start with the interviews."

Peter swung his feet onto the seat, leaned against the wall, and began to read. As always when he concentrated, the world around him faded, the glorious tumult of Draconi's dimming into a blurred backdrop. He read leaning back, he read hunched over, he read reclining. He read sitting on the table, he read standing. He found a chewed ballpoint pen in his jacket, and twirled and tossed and munched it.

How interesting! He'd never worked through interviews before, but quickly got the hang of it, cutting to the meat of each one, decoding the moods of the interviewees and interviewers.

Scientific Money had only been in its new headquarters for three years. Peter knew it well, everyone in the city did; a gleaming squat edifice dominating the skyline across the river in Southbank, its red-and-gold logo encapsulating perfectly the company's fairytale success. And the building's security system suited a murder investigation. All staff were issued passes that had to be scanned for entry or exit, and every use of a pass was recorded on the computer system.

With his feet tapping on the floor like a tattoo artist's needle, Peter mentally summarized. At the assessed time of the murder, 10:30 on the night of Friday, April 30, 1999, only four other people remained in the building. An examination of the computer activity log ruled out two junior staff on the first floor. Of the other two, Marcia Brindle, the company's accountant, left around 11:30. Her computer log was silent during the critical period. She claimed to be working on accounts the whole time. Benedict Dancer, another exec, logged out of the front exit around the time of the murder, and claimed to have seen nothing.

But that wasn't the end of the story. The building had one

emergency exit in the basement, for genuine emergencies. And the security system records showed that on the night of the murder, one unidentified person used this exit at 10:37 PM.

Even more intriguing, the security system's software allowed for "invisible" security passes to be created. Such an invisible pass enabled the user to enter and exit without leaving a computer record. In interview, Scientific Money's founder and Kantor's brother, Rollo Keppel, stated that the company's owners, the Keppels, were in and out of the building so often that monitoring their movements would clog up the more important records of staff. Only three invisible passes had been created. Rollo himself had one, as did his wife Bella, and Kantor's invisible pass had been found next to his body.

Rollo Keppel claimed to have left the building at 8:30, a time confirmed by his staff. Bella stated that he arrived home at their Southbank apartment by 8:40. Both agreed that they stayed in the apartment until the police woke them at 3 AM. But they lived so close to the office, Peter mused, that either could have sneaked out in time to ambush Kantor.

Occasionally, Peter surfaced from deep reading, and idly took in the sounds of chairs scraping on floorboards, coin tips clattering on saucers, the tractor sound of coffee grinders. He watched Mick. The ex-cop sat perfectly still, bristly hair soft in the glow of Draconi's lights, working his way through the document page by page, writing in a spiral notebook. Of course he wouldn't have Peter's powers of concentration, but his progress seemed quick. The police training, no doubt.

Peter's interest quickened. A threatening email had been found on Kantor's computer. At least, the police presumed it to be threatening; its meaning was unclear:

To: KantorKeppel@scientificmoney.com.au
From: j2z3dfj666@postbox.com
The natural order is there for the good of all. If you transgress, the fury of the heavens will descend.
B

The police had determined that the sending mailbox address was a dummy one. The email did sound threatening to Peter. B for Benedict, perhaps?

He rubbed his eyes. The restaurant was packed. Their booth could seat four, maybe even six, so that in any other restaurant they'd have been asked to make room, but Hector treated Peter and the other members of the Skulk Club like family.

Peter had entered the phone number of Imogen Keppel, the widow, into his Palm Pilot.

"Hello?" A polite, firm voice.

"Mrs. Keppel? This is Peter Gentle. Mr. Bishop will have told you about me."

"Yes indeed. Young man, we need to meet. Would noon be suitable?"

Peter glanced at his watch and gulped. An hour and a half. How could he survive without lunch?

Intimidating, he thought, as he took down the address.

Peter grinned at Mick. What was so difficult about detective work? The facts seemed clear enough. Some more digging, apply decent analysis, and the solution would be obvious. Why didn't the police force employ intelligent people?

CHAPTER 3

What took hold of Mick Tusk, after he succumbed to Gentle's high-pitched appeals, felt so strange that it took some time to recognize. Sure, he knew part of it was sheer pleasure. The pleasure of working through case documents once more. The joy of unfurling his half-filled spiral-bound notebook. The ritual of inscribing notes in his spidery handwriting. The sweet feel of exercising rusty case skills. But beyond all that, something else gripped Tusk. His heart beat faster. His hands felt light. The surging drive of Nirvana's "Smells Like Teen Spirit" filled his inner ear.

Regularly, he checked out his new so-called partner. Peter Gentle had been a mad bugger in school, all that time ago, before the fucking troubles. A crazy dervish of a nerd. As far as Tusk could make out, the only change since then was the stubble under Gentle's chin. Still the crazy rocking and irritating tapping of feet. The hands that never stayed still. And the posture! Half the time Gentle hunched so far down in his seat, only his wild black hair was visible.

Still handsome, almost beautiful, with that long bony face, a hint of buck teeth behind those full lips, the lidded green eyes. Even that bloody hair, down to his shoulders, made him look like a rock star. Pity he was so thin and slouchy, so excitable and shy looking. More like a rock star wasted on drugs, Tusk mused. And one other change—a small paunch, a slacker's paunch.

A man-child, that's what Gentle was. On a crusade to become a private eye.

Tusk checked his watch. 10:36—time to compare notes.

The owner of the yuppie restaurant appeared out of the gloom. Creased face, eyes certainly sharp enough for an ex-judge. Gentle ordered coffees, took command as Tusk expected.

The nerd hadn't bothered to take notes, as expected, so Tusk scribbled as he listened to the breathless delivery.

"Okay. Scientific Money was founded five years ago in 1994. I remember it well, the press gave it a big bang write-up. The two founders, Rollo and Kantor Keppel, had huge reputations coming into this new venture. Rollo Keppel was one of Australia's most respected investment bankers, and had only recently resigned as top dog in Coombs Holcomb. The stiff, Kantor that is—" Tusk raised an eyebrow at the term, saw Gentle catch the expression and smile with adolescent glee "—was one of our most respected economists until he joined the funds management industry eleven years ago. Then he came up with this bright idea, to form Australia's first quant fund."

"What's a quant fund?" Tusk asked above the never-ending din of the restaurant. "Sounds like something from physics."

"It's short for quantitative. In nearly all funds management companies, your money is managed by people, who decide which stocks to buy or sell. In a quant fund, it all works by formula. A quant fund claims that its science is better than the judgment of mere mortals, with all their foibles and flaws."

"So it's like giving your money to a computer?"

"Right. And in fact you've hit upon what Scientific Money has done. Kantor developed a new economic theory, call it a formula if you like, that relies upon a very detailed analysis of the Australian economy and the companies operating in it. So Scientific Money has a huge array of computers linked together. They claim to have the biggest firepower used in funds management in the Southern Hemisphere."

By now, the table lay hidden under papers. On Tusk's side, neat piles and his notebook. On Gentle's side, a mass of papers, heaped and scattered, coffee cup rings all over them.

"Who'd give their money to a machine?" Tusk said.

"Good question." Gentle smiled, a teacher rewarding his student. "That's exactly what the financial world said when the Keppels did a big song and dance about their new fund in '94. The prevailing view was that Scientific Money would sink without a trace."

Their coffee arrived. Tasted superb, Tusk had to admit.

"But what the establishment didn't realize," Gentle said, "was that the investing public was ready for a new paradigm."

"Explain."

"Well, a paradigm is a new way of looking at things—"

"I know what a bloody paradigm is. I meant, keep a move on. We haven't got all day to prance around."

Gentle looked at him with exasperation.

"Okay, okay." Gentle tugged at his hair—why didn't he get it cut? "After the '87 sharemarket collapse, people were ready for new ideas. And research shows that most fund managers can do no better than just investing in an average group of shares. So the upshot is that Scientific Money's first fund, Quant Fund #1, quickly became a success. It now has over $5 billion invested in it, which is amazing. Rollo's one of the most feted men in the industry."

Gentle waved at a passing suit. Plenty of people seemed to know him here. A waiter cleared their cups. Tusk shook his head when Gentle ordered yet another coffee.

"And Kantor?" Tusk said.

"He's not... wasn't nearly as famous. He was the quiet bright guy behind the scenes, one of the brightest men in Australia."

Besides yourself you mean, Tusk thought. He flipped back through his notebook and took over the running.

"The crime scene's not all that helpful," he said. "Kantor Keppel was found at 12:30 AM by a security guard doing a routine inspection. The body was lying at the top of the stairwell leading down to the parking garage. A mess, blood everywhere. The security guard freaked, called the police. Estimated time of death 10:30 PM—"

"That lines up with the fact that he logged off his computer at 10:30," Gentle said, hands flying.

"Cause of death: a single blow with a heavy blunt object. Soot particles suggest a fireplace poker. Not found yet. From the body positioning, the police think the victim must have been at the top of the stairs, turned as his assailant opened the door behind him. They lifted fingerprints off the stair railing but they're all of people who'd be expected to use the stairs, so that's no help. No useful prints on the doorknobs or the body itself. No footprints. Oh, and Kantor's briefcase was taken. No trace of it yet."

Tusk blinked, momentarily pierced by memories of cases long gone. He listened intently to Gentle's summary—impressive, no notes yet minutely detailed—of the email and the security system with its implications.

"Anyone traced the email yet?" he asked.

"They've tried but without any luck. It's not hard, you know, to set up a chain of anonymous email addresses that just can't be unwound."

"Show me the case documentation on it." Tusk read the email, shook his head. "See this note in the margin? Random junk, it says, and they're right. It just doesn't have the tone of a threat to a big time exec."

Tusk tried to ignore the growing hubbub of the restaurant revving up for lunch. Why did he find it so noisy when he'd spent years standing in pubs that must surely have had as many decibels? I've become a suburban git, he thought. And why not? What's the city ever done but fuck me over?

"You know, it all seems pretty simple to me." Gentle sounded like a squeaky wheel in his excitement. "There are only four people who could have done it. Rollo or his wife Bella—what kind of a name is that anyway? Benedict Dancer, who I gather from his interview was pissed off at Kantor because of a salary dispute. And Marcia Brindle. All we have to do is figure out who had the motive, and we'll solve the case, bingo."

Christ! Tusk nearly shouted it. He felt fifteen again, spiked with irritation, not at the smart-arse intellectualizing itself—he realized he rather enjoyed the stimulation—but at the arrogance.

"What about the emergency exit?" Tusk said.

Dunce cap time, Gentle's smirk said. "None of the staff with normal passes could have used that exit, otherwise they'd have been registered as going in but not coming out. The police went through the security system records for all staff in the office that day and found an entry record and an exit record. I guess Rollo or Bella could have gone in using an invisible pass, and then left through the emergency exit, but to what point?"

"Maybe," Tusk said, "the perp wanted the police to think that it was just a vagrant squatting in the stairwell. Because that's exactly the position the police are taking at the moment, at least from my reading of the case file."

Gentle flushed.

Gotcha, Tusk thought. "I doubt it would be difficult to slip into the building with a crowd of staffers. I bet you or I could do it without any problems."

He had to give Gentle credit—recovery was instantaneous. "In that case, there are a couple more suspects the police have interviewed. Willy Keppel, the third brother, doesn't seem to have been a popular sibling. And a guy called Robert Friedman, who's been hounding Kantor for years. Do you give the hobo theory any credence?"

"It's possible. The taking of the briefcase supports it. But no." The pulped face loomed in Tusk's mind. "You saw the face. That was no random killing, even by a nutcase. In fact, I definitely get a sense of something not quite right from the case file. Sam Vinci, the guy in charge, is a hell of a cop, yet they haven't covered all the bases hard enough. Maybe the widow is right to hire some extra help."

And he'd noted his old friend Deirdre was on the case. Promoted to Senior Constable Lasker now. Maybe useful, maybe not.

Gentle leapt up. "Speaking of which, we need to dash."

Tusk's body felt relaxed and well oiled as he followed Gentle past the jam-packed bar.

"You don't pay here?" he asked.

"Jesus, forgot again. Never mind, Hec will keep a tab."

Outside the bright autumn light in gentrified Block Place made Tusk blink. Isolated yellow and red autumn leaves lay underfoot. Christ, he could remember sleeping in one of the doorways here, back in the days when this was just a shabby shortcut. Now glasses clinked as mineral-water businessmen sat under restaurant umbrellas crowding the paved laneway. A tanned businesswoman strode past.

Boy Wonder grinned inanely, as if he was a tour guide showing off the lane. He was slouched, one hand in pocket, the other clutching his mobile. Tusk tucked in his stomach, grabbed Gentle's mobile. He'd been dreading the call home, but found himself jaunty as he told Dana he'd be out all day. Reason unspecified.

"One thing," Gentle said when they reached Collins Street. "I'm going to look at the theory, the magic formula, behind Scientific Money. If Bishop's right, there may be a connection."

Tusk observed the scurrying people. Green-and-yellow trams. A beggar against a wall, head down. "Waste of time. Suspects are the key, not some bloody theory."

"You're completely wrong." Gentle tossed coins into the beggar's cup. "Let me tell you why. Firstly—"

"Shut up for a change," Tusk grunted. He watched Gentle's face fall, felt a surge of affection for him.

Time check—11:29. As Gentle scythed ahead with his loping stride toward the parking garage, Tusk finally recognized the odd sensation lodged inside him. An R.E.M. lyric did it: "Aluminum tastes like fear, aluminum pulls us near." For the first time in so long, he felt the reckless pulse of pursuit.

I'm excited, he thought.

Halle-fuckin'-lujah!

CHAPTER 4

"This place must be worth a couple of mil," Peter said.

Mick didn't respond. Peter watched him head along the high white stone fence blanketed by ivy. Willow branches hung over the top. Unlike the huge two-story mansion next door, the frontage of the Keppel residence wasn't wide.

In the car, Peter had thought of asking his partner how to conduct interviews. How did one approach a potential suspect? Hi, I'm a private investigator, I'd like to ask you some difficult questions? But it all sounded too basic. Instead they'd discussed the facts of the case and their tactics.

Peter's stomach grumbled. He shaded his eyes to look down Mathoura Road toward Toorak Road. He'd noticed a busy restaurant on the corner, Toorak socialites sitting outside in full battle dress, sipping wine. He wondered if he'd have time to stop off there after the meeting.

"Hey, genius," Mick called.

An alcove was set back in the fence to enable a car to be parked, and there Mick had found an imposing gate with an intercom.

Peter knew a bit about real estate—it was a frequent topic at Skulk Club meetings, some of the guys were near-professionals—and he'd learned that while Toorak had always been Melbourne's most prestigious suburb, there were really two Tooraks. To the north and east, wide leafy streets held the greatest concentration of property wealth outside America's Beverly Hills. Here in the southwest of the suburb, the standard was still high, but down a few notches. Garish new townhouses, squeezed onto smaller blocks, coexisted with old wealth in large houses. Off-street parking was at a premium, and BMWs and Mercedes Benzes lined Mathoura Road.

"Yes?" Peter recognized the client's imperious voice over the crackling intercom.

He attempted to tidy up his hair. Old-time actuarial consultants had told him they always remembered their first clients. Would he recall this moment in twenty years?

"Mrs. Keppel? It's Peter Gentle." Should he have mentioned Mick? He glanced at Mick to check whether he was offended, but the ex-cop stood stretching his arms like a bodybuilder.

"I've been waiting for you, Mr. Gentle. You're late."

The gate swung open.

"Yeah sure, Tusk & Gentle are late," Mick said. "At 12:06."

Inside, Peter stumbled on stone paving, his eyes struggling to adjust to the murky light. A small garden area had been transformed into a minor courtyard. A paved path curved to the house, lined by thickly planted trees on one side and red rose bushes on the other. A small fountain stood silent in the middle. He inhaled the sweet, earthy aroma of autumn leaves. A Siamese cat watched them for an instant, then slipped behind a half-hidden statue in the undergrowth. All sound from the outside world had cut out. Peter felt a chill on his neck.

He climbed wooden steps to a small creaky veranda decorated with iron lacework. Next to them a new bay window showed an easy chair with lush cushions. Yellow leaves on the floorboards rustled at their approach. The front door, clearly original and repainted a deep brown, with a grandiose brass knocker, stood ajar.

A polished gold sign beside the door read "The Island."

"Get it?" Peter whispered. "Great Keppel Island, the resort island on the Great Barrier Reef. That must have been Kantor's sense of humor."

He nearly gasped when they walked in. The long hallway had been completely renovated. He admired the gleaming pine floorboards, the vibrant paint, and the oil paintings caressed by recessed lights. Everything glowed. This is success, he thought.

"Do come this way," the widow said.

Peter grinned with relief as his client came forward. Imogen Keppel looked nothing like the Sunday school teacher he'd expected. If anything, she seemed younger than her fifty years, with curly auburn tresses streaked with minimal gray, and clear unwrinkled skin. She wore a severe black jacket and trousers over a white blouse. She must have been beautiful once, Peter thought. But the blue eyes that flicked from him to Mick in rotation were muddy and inflamed simultaneously, fired with—with what? Grief? It seemed more like anger. A tortoiseshell cat circled her cream shoes.

The hand she extended felt dry as newspaper.

He introduced Mick before they sat down in the room with

the bay window, a large living room with a high ceiling. A vase bursting with an extravagant flower arrangement stood on the floor, and his nose itched at the heady perfume. Huge old lounge chairs and a deep brown coffee table, under which a plump gray cat slept, contrasted with pristine walls lit by lights on tracks.

Lovely, Peter thought. But so impersonal.

"Please help yourself to coffee and cakes," Imogen said, moving to a lounge chair.

"You have a lovely home, Mrs. Keppel," Peter said, trying to sound like he knew how to start. "Have you been here long?"

The tortoiseshell cat rubbed against Imogen's legs, and another white cat entered and surveyed them, its tail waving. Peter's older sister Julia had once brought home a black stray cat, a fierce creature with half an ear missing. They christened it Sooty and Peter grew to like it. Other than that, he had little experience with cats. He found the Keppel cats vaguely disturbing.

"Thank you, Mr. Gentle," Imogen said. "My husband and I put so much time into the design here. We bought it in 1991, but only redesigned it a couple of years ago. We were so happy here."

Peter assuaged his hunger with a large vanilla slice. Pastry flakes drifted onto his suit.

"I am so glad that you have taken on this assignment," the widow said. "Mr. Bishop spoke so highly of your record and your skills, although I must confess he did not tell me that you would be so young."

Peter noticed Mick's face twitch. Bishop had clearly sold them on false premises. The sugar hit of the icing kicked in and Peter rubbed his thumbs together to stop himself leaping up to pace.

"We're older than we look, Mrs. Keppel," Peter said. "What can you tell us about your husband?"

Imogen twisted a pink handkerchief in her hands.

"My husband was a special man. He swept me off my feet when I was young. Are you aware we have been married thirty-two years?" She twisted her handkerchief harder. "He was a genius, Mr. Gentle, a genius. His company relied upon him absolutely. I just don't know what they're going to do without him. He revolutionized investment. He has awards from all over the world. He deserved a Nobel Prize. And the police are simpletons. I have never in my life seen such incompetence, never in my entire life."

Peter knew the raw history, from the case interviews and his own memory. Kantor had married Imogen in 1967, just before moving from Melbourne to the Australian National University in Canberra, to start his illustrious first career as an economics professor. In the mid '70s he was a visiting fellow at MIT in Boston, during which time there had been talk of a possible Nobel Prize. He returned to Melbourne in 1980 to take up a local academic post, and in 1987 moved to join his brother Rollo at the major investment bank, Coombs Holcomb. And what a second career!

Peter looked at Mick, so still he could have been carved into the lounge chair. Say something, big guy, he thought.

"Mrs. Keppel," Mick said on cue. "How many children do you have?"

"Only one. The light of my life." Imogen looked to the door. "Come in, dear."

The woman who stood in the doorway struck Peter as a

spectre, white on black. Her jet-black hair formed a shiny halo around a perfectly oval face, pale as hotel marble, and she was encased in black from neck to feet. She stood immobile, green saucer eyes focused somewhere above Peter's head. Purple lipstick glistened, a smudge trailing down her chin. She wore a black dress elaborate enough for a ballroom, highlighting large breasts. Her belly strained at the dress and the skin on her white arms hung slack. Silver crosses dangled from her ears. Black boots and black gloves with ties running up her arms completed the picture. How old is she, he wondered, eighteen or forty?

"Straw dear, do sit down," Imogen said.

Straw sat down next to her mother, shoulders slumped, a tiny second chin incongruously at odds with the smooth skin of the oval face. Her eyes never met Peter's, and he knew immediately that she wouldn't speak.

"Mrs. Keppel, do you know anyone who would wish to harm your husband?" Mick asked.

"Mr. Tusk, my husband was one of the most respected men in Australia, loved and admired by so many. All he sought was the best for his family, not just Straw and me, but all his wider family. And he often said his aim was to bring light to the lives of ordinary Australians."

Peter's feet began tapping silently on the carpet. He couldn't stop glancing at Straw. A botched statue, she sat unstirring. A hairless cat, skinny and freaky, jumped up on her lap and purred. She didn't touch it.

"But talent attracts envy and hatred." Imogen's voice lost its careful tone, taking on an accented harshness. "The police seem to think some random tramp snatched his life away. Did you see him, Mr. Gentle? Did you see what some animal did to him?"

Peter looked into Straw's movie screen eyes, willing her to comfort her mother, but she sat calmly. Surreal, he thought.

A shimmer of tears appeared in Imogen's eyes. "Someone who hated him killed my poor husband. Someone… I want you to find him. Talk to that crazy man, Friedman, always ringing my husband up at home. Talk to my husband's no-good brother, living a life of sin."

Her voice rasped, nearly hoarse. Peter felt pity as she picked up a cup of tea with trembling hands. Her eyes locked onto his, burning with intensity.

"Mr. Gentle, the world is a wicked place. Cast your net wide. Consider Scientific Money's competitors, I know what big companies will do to stop the new stars like my husband. And he argued with that neighbor of ours, what's his name, Straw dear?"

She didn't seem to expect an answer, never glanced sideways.

"And his work colleagues?" Mick asked.

"Yes, talk to them. They resented him."

"Who in particular, Mrs. Keppel?"

Imogen swallowed. She now refused to look at Mick. "Rollo will know their names. My memory is not as good as it used to be."

Odd, Peter thought, not knowing Kantor's colleagues.

"Mrs. Keppel." Mick's persistent voice sounded like an accusation. "How did Kantor relate to Rollo?"

"My husband adored his brother. He did so much for Rollo. If it hadn't been for his mind, where would Rollo be today?"

"Was Rollo resentful of Kantor's brilliance?"

"Never. Rollo is such a fine man. So considerate. His wife is a hussy."

Peter was stunned.

Mick inclined his head. "Did Kantor know Bella Keppel well?"

Imogen continued to stare at Peter. "No. We did not mix with her."

"Willy Keppel?" Mick asked.

"Vermin. A drug addict. If you could have heard what he said to Kantor…"

"Recently?"

"No, no." Imogen paused to sip tea through bloodless lips. "That was in Boston."

No wonder Bishop called her a dipstick, Peter thought, then regretted his callousness. Her husband was only a few days dead.

"Find the beast who did this, Mr. Gentle," Imogen spat. "Find him. And please ring me twice a day."

She rose abruptly. But Mick hadn't finished. Smoothly, he stood and somehow blocked her exit.

"Two requests, please, Mrs. Keppel," he said. "And then we'll get to work catching the perpetrator. Would you be able to ring Rollo and smooth the way for us to ask around in the company?"

"Certainly." Next to Mick, Imogen looked frail. The tortoiseshell cat arched against her. "When shall I tell him that you will visit?"

"Straight away," Mick said.

Really, thought Peter. Who's in charge here? But he smiled in admiration. Mick might look like the Terminator, but he sure could extract data.

"And can we look over Kantor's bedroom?" Mick asked.

Peter saw Imogen wince and wondered how Mick dared presume the murder victim had his own bedroom.

"Of course. It's the first on the left upstairs."

Imogen moved stiffly toward the door. She paused.

"And Mr. Gentle, please don't bother Straw. She's not well. She hasn't spoken in years, and lives a solitary life stuck in this house. This must be a great shock to her. I don't want her to revert."

She hurried out of the room. The cats had disappeared, but Peter could still smell them over the reek of flowers. Following Mick's broad back, he stole a final glance at Straw. Resting unnaturally still in that pristine face, Straw's eyes had turned toward the dappled light in the window. Peter resisted shaking his head.

Jesus, he thought. How did Kantor put up with this?

CHAPTER 5

Tusk loved music. Real music. Rock music. Always had cherished it, always would. Hearing a new song on the car radio, he'd pull over and listen, searching for the song's heart. Hoping for another "Boys Light Up" to share his life with.

Although he didn't have the mental capacity of Gentle, he possessed a deep memory. He remembered important events with a level of recall that could frighten. So when he met up again with the slouched nerd, naturally Tusk asked about music.

They'd found a couple of spare seats in the Matthew Flinders, one of his favorite pubs of yesteryear. The swirling smells of hops and cigarette smoke beckoned his abandoned addictions.

"Remember that song we'd sing together?" Tusk said. "'Brass in Pocket' by The Pretenders?"

"Sure." Gentle was in the middle of spouting his life story. A real middle-class tale of woe, though Tusk managed to feel sympathy for him. Being skewered could ravage a man.

"You kept up with rock music?"

"No, not really." Gentle sipped his beer like a glass of wine. "I'm more into jazz now. Oh, and I like those Lloyd Webber things."

Tusk couldn't stomach jazz or the sanitized rock pap of Andrew Lloyd Webber, but he hadn't been surprised. Most people he knew from his youth had drifted away from the raw music they grew up on. Lesson: maturity dulls.

Tusk recalled that moment as he headed for the stairs in the dead man's plush house. Time check—12:22. A glimpse of a kitchen with gleaming steel appliances, naturally enough with a servant bustling around. A living area with low-slung leather furniture, another bloody cat sprawled asleep on the carpet. A song even then lodged in his mind, the calculated distortion of Silverchair's "Anthem for the Year 2000."

At the foot of the carpeted stairs, Gentle grabbed his arm. "That was our client back there. You were pretty rough on her."

Down the other end of the hallway, the nutcase daughter stood watching them. Could she hear them?

"Look, mate," Tusk said, exercising patience. "She's an alkie."

"An alcoholic? How do you know?"

"Didn't you see the spiders' webs around her nose?"

Tusk almost felt sorry for Gentle. A certified genius, but at sea in the real world. Truth was, the physical evidence of alcoholism had been muted. But one drunk, even an ex-drunk, can always spot another. Perhaps that was why Imogen had talked at Gentle the whole time.

"Jesus, that's good." Gentle's eyes were bright. "And what about the single bedroom?"

Tusk headed up the stairs. "Bit of a gamble. But I bet those two hadn't slept together for years."

He stopped at the curve of the stairs under a large studio photograph. A happy Toorak family: Kantor Keppel the patriarch, Imogen beaming from a two-scotch breakfast, Straw vacant in black.

Here's what you looked like alive, Tusk thought.

He could see where Straw's face came from. Kantor's was smoothly oval, topped by gray hair swept back. Round-framed academic glasses, bright brown eyes exuding energy. Short, a stoop in his shoulders. Goatee beard. New tweed suit.

He flashed on Kantor's corpse in the morgue. Christ—another snapshot in his personal gallery of murder victims, lined up with all the other poor bastards. A beast, his widow had called the killer. Beast, I'm on your trail, Tusk promised, eyes on the photo. His skin prickled across the shoulders.

"Looks like a nice guy," Gentle said.

"Don't they all in Toorak."

Four rooms fanned off the landing at the top of the stairs, Tusk guessed three bedrooms and a guest room. Next to Kantor's room the door was shut, Imogen drinking perhaps. A black-and-yellow cat slunk through Straw's double doors at the end.

Kantor had kept his bedroom in good nick. Cream walls, large windows looking out to a swimming pool behind a fence. Bouncy pile carpet. The stale dusty smell that always moved in when someone died. The autumn light cast the room in a pale gloom, so he switched on the lights, which must have cost a fortune: a central chandelier, recessed lights above the walls. Tusk moved around taking notes, thankful that Gentle had stopped in the center, rocking from one foot to the other.

The bed looked new. Surprisingly, no books on the sideboards. A couple of prints on the wall, bland, as if chosen by an interior designer. A half-empty bookshelf, mostly old novels. Next to it a large photograph, an earlier version of the one in the stairway.

"Wow, look at her," Gentle said.

Better days for sure. Straw looked luminous, her face firm and porcelain, the green eyes staring right at the camera. She wore a short yellow skirt that showcased slim legs. She took center stage, arms linked with her parents. Imogen's cheeks were rosy and Kantor's hair had only flecks of gray.

"Straw sure was a good looker then," Tusk mused. "Must have been ten years ago."

"She's still good looking."

"You're joking. Gone to ruin."

"Straw's clothes," Gentle said. "They remind me of something."

"Goth rock. From the '70s, although it's being revived now. You can tell from that garish lipstick, can't recall the brand name. Remember The Mission? Sisters of Mercy?"

"Who?"

A lost cause, Tusk thought.

An exercise bike faced a small television. When Tusk climbed on, the wheels turned with difficulty, nearly rusted up.

Christ, working again feels fantastic, he thought. Body light, mind clear, senses alert. If only I could bottle it.

"Big guy, come over here," Gentle said.

A medium-sized desk strewn with papers: household bills, bank statements, junk mail. Gentle was peering at a small faded photograph in a cardboard frame. Tucked behind a digital clock, as if to conceal it from casual eyes.

Kantor and family at the seaside, foaming water and striped beach umbrellas behind them. Kantor beamed, a smile that traveled the years. His body thin and wiry, wet hair standing up. A different Imogen held his hand, a laughing young woman with curly auburn hair, milky skin, and glowing cheeks. A striking, moon-faced girl with long black hair and green eyes. Straw.

"Who's he?" Gentle said.

Holding pride of place in the middle posed a boy, no more than six or seven years old, clutching a bucket. His brown body covered with sand. The Keppel oval face and flashing white teeth. Tusk eased the photo out of the holder. Scrawled on the back an annotation: "Portsea 1980." He slipped it into his jacket pocket.

"What are you doing? That's theirs!" Gentle whispered, his lidded eyes shocked.

"Evidence," Tusk said. "Any mention in the case file of a son?"

"Nope."

"Nothing much here, is there? His office will reveal more of the man."

"How do you know?"

"Experience, Gentle, experience." Ah, the pleasure of winding the guy up. "Let's go and collar the hot-shot brother."

"I suggest I handle Rollo," Gentle said as they left the room. "We're in the same industry."

Tusk grunted. "Maybe. But you'd need to do a better job than you did with the missus."

He glanced back, hoping to catch annoyance, but it was all water off a duck's back. Gentle was scratching his balls.

Time check—12:55. Half a day gone, four and a half to go.

"Who on earth is that boy?" Gentle said.

CHAPTER 6

When Peter was fifteen years old at Mont Albert Grammar School, he was undisputedly the most intelligent of the top tier. So he reacted badly when the new boy, a brute who never said anything, sat down next to him in History class a couple of weeks into the year.

"Hey," Peter said. "That seat's taken."

The new boy had straw-colored hair, cheeks like a Russian ballet dancer, a wide chest, and meaty hands. "Hi, I'm Tusk."

Peter didn't need to introduce himself.

"Look, you don't get my point," he said. "Someone else sits there."

Mick leaned over, blue eyes mild as talcum powder. "You want me to fuckin' thump you?"

Peter was startled. Already the Baltic boy had ended up in three fights, winning them all.

"All I want is to sit up front in this class," Mick said. "I like History."

"I don't."

"That's bloody obvious." A snort. "Why doesn't a brain like you like History?"

Peter heard the scuffle of shoes as the rest of the class scrambled in. "History is just facts. You don't need to think."

Mick fell silent.

So, Peter thought, the thug can be bloodied by words.

They became friends. At school they rarely mixed except in History, but Peter invited Mick home to listen to his Blondie record; Mick brought along The Clash. Sometimes Peter would watch Mick's ruthless grace at sporting events.

Mick called Peter by his surname, as he did with everyone. In accordance with their adversarial rough humor, Peter hailed Mick as "Big Guy," or less frequently, by his first name.

Everything changed the following year. Mick found new friends and began warring with teachers. Soon he sat at the back in History classes. Like many school experiences, neither the unexpected flowering nor the fully expected withering of their brief friendship seemed out of the ordinary.

***

Peter knew he could be easily distracted. He often slipped up in daft ways, like leaving his fly undone or losing his briefcase on a tram, and he remembered his father saying to him, in full seriousness, "Peter, if you can't learn to put on two shoes from the same pair, how can you expect to get a job?" But the absentmindedness was part and parcel of his superior brain, and he regularly and deliberately slipped into a twilight of whirring thoughts.

So when Straw appeared beside him, during his reverie about Mick, to lay a light hand on his shoulder, he jumped.

"Jesus," Peter said. He could see Mick's ramrod back, already halfway down the stairs. "You frightened me."

Close up, he could see what Mick meant. The perfect pale skin of the earlier photo looked puffy in real life. He saw discolored pouches under Straw's eyes, and pores in the skin around her mouth. Her eyes had lost their stillness and darted in all directions—all directions, he realized, except into his eyes. A sheen covered her brow.

"Are you okay?" he asked. Alarm and pity commingled in his thoughts.

"Smart," Straw said.

"Wha—" Peter gaped. She talked! At one level he reacted viscerally, at another his mind raised possibilities. What if she knew something about Kantor's last days?

"Hang on," he said, and ran down the stairs to Mick standing in the hallway, arms folded.

"Wait for me outside," Peter hissed. "I think I'm onto something."

Without waiting for a response, he ran back up. As soon as he rounded the corner onto the landing, Straw grabbed him. The scent of strawberries, mixed with cigarette smoke and stale sweat, assailed his senses. Her eyes closed, she pulled his head down, and her lips seized his, sliding frantically, tongue stabbing.

Gasping, he wrenched away. Holy shit, her mother was just behind the door.

"No. Slow down." His whisper seemed to fill the landing.

Her breasts heaved, threatening to burst from her dress, and her hair shone with sweat. She opened her eyes and for the first time fixed those bruised, green marvels onto his. He gaped.

Then something furry snaked around his legs. He kicked it

away. A cat. No, two of them, slim black creatures entwining his legs. Another one, a plump white one, stared at him from the open door of Straw's room, its eyes a mirror image of Straw's. He felt sick.

This was madness. Peter stumbled back against the wall.

"Straw." His lips smarted.

"Magical Mister Mistoffelees," she intoned in a soft high-pitched voice. Her arms hung slack.

"What's that?"

"Smart."

Peter thought of a robot, if a robot could be programmed to sound like a schoolgirl.

"Find Macavity?"

Huh? Peter strained to make meaning of it all. He held up one hand to prevent her approaching, and with the other righted his suit. A lock of hair hung over his eyes and when he shoved it sideways, it stuck on his forehead.

Then it dawned. "Are you the Gumbie cat?"

T. S. Eliot, of course. She was quoting feline characters from Eliot's poetry on cats, she was crazy about cats. Peter's sister Julia had read Eliot to him when he was a tot, and he'd seen the musical. Mister Mistoffelees was the clever conjuring cat, Macavity the master criminal cat. He'd got it right, the Gumbie cat was the one who sat all day.

"Are these the Jellicles?" he said, pointing with a trembling finger at the circling cats, and a faint smile crossed her face.

"Smart."

"What can you tell me, Straw?"

He had to recover from the near-disaster. Or had Imogen

heard their gasps from behind the door, was she even now ringing Bishop to cancel the contract?

"Uncle Rollo." She picked up a black cat and held it purring across her arm flab. "Bad."

"What? That's not what your mother says."

"Bad." She lifted the cat to her face. Peter watched the green eyes fixed on him through cat fur. Nausea returned.

"Who killed your daddy?" he asked, thrilled at his own audacity. Would she flip, as Imogen had said?

She regarded him, stroking the cat.

"Come. Tomorrow morning. Eight." She jutted her lips at him in a warped parody of a harlot, and then turned. Peter heard her door click shut.

The landing pulsed silently. The cats had disappeared; how did they do that?

He breathed to steady himself, descended shakily. His footsteps echoed in the hallway. Nothing stirred.

The front courtyard brooded in shadow. Mick stood by the fountain, his stillness a hundred questions.

"Fuck me." A smile appeared on Mick's face like a desert sea after the big dry. "Who'd believe it, my mate from History class. How was it?"

"What do you mean?" Peter's cheeks flamed.

"We never used that technique in Homicide."

"Cut it out. Nothing happened."

"You often smear lipstick over your face?" Mick inclined his nose. "And phew, you smell of it."

"Look, she came onto me, but nothing happened."

"Yeah, yeah."

"Look, believe it or not, nothing happened."

Through the red leaves of a Japanese maple outside the bay window, Peter saw the tortoiseshell cat propped motionless behind the glass. The Island seemed like a world removed—part sanctuary, part haunted house. He soaked in the scent of trodden autumn leaves as he walked alongside the pruned low hedge. Although miffed at Mick's jibes, he couldn't help feeling a tiny bit triumphant. Who's a closet intellectual right now, he thought.

"She asked me to come tomorrow," Peter said.

"I bet she did."

"No, she implied something about Rollo. I'm sure I'm onto something."

"Your objectivity is not exactly a given here. But yeah, worth pursuing. People like Mister Rollo Keppel are always prime suspects."

"Why? You haven't even met him."

"Those guys at the top are always dirty. And couldn't you smell it in the case file?"

"I don't sniff files. I analyze and reason."

Mick's chest shook, his laugh an octave above his speaking voice. "Gentle, that's not all you do, that's for sure."

The wooden gate creaked when they emerged from The Island. Peter took out his handkerchief.

"Where did you say the lipstick is?"

***

"I really am sorry, but Mr. Keppel's busy."

Peter shifted from foot to foot, wilting under the woman's scowl. Considerably shorter than him, she looked impossibly dainty and severe at the same time, a green outfit snug on her slim frame. Large black-rimmed glasses highlighted her brown eyes. Mika Hashimoto, Personal Assistant to Chief Executive, her card said. Her musky perfume enveloped them.

"It's imperative that we speak with him." Mick's deep voice carried, and Peter smiled at his persistence. Peter had been prepared to let it go and try again later. He needed thinking time. Time to sift the data. Time to look for patterns.

He'd never been in Scientific Money House, let alone the semi-circular reception area on the top floor. The in-your-face style, all dark woods and gold trim and huge posters, reminded Peter of the offices he'd noticed in Hong Kong. Certainly the floor-standing Scientific Money logo, a red-and-gold affair that stretched from the patterned carpet to the ceiling, wasn't typical of Melbourne offices. A receptionist busied herself at a black glass-and-metal workstation. Peter smelled money; but then again, he often smelled money.

"I'm sure that's the case," Mika said. "But I repeat, he is in a meeting at the moment."

A door slammed back. A man plunged into the reception area, gesticulating. Peter immediately recognized Rollo's bald pate, oiled and fringed by gray stubble, though he was more portly than he seemed in the press. Deep blue eyes and a sweeping nose dominated that Keppel oval face.

"Shorty," Rollo said to the stooped Chinese man in uniform behind him, "when we get to the apartment, you'll need to bring the car around the front while I change."

"Mr. Keppel," Mick said.

Peter waited for Rollo to stop at the authority in Mick's voice, but Rollo's eyes never noticed the two of them. A ball of ferocious energy, he swept past and punched an elevator button.

"I'll need that letter first thing after lunch," Rollo barked at Mika, who had scurried to his side. "Fit in a meeting with Marcia. Cancel the ad agency. Book a flight—"

Peter panicked. "Um… Mr. Keppel, Kantor's widow asked us to talk to you." His voice sounded reedy next to Rollo's powerful tones.

But it worked. Rollo's eyes swung to his. Mika's mouth tightened.

"Did Imogen ring you?" Peter asked. He knew how these whirlwind executives worked. One had to puncture their bubble to gain their attention.

Rollo wore an expensive gray suit and the gold chain of a pocket watch hung from his vest. His eyes raked over them.

"Ah, yes." Rollo's voice was mellifluous and unaccented in the way of investment bankers. "You must be Messieurs Gentle and Turk."

Rollo locked eyes briefly with Mick to signify, Peter was sure, that the misstated name was deliberate. Mick gave no sign of having noticed.

Rollo waved them through the elevator door held open by the wrinkled Chinaman and took the central spot. Everyone, even Mika, instinctively drew away toward the sides. Peter quailed under the Chief Executive's scrutiny.

The last time Peter had physically seen Rollo Keppel had been at an industry luncheon, back when Peter had a job. Rollo had mesmerized the large audience, or at least had mesmerized Peter, with an eloquent speech on business principles and the power of commitment.

Rollo had proclaimed, "The funds management industry has all the technology it will ever need. What it needs more of is talent. Bright talent. Committed talent." And Peter had smacked fist in palm and breathed: yes!

"You must all aspire to leadership," Rollo boomed that day, and Peter had nodded.

Now Peter stood in the same elevator as Rollo Keppel, one of his heroes, helping him by tracking down his brother's killer. Although the man didn't seem to value the assistance.

"My sister-in-law is most remiss in pursuing this course of action." Rollo clasped his hands together, as poised as Mick, but instead of the wariness of a coiled animal, his stillness bespoke the patience of the powerful. "My brother is less than a week dead, and we've not only the police on our doorsteps, but now private detectives. It's most distressing for family and friends."

Peter was struck dumb. He appealed to Mick with his eyes, but the leviathan had reverted to stone, and Peter's face reddened as they descended in silence.

As soon as the elevator doors opened, Rollo sped across the marble foyer, acknowledging a waving security guard with a nod. When they emerged along Southbank, Peter barely had time to snatch a glance across the Yarra River at the office skyline challenging gray clouds before Rollo rushed along the front of the restaurants.

Rollo suddenly stopped in sight of the rippling river and Peter nearly stumbled. The dull roar of traffic behind the buildings competed with the chatter of tourists heading toward the casino. Businesspeople streamed across the river on the zigzag pedestrian footbridge. Peter loved this scene but all his energy was focused on Rollo.

Rollo faced them with hands on hips. With Mika frowning on his right, and the bowed Chinaman on his left, he looked like a surreal gang leader.

"You," Rollo said to Mick. "I don't approve of ex-policemen continuing their careers as gung-ho militia, and I won't have you trampling all over my company. Understand?"

Mick nodded. His mild eyes blinked.

Jesus, how does he know Mick's history? Peter thought. Rollo's eyes swiveled to lock onto him.

"But I feel obligated to help in easing Imogen's mind," Rollo said. "I fail to see how you can help the police, but if there's any improvement in the odds of catching my brother's killer, I'll support you. I'm partial to actuaries, Mr. Gentle. There are too few intellectuals in this industry. So you, and you alone, can have access to the company's senior executives."

Peter gulped.

"I expect any interviews to be cordial and professional," Rollo said, "and for your investigation to be concluded speedily. See Mika to arrange a pass and a schedule."

And he was gone, charging along the riverbank with Mika and Shorty in tow. Mick stood immobile. Hair flapping, Peter ran after the incongruous trio.

"Mr. Keppel?" His chest heaved. "May I see you this afternoon?"

Rollo stopped mid-stride and turned, eyes sparking. His lips tightened for an instant, then relaxed into a smile.

"Very well. I've a full schedule but will fit you in at 2:30 sharp in my office. Mika, look after it. Now I must go. Shorty, you'll need to drive like the wind."

Peter walked back through the milling crowd, legs unsteady. He found Mick staring over the railing across the water at the rusty green dome atop Flinders Street Station, the man so still that Peter found himself fearful of his partner's reaction to being excluded.

But Mick took a different tack. "He thinks he can manipulate you, Gentle. You'll need to be sharp. He's managed to push me out at the start. Smart."

The Melbourne skyline towered above them as they organised the afternoon's work. They would work apart, Mick taking his Peugeot, Peter retaining his mobile.

Seagulls cawed. Southbank pulsed, spilling out toward them at the water's edge. Peter had never felt so hungry. Suddenly weary, he drank in the vista of skyscrapers. There was no doubt—he loved this city, with its mix of ease and fieriness. Having lived and worked in Sydney, New York, London, and Hong Kong, no other city would do. And somewhere in his city stalked a monster, a genius killer. Only he, Peter Gentle, could track the murderer down.

With his partner, of course.

"You having fun so far?" Peter asked.

Mick's smile transformed his face for an instant. "Yeah, actually. This case has already gotten under my skin. Who the fuck killed him, eh?"

"I don't know." A whistle sounded and Peter watched a cruise boat pulling away from the riverbank. "But I reckon the answer isn't far away. Just a bit more data."

The passengers glanced up at Mick's sudden laugh. "Man, you haven't changed. So confident you can know it all. Well, we'll see. I hope you're right."

Peter did the leadership thing and raised a hand in the air. Their palms smacked together.

"Ciao," Peter said, and set off back toward Scientific Money House.

"See you," Mick said. "Say hi to your dad tonight."

"My father?" Peter yelled, but Mick was scything through the crowds.

How the hell did Mick know his father?

CHAPTER 7

Time check—2:30 on the dot. Time for interview number one.

"A beauty, isn't it?"

The speaker approaching Tusk looked like a dodgy salesman from tip to toe. Rumpled tan suit, a white shirt with frayed buttonholes. Wary black magpie eyes. Mousy brown hair. A flush suffusing his cheeks. A leer glued to his face, revealing stained teeth.

The man panted and one leg dragged slightly. He thumped the roof of the Toyota next to Tusk. "A 1994 model, from a deceased trust. As reliable as they come." A vaguely European accent. "You interested in such a model?"

Tusk wiped dust off the car roof, inhaled petrol fumes from the choked-up traffic throbbing on Sydney Road behind him. In the distance, over the row of car yards and car repair shops, loomed dark gray stone and coiled barbed wire. Coburg: the old migrant suburb bisected by Sydney Road heading north to become the Hume Highway, pathway to Sydney. And in this wing of Coburg, Pentridge Prison, once the collection point of all the criminal sludge of Melbourne. Here they buried the body of Ned Kelly the bushranger, and in modern times, parceled the scum into separate doom-ridden blocks. Occupying a huge area, the prison had been closed for two years, and now thousands of spectators toured its bloodstained corridors. No doubt Kennett—bloody Premier Jeff Kennett—would sell it off soon, like everything else in the state of Victoria.

"I'm not here to buy a car," Tusk said, delighting in seeing the man's smile fall off his face like stripped paint. "Mick Tusk, Private Investigator. Can I ask you a few questions?"

"Why should I answer?"

The man cocked an arm on a hip and glowered. A nasty piece of work—the prospect of pressuring him beckoned Tusk like a long lost pal.

Tusk breathed to expand his chest. "My partner and I have been engaged by Imogen Keppel. You're her brother Albert, right?"

"Why didn't you say so? Mr. Tuck, Albert Strasser at your service."

"Tusk."

"Tusk, yes." Strasser's handshake was all flourish.

Strasser led Tusk through cramped cars. The car yard was little more than a small parking lot, nestled between two repair shops, the office just a wooden shack raised a few feet off the ground. Inside, a reek of sweat, smoke, and stale onions. A small, piled-up desk, a bulging filing cabinet. Hardly room for the one extra chair, which groaned when Tusk sat down.

Strasser beamed and scratched what Tusk realized was transplanted hair. "So amazing that Imogen would hire a private detective."

Tusk pulled out his notebook and ran his eyes down the questions he'd prepared.

"Mr. Strasser, how old are you?"

"Fifty-two. I am the oldest child of our parents. Imogen was born two years after. There are no others."

"What can you tell me about your childhoods?"

"What do you want to know? It was an okay childhood, quite hard. Our parents migrated from Germany after the war. You imagine what it was like to be a German in Melbourne then. My father died when I was fourteen. I left home young, at fifteen. You had to in those days to earn a quid. No fancy education for me, that's for sure."

"Have you lived in Melbourne all your life?"

Strasser tapped a cigarette out of a packet and raised his eyebrows. When Tusk shook his head, he lit up, blowing smoke toward the small open window. Tusk curbed a sudden urge to reach over and grind the cigarette out. Maybe later.

"Yes. I've been a businessman all those years, mostly here in the north. Very successful, I can say."

"Were you and Imogen close?"

"Imogen and I were separate our early years. Both struggling in life. Then when she came back from America and they had that tragedy…"

The boy in the photograph! Tusk felt success surge through him. Christ, I love this work, he thought.

***

When he'd risen to stretch that morning, Tusk's first thought had been, Bugger him. Ring the bloody geek and tell him I've changed my mind. I don't check out bodies anymore.

His pulse buzzed. As he donned running shoes on the grass out back, Bully licked his face and slammed his rump against Tusk's legs.

Dawn in Belgrave: peach fuzz on the horizon bringing the silhouettes of eucalypts into relief.

They headed down to the gully, his body creaking at first as he ran slowly to raise a sweat. His nose flared for the sniff of lemon from the first stand of gums. Early morning exercise was his mantra, his ritual to refresh after troubled nights. Increasing speed, his muscles sang. Bully alternately bounded ahead to gain sniffing time, then sprinted to catch up, occasionally looking up at him with raw pleasure.

An hour later he sat on a towel in the family room to cool down. Bully panted by his feet, tongue lolling. Tusk unpeeled the plastic over *The Age* and checked the weather forecast: sunny periods, then a cool change with thunderstorms. A headline in the business section caught his eye. "Scientific Money Fund Wins Award Despite Death of Founder."

Christ, Tusk thought. Trust the Brainiac to take the highest profile case in town.

Uncertainty gripped him. Yes or no?

In the end curiosity won. Who killed Kantor Keppel?

***

Tusk asked Strasser, "You mean the son?"

"Yes, did Imogen tell you about Walter? A tragedy, drowning right before her eyes. After that, Imogen needed family and looked me up. We have been close since then, maybe for fifteen years."

"You knew her husband Kantor?"

"You bet." Strasser's face tightened into a scowl. "He was a no-good son-of-a-bitch, and I tell… I told Imogen every time I saw her."

"Why do you say that?"

"Hey, I know." Strasser waved his cigarette in the air. "Believe me, I know. When they came back from America in the early '80s, I was good enough to give Imogen a share in a business of mine. You know business is a lottery, Mr. Tuck? Some win, some lose. Well, this one went down for a while, had cash flow problems, but it could have got up over time. But that mongrel Kantor refused to contribute more capital."

Tusk had met a hundred Strassers on the job, small-time hustlers and rip-off merchants. Maybe the guy had taken advantage of Imogen after the mysterious Walter's death.

"He never talked to me again." Strasser's face was alive with indignation. "His own flesh and blood. Well, it was no skin off my nose, I can tell you. He was always stuck up, looking down on anybody outside the bloody Keppels."

"You know Rollo?"

"What do you think? He's a Keppel, never had time for me."

The indignity of it all sent Strasser silent. He drew on his cigarette and squinted at Tusk, as if trying to see behind the sunglasses. Tusk waited and his patience paid off.

"The world thinks the sun shines out of the Keppels' arses," Strasser said. "But me, I know the inside story. I bet Lord Keppel told you how much he loved his goddamn brother, eh?" The voice at high pitch, sweat over the lip. "Well believe me, Rollo wasn't always the loving brother of Kantor. Kantor was the clever one, and Rollo hated that. Not until he needed Kantor's brains, then it became all sweet and light."

"You suggesting Rollo killed his brother?" Tusk leaned forward and was rewarded by Strasser shrinking back. The room swam with cigarette haze.

"Not me. I am suggesting nothing."

Tusk changed tack. "What about Willy Keppel?"

"Ha!" Strasser thought this hilarious. "Have you met him yet? That's one bad man. Did you know he was on drugs? Did the high-and-mighty Keppel brothers help him? Like hell. Just like they treated me, they treat their own family like crap."

"Would Willy harm Kantor?"

"Would he? Who would not?" Strasser smacked the desk, setting it shivering. "Maybe I wanted to kill the mongrel, eh? Over the years, maybe I wanted to?"

"Did you, Mr. Strasser? Kill your brother-in-law?"

Strasser's face turned sullen. "No. I already told the police, I was at a party."

Tusk felt suffused with power. Five days, he thought. I've got five days and five days will solve it. My focus plus some of Gentle's brainpower. We'll bring down the perp.

"What can you tell me about Imogen's daughter?" he asked.

"Straw?" Strasser licked his lips. "As if my sister doesn't have enough to worry about. I always told her to put Straw in a home. It's not right to have her just sitting around all day, never saying anything. But Imogen, she has a heart of gold. She would never hear of it. Me, I don't know Straw well. She spent all her time with Kantor. I guess she's another Keppel really, even if she is loony."

"How often do you see Imogen?"

"Me? Maybe once a month. Sometimes I go to her house, sneaking in like a common thief because Kantor forbids me to come into his castle. Sometimes she comes to see me."

"When was the last time?"

"Not since April."

Tusk had everything he needed. The police file made it clear that Strasser's alibi was strong. He hadn't killed Kantor, though he was glad someone had. Tusk handed Strasser one of the makeshift business cards he'd written out.

"Thanks, Mr. Strasser. Most helpful. If anything else occurs to you, ring me."

Outside, he gulped fresh air. Gray clouds had built up. 3:01—how much easier without Gentle. He was on Sydney Road when he heard a shout.

"Mr. Tuck." Strasser wheezed as he lurched out of the car yard. "You asked if I thought of anything else…"

"Yeah?"

"That wife. The wife of Mr. High-and-Mighty. Take it from me, she's no angel. I hear she's a right whore."

Tusk flipped open his notebook. "What do you know?"

"Hey, nothing personal, though she's some hot stuff, if you know what I mean." Strasser winked. "But I hear things, and you can take it from me, that lady puts it about. For sure."

Heading up Sydney Road toward his parked Peugeot, Tusk glanced back. The brother of his client waved and scratched his fake hair. The black eyes shone with pleasure.

CHAPTER 8

"Take a look at the old center of Melbourne, Mr. Gentle."

From his top-floor office window, Rollo Keppel gestured in his familiar four-fingered style—everyone in the business world knew the story of the loss of his ring finger in Vietnam—across the river to the two humps of Melbourne's skyline, poised under darkening gray-purple clouds. Rollo's long nose and gleaming head made Peter think of a Roman emperor. Even his discovery of Rollo's plumpness, now that he could see Rollo without jacket and with unbuttoned vest, failed to diminish the image.

Peter sniffed for the scent of coffee, without success, and sighed. He'd managed a second-rate focaccia in the Southbank food mall, but there hadn't been enough time for a glass of wine or a hit of strong coffee at Draconi's. No doubt Mick had skipped lunch altogether, to plot his interview questions in that bloody notebook, a task that hadn't occurred to Peter until Mika had handed him a security pass in the Scientific Money House lobby.

"Collins Street, Bourke Street, that's where the companies that built up this great city were located," Rollo said. "There, see the Rialto, Mr. Gentle? All the big fund managers once kept offices there. I worked there for years and years."

Peter was a keen observer of offices. When he'd started out at Rock Mutual, he'd seen how the huge insurer allocated offices using a precise formula, one's rank determining not only size and position, but also the size of the desk, the type of chair, and even the painting on the wall. His next employer, Thompson White, saw itself as a modern consulting firm and eschewed such conservatism, but even there one could tell the seniority of the partners from the relative opulence of their offices.

And Rollo's office was definitely opulent. It was huge, occupying half of the top floor's north-facing wall. A heavy redwood table, almost a mini boardroom table, surrounded by oak paneling inlaid with velvet and hung with ornately framed paintings, had confronted Peter when he entered. This area opened out into a casual expanse with large settees around a smoked-glass coffee table. Reds and greens abounded, and an enormous television screen dominated the wall over a small fridge. Finally, at the end of the room, gleamed Rollo's work area, a polished metal desk surrounded by workstations.

Rollo continued to declaim. "The old school is now under threat. Nearly all of Melbourne's fund managers have moved their headquarters to Sydney. The big life insurers are just about all Sydney-based. Rock Mutual's the only major left here. Even our own State Premier has publicly conceded that Australia's financial capital is up north."

Peter couldn't keep his hands still. They flitted through his hair, across his cheeks, into his pockets. He'd never come this close to a business demigod before.

"You know," Rollo said. "When I decided to build my company's headquarters south of the river, Kantor said I was crazy. Now the very pulse of Melbourne beats in Southbank, and it all revolves around Scientific Money House."

Peter noted that Rollo referred to his company, not their company. It was clear who'd been the boss out of the two brothers. And why not? Rollo owned nearly all of its shares, while Kantor had held only ten percent.

The Chief Executive's handshake was vigorous. "Call me Rollo."

"I'm… I'm Peter."

"Well, Peter, if you've studied the great cities of the world, you know that what attracts capital and prosperity to a city is a combination of politicians and enlightened businessmen. Now that my brother's genius has generated such success, I feel a heavy weight on my shoulders. Remember that, Peter. It's not too extreme to say that Scientific Money is the key to the fate of Melbourne."

Rollo's speech finished, he directed Peter to a couch, and then sat so near that their knees almost touched. Close up, Peter saw hollows rimming Rollo's eyes, and creased skin around his mouth; the realization that Rollo was exhausted made Peter admire the man and his energy even more.

Jesus, Peter thought, how should I kick this off?

Rollo saved him the trouble. "Now to business. On the way out Mika will give you an interview schedule. I've an appointment at three o'clock, so you have fifteen minutes to quiz me. Go ahead."

Peter felt dazed at the power of Rollo's eyes, intimate and

piercing at the same time. He asked the first question he could think of. "What were your movements on the night of... of the 30th?"

Rollo chuckled. "Get right into it, why don't you? Well, I left the office at 8:30, earlier than usual, and walked home to our apartment. Bella cooked and we spent the evening together. I was tired, this has been a hectic time for me, so we retired early, just after eleven. The police woke us up at 3 AM."

Peter began to tap a foot on the carpet. "Did your secretary see you leave?"

"Personal Assistant. Why don't you ask her?"

Peter smelled coffee, and that musk perfume, and looked up to see Mika glide in, bearing a tray with two mugs and a plate of biscuits. She glared at him.

"Mika," Rollo said, "what time did you leave the office on the night of the murder?"

"6:30."

Rollo and Mika looked at each other for an instant, and Peter flushed. They're laughing at me, he thought. He heard the door latch shut as Mika left.

"Mr. Keppel, who wished Kantor harm?"

"That's what I've been pondering ever since, Peter. In the industry, he was universally respected and liked. Universally. Kantor just didn't make enemies."

Rollo had this way of sitting still and cocking his head to listen, as if the questions completely absorbed him, and Peter noted how soft and modulated Rollo's voice was, so different from his passionate oratorical style. Peter began to relax.

"Were you close as brothers?" he asked.

"Very. As children, not so close. I was five years older and we were very different in personality. He was the bright one, I was always the ambitious one. But ever since he got back from America in 1980, we've been as close as brothers get."

Peter decided the taste of the coffee didn't live up to its inviting aroma, but the chocolate biscuit was delicious. "Did your two families get together a lot?"

"Not often. Bella's very different from Imogen. But since we started Scientific Money, Kantor and I almost lived together in our office, first Queen Street, now here."

"In what way is Imogen different?"

"Don't put words in my mouth, Peter. What I meant is that Bella's very outgoing. Imogen… Imogen keeps to herself these days."

Peter had an idea. "Would that have anything to do with her son?"

Rollo smiled, as if in approval. "Did she tell you about Walter?"

"A little," Peter lied.

"Walter drowned down at Portsea. He was just seven or eight. It must have been twenty years ago. Ever since, Imogen has been slowly withdrawing." Rollo sighed. "But she's still family, and I'm a strong believer in families, Peter, which is why I've consented to this project of hers."

"What about Straw?"

Rollo narrowed his eyes. "What about her?"

"Do you see much of her?"

"Have you met her?"

"Today." Peter cringed inside at the memory of the smudged purple mouth, the breasts pressing against him.

"Straw hasn't talked to anyone since she failed to turn up at her wedding ten years ago. I remember the poor groom waiting at the altar—a beefy young man. I gave up trying to communicate with her years ago."

"What's wrong with her?" Peter asked.

"Who knows? Kantor had all the psychiatrists in. Before the wedding she just seemed a bit strange, but afterwards... It seems she's close to autistic in behavior, although I gather she copes with everyday life, stuck in their house, well enough."

"Did Kantor get on well with her?"

"He idolized her. Like he idolized Imogen." Rollo wiped a hand across his mouth, eyes wide. "He was a full-on family man. I couldn't put so much energy, for so little response, into a daughter like that. And... and what he did with me... so we could achieve..."

There was no doubt—Rollo's eyes glistened.

Peter glanced away. He snatched a chocolate biscuit, somehow the last one on the plate.

"That's why I can't imagine anyone doing... that." Rollo clasped his hands together, under control again. "You know about the emergency exit?"

"Yes."

"The police think maybe Kantor surprised a drug addict who sneaked in for a warm place to sleep, and panicked. It sounds crazy, but I can't help believing they're correct. Peter, no one, but no one, hated Kantor. He was a genius and, in his own way, a saint."

"Did Willy want him dead?"

Peter regretted his bluntness immediately, but Rollo simply looked at him quizzically.

"I'll assume you ask the questions you do out of ignorance, Peter."

"I'm sorry, I—"

"Willy chose a different path and we see little of each other. But to imply he'd assault one of his brothers… you just don't know the Keppels, young man."

Peter's cheeks flared at the rebuke.

Rollo stood up. "We're out of time, I'm afraid. Let's see Mika."

Dozens of questions suddenly spilled into Peter's mind.

"Just two more questions, please," he blurted as he rose.

"Make them snappy."

"Was Benedict Dancer upset at Kantor?"

Rollo shook his head. "Benedict wanted a salary increase, but the thought of him killing Kantor is ludicrous. When you meet him, you'll see. Last question."

"I had hoped to ask you more about Scientific Money."

Was it his imagination that Rollo flinched?

"It's all on the public record," the chief executive said. "Except for the detailed implementation of Kantor's model on our computers, and that's commercially sensitive. Anyway, I'm just a figurehead. Ask my management team. Now I really must ask you to leave."

Rollo took Peter's elbow and guided him through the long office.

What a debacle, Peter thought, where did my time go? "Who understands the workings of the model now that Kantor's gone?"

"No one needs to. Relax, Peter. The software does it automatically. Mika, look after Peter, will you?"

"Mr. Keppel. The email—"

The big door cruised shut with a click.

"Shit!" Peter hissed.

"Excuse me?" Mika's voice was full of the imperiousness Peter hated in a certain sort of secretary.

"Your coffee," he said. "It's over-brewed and tastes like shit."

Her smirk vanished.

CHAPTER 9

Time check—3:30. Bell-ringing time.

After a single chime, one of the double doors was flung open. Mick Tusk's immediate thought: Now there's a motive for murder. Followed by an erection.

"I'm on my way out."

The woman swung her handbag, clearly annoyed.

Tusk's second thought: Nine out of ten. She was tall, poised. Shoulder-length black hair, a petite olive face, glistening red lipstick. Green I-know-what-you're-thinking eyes. A long fur-lined black coat, open at the front to show skimpy black shorts. Long slim legs, black high-heeled boots. A light brown handbag dangling from a dainty hand.

His third thought: Why do I still do that, rank every woman I meet, like a twenty-year-old?

"Mick Tusk, Private Investigator." Tusk hoped she wouldn't catch the heat on his cheeks. "I wonder if I could take a few minutes of your time."

"Ah." Even her throaty voice carried allure. And danger. "Rollo rang to say someone might visit. Can it wait?"

"I'm sorry, ma'am. It'll only take a few minutes."

She appraised him. "If you have to."

He caught a glimpse of breasts held loosely in a black silk top as she swiveled.

A penthouse apartment in Southbank was bound to be swanky, but Tusk had to stifle a gasp. Expecting a hallway, he stared at a large open space of polished pine boards that could have held fifty people. On the wall, dozens of photos of the woman and Rollo and others. Steps down to a recessed area in front of floor-to-ceiling glass windows, with two mammoth groups of settees, one brown, one black. On his left, a stunning redwood dinner table on the edge of what looked like a large dance floor. On his right, a huge television in the wall, overlooking small couches and coffee tables. A wide fireplace—he recalled the police had checked the poker.

She poured herself a glass of wine from an already open bottle and began to pace. He could smell her perfume—Dune?—over the scent of fresh floor polish.

"We designed this place ourselves." Unlike Rollo's, hers was pure Melbourne, broad and Australian. "Why live in the city if you can't entertain? The bedroom's back there, and on the other side is the kitchen."

So this is what the rich see from their living rooms, Tusk thought. Straight ahead, over the wide balcony, the lazy Yarra River curled into the distance. Swathes of green parkland, then the endless suburbs, finally out to the dusty blue Dandenong Ranges. On the left, above the Southbank bustle, the city skyline brooded under gray skies. To his right, a glimpse of the blue and green bay, dotted with yachts.

"Some view," he said.

No offer of a seat or even a drink. He didn't mind.

"You really a private dick?" she said. "Or just an out-of-work stuntman?" A tight smile to show she was joking.

"Mrs. Keppel—"

"It's Bella. And… Mick, right?"

Tusk took out his notebook. He could hear dishes clattering in the kitchen. Bella's boots clicked as she paced. Like a restless leopard, he decided. The well-developed calf muscles told him she worked out.

"What nationality is Bella?" he asked.

"Italian. But I hardly speak the lingo. You come here to survey ethnic background?"

"Is your family close to Kantor's?"

"Kantor himself, yes." No grief at all on Bella's pixie face. "He spent so much time with Rollo, I saw him often. I liked him, he was like a cuddly teddy bear. The police caught the murderer yet?"

It's all part of a game, Tusk thought. With that beauty, every encounter with a male has been this flirting, tough-arsed tussle. She was more similar to him than she knew.

Careful politeness would get him nowhere. "No, the bastard is still out there somewhere. Laughing. Did you really like Kantor?"

She paused her pacing, her eyes re-evaluating. "Hey, don't give me that look. You think I'm glad he was killed? Yeah, he was nice. You want me to break down and cry in front of you?"

"No," he said. "What about Kantor's family? See them often?"

Bella tossed back her drink. Tusk could see something

feverish in her round, bright eyes. The case file referred to loss of her license on reckless driving charges. Grog? Drugs?

"Never. Imogen has this thing about me, won't even talk to me. As if I care, she's a frigid bitch. And that nutcase Straw…" A derisive laugh. "Maybe Kantor killed himself to get away from them."

She was provoking him now.

"Bella, who hated Kantor?"

She yawned exaggeratedly. "No idea. Next?"

"No idea at all?"

"Look, I told you. He was like a cuddly bear. You know anybody who kills teddy bears?"

She was twenty years younger than Rollo, he knew, but looked younger than Tusk himself. He knew from the case file that they'd been married fifteen years. A song came to mind— "Honey Child," Bad Company's chugging ode to a seductress. Had Rollo ever had a day of peace?

"Willy Keppel," he said. "What can you tell me about him?"

He was watching, so he caught the minute stiffening of her posture.

"Willy turned his back on the family years ago. He's like the black sheep of the family. I don't know him and we don't have any contact with him."

"Not even Christmas cards?"

A snort. "Willy? Christmas cards?"

"Would Kantor have been in touch with him?"

"No idea. Next?"

"Did Kantor have any money problems?"

"As if I'd know. But does this look like money problems?"

She flung her arms wide, teeth flashing. "You know Rollo and I are building Melbourne's most expensive house? In Toorak. Mick, are we finished?"

His old police buddy Cap had a saying to cover every situation. Tusk pictured Cap flicking ash from a cigarette: "Whatever you do, leave your boner at home." Recalling Cap's advice didn't help. He was still hard, watching her toss back her hair, staring at her lipstick, smelling her perfume while she paced. Jesus, he thought, that's what her life's like. Every bloody male within sniffing distance…

"Nearly done," he said. "Tell me about the murder night."

She paced. "What's to say? Rollo came home just after 8:30. I know because I'd just started watching *The Drew Carey Show*. The cook fixed us dinner and we ate it in front of the TV. Rollo did some work while I read magazines. Then we went to bed, quite early, around eleven o'clock, and we fucked."

Her eyes probed Tusk's reaction to the language.

"So your cook can verify you were here all evening?" he asked without a pause.

The green eyes narrowed. "Look, we've been through all this with the police and they're bloody satisfied."

"I just need to be clear on the facts. The cook?"

"No," Bella conceded. "She left about seven o'clock. I microwaved the dinner."

"So no one saw you two all evening?"

She stopped to gaze distractedly out the window, chewing on a fingernail. Tusk registered that all her nails were gnawed down to the quick.

"Bella?" he prompted.

For the first time she looked at him with something other than amusement. The look, the twitchiness, the nails… I know you, he thought. Brittle, hardened, shallow as shit, but underneath—the void. The void Tusk had known and accepted as his lot until a decade ago.

"I've never heard so many dumb questions in my life," she said. "Time for you to piss off and waste someone else's day."

As a copper, Tusk would have hauled her down to the station to apply pressure. As a powerless private investigator, he had to call it quits. Stepping outside, he caught another odor over Bella's perfume. The experts said you couldn't smell it, but he'd always disagreed. The animal scent of fear. He took a step toward her.

"Rollo resented Kantor's brains, didn't he, Bella?" he said.

"You've got some nerve."

"I reckon they competed against each other."

Burning green eyes, twisted red mouth. "Piss off, you wrestling reject."

The crash of the door echoed in the lobby.

Time check—3:57. How clichéd life can be, he thought. The rich bitch in her penthouse.

Waiting for the elevator, Tusk leaned against the wall to stretch his calf muscles. Christ, he thought, how good it feels to be back on the job. Hope Boy Wonder is doing okay.

CHAPTER 10

"Come in, Mr. Gentle, come in. Sit yourself down."

A short, stocky man bounded out to crush Peter Gentle's hand. Benedict Dancer, Funds Manager by title, wore a black pinstripe. His tanned, rectangular face seemed permanently thrust forward. Neat, wavy brown hair, streaked with gray, receded along both sides of his head. Light-framed glasses accentuated shrewd brown eyes, which, combined with a high forehead scored with deep lines, gave Peter an impression of a face uncommonly large for his body.

Dancer's office was much smaller than Rollo's, but still impressive by Peter's standards. Peter took in the wall covered with tombstones, plastic-encased announcements of large deals collected by investment bankers as mementos. The two of them seated themselves around a small table, from where Peter could see the distant bay.

"Now." Dancer spoke with the transatlantic accent Peter associated with businessmen who had worked in several countries. "What can I tell you about Scientific Money?"

Peter mentally reviewed Dancer from the case file. A

decidedly impressive investment banking career—seven years at BT, seven working for Citibank in Melbourne, New York, London, and Sydney. Then Rollo enticed him to Coombs Holcomb, and he joined Scientific Money just before the launch. The interviewing policeman had scribbled "high roller" in the file. A bank account review had unearthed a mountain of debt.

"I'd like to hear about the daily investment cycle," Peter said. "What actually happens each day to result in a particular investment? And who are the key people who make it happen?"

Dancer unwrapped a stick of gum and thrust it into his mouth, in one precise movement. He hunched forward.

"You've come to the right person. That's my job, monitoring the Quant Fund investments, though in fact it's more properly explaining afterwards what the computer program did. Actually, five of the senior execs get together daily to check what the computers are investing in. Sorry, that's four, now that Kantor is unfortunately no longer with us." Peter noted an odd expression flit across Dancer's face as he mentioned Kantor, almost a smirk. "The four are Rollo, myself, Weiqing Chang our Research Manager, and Marcia Brindle our Chief Financial Officer. We call ourselves the Investment Committee, although we don't actually do any investing."

Dancer spoke rapidly, chomping on his chewing gum.

"What happens is this. The research people are constantly feeding economic, market, and company data from around Australia into the computer. The artificial intelligence built into the system determines how often the investment model is run, but typically it will be every half day or day. More frequently if some unexpected market news hits our desks. The program model then determines what sectors the portfolio should be weighted toward, and also which stocks to buy. The program issues a complete portfolio listing we should aim for, then we buy and sell shares to achieve the target portfolio as soon as possible. These days, some of the buying and selling can be done computer-to-computer, but most of it is implemented by our trading department."

Dancer stared pointedly at Peter's hands drumming on the table. Peter stilled them.

"So you can see why we need such massive computer firepower." Dancer smiled even as he chewed, a tight expression that suggested pain rather than warmth.

Peter grinned. At last, he thought, someone helpful. "Does the committee ever intervene to change the decisions made by the computer?"

"Of course not. That's the whole point of a quant fund. If we allow humans to intervene, even in exceptional circumstances, we introduce the possibility of human error."

Peter brushed back his hair and switched focus. "What were your movements on the night of the murder?"

The smile vanished. Dancer stopped chewing gum in mid-bite.

"Who are you?" His voice held a quaver.

Peter shifted in his seat. What the hell was going on? "Peter Gentle, Private Investigator."

Dancer reared, sending his chair flying backward to crack against his desk. Crimson surged on his cheeks.

"That bloody Mika. Well excuse me, buddy, I thought I was talking to an investment consultant. I'm well within my rights to ask you to leave."

Dancer's accent had turned American. He held the door open.

Peter leapt up. "Look, all I want is to ask a few questions."

He was startled to observe Dancer's hands shaking. "I'm sure you do."

"What's the problem with—"

"Out," Dancer said through clenched teeth.

Retreat, Peter thought, retreat and ask Rollo for help with this one. But how can I catch a killer if nobody talks to me?

"Did Kantor screw down your salary, Dancer?" he said, rocking on his feet, heart charging. "Did you two quarrel?"

Dancer lunged and grabbed Peter's jacket. Spittle sprayed Peter's face, and he smelled spearmint before being launched into the corridor. He gasped and staggered to stay upright.

"I had nothing to do with the murder," Dancer shouted. His face, shiny with sweat, was contorted into a rigid mask. "Stay away. I've got enough to worry about without some hippie private eye bugging me."

Something wet hit Peter on the cheek. He heard the door slam. A couple of men came out of their cubicles to stare. He straightened, felt the object catch inside his collar. He fished it out. Sodden chewing gum.

Hippie? What did he mean hippie? Peter smoothed the crumpled fabric of his jacket.

Shit! He hurled the gum at Dancer's silent door.

CHAPTER 11

"Did that Keppel bastard send you?"

Tusk stood on the muddy drive of the near-completed shell of an apartment block, surrounded by new condominiums and construction sites. Black storm clouds scudded across the sky. A billboard proclaimed that the Seascape Apartments would be luxurious Port Melbourne treasures close to the city and transport, only a stone's throw to the water, an investor's dream. The smaller print: Developer and Builder—Robert Friedman. In luck at 4:20—Friedman's secretary had suggested Tusk seek the developer on site.

Tusk raised his voice over the rasp of a concrete mixer. "No, my partner and I have been engaged by Kantor Keppel's widow."

"She's no friend of mine." Friedman took off his hard hat. He was a sturdy man with wavy, carrot-colored hair, straggly over his ears. Tidy orange mustache, a rugged face littered with freckles. Tufts of hair poking over the top of his short-sleeved shirt. Jeans and short brown boots caked with mud.

Friedman's slitted eyes peered over baggy pouches. "Let's see your license."

"Don't have one yet. This is my old police photo."

Friedman glanced up the drive at the men watching them. "I don't have to talk to you."

Tusk popped a knuckle. "Technically no, Friedman. But I want to catch Kantor's killer. I'll pursue every lead to hell and back. You want me on your back?"

Friedman shook his head. "Christ, no. You believe in justice, mate?"

So unexpected.

The question rattled among Tusk's memories. He stared at the scuffed city skyline.

***

Tusk had just finished dinner at Cap's rundown house in Frankston. It was the fourth time Cap had invited him over to celebrate an anniversary of donning the blue and white uniform.

Tusk worked on a chilled beer. "Cap? You ever get down, working in the Force?"

The grizzled face of Tusk's savior, mentor, and mate turned toward him.

"Sure. It's hard to keep the motivation up. What's bothering you?"

"It's the grind, Cap. The endless hours. The weekend shit. I mean, I like the hard work, but no one ever thanks you, you know what I mean?"

"You believe in justice, Mick?"

"I'm not sure. I don't think, 'justice, justice,' while I'm talking to some woman about her basher husband."

Cap's chair scraped on the uneven linoleum. He went to the fridge for another stubby.

"That's why I'm in this game, Mick. Not for the glory. Or 'cos we're saints. Christ knows it's not the money. No, someone has to work for those on the down and out. Someone needs to stand up for the victims of the con men. Someone needs to be there for the old lady raped in her home. And someone needs to speak for the poor bastard killed by some scum who thinks he can get away with it."

Tusk stared. Heart pounding. Almost a soapbox speech, and yet the older man clearly meant every word.

"You should know," Cap said, and as he spoke, Tusk clamped his jaw shut tight to stem tears. "You should know what it's like being the guy without a voice. The guy on the outer, kicked around by the whole world. Someone had to stand up for you, Mick. Now it's your time to stand up. And that's called justice."

Tusk listened to seagulls quarreling outside.

"You know, Mick?" Cap smiled. "I reckon you should join Homicide."

***

"Yeah," Tusk said dreamily. "I believe in justice."

The developer looked at him steadily, then nodded almost imperceptibly. "Come on then."

Friedman carried himself with a workman's gait, strong-legged and efficient. He walked past Tusk's parked Peugeot to a battered Range Rover. As Friedman drove down the pot-holed road, he switched on a tape of Queen's ancient classic, "Bohemian Rhapsody." Tusk approved.

One of the overt symbols of bloody Jeff Kennett's so-called new Melbourne was the transformation of Port Melbourne, on the mouth of the Yarra River. Once the semi-slum province of working-class dockers, Tusk saw from the rows of gray-and-white double-story townhouses that the property fat cats had nearly completed their invasion.

But Friedman seems okay for a developer, he thought.

Friedman drove to a deserted milk bar, where they sat at an outside table, on warped metal chairs that refused to rest flat. Friedman bought a Coke, Tusk a mineral water.

"He killed my brother Stan." Friedman wrapped both arms fiercely around his body. "Kantor fucking Keppel killed him. And now that the bastard's dead, I don't know whether to cheer or shoot myself. I've been trying to nail him for so long, I think I've gone a bit crazy."

"Tell me about Stan," Tusk said.

"What's there to say? He was a year older than me. We were close, real close for brothers. He was the bright one, went to university, became a real star. I was the moody one, always getting into trouble. And you know what? He always stood by me, helped me pick myself up."

This is a tale Friedman would tell anyone, Tusk thought.

"After he left uni, he joined one of those funds management firms, I can't remember its name. He was the economist. Stan did real well then. When he was thirty-four, he joined Coombs Holcomb, just to work with Kantor Keppel. I remember how excited he was to be able to work for the man."

"Was he married?"

"No. Too shy. You know, the way super-bright guys seem to be."

Sounds like Gentle, Tusk thought. A breeze stung his face.

Friedman seemed impervious to the cold. "I never saw Stan happier than in those days. They were good days for me too. I finally got my act together and started my own building business, and my kids were born around that time. Stan would come over to our house on weekends for dinner. He always talked nothing except work. Lived for his work, Stan did."

"Did you ever meet Kantor?"

"Not then. Hah! You reckon Keppel would mix with the likes of me?"

Friedman rubbed his forehead, lined as if someone had scored it with a knife.

"Then Stan and Keppel left to start up this new business. Stan was so bloody excited. He brought around a bottle of champagne one night to celebrate. Called it his chance for the big time."

A handful of seagulls ventured closer, hoping for tidbits.

"That was back in '92. And things went okay for a while, Stan seemed really happy. But in early '93 I noticed a big change. I think back now and wish I'd been more alert. You know how sometimes you feel something bad is happening, but it doesn't strike you properly."

Friedman sipped at his Coke, lost to the world.

"He was working on some theory. I never took much notice of his technical talk, what did I know? But Stan was slaving away all hours, hardly sleeping or eating. He called it the theory to end all theories, and he was obsessed by it."

"So he was helping Kantor on the theory for the new company?"

"Helping?" Friedman growled. "That's the story now, for sure. Keppel the bloody genius. I've got a file this thick with articles all saying the same thing. Well, they're lies. My brother was the one who came up with the theory. He was working for Keppel, but the ideas were his. I know, because Stan told me Keppel was reviewing his work. He said even Keppel found it daunting. That was his word—daunting."

"That's a serious allegation, Friedman," Tusk said. "But your brother was working for Kantor, so doesn't the intellectual property belong to the Keppels?"

"It's not a question of money," Friedman said. "The word is justice. But it's also important when you hear what happened next."

"Like?"

"As I said, in early '93 Stan became troubled. Lost weight and looked ill. And he clammed up, never said much when he came to our place for his weekend feed. Then on a Sunday in April, I managed to get him to down a couple of beers and he opened up a bit. Told me the work wasn't going so well. He said it was ninety percent done but the last part was too hard. That was my line, you see, I was the one who always said things were too hard. Stan never said that. Just put his head down and kept going. That's why I remember his words so clearly."

"What did you say?"

"What could I say? The usual encouraging stuff. That was the last time I saw him. A schoolgirl rowing down the Yarra spotted his body the following Saturday morning. The police couldn't figure out where he entered the water, but it must have been farther upstream. No one could find evidence of violence on his body, but I know he didn't just fall in. Couldn't swim, you see. The coroner put out a verdict of death by accidental drowning, but I know that Keppel pushed him."

"Why do you reckon that?"

Friedman's red eyes stared unseeing. "Who else could it have been?"

"What about suicide?"

"Stan? Come off it."

"Most families say that after a suicide."

Friedman sighed and shook his head.

"Did he have any enemies?" Tusk asked.

"Stan? None. He was just a quiet, intelligent man. No one stood to gain by his death except Keppel. He killed him to steal the credit for the work Stan had done. I spoke to Keppel about this and I could see the murder written all over his face."

Tusk rolled his shoulders. "So you've been pursuing Kantor ever since."

Friedman rubbed a hand across his chin. "So you've heard. I tried everything. I've been to the police so many times they know me like a regular crim. Hocked my house to pay for legal challenges to the rights of his work. Managed to get an article published in the *Herald Sun*. I even hired a private investigator, spent thousands of dollars finding out nothing much, except that Keppel didn't have an alibi the night Stan died. He killed Stan, I know it. I know it in here."

Friedman thumped his chest.

Tusk injected menace into his voice. "Kantor Keppel was bashed to death on April 30th. Your brother died on April 30th, six years ago. Did you commemorate the anniversary of Stan's death by smashing Kantor's head into a pulp?"

The eyes Friedman raised to stare into Tusk's were hot and hurt. "No way. I tried to see Keppel in the afternoon but only managed to see Morrison, the company's lawyer. He fobbed me off as usual. Mate, I've thought of killing Keppel a hundred times, and by Christ, maybe I might have done it too. But I didn't kill him that night. Someone saved me the pleasure."

"What time did you visit Morrison?"

"Three o'clock. I was gone by 3:15."

"What did you do after that?"

"I drove out along the bay and mulled things over. Done a lot of that over the last six years."

"You just drove around?"

"Believe it or not, I did." Friedman glared. But there was no violence in his body. "Ate some fish and chips and then drove around. Parked by the beach and walked. God help my family, sometimes they hardly see me, I'm so twisted by this business."

Tusk knew from the case file that the police hadn't been able to verify when Friedman drove out of the Southbank parking lot. The fish and chip shop owner couldn't recall him. His wife had been fast asleep at whatever time he returned home.

"You know, Stan used to like to walk," Friedman said on the drive back to the building site. "Hours and hours, he walked some nights, said it helped him think. That's what happened, I can picture it. Keppel went for a walk with him that night, pushed him into the water, and watched him drown."

Who are you, Kantor? Tusk asked the corpse in his mind's gallery. The sainted family man? Or a murderous thief of ideas?

"Bob," shouted one of Friedman's workmen when they arrived back at the site. The air had cooled. The storm clouds looked swollen. "Come and look at this."

"Friedman, do you have the Internet at home?" Tusk asked.

Friedman gave him a confused look. "Yeah. Why?"

Tusk scribbled in his notebook: Friedman is called Bob, could have written the email.

Friedman's parting handshake, with a hand even more callused than Tusk's, seemed almost grateful.

Tusk handed Friedman a business card. "Call me if you want to talk again."

"As if."

As Tusk drove off, wheels spinning in the dirt, he wondered how he could explain Friedman to Gentle. The developer had the motive, that was certain, and perhaps he could have hidden in the office to kill Kantor, but Tusk felt certain the man was innocent. Intuition, it was called, but how to explain that in polysyllabic words of logic?

CHAPTER 12

Peter tried panting to counteract sudden breathlessness. It didn't work. The clatter of cutlery and voices cascaded all around him. Even halfway through the afternoon, the lunch crowd hadn't dispersed. He dialed.

"Mandy Fitzgibbon."

Peter gulped at the sound of the slightly husky, confident voice. "Hi, Peter here."

"Peter." She still had some of her bush accent. "Sounds like a long lunch. Some people have all the luck."

Did she sound happy to hear from him? He cupped a hand over the mobile. "I'm in a restaurant in Southbank. E Gusto. Do you know it?"

"I've walked past it. Looks good."

Why on earth had he fallen for someone so different from him?

***

Harvey Jopling, President of the Skulk Club, party animal extraordinaire, and workaholic investment banker, had been his savior back when 1998 drew to a close. Out of work and hating every minute of it, Peter leapt at the opportunity when Harvey offered him a contract with a Merrill Lynch acquisition team in Hong Kong. It proved to be backbreaking work around the clock, and at the end of every day, he'd come home and collapsed.

On a warm December morning, he trudged up to Merrill Lynch at 120 Collins. Hands deep in his pockets, he scowled at his reflection in the glass of Harvey's office. I need a proper job, he thought. Waiting around for a bloody check isn't my idea of life.

"Mr. Gentle?" Harvey's secretary interrupted his thoughts. "Mr. Jopling just rang. He's on his way from the airport. He'll be with you in ten minutes."

"He won't get to be a director with that kind of service," Peter said.

"I'll try to get him a police escort."

Startled, he looked over at a long, raw-boned face whose intensity belied the sarcasm. She was a tall, lanky woman with long black hair, smart-looking in a loose yellow top over a green skirt. Peter was drawn to her eyes, wide and strong.

"Just a joke," he said. "Harvey and I are old friends."

"Oh, are you in that club of his?"

Peter straightened his shoulders self-consciously, smoothed his hair. His stomach fluttered. "You mean the Skulk Club?"

"Yes. I've just started to type up the minutes. Can I ask you a question? Exactly what is the club about?"

Peter grinned. "It's hard to say really. We're a group of finance professionals of about the same age, who like to get together every month."

"The minutes sound flippant. As if it's all a big joke."

He flushed. "Well, in one way it is. It's good fun. But in another sense, it's very serious. We're likeminded. We help each other."

"And why is it called the Skulk Club?"

Peter felt infinitely shy. "My nickname is Skull. Because I'm the most intelligent. You know, skull as in brain. And someone mispronounced it as Skulk Club, and it stuck."

"How quaint." Her mouth held the faintest hint of a sardonic tilt. "And this place Draconi's, where you met in November. Is that always the location for the Skulk Club?"

"Always." He walked over to her desk. "It's the center of the universe. Haven't you been there?"

Her fingers, resting on the keyboard, were long and harshly bony. "On a secretary's wage? My name's Mandy, by the way. Mandy Fitzgibbon."

"I'm... I'm Peter." Seized by a mix of terror and abandon, he plunged in. "Would you like to... I mean, can I take you to Draconi's for lunch? Background for your minutes, you know."

"Peter." Harvey stormed down the corridor, fresh and vital. "Let's do it."

It took Peter ten minutes of banter to extricate himself from Harvey, check in pocket. On the way out, he stopped at Mandy's desk. He struggled to speak.

"Sorry." She smiled and Peter was struck by how wild her face became when it opened up. "You seem like a nice guy, but I'm taken at the moment."

Later, he found out from Harvey that she'd moved to Melbourne from Ballarat a year earlier, that she was a single mother, that she was a great secretary, that she was writing a novel, and that she wasn't taken at all.

***

"Today's been lousy so far," Peter said into the mobile, struck by how glum he sounded. Where was the keenness he'd felt in Bishop's office? "But hey, Mandy, I've got a great new job."

"That's wonderful," Mandy said.

"I'd love to celebrate." He stalled, mouth dry as a drunk's. During the months since meeting Mandy, he'd used every pretext to visit Merrill Lynch and chat with her. But courage to ask her out had failed him. But now he was a private detective… "What about Friday night?"

The mobile fell into silence. He strained to hear.

"Peter Gentle?" A short woman stood over him. "I'm Marcia Brindle."

"Mandy?" he said.

"I'm still thinking," Mandy said.

"I've got to go, I have an interview. I'll ring you back."

"Okay, then the answer is yes."

Yes! Peter beamed as he hung up and unwound his slouched frame to stand.

"You look like you've just won the lottery," Marcia said in a gravelly voice.

Peter's impression of small stature faded the instant he shook her hand. She stood straight-backed, as if accustomed to commanding, in a severe gray jacket over a matching skirt. Blue eyes sized him up from under hair as white as any he'd ever seen, cut short and immaculate. Her face was craggy rather than what

Peter would have called pretty, but it was an alert face, animated with activity.

"It's a bit like that," he said. "How did you know it was me, in all this?" He indicated the frenetic restaurant.

She placed a gray leather folder on the table and chuckled. "Rollo said you have hair like a rock star."

Peter liked her instantly. It helped that she'd arranged to meet him at a nearby restaurant, rather than in her office, but there was also something recognizably decent underneath the imposing exterior. He knew her background. At age fifty-five, she was the company's financial controller, and had taken care to inform her police interviewer that she was one of the few female accountants in Australia to have such a coveted position. She had known Rollo from his Coombs Holcomb days, in fact had been there when he joined in 1978, and had moved with him to Scientific Money. She was a passionate advocate of women in business, and a member of various groups of corporate women.

They ordered coffees. He had taken a table outside, beside a vertical heater. Blue-black clouds hung over the higgledy-piggledy skyline across the river. Gulls wheeled over swirling brown water.

Marcia drummed fingers on the paper tablecloth. Peter told himself to resist, but his renewed buoyancy made it impossible. He started up his own tattoo on the carpet.

"Marcia, who would want to harm Kantor?" he asked.

Marcia's hands trembled momentarily. She lit a cigarette. Peter noted puffy bags under her eyes. She asserted control and exhaled over her shoulder. "Absolutely no one, Peter. I still can't believe it even happened. In all my years, I've rarely found anyone who was genuinely liked as much as Kantor was. At times he'd come across as a bit arrogant, but all academics have a dose of that. It must be something they inculcate at university. But if anyone was entitled to a touch of superiority, it was him."

"How did Rollo get on with him?"

"Like twins. That's the way I can best describe it. Always together."

"Did they ever quarrel?"

"At work? Never. They'd argue, that's for sure. Rollo's such a hardhead. He argues with all of us."

She smiled wistfully.

"Marcia, you were in the office on the night of the murder. What were you working on?"

"Our April management accounts were a day late, so I stayed back to finalize them. And no, I don't have any verifiable account of myself at the actual time of the murder. I was just at my desk, actually at my work table, poring over numbers."

A party of schoolchildren peered over the flower boxes cordoning off the restaurant.

"You were seen talking with Kantor at about six. What were you arguing about?"

She squinted at him. "I've been through the third degree with the police on this, Peter. Kantor and I discussed the format of a management report. Nothing more. We got animated, but it was strictly professional. Do you know what it's like to work in an office?"

What did he look like, a truck driver? "Of course I do. I'm an actuary."

Warmth flooded Marcia's face as she smiled. "Really? I've never worked with an actuary. I always liked that joke. What do you call an actuary? An accountant without a personality. I've never been sure if it's a joke on your profession or mine. Anyway, you must know what a constructive discussion in the office looks like."

Peter could concede that. If anyone had watched him at Thompson White, they would have seen him waving his arms like a dervish ten times a day.

"Marcia, how do you sign your emails?"

"What an odd question. I sign everything, memos, emails, the lot, except for official accounts, just with a B for Brindle. Sounds stuffy, but one of my early bosses suggested it as a way for a female accountant to appear tough. Why do you ask?"

"Just curious," Peter said. That bloody email to Kantor could have been written by anyone, he thought. Benedict Dancer, Bella, even Marcia. "Look, I'm fascinated by Scientific Money. Could I take a good look at the accounts?"

Her fingers went still. She reached into her folder and handed him a thick, glossy document. "Our latest accounts."

"What about something more detailed than the published accounts?"

"Sorry, no can do."

Crap, he thought, but pressed on. "The Investment Committee meets daily, I gather. What exactly does it do?"

"What does this have to do with the murder, Peter?"

Peter sat up, surprised at how low he'd slumped in the metal chair. He decided to confide in her.

"I have a theory that the killing is tied in with Kantor's

unique role in the company."

"Nonsense." Marcia glared. "Do you think a competitor would kill him to harm us? Far better to kill Rollo. Kantor was critical when we started, but no longer."

"I'd like to look at Kantor's theory—either read some detailed documentation, or even sit down in front of a screen with the software program itself."

"Peter, excuse my French, but that's bullshit," she said. "Check with Ross Petrov. Systems are his area. But you'll just be wasting his time and yours."

"Would the theory documentation have value? Did somebody maybe try to steal it?"

Marcia snorted. "Very unlikely. There are dozens of quant funds in the States, so anyone wanting to get into it could readily track down a good theory."

She checked her watch. "Peter, hope I've been of help, but I need to dash. We're getting ready for the year-end rush. Here's my card. Anything I can do to help catch whoever did this…"

As she wended her way through the tables, her white hair and confident gait attracting diners' glances, Peter reflected on the interview. Mick, you'd be proud of me right now, he thought. Marcia is definitely no murderer. But why did she avoid talking about the Investment Committee?

CHAPTER 13

The corridor smelled of piss and vomit, the carpet was more patches than fabric.

"Keppel," Tusk barked as he rapped. Time check—5:34. No need to worry about disturbing the other guests. "Willy Keppel."

The address for the mysterious third brother was the Faulkner Hotel, one of a number of seedy dives on Spencer Street, on the western edge of the CBD, across from the bustling railway station. Plenty of cop memories in this end of town.

"Shove off." An accent from New York movies.

"We need to talk."

"Suck my dick."

"I'll make it worth your while." Positive silence. One of the few advantages of working outside the law was you could freely use money to open doors.

"Two questions. Who the hell are you and how much?"

Tusk smiled. "Mick Tusk, Private Investigator. I'm working for Imogen Keppel. Twenty dollars."

"Stick it."

Tusk looked out the small fifth-floor window over the sprawl of the railway yards, Colonial Stadium in the distance. An early dusk under black clouds.

"Fifty," he said.

"You've gotta be kidding, man."

"Hundred."

The door creaked open. Tusk smelled waves of sour spirits. The man in a tattered green robe looked nothing like Rollo nor Kantor. Perhaps the face was oval beneath the wild, graying black beard, the long Grateful Dead hair, the mustache. Tusk took in the coal black eyes, rimmed blood red, glaring from behind small glasses. Deep lines etched in the face. Mashed nose.

"Come in, pardner," Willy said.

The room smelled like the end of the road. A couple of weak globes in the low ceiling bathed the peeling wallpaper in sickly yellow. A greasy mattress peeked from under scrunched dirty sheets on the low box-spring bed. A chair, a tiny closet, a dresser with one book, and a small sink. In one corner, two scuffed saxophone cases.

The file said Willy had returned in 1997 after many years in the States. He played jazz sax under the name Willy Willard. Tusk had never heard of the performer.

"Man, you look like those old cartoons of the Incredible Hulk," Willy said, loud in the constricted space. "I bet you rip your shirts like he did. Let's see the color of your money."

He licked his lips, again and again, feet tapping the blackened carpet. Tusk counted out fifty dollars. Willy snatched it.

"The rest at the end," Tusk said. "Tell me the truth and it's yours."

The chair creaked when he sat down. Willy remained standing, pulsing with energy.

"Okay, man. Fire away."

"How old are you compared to your brothers?" Tusk asked.

Willy chuckled without mirth. "Can't tell, can you? I'm the youngest, five years younger than Kantor, ten years younger than Rollo."

"I've heard you brothers don't get on."

"You heard right." Large, weathered hands crossed in front of him. Lick, lick of lips. "Rollo hated me from birth and has treated me like a pile of dog shit ever since. I left home at fifteen to be a musician and life's been tough, but I ain't never got a damned cent of help from him. As far as he's concerned, I don't exist."

"And Kantor?"

"He was okay when he was younger. I used to see him now and then before I went Stateside, and then I'd touch base whenever I did a gig in Boston while he was there. Intellectual cocksucker, as ashamed of me as Rollo, but at least he talked. And he helped me out a couple times when I was in rehab. But ever since he came back to Oz, he's been close to big brother and a real prick."

"So you're not exactly mates with them?"

"Hope they roast in hell," Willy said. "Even wrote a song for 'em."

Willy dashed to the closet, hauled out a suitcase packed with trophies, plaques, and compact discs. He brandished a CD.

"See? From my '94 release. 'Devil's Brethren' I called this track. Man, I think of them two every time I play it."

"Maybe you hated them enough to sneak in and crush Kantor's face," Tusk said, standing up.

Willy placed hands on hips and glowered. "No way. I'm not a violent man."

"Yeah? You've been charged with assault. Twice."

"That was in my younger days. I ran wild then, but now I'm a pussycat."

Sure, Tusk thought. He knew about running wild as a youngster. He also knew the urge to hit never left you. Not fully.

"What were you doing the night of the murder?"

"Same as every day. I sleep in the afternoon until just before my show. Got a gig at the Mingus Club."

"Can anyone verify that? Hotel staff? What time did you get to the club?"

"The staff here are as pissed as the guests. I got to the club at 11:30. The pigs tell me that's not enough to clear me. But I didn't kill Kantor. Man, I'm no killer. Now give me my money and head back to your Gestapo HQ."

For the first time in the day, a tendril of anger snaked through Tusk's guts. "If you're not a killer, who is?"

"How the hell do I know? Hey man, it could have been Rollo. They may have looked bonded at the hips, but when we were kids, they were no closer with each other than with me. Rollo was always pissed as hell at Kantor's brains, and Kantor was decent then, couldn't stand Rollo's bloody money hunger."

Tusk felt queasy from the smell in the room, a mix of sweat, booze, vomit, and cum. "When was the last time you saw them?"

"Rollo in 1981, at our father's funeral. I was gonna speak to him but the slimeball just told me to stay clear. Kantor… I saw him in '97, just after I got back, but he pissed me off as well. I hope hell is a damn hot place for him now."

"What about their families? Bella? Imogen? Straw?"

There! Tusk had been watching for it. Willy stopped licking and stared. "Never met Rollo's wife. Saw Imogen at the same time as Kantor, she'd gone all cold. Straw? Last time in the late '70s I guess, in Boston. That chick plays her own jazz, weird."

Tusk stared at the wreck in front of him. Why did all families end up so twisted? Willy was lying about something, somewhere in that skein of brotherly hatreds.

Willy's hopping had slowed to shuffling. "Now cough up the money and move along."

"Keppel, you're holding out on me," Tusk said. "Give me a ring when you're ready to talk, and you'll get the rest of your money."

He closed up his notebook, tossed over a card, and walked out, eager for fresh air.

"Creep!"

The door slammed behind him.

Outside it was nearly dark. The wind had picked up, sending dust swirling along tram tracks. Crushed cans and cigarette butts in the gutter. Motorbikes parked on the footpath. Office drones fleeing, leaning against the wind as they rushed toward the station. The smell of imminent rain.

Time check—6:00. A productive day, he thought, plenty of data, as Gentle liked to say. His energy was deserting him. His right shin, sporadically sore since his last half-marathon, twinged.

Strange, he thought, all my life this city pumped me up. I knew the rhythms of every alley. Now all I can think of is to get home, wash off the stink, play with the kids, smell the grass. Is this what Dana calls healing?

CHAPTER 14

After Marcia Brindle left, Peter had no more meetings arranged until the following morning. He decided to research Kantor's investment theory. Clutching the Scientific Money annual report, he rushed along the riverbank and up the steps to catch a tram along Swanston Street.

A headline caught his attention. The tram clanging across an intersection, he hung onto his strap and stood on tiptoe to peer over the shoulder of a man reading *The Australian Financial Review*.

"Consultants Quiz Quant Fund King"

The man snapped the newspaper shut and glared at Peter, but not before he'd skimmed the article. It quoted a number of investment consultants queuing to ask Rollo about the impact of Kantor's death on the company.

Spot on, Peter thought, exactly the question I'm pursuing, though in a different fashion. Mick would label this trip a waste of time, just as well we're apart. But why hasn't he rung me?

When the tram crossed Collins, he gazed at the Town Hall, stark under the threatening sky. Swanston Street had once been the main north-south avenue through the city. A few years back, it had been converted into a traffic-free zone, and now only trams made their way up toward the universities. Somehow it had resisted being converted into a mall. A handful of classier cafes had moved out onto the footpaths. Some of the Bourke Street Mall street performers had shifted to Swanston, but the greasy cafes, sex parlors, and two-dollar shops remained. The street reminded Peter of a shabby tourist strip cleared by a bomb blast.

He alighted at Latrobe Street. Pigeons scattered when he climbed the steps up to the Roman-columned State Library on its hillock. Inside, his footsteps echoed amongst the voices of tour guides. He sat before a large screen in the Information Center and began his search.

He ordered some journals, scampered up the worn stone steps to the Domed Reading Room, a round cavernous space lit by green lights on wall sconces. In an ancient wooden cubicle, he screwed up his brow and read. He tapped his feet, squirmed in his seat, chewed his pen. Occasional grunts escaped him.

He took no notes, preferring the chain of reasoning to stay inside his head. He rushed back and forth to obtain more material. Some of the relevant papers were unavailable, but the web of cross-referencing left him satisfied with what he had.

When he took a break after an hour and a half of concentration, his throat ached for liquid. He bought a can of Coke from a vending machine and sat on a seat outside the library. The world had darkened prematurely, massed purple clouds hung like swollen plums over Melbourne Central. The office workers hurrying into Museum Station all carried umbrellas.

It took him a moment to realize the trilling mobile was his. Rollo asked whether his day had been useful.

"Quite productive, but Mr. Dancer was very rude."

"So I heard." Rollo's voice was smooth. "A misunderstanding. Tell me, Peter. Any progress in your thinking?"

Away from Rollo's searching eyes, Peter's awe of the Chief Executive had dimmed enough to embolden him. "No, it's way too early. Would it be possible to spend some more time with you tomorrow?"

"Sorry, the diary's full. Where are you?"

Peter heard the urgent dongs of a tram driver's warning bell, followed by the skid of tram wheels gripped by sand. On Swanston a tram juddered to a halt just in front of a turning car.

"The State Library."

The tram driver leaned out of his cabin and screamed at the car driver.

"The State Library? Why on earth—"

"What about 10:30 tomorrow, Mr. Keppel, after my morning meetings?"

"Sorry, no, I've an appointment. Peter, stay in touch."

Peter nursed the silent mobile. Both the tram and the car had gone. He finished his Coke, gritted his teeth, and headed back to his cubicle. The world receded again as he applied his mind to the job.

His pulse quickened when he found a reference to a conference paper by Kantor and Stan Friedman, the drowned brother of the man who'd been pestering the Keppels. He sighed with frustration when he found that the library didn't hold that paper. A search showed that none of the university libraries did either.

By the time he walked down the front steps, yawning and stretching stiff legs, night had fallen. He glanced at his watch—6:30. He looked up Bishop's phone number on his Palm Pilot. The lawyer answered on the first ring.

"Good work," Bishop said after Peter filled him in on the day, glossing over the early interview difficulties. "And the beefcake?"

"Mick hasn't contacted me."

"Better lines of communication, Peter, that's what you need. Thanks for the bulletin."

A thin man with ropy hair, carrying a cardboard sign, shuffled up. Peter gave him some change and dialed Imogen Keppel. The phone rang for a long time before she answered, her voice slurred.

"Mrs. Keppel, does Straw ever talk?"

"Straw? Never. What's this nonsense in aid of?"

"Nothing, just an idle query."

He updated her on his day.

"I must say that progress seems to have been slow," she said.

Hardly an encouraging client, Peter thought, though he could see her perspective. After all, it was her husband in the morgue. He promised to keep her up to date.

A bolt of lightning blazed in the black sky, and a chill wind whipped up leaves and chip bags. He dodged trams across Swanston, and reflected on the day as he stood amongst hundreds of bodies crammed on escalators descending into the bowels of Melbourne's short subway system. A dreadful start, he thought, but a decent finish. He should have taken better notes. His crumpled suit felt heavy on his shoulders.

The Belgrave train was packed. Peter held onto a waist-high

handle jutting from a seat, jammed between a mustached man reading a newspaper and a plump woman chewing her lip. When the train emerged from the subway tunnel, a deluge of thick rain smashed down on it. He could barely see the Melbourne Cricket Ground. Lightning blazed and thunder answered, and the train sped through a sky of water.

Why were the Scientific Money executives so evasive about the investment process? Peter's short burst of research had helped define what he was up against, but in the end it raised more questions than it answered. Modern Portfolio Theory, as the theory behind formula investing was known, had a firm mathematical basis, but for all its proponents, there were as many critics who questioned its very foundations, the assumptions that underpinned it. Kantor's theoretical basis was sketched in two papers, both reputable, but the details were simply insufficient. How was it applied in practice? Peter knew the key was to get into the actual software programs.

He almost missed Box Hill Station, just managing to squeeze through the gap of the hissing doors. Outside, the rain had ceased. He gingerly stepped over the puddles on Station Street, trying to protect his shoes. He smelled the familiar spices and Asian vegetables, smiled at the neon of the Chinese restaurants glowing in the pitch-black sky. His hands stung with cold.

How strangely it had all panned out. When Peter's parents moved to Box Hill in the '70s, it was a post-war Anglo-Saxon suburb, complete dullsville. Now, though he still couldn't stand the brick veneer streets, and though his parents didn't eat Asian food, Box Hill had metamorphosed into a multicultural dining heaven.

At a Skulk Club meeting, Peter had argued vociferously that Box Hill's restaurants were better value, more atmospheric, and more competitive than those in the celebrated Chinatown district of the city.

"Crap," Harvey Jopling had shouted. "You just like it because you grew up there."

Peter smiled at the memory. He hunched his shoulders against the wind, pushed hands deep into his pockets. Away from the shops and restaurants, Box Hill sat quietly. Occasionally cars drove past, tires spraying water, their headlights bright.

He smelled bacon as he turned onto Lesdale Street, wondered what his mother would have ready for dinner. A car pulled along the curb just in front of him. A thin man got out and headed for a house. Peter walked past, skirting a large puddle. He felt lucky to still be dry.

Something smashed onto his right shoulder, pitching him forward, and then a hand gripped the back of his suit with fearsome strength. He cried out.

CHAPTER 15

A decade ago, Tusk's father had retired after thirty years' service with the tramways. As far as Tusk could figure, the old man never enjoyed a single day at the helm of the clunky vehicles that spanned Melbourne. But when he finally slammed on the air brakes for the last time, for some reason he decided to be melancholy. He threw a farewell party at his rickety place in Collingwood.

They'd both begun to recover from the wars of Tusk's youth and were talking again. Not often, but enough for Tusk to accept the invitation.

The day of the party, he had worked a long shift in the squad car. He'd been a policeman for three years, loving every minute, working as hard as shit to make up for his late entry age. At nine o'clock he stepped into the smell of pickled fish, dumplings, and vodka. Cigarette smoke swirled toward the open windows.

His father slapped his back. In the living room, thirty balding trammies drank and shouted. They called his father Arnie, a distortion of his Estonian name Arne, or just as often he was "the fucking Balt." His mother periodically brought out plates of food from the kitchen. Tusk didn't speak to her.

He drank beer and pictured Mercy, the woman he was seeing at the time. The image of her hot body sent him edging toward the door, just before the pumpkin hour.

"See you, Arne," Tusk said.

Sour vodka breath. "Eh, where you think you're goin'? This is my party."

"Got someone to meet."

"You screw around too much."

Tusk opened the sagging screen door, held out his hand. "Congrats, Arne. Free as a bird now."

A stiff finger poked Tusk in the chest. "You can't fool me, Mihkel. I seen the way you look at my mates. You think you're too fuckin' good for us. Us workers."

The house inside had fallen silent. Next door a cat wailed. Tusk looked at the finger digging into him. An electric current buzzed in his arms and legs.

"You weren't so high 'n mighty when you lived on the streets." His father's eyes burned. "Then you were happy to see your father's money when you came begging. Now that you're a copper, you think we're dirt. Right?"

To respond would have prompted their first fight since the big one all those years earlier. And Tusk was in uniform. He drove off to find Mercy, didn't visit his father for months.

***

Time check—6:06. Dark outside Scientific Money House, the lobby inside lit by golden lights on stalks around the walls.

Arne was wrong, Tusk thought as his footsteps clopped across the marble floor. In fact, being a copper had convinced him that workers were the salt of the earth. Take security guards. No one ever noticed them. Cunts like Rollo Keppel looked right through them, but security guards were the ones who really knew what was going on in offices.

"Is Shao Yang on shift?" he asked.

The man behind the security desk needed a shave. "Who wants him?"

Tusk flipped him his police merit badge and was led into a cramped back room reeking of sweat. A thin Asian man sat surrounded by screens.

Yang's hand trembled in Tusk's. About forty, long face pitted with acne scars. Black hair with strands of gray. Watery eyes peering over thin spectacle frames.

"No trouble, please," Yang said.

"No trouble, Mr. Yang. Tell me about the night of the 30th."

Yang's chair creaked as he leaned back. "I already tell the police but okay. I am doing late shift, start nine o'clock, finish five o'clock in morning. I do this job one year, since coming from Taiwan. I like night shift, very convenient. I very loyal, very hard work. This night same as others. No trouble. 11:30 I do routine, visit all floors, start from bottom. No problem, no trouble."

Yang's voice dimmed to a whisper, barely audible over the sputtering air-conditioning. "When I finish fourth floor, I open door to stairs. I see man lying down stairs. On his side, feet and knees on landing, rest down stairs. I lift body. Terrible. Terrible."

The man's voice quavered. He took off his glasses and rubbed his eyes, as if to make the scene disappear.

"I see it Mr. Kantor. His face smash in, terrible. I feel blood on my hands and I see it on stairs. I… I scream. It's not proud to say that, but I did. I think maybe his soul screams. His face…"

No wonder the crime scene yielded so little, Tusk thought. Yang had trampled all over it. "Anyone come to help?"

"No, no other guards then. I ring police on mobile. I sick on stairs."

"Objects around the body?"

Yang breathed noisily. "Just security pass, lying on second step. In blood."

Tusk gestured at one of the screens with scrolling characters. "I assume that shows security passes being used, real time. Do you watch people coming in or out?"

"No, no point. Only sometimes I check if someone come in late, but that night nothing special."

"Anyone in the building when you did your sweep?"

"The building empty. Just me. And dead Mr. Kantor."

"Any security cameras in the stairwell?"

"No."

"Why not?"

"It a small building, sir. We never have trouble on stairs. Until now."

"I'd like to see the stairwell," Tusk said.

"I refuse," Yang said.

Tusk looked at him, keeping his face blank. The Chinaman squared his shoulders and stared back. Seconds ticked by. A minute. Yang's fingers began to tremble. A shrug.

"Okay."

"Good choice," Tusk said.

Yang led him through the lobby. At the elevators, Tusk

looked back at the security desk. The desk wasn't ideally located. The guard had a clear view of the front revolving doors and the elevator area, but was too far away. Like Tusk had told Gentle, it wouldn't be hard to sneak in with other people during the day. Not at nighttime, though.

Tusk quizzed Yang about the security pass readers. One in each lobby elevator, occasionally outside high-security rooms, and one by the basement exit.

On the top floor, he followed Yang along a dark corridor lit only by night panels. The dark, the quiet, it felt like back on the job.

At the end of the corridor Yang gestured. Face pinched with fear. "You go. I stay."

Tusk shrugged and pulled back the door. It opened silently. The stairwell, unlike most, was well lit by overhead fluorescent lights. He took in the khaki green walls. Musty air, no other smells. The echo of his footsteps—loud, so Kantor must have heard his assailant. Dark stains covering half of the first three concrete steps.

Tusk walked to the second step and stood still. Sam and his team had got it right. Kantor had been there when he heard or saw something. Tusk turned his head, mimicking Kantor hearing footsteps behind him. Like an actor, he relived the moment, saying something, eyes wide, then reeling with shock as the killer came at him. Too slow to raise his arms, the blow to his head, staggering, already close to death, falling backward down the stairs. Then the killer stepping past the body and running off.

An insistent rhythm, like a techno beat. His heart. Too many memories, released like an egg hatching. He shouldn't have come here. No sleep tonight. Or he should have brought Gentle, showed him this was no game of Cluedo.

He trudged back to the corridor. Now the murder resided in him, stacked alongside all the others. Yang must have seen it on his face. The security guard held his hands up in the ghostly light. Tears slipped down his cheeks.

"Blood everywhere," Yang said. "It all over my hands and I must touch my face, I see it there. Sir, I cannot forget."

***

On his way to the parking lot, Tusk paused halfway across the Yarra River pedestrian footbridge. He entwined his fingers and stretched his arms above his head, a delicious pull of muscles, while he looked back. To his left the affluent glitter of Southbank, to his right the green disk of the Casino, Melbourne's new icon of greed. Near the middle, beckoning like a lighthouse, the red-and-gold logo atop Scientific Money House. Savage Murder House, he thought.

He walked on. The city cast its tendrils deep. He grew up on its outskirts, came down here to raise hell as a teenager. Later, in the dark years, many a time he passed out in a gutter surrounded by skyscrapers. And as a copper he grew to know every one of the myriad narrow lanes in the cracks between office towers. The building spines, dark and lit at the same time, filled him with a stew of dread and excitement.

Walking along the dank passageway that ran along one side of the station, he kept tripping back to the stairwell. He took out the beach photo, and tried to imagine the professorial face, accustomed to musing over a desk, raised in terror at the looming killer. As well as fear, Tusk sensed disbelief. "You!" Kantor had known the killer.

When he came out into Flinders Street, rain had begun to pour down. As he waited for the lights to change, he sank into familiar reverie.

***

Sometimes Tusk labeled his life as before and after William Bell.

In 1994, when his daughter Yolanda was born, Tusk had wept with joy. Even with his long and irregular Homicide hours, whenever he was home at night, he sprang up when she cried, changed her nappy, and brought her into the bedroom for Dana to breastfeed. On one such night, wind slapping branches against the wooden house, he'd been rocking her when the phone rang. The dispatch officer was curt.

"Dell Road in Prahran. A messy."

He pulled up outside a cramped terrace house in the shadow of the Prahran Town Hall. Blue and white tape, tossed by wind, held back a dozen spectators. Fingall, the toughest of them all, motioned him toward the open front door.

Tusk's footsteps sounded on the tiny front veranda. A fetid stench hit him. He blocked off his sense of smell and eased in. Tiny bedrooms, barely room for a bed, off a dark corridor. A body in the living room, on the floor. A naked bulb high overhead. Dancing shadows. A television hissing white noise, two couches—one cracked underneath, a coffee table covered with magazines, an impressionist print on the far wall, peeling green wallpaper. And the body…

A cap lay a couple of meters away, but Tusk didn't need it as confirmation. It was a teenage boy, face smooth and finely featured, eyes blank and somehow uncolored, cheekbones honed as if in a sculptor's workshop. An innocent's face.

The rest was fucked. The boy's hair had been shaved off and lay in tufts over the floor, caked with matted fluid. Arms bound behind the back with wire. So too the ankles. His clothes, Tusk identified later as a school uniform, folded on a couch. Burn pockmarks dotted the upturned chest and down the arms. Thin crosswise cuts up both legs, a precise handiwork. Entrails oozed from a gaping hole where his belly button would have been. A jagged cavern had been ripped in his groin, dark red; where was the poor sod's cock?

Tusk stood motionless, playing out the horror perpetrated on this boy.

The autopsy revealed that the boy had died over a number of hours, all of them in extremis. He'd gone missing after school, but his parents had failed to ring the police. His name? Tusk sighed, his neck muscles bunched, spelled the letters now. William Bell.

Before that night he'd seen many vile deeds. Helped solve, or not solve, more than a few gruesome deaths. But no event so clearly signaled to him that the world was amiss as that boy's face framed by a monster's artistry.

Tusk and Fingall were the only observers who failed to spew after the sight. Fingall was a hard case, inured to anything. Tusk? "Fuck it," he muttered as he kneaded his neck, "I was so cool, but that was the beginning of the end."

***

An Indian woman looked sharply at him and moved away. He must have spoken aloud. Head like a boulder, mouth bone dry, the dry before a beer. Tusk jogged across Flinders Street, through the rain, then made his way to the parking lot. He drove numbly.

The rain had given up by the time he reached the outskirts of Belgrave. Belgrave: end of the railway line, a suburb more rural than residential. Nearly home. He sniffed the freshness of the air, sped past silent, wet lawns.

The car crested the driveway of their home, a weatherboard house with a wide back veranda overlooking a large block. He saw the front door open and his heart pinged. Like a bear in a stream, he shook his head to clear it. Mustn't let Dana see me in this state, he thought. Christ knows she's seen enough of it.

"Daddy!"

Yolanda raced across puddles to leap toward his face, her arms wrapping around his neck. He lifted her up to his chest, inhaling the soapy smell of her hair, driving out William Bell and Kantor Keppel.

"Daddy!" Nelson was clutching his legs.

"Hey," Tusk said, squeezing Yolanda before lowering her. Nelson squealed when Tusk roared his fake lion roar and bent down to kiss the hot cheek.

"Got you," he said, reveling in the matchstick arms grabbing him, the kicking legs at his stomach.

"What about me? Where's the hug for the woman of your dreams?"

He gazed mock-seriously into Dana's brown eyes. "My Belgrave woman."

"You've got one in each suburb?" Dana's voice cut through the quiet of the driveway like a megaphone. The voice that had made him stare across the room at the police ball the night they met.

"Nearly, m'dear, nearly." Tusk laughed, a silly giggle that he couldn't contain, and the children chimed in.

Dana's hair, masses of dancing black ringlets, shook as she laughed. She wore a tracksuit, signaling that she'd been to the gym earlier in the day. He stared at her beak of a nose, marveled yet again at his good fortune. Nobody else could have done what she'd achieved. Tackled the violence. Calmed the spirit. Took him off the cancer sticks and the hard liquor, cold turkey. Gave him a reason to live.

He hadn't told her much when he left in the morning, just that his old mate Gentle had an idea for a job, but she must have sensed what that might mean.

"I've got work," he had said. "If it goes well, it'll mean a lot of money."

"That's great news," she had said, giving him an uncertain smile. Tusk had learned to keep to himself, but Dana never hid a single emotion. Christ, he loved her.

"Gate noos," Nelson had echoed.

Tusk hoisted Nelson under his arm, and with Yolanda in tow, took them inside to brush their teeth. He read to Yolanda, wrestled with Nelson, and then switched on the television in the family room while Dana bustled in the abutting kitchen. While he scanned his long list of To-Dos in the notebook, Dana filled him in on her day. Ever since she gave up teaching with the birth of Nelson, she'd built up a network of friends in the local community that amazed Tusk. In this world far away from the city, she was a ball of energy, out and about continually.

Bully barked at the back door. When Tusk let him in, the German Shepherd raced around the room and leapt up to lick Tusk's face. Tusk gave him a stomach rub, watched the start of

Water Rats, another useless cop show.

He rang Gentle's mobile. No response. He rang his sister. As usual, Elizabeth did all the talking. A social worker's life seemed as busy and wrenching as a copper's.

"You sound happy, Mick," she said.

"Do I?"

"Dinner," Dana called.

"Gotta go, Liz."

"Take care now." He crossed the task off his To-Do list.

With the television still on, they ate an aromatic Mediterranean stew, looking out onto the dark expansive garden. His favorite room, so open and comfortable, with its high exposed timber ceiling. As always, he marveled at the portrait photograph on the wall, the blonde pale Estonian gravely holding hands with the olive-tinted Greek with jet-black hair.

"So come on," Dana said. "Cough it up. What's this great new job? Should I book a dirty weekend at a hotel?"

Tusk felt a weight in the pit of his stomach. "You're not going to like it."

"Let me be the judge of that. Have I met this Gentle what's-his-name?"

His fingertips etched patterns on the condensation on his beer glass. "Peter Gentle. I was friends with him for a year in school. Before I went off the rails."

Dana was the only one who knew all about those years.

"A strange guy," Tusk went on. "One of those genius types, thin and always thinking. A real brain. Hardly grown up at all, still soft and unreal, still mouthing off. Not my type of mate at all, really."

He swigged the last of his beer and smiled. "But he's got something. I can't describe it, Dana. Half the time I feel like laughing at him, half the time he gets me excited. He's got some crazy enthusiasm that I love."

He watched Dana's wide hips swinging on her way to the kitchen to pull out a steaming pie from the oven.

This is heaven, he thought, biting into fresh apples and crisp pastry.

"Okay, he sounds interesting, Mikey," Dana said. "So what kind of job has he lined up for you? What does he do, anyway?"

Tusk couldn't bring himself to explain what an actuary was. "He's unemployed like me. Been off work even longer. It's a lucrative assignment together. A private detective assignment."

There, he'd said it. He retrieved another beer from the fridge. Dana sat back, arms folded under her breasts. Her eyes were wide and wounded.

"You've got to be joking," she said. "How many times have you said you don't want that kind of work?"

"This is different. Those offers were for regular work, crap work like following people, that kind of stuff. This is different. We're just doing one job. Investigating a murder for a widow."

"Murder." Bully's ears pricked up at Dana's harsh tone.

"Yeah. You might have read about it, a city exec beaten to death." The stains on the stairs, that smashed waxen face... "The widow isn't satisfied with police progress. Dana, it's not like police work. We just snoop around. When we figure who it is, we let the police mop up."

He was repeating Boy Wonder's pitch. The difference was that Gentle actually believed it could be that simple.

He wanted to say so many things to Dana. So many things left unsaid for too long. Like: Look at me, Dana. Tossed on the bloody scrapheap at age thirty-four. Driving taxis, digging swimming pool holes, even training to be a masseur, for Christ's sake.

Like: I miss every minute in the Force. This morning in the autopsy room, smelling that special stench of a days-dead corpse, it felt like a welcome childhood memory.

Like: If there's a God, until last year I was doing exactly what He ordained, until those sanctimonious pricks screwed me.

Instead, he took her hand. She was breathing hard. Try the trump card, he thought.

"Dana," he said. "I've agreed to try this for five days. If it's a flop, or if I don't like it, I can pull out then."

"You won't." She yanked away her hand. "I can hear it in your voice already. You're back playing cops and robbers. And you love it."

He stood up and moved behind her. He massaged her rigid shoulders, felt them relax. Her hair tickled his nose while he talked in her ear.

"Just five days. And if we're successful, my share is $40,000. Imagine that. The lucky break we need."

His hands slid down to rest on her breasts. He felt her deep breathing against his chest. She turned to look him in the eyes.

"Okay," Dana said. "Five days, you say. Okay, but you talk to me, Mikey. Talk to me every one of those five days and tell me what you're feeling. I will not see you slide down that slope to craziness like before. Got that?"

"Dana." He lifted her hair up and ran his lips across the back of her neck.

"Is that a yes?"

"Yes, yes, yes."

She pulled away and stood with arms on hips.

"And just because you persuaded me to go along with this madness, doesn't mean I'm happy about it. I thought we had put all that…that life behind us. Now I get to worry about you again, every bloody hour of the day."

"I know, Dana." He wanted to reach out to her, but knew he shouldn't. "Thanks."

She headed into the kitchen. Tusk directed a sleepy Bully outside and rang his uncle.

"Uncle Mart, I can't take the cab out for a week."

"What, you're not liking to work for your old uncle?"

His uncle owned three taxis. Should have sold out years ago, but still drove one of them. Tusk liked working for him, enjoyed the ease and trust.

He stayed up to watch the 10:30 news. Interviews with a few of the four thousand Kosovo refugees about to board flights to Australia. Five hundred days until the Sydney Olympics. Boring predictions about the State budget the next morning. No news about Carlton, his football team, bastards had only won three of their six games this season.

The bedside lamps were on when he slipped under the blankets. Dana laid down her magazine and slid onto him, wet and trembling. Sweet vertigo flooded his body.

Paul Rodgers' soulful, aching vocals—Free's "Be My Friend"—welled up in him. The first time they'd made love, he'd chosen it, or rather it had chosen him, as his secret song to Dana.

She fingered the bullet hole scar on his belly and the long white scar down his arm. He shivered.

"No more of these," she breathed into his ear. "Got that, Mikey?"

CHAPTER 16

Peter Gentle cried out, "Hey!"

He attempted to turn toward the person gripping the back of his suit. Another figure came from the front and thrust a cold hand into his face, across his lips, cutting off all sound. The Scientific Money annual report flew from his hand. Horror flooded him. His two assailants jammed up close. Grunts, the smells of garlic and aftershave. Although he squirmed, they wrenched him sideways with ease, and then his forehead struck a car door frame as they shoved him in.

One of his attackers plunged into the car with him, shoving Peter's body aside for room. Sharp pain seared Peter's head. Take my money, he tried to yell, but a hand forced his face down, and another throttled his mouth.

Doors slammed. The car jerked as its engine roared to life, and then they were moving. The man was sitting on Peter's feet, leaning over to restrain him. Peter smelled petrol fumes. He thrashed, desperate to be gone from this nightmare, to find himself strolling down his street again, but something hard, it had to be a fist, crashed into his side. He doubled up in pain. A rent in the car seat cut into his cheek, the hard shapes of his mobile and Palm Pilot pressed into his side. Warmth flooded his groin; he'd pissed himself.

"Don' move." The voice was hoarse and deep. An Italian accent.

God help me, Peter moaned silently. His heart hammered in his chest. He curled into a fetal ball and shuddered uncontrollably.

After what seemed only minutes, the car bounced. A squeal of tires and they stopped.

"Out."

The car door was flung open. He was thrown onto the ground like a limp puppet, wet gravel tearing his hands. He ended up on his side, winded, cheek resting in water, right knee pulsing with pain. He'd never realized the ground could be so hard. His eyes at ground level, he saw puddles of glinting water, a chain fence in the distance, and next to him two feet in Reeboks, and a knee on the ground, the tracksuit fabric darkened with water.

Images spun through Peter's numbed mind. Home, not his parents', but his apartment—the kitchen, the bed. Draconi's. Harvey Jopling smiling. Mick running toward him. Strangest of all, his father's worn face.

He began to sob, wrenching exhalations of terror. He tried to get up on his elbows, but a hand shoved him down.

"Please." Snot bubbled in his nose.

"Shut up." The man with the hoarse voice again, only this time the voice held pleasure.

The ring of Peter's mobile sliced through the quiet. Relief pierced him; it had to be Mick.

"Fuck." The man Peter thought of as Hoarse snatched the phone from Peter's jacket pocket, smashed it into silence on the ground.

Any hope left in Peter died.

A savage pain tore at his back. A shoe. Another kick wrenched a scream from his mouth. He thrashed under the strong hands of Hoarse, then another kick crashed into the back of his neck, and he tasted blood in his mouth. His head swam.

A finger traced the tears down Peter's cheek. He jerked onto his back to look up into a thin face dominating the sky, a thin face dark as the night above it, no features visible except for a pointed chin. He smelled aftershave, something familiar.

"Hey, cock suck." A sibilant voice, almost loving in its slowness. "No one's gonna come to grief here, understand? Just listen. Just listen real good. Okay?"

Peter nodded. Pain ballooned from his back and neck. He tasted vomit in his throat.

"Playing at detective. It's gotta stop. Okay?"

"Yes." Peter's voice came as a wheeze. He blinked tears from his eyes, trying to focus, to stay alive.

The man leaned over. "You wanna play cowboys, this is what you get."

Peter saw teeth glint. The maniac was smiling. Peter wanted to say yes, anything, anything you want, but never managed a sound as the thin man gently picked up his wet left hand and deftly snapped the little finger back with a crack and a surge of pain.

Peter screamed and arched.

His assailants stood up. Hoarse chuckled. The two of them loomed over Peter, black shadows of death, one thin, the other thick, faint light framing their silhouettes.

The thin man bowed, hands behind his back.

"Lesson number one," he said. "Lesson number two, I cut out your eyes."

The hissed words penetrated into the deepest recesses of Peter's mind. He jerked in terror and writhed away on his back.

Then Hoarse and the thin man were strolling away. As Hoarse turned at the car, a patch of light caught the left side of his face, smooth except for a depression where the ear should have been.

"Fuckin' weed," Peter heard Hoarse say to the thin man. They both laughed. Doors slammed. The engine revved, tires spun, and then they were gone.

Peter lay on his back, soaked, sobbing at the black roily sky. A drop of rain hit his face, then another, then the heavens opened. He sat up in the pouring rain, gasping at pain from his back and neck and knees. The broken little finger throbbed, though with less pain now. He felt it, loose as a bird's wing, already puffing up.

"Help," he cried as he struggled to his feet.

He was in the parking lot of a warehouse, two lampposts casting a feeble light onto uneven gravel. Utter emptiness and blackness otherwise, no sounds other than dull traffic somewhere far off. His Palm Pilot lay in a pool of water.

"Help!" he roared, standing hunched in the rain, cradling his left hand, snot and tears and water slicking his face.

No one answered. He pushed back his sodden hair and wept.

CHAPTER 17

Mick Tusk yawned over his mug of coffee. Eleven o'clock at night, already falling asleep. Another song started up over the speakers. That familiar organ-led riff, the precision drums, then Ian Gillan began singing, his voice moving from deep to screech with ease. At last a newie from Deep Purple, the icon rock band—"Abandon," their first genuine release in years. Old men now, but as full of life as ever. Pity Ritchie Blackmore, the magical guitarist, had thrown another tantrum and left the band for the thirty-fifth time.

"Mikey, phone," Dana called. "It's Peter Gentle."

The kitchen was full of the aroma of biscuits baking for a kindergarten stall. What did Einstein want that couldn't wait until tomorrow?

"Mick." The voice sounded strained. "Someone attacked me."

"What?" Tusk's tone drew a worried look from Dana. "What happened?"

"On the way home. A couple of them. They pushed me into a car and took me to a parking lot and... hurt me."

"You're fucking joking."

"No joke, Mick."

"You okay?"

"Yes. No."

"Where are you? At the police station?"

"No, at home. I...I don't want to go to the police. I'm quarreling with my father right now."

Tusk could remember Trevor Gentle's insistent style. "Hang on. I'll be right there."

Dana had hands on hips and a knowing look in her eyes. "Where are you going?"

Tusk rubbed Bully's head as a farewell. "Just to Gentle's place. Box Hill. The useless sod's been beaten up."

"It's this case, isn't it?"

"Could be, could be just local toughs."

She kept that you-can't-fool-me look on him as he kissed her cheek. The smell of cinnamon lingered in his nostrils as he drove through bucketing rain. Traffic was light, by 11:30 he was pulling into the Gentle driveway. Instant deja vu, though the clinker brick house was recognizably more careworn than he recalled from fifteen years ago. Front door open, presumably for him. Voices in the kitchen, the aroma of instant coffee disturbed by antiseptic. Gentle's old man, Trevor, and his wife—what was her name?—in pajamas.

Gentle's face shocked him. Pale and so thin. The brown eyes wide, not hooded as usual, a stunned look Tusk recognized as shock. A tangled mess of hair. Striped pajamas and a shiny bathrobe. Reedy body slumped in a chair, no sign of the usual manic twitching, glass of wine in his hand. Christ, a splint on the two smallest fingers of the left hand.

"Tusk." Trevor rose to shake Tusk's hand. "This lunacy has to stop. Can you talk my son into seeing reason?"

Tusk read the appeal in Gentle's eyes, and signaled with his head: Out of here.

Gentle winced as he stood up.

"Hey." Imperious Trevor. The wife wringing her hands. "Sit down and talk to me."

"We'll be back," Tusk said.

Gentle led them down a dark hall to his poky bedroom, crowded with books and a computer. To Tusk it seemed unchanged from his teenage memories. Christ, he could recall pushing Gentle to try a smoke here.

"Big guy, am I glad you came," Gentle said, after they sat down on the bed. "They've been at me for an hour."

"They're probably right."

Tusk took Gentle's injured hand, raised his eyebrows.

"A broken finger. The little one."

Tusk heard out Gentle's story. The poor dork angrily brushed away tears as he described the kicks and the finger-breaking. For a moment, Tusk felt like hugging him.

"When I saw no one would come to help, I walked out and found myself down Maroondah Highway a bit. I ended up walking home. Dad rang the family doctor, who set the splint. Mick, why?"

"Nothing else broken?"

"No, but my body and neck feel like they are. Answer me— who's done this and why?"

Tusk felt calmer. Minimal damage, although Gentle wouldn't see it that way.

"Someone wants to stop you from asking questions," he said. "Someone with enough money to hire muscle. There's a positive side to this. You must have done a good job today and really got up somebody's arse."

"Thanks a lot. I'll try to get beaten up some more. The whole thing is so barbaric."

"That's one way to describe it. How'd they find you?"

"Easy. Telstra White Pages on their website. I checked a month ago, it has my change of address."

"Now tell me again why we shouldn't let the cops handle this."

Gentle's right hand gripped into a fist. "Don't you see? We haven't even got our licenses yet. The police will tear us apart. We could lose days."

"What if they have another go at you? Doesn't that worry you?"

"Of course it does." Gentle shuddered. "The thin one said he'd cut my eyes out."

"Calm down. That's just a drama queen at work."

But Tusk's disquiet was rising again as he absorbed the events of the night. These hoods had been so businesslike...

"I'm scared, okay?" Gentle's voice caught. He stuck his jaw out. "But we're not going to stop. I won't go to the police. Got that?"

Stubborn cunt. No budging him. Tusk held up a hand. "Okay, okay. It's borderline. I'd hate to front up to the cops either. Now, Doctor Tusk prescribes sleeping in tom—"

"No can do. I've appointments at Scientific Money from nine, and Straw wants to see me at eight. Can you pick me up at 7:30?"

"Guess so. Two last things. One, tomorrow we work together, not apart. Two—tell me again, you reckon they were Italian?"

"Yes. At least, the first man was. Definitely."

Tusk's unease grew. He rose. "Get that beauty sleep, okay?"

"Mick? Thanks."

"No worries." Incongruously, a smile bubbled inside Tusk. "Didn't I—"

"—say it would be dangerous? You're so predictable."

Gentle's fleeting smile stayed with Tusk as he headed down the hall. A babe in the woods, he thought. And guess who's got the baby-sitting job?

"Hey. One thing…" Gentle had come to the door. "There was something strange about the first man. I can't be sure, they both did a good job in keeping their faces hidden, but he had something wrong with his ear. His left ear."

Tusk's gut tightened. Christ, who would have believed it?

"What do you mean, wrong?"

"As if the ear was really tiny. You know him?"

Something must have shown in his body language. Tusk felt a gamut of emotions. Triumph, for his memory was as good as ever. Rage, because right now he wanted to smash the bastard. And fear…

"Yeah, I may know the guy," he said. "Something to talk about tomorrow."

He headed straight out the front door.

"Did you persuade him to ring the police?"

Trevor was waiting on the small front porch. It was still pouring, water cascading off the porch roof. Trevor had been Assistant Commissioner of Police when he'd retired in June of the previous year. Tusk had wondered more than once whether he might have kept his job if "Rough" Gentle had still been there on that fucking day in November. Now Trevor seemed diminished, in the way that long-time cops went when they left the brotherhood. Tusk towered over him.

"No cops." Tusk longed to be away, because the man was right, especially with this new info.

"I don't approve of this gumshoe fantasy of Peter's." Rough Gentle's voice rose. "For God's sake, he's an academic. No idea what the real world is like. And on his first day, he's assaulted! This one's for the coppers, Tusk, and you know it."

Tusk bristled. He liked Rough, but the ex-boss was treating him like a cadet.

"He's an adult now." Tusk took a step back, rain plastered his head. "Most of it's just scratches. What he needs from you is support, not bloody nagging."

In the Peugeot, he dredged up an image of the one-eared scumbag's face. Con Marcantonio, a beefy stand-up man with a record as long as his attention span was short. Problem was, Marcantonio wasn't a contract man, he was a company man. Tusk smashed a hand on the dashboard. If he'd guessed right, and he knew he had, he knew the other assailant as well. Hatred and alarm welled up. Marcantonio frightened only the weak, like Gentle, but Pasquale Bertoli frightened even coppers. Tusk had interviewed him once, still remembered the hatchet face and cold eye-slits.

Thing was, Bertoli could only be described as a hit man, one of the smart ones who'd never been convicted. And Bertoli worked for Sergio Scaffidi, a crime boss in the north of the city.

Scaffidi was very different from a couple of hoods roughing Gentle up. Scaffidi was organized crime, the full weight of it.

The oily, wet streets gleamed as he drove home. Gentle, he thought, what have you got us into?

CHAPTER 18

Sleep refused to come. Peter's heart was a thick jungle beat, equal parts righteous anger and fear. The fear was easy to spot; he only had to hold out his hand and watch it flutter.

He heard voices over the ever-present television. Even without distinguishing words, he recognized the sounds of argument. Every part of his body ached in a concert of torment dulled by painkillers. He rose from bed and listened from the hallway.

"I won't have it," his mother was saying.

Peter sighed. He loved Mum, always had, but living with her these past two months had been hellish. He pictured her lean face and fiery eyes. No doubt she was pacing backward and forward in front of his father.

Peter had resisted moving back into brick veneer heartland, even as the months passed after losing his job. But after Christmas disappeared without a sniff of work, he had finally ceased pretending he could keep up the hefty mortgage on his city apartment. Egged on by his mother, he'd leased out the apartment and returned to his gloomy bedroom. He'd regretted it ever since, and registered his distaste by rarely staying home, other than to sleep.

"How many of our police friends are still married, Trev?" he heard his mother ask. "Tell me that. I'm one of the precious few who have stuck with it. Now I'm expected to start the whole cycle again with my son?"

Harvey Jopling had a theory that everybody needed one parent to hate. In Peter's case, it was his father. He'd never grown to hate him, actually. But sometime in his teens Peter had crossed a line and disavowed everything about Dad: the police force, the disdain for pencil-pushers as Dad called them, the reverence for austerity, the hard line on nonconformity. It was never a policy decision as such, just a gradual and near-complete withdrawal of communication.

Peter had especially dreaded returning home and having to put up with his father in retirement. But retirement hadn't suited Trevor Gentle at all, to Peter's advantage. Dad was still sturdy, only a little thicker about the waist, and his black cropped hair had held most of its color. No, the only thing that had changed since he'd left the police force was his attitude. While at work he'd been a dynamo, always rushing off, always declaiming in public. Now he was silent, sipping whisky in the living room as he watched television with flat eyes, rarely moved by anything except his weekly get-togethers at the Retired Police Association. Which suited Peter fine.

There was a pause in the living room. Peter pictured his father preparing to agree. Considering how well Dad had done in his career, it always amazed Peter how his mother dominated the family. And just half an hour earlier, Dad had harangued Peter in concert with Mum.

But his father surprised him. "Emily, he's grown now." The gravelly voice sounded as firm as Peter had heard for months. "If he wants to mess with things he's not born for, let him. I never could get him to change his ways, and I guess I never will."

Well, well, well, Peter thought.

He went back into his God-awful bedroom and lay down on his sagging bed, under faded pictures of Fermat, Laplace, and other famous mathematicians which his parents had insisted on not removing.

I should have grabbed the wine bottle, he thought.

He drifted toward sleep, into a dream-memory he hadn't experienced for years.

***

He was a boy, a skipping boy. The sky shone white and blue. Dad's hand encased his, and the deep voice hummed as Peter skipped along a footpath lined with cars. His only thoughts concerned the ice cream he'd just shared over a plastic table and the jerky rhythm of his skipping. A joy to be here, right now, with his dad. Big, gruff Dad, chocolate smeared on his upper lip.

A bang punctuated the air. Dad wrenched his arm down. He saw Dad's face right next to his, crouched behind a car.

"Dad, what—"

Another bang. A clang nearby and Dad's grip was steel. Fear rose in Peter like motion sickness.

"Listen, Peter." Dad's voice was all hot breath, and Peter grabbed an arm covered with soft hairs. Dad pried him loose. "Just stay here. Low. Don't make a single move. Can you do that for me?"

He shook his head, but was already alone, pressed against the warm car door. A rusty blemish scraped his cheek. He trembled and waited.

Then he heard voices running, heavy steps not at all like Dad's. He curled into the smallest ball he could achieve, shaking. He'd wet himself.

"Bugger me, what have we got here?" A high whisper through panting.

Peter crushed himself lower. A hand grabbed his shirt. He whimpered. Smelled cigarette. The hand twisted and lifted him, and his writhing meant nothing. He screwed his eyes shut. This was a nightmare he'd never wake from, everything in him was braced for...

After that the dream was blurry, as if it was a dream after all. A harsh bang filled his ears, and the hand released him with a grunt and what Peter later recalled as a sigh.

Dad's footsteps, Dad bellowing. Horrid smells. His body shaking so fiercely it filled his mind.

***

"Peter."

"Jesus, Dad. You scared me."

His father, straight-backed in his blue bathrobe and old brown slippers, held a wine bottle and two glasses. He'd always had the ability to move stealthily, to suddenly appear and disappear. Only the red spots on his cheeks signaled the quarrel with Mum. He sat down on the edge of the bed, idly fingering Peter's latest Ruth Rendell paperback. Peter marveled at how his spotted hands were the only part of him to show his fifty-eight years.

The dream, Peter thought. Maybe that's why I rejected Dad's occupation. Ever since that episode, he's represented violence and fear to me. Jesus, no wonder I was so scared tonight.

"Sorry about the fuss Mum and I made." His father's voice rasped. "This was just so unexpected. And Mum… well, she was thrilled when I quit the Force, and now this…"

"But—"

"No, I didn't come to argue."

Dad filled the glasses, handed one to Peter, and took a mouthful.

"All I came to say was good luck with the venture. Odd choice, but you always went your own way. All of you children did, it seems. Just remember, if you need any help, I'm the one who knows where all the skeletons are hidden in the Force. Just ask."

"Thanks, Dad." Peter was stunned. "Thanks a lot."

When his father reached the door, Peter remembered Mick's easy familiarity earlier.

"Dad? How well do you know Mick?"

A smile tugged at Dad's mouth. "Well enough. A fine copper. I was the one who hired him. He came to the force late, but I knew a good man when I saw one. Became a homicide star. Pity about all the troubles."

"Troubles?"

"No doubt he's told you. Internal Investigations nabbed him on the shooting of a suspect. He got off, but they ended up retiring him soon after. He'd become obsessive, involved with the victims. Like I said, Peter, he's a good man. Just watch that temper of his."

Trust Mick not to tell me he'd shot someone, Peter thought. His eyes watered with fatigue, but his mind had begun to whir. He hunched over the computer on the corner desk, piled with investment and wine magazines, research papers, business bios, science fiction and crime novels. He logged onto the Internet, found his latest game of Diplomacy, checked out the battle situation.

Games felt trivial. He mentally reviewed what he'd gleaned in the State Library, certain of his instincts. How could he understand, really understand, why someone would want to kill Kantor, unless he understood the man's mind? But he needed more general theory.

Surging with energy, he knelt on aching knees to pull out cardboard boxes of files and books from under the bed. He found the actuarial journals and quickly tracked down three papers explaining modern investment theory.

He was pushing boxes back under the bed when the phone in the kitchen rang. At this hour it could only be for him. He rushed down to answer before it woke his parents.

It was Rollo Keppel. "Why did you turn off your mobile?"

"Sorry, Mr. Keppel." For some reason, Peter didn't mention his trauma.

Rollo slurred. "Thought you'd like to hear this. Kantor's funeral, Friday. My eulogy. Smarter man never walked the grand streets of Melbourne, nor one truer or finer. Sounds good?"

The phone went dead. Why on earth had Rollo rung him?

Peter switched on the kitchen light, checked the time, decided that Harvey Jopling would still be up

"My God," Harvey breathed when Peter filled him in.

The next ten minutes were spent resisting Harvey's insistence that he report the incident to the police, but when he hung up and returned to his room, he felt stronger. Harvey always did that.

Two hours later, he was still reading, squirming in the grip of his thoughts, the bottle empty, brow screwed up and mouth open, his mind unscrambling the symbols, testing the notions. The house was silent. Data, that's what he desired, data.

CHAPTER 19

As soon as Tusk arrived home, Bully whimpered at the back door until admitted. His tail thumped against the couch while he licked Tusk's hands.

Time check—1:20. Silent house. Fingers poised over the phone for nearly a minute before dialing.

"Candle," said a dry voice.

"Candle, mate—"

"Ivory!" No mistaking the pleasure in Candle's voice. "Where've you been?"

Detective Inspector Balthazar Candle of the Organised Crime unit. Tusk pictured him. Thin, almost gaunt. Eyes neutral after twenty years in the Force. Twice divorced.

"Sorry I haven't been in touch."

"Sorry, Ivory? Six fucking months sorry!"

Tusk licked his lips. Why feel pressure ringing an old friend? Even the brotherhood nickname of Ivory disturbed him. "Yeah, well. They rolled me, Candle, rolled me. It's been hard to keep the faith."

Silence.

"Yeah, mate," Candle said. "But now you've made the call, eh?"

"Tell me about Sergio Scaffidi."

A longer silence.

"Why?"

This time Tusk said nothing.

"Fair enough," Candle said. "Same old, same old. Scaffidi is still strong around Fitzroy and Collingwood, steady growth, no real trouble with his neighbors. Careful son-of-a-bitch, I'll say. Not on our target list right now—not ambitious enough to make waves, too smart to trip over his own feet. Not to be messed with though." A pause. "But you know that, eh?"

"Does Bertoli still work for him?"

"Bertoli? Fuck, now there's a bad memory. Last I heard he was in Queensland, hiding after the Rivers hit."

"Thanks, mate," Tusk said. "I'll ring you for a beer."

"Hey, Ivory—"

"Gotta go."

Tusk massaged his brow. Buckingham was easier.

"Who has the pleasure?" Buckingham's dandyish voice brought a smile to Tusk's face.

"Anything floating around on Sergio Scaffidi and his crew?"

Gentle would remember Justin Buckingham from school. Not with any pleasure. A thin rebel with a cruel streak, Buckingham became Tusk's mate after Gentle. He was eventually expelled for locker theft. Now he worked hard as a drug dealer.

"Well well, if it isn't Tusk. How are they hanging?"

"Yeah, good to talk to you too. Is everything okay?"

Buckingham barked. "Tell you about it one day. Scaffidi.

Mmm… why's a sacked psycho cop need to know about the philosopher-king?"

"A job." Last time Tusk had seen Buckingham, he'd looked wasted, as if he was using again. That had been months ago, a brief beer—Buckingham was one of his secrets from Dana.

"Bugger me. I'll need to ask around. Something in it for me?"

"Yeah, sure. Ring me tomorrow?"

"Yes sir, no sir, three bags full sir," Buckingham moaned. "You think I've got nothing else to do?"

Tusk stared at Bully, dozing across his feet.

"You'll fill in the gaps sometime?" Buckingham said into the silence. "I'll ask around. But you understand I've got to be careful around Scaffidi. You fly carefully too, n'est-ce pas?"

So good to have his feelers out again, after so long. But when Tusk donned his headphones and turned off the light to revel in the wall-to-wall guitars of Oasis, the dark pressed down like a tumor.

***

On his back, the family room floor unyielding. Bathrobe, warm socks. Eyes closed but no sign of sleep. Fingers tapping on the itchy carpet, rocking to the crashing chords of Guided By Voices, his latest find. Unknown in Australia, but the swooping voice of its genius, Robert Pollard, would one day rule, he was sure of that.

Images flowed haphazardly, as they always did on these vigils. Dana's wounded eyes. His mouth sliding on hers, thanking her as best he knew. Gentle, waving arms in the air as he spoke like a machine gun. Gentle cradling his hand.

A fanciful image, like a mirage in the distance. Kantor Keppel, staggering backward, arm up defensively in the harsh light of the stairwell, beard raised toward Tusk, mouthing a word over and over again.

Tusk rose and took off the headphones. 2:49 on the green oven clock. Time for something more classic, to quiet the blade of anger inside his chest. Maybe some Springsteen.

He switched on a standing lamp to change the CD and blinked. The cover of the latest *Women's Weekly*, sitting on the coffee table. Rollo Keppel in tuxedo, accompanied by Bella in a stunning red outfit. The caption: "Party of the Year. Exclusive Pics." Some orphanage the Keppels supported.

The victim's brother. The tycoon. The man who had called him gung-ho militia.

He traced the oval face on the shiny page. Yawned and mouthed, How guilty are you?

***

Time check—5:15. Head pounding from almost no sleep, sweat pouring. Lying on a bench, panting after warm-up cycling. The clang of weights, ceiling fans whirring, shouts of encouragement. Not a fully equipped gym, like the police gym had been, and the patrons were amateurs, but the best he could do close to home.

150 kilograms on the bar. A faint odor of liniment. The night hadn't soothed; now he'd bench press himself to some feeling of settlement, so he could start the day calm. But as he hefted the bar, muscles quivering, he couldn't banish the image of useless Gentle lying in the rain, vague figures above him, identikit

images of Marcantonio and Bertoli, and the shadowy outline of Sergio Scaffidi.

A burst of fury fueled his lifts. Exhale! Scum! Exhale! Scum!

***

"Jesus, big guy," Gentle said in the Peugeot's passenger seat. "Are you sure?"

Gentle's face had lost its deathly pallor. The prodigy looked vaguely presentable: pressed suit, blue this time, hair washed and neatly flowing. Sleep must have done him some good—he'd started fidgeting again. The bulky bandage on his finger had been exchanged for a smaller one, and although Tusk saw him wince once, he did a good job of hiding any pain. But the flitting eyes told Tusk he was panicky inside.

"Can't be sure," Tusk said. "But everything checks out. Marcantonio had his ear bitten off in the Pentridge exercise yard some ten years ago."

Time check—7:37. Tusk's arms and shoulders ached sweetly from the workout. He recalled Dana's fretful eyes and Nelson's little hand waving as he left home. Peak-hour traffic crawled along Canterbury Road. The majesty of the new Jimmy Page and Robert Plant collaboration, Eastern-tinged hard rock a la Led Zeppelin, roared over the car speakers.

"This Bertoli character's a hit man? Someone who actually kills others for money?"

"No, not for money. At the orders of Scaffidi."

Tusk glanced at *The Age* lying between them. Inspector Sam Vinci was quoted as saying he was hopeful of an arrest soon. That they suspected a vagrant. Spare me, he thought.

"And this Scaffidi is, like, Mafia or something? What connection could he have with Kantor Keppel? I can't believe this." Now that Gentle had names for the thugs, indignation seemed to have replaced some of his fear.

"Hey, relax. It's not as bad as it sounds," Tusk lied. "They're just trying to frighten us."

"Why aren't these animals behind bars?"

"Marcantonio has been—often. Bertoli, now there's a clever fish."

Tusk squeezed the steering wheel.

CHAPTER 20

"Straw?"

Peter Gentle listened to the crackle of The Island's intercom. Toorak throbbed with the noise of the AM commute. After the rain and cold in that parking lot last night, the touch of the morning sun on his cheeks felt like a benediction. His body ached in a thousand places. If Imogen hears me at the other end, he thought, calling her daughter who is supposedly mute, I'm cactus.

The gate clicked open. Mick nodded once to him before resuming his careful scrutiny of Mathoura Road. As soon as Peter entered the murky courtyard, separated from the safe bulk of his partner, his fuzzy nervousness returned. A Siamese—was it the same cat?—sat on top of the dry fountain.

Straw stood in the doorway, a finger to her lips to shush him, her green eyes large and still. Her black outfit looked unchanged, but no boots or gloves this time, instead a studded collar around her neck. Her lipstick was thick scarlet, her hair disheveled.

Peter mounted the veranda steps, bandaged hand in his pocket. Her face expressionless, Straw swayed her hips in a parody of sensuality. She took his hand by the fingertips and chunkily shuffled backward, drawing him inside.

The Island was shadowy and silent. Straw led him along the hallway and up the stairs, moving quickly on bare feet, her only sound the swishing of her dress, exhibiting purposefulness completely out of character with the public persona Peter had seen. He tried to keep quiet, and though his footsteps sounded loud in his ears, nothing stirred in the sleeping mansion.

The size of her bedroom staggered him. It had to take up an entire side of the house, yet it was packed with couches and chairs, some new and sleek, others tattered and high-backed, through which Straw wove, stirring up dust that spiraled in the sunlight streaming through half-drawn curtains. The walls were covered with posters depicting what he took for Goth-rock images—maidens draped over chairs, dark-haired men in black. Near a massive, unkempt bed, a computer screen on a corner desk showed a website covered with moving cartoon cats. A towering cabinet, containing video equipment and a huge television set, dominated the center of the room. Melodramatic rock music played softly in the background. Coals smoked in a fireplace by the window.

Everywhere—on the thick carpet, on lounge chairs, on the bed—cats slept or groomed themselves. Peter stopped counting at ten. His nose bristled at the stew of odors: cigarette smoke, cat fur, incense, and general mustiness. He felt a curious kinship with Straw as he took in the crowded, obsessive nature of the room. It's a world, he twigged. A coherent, complete world. To society, she's a mute marionette. Here, she's...she's the Straw she wants to be.

"Straw. Why did you invite me here?" His whisper sounded so surreptitious.

"Magical Mister Mistoffelees."

The disembodied voice sent goosebumps scurrying down Peter's back. He was mentally prepared to resist another advance, but she surprised him by lighting a cigarette and peering at him, eyes motionless, through the smoke.

A wide mantelpiece by the window held half a dozen cat statuettes, and in the middle a larger, Egyptian-looking, brass one. Desperate to strike up conversation, Peter pointed. "What's this?"

Smoke filled the air as Straw waved her cigarette at a poster on the wall.

"Bastet," he read aloud. "Egyptian goddess of cats. Sworn enemy of the serpent Apepi. How interesting. Where did you get this?"

"Shout," Straw intoned. Her moon-eyes glowed, placid in her placid face. "Uncle. Shout at Daddy."

"When?"

As if on cue, all the cats went still. Straw's face snapped toward the door. Without a word, she took his hand, pulled him out onto the landing and pointed toward the stairs. Peter could find no alarm on her face, no emotion whatsoever.

"Straw…" She was gone.

He hurried downstairs. Quietly shutting the front door, he heard a voice calling, "Straw?" Imogen.

The cold, still air in the courtyard set off a shiver. Talk about wonky data, he thought.

There was more to Straw than he, or even her mother,

understood. He sensed that she revealed only what she wanted to. Her vague accusations against Rollo surely had no basis, but why was she coming out of her shell to talk to him, a complete stranger, unless something underpinned them?

Peter spotted the Siamese cat judging him from the fountain. He scooped up a stone, but by the time he rose again, it had disappeared.

***

The tourists had arrived at Southbank, busloads of them, snapping photos, milling on the walkways down to the cruise boats. Peter shuffled nervously when he reached the revolving doors under the red Scientific Money logo. He watched Mick take up position and begin scanning the crowds.

"Two hours, then I'll come in to get you," Mick said. He'd been silent on the drive into the city, seemingly content to let Peter think out loud about the data.

"I won't get attacked in there, surely."

"Kantor was."

A shudder twinged Peter's stiff neck and he grimaced. He headed through the lobby and up to the second floor.

Ross Petrov, Customer Services Manager, was a wiry man with a chunky head and straight black hair. His manner was somber.

"Mate, the place has felt like a hospital ward ever since Kantor…"

He offered Peter a mint from a bowl. They sat around a small table next to a whiteboard covered with an untidy flow chart. Petrov undoubtedly had more people reporting to him than any other executive in Scientific Money, yet his office was small. Typical, Peter thought, the fund managers and marketing people are always the stars with the big salaries and swanky offices.

The office faced away from the river. From his chair, Peter could just see the dome of the Shrine of Remembrance poking through trees, bathed by balmy sunlight.

Petrov proved to be of little use. Yes, Kantor and Rollo got on well, "like two hands on the one body." Yes, Kantor got on well with Dancer, though Petrov's body language begged to differ. Yes, Kantor got on well with Marcia Brindle.

Petrov was in charge of the technology department, which looked after the security system.

"So your people program the invisible passes?" Peter asked.

"Yeah, in theory, but they've never actually programmed one under my control. The three invisible passes in existence were all originally programmed by Weiqing Chang in '94, when the company started."

"But he's the Research Manager."

Petrov chuckled. "Now he is. When the company started, everyone did odd jobs. Chang's one of our bright boys and he installed the security. There's nothing much he can't do, our Chang."

Weiqing Chang wasn't on Peter's agenda of interviews. "Who looks after the security of the central computers?"

"Yeah, me. It's like Fort Knox over on the other side of this floor. Special passes, a select team of operators on twenty-four-hour rosters. Security checks like the bloody secret service. And guess what? Even I'm not allowed in the most sensitive area. No one is, except the Investment Committee."

Peter grabbed one last mint before going back down to the ground floor, behind the elevator area, to find the company's Marketing Manager. Penelope Wilkins was a slick woman who knew little about how the investing was done and had hardly known Kantor. She painted a picture of a harmonious management team.

John O'Halloran, Scientific Money's Legal Counsel, was the last member of Rollo's executive team on the agenda. A dapper man with curly white hair, he also knew little about the inner workings of the investment process. In his ornately fitted office on the fourth floor, he spoke eloquently about Rollo as the company's visionary, and Kantor as its guiding intellectual. Peter quizzed him about Robert Friedman.

"Aye, a right nuisance," O'Halloran said. "He's tried everything to push the line that he owns our intellectual property rights, that his dead brother invented it all. Hasn't got a leg to stand on. A couple of years back, he tried to interest the press in the ridiculous notion that Kantor killed his brother. But lately he's been quieter. I'd wager he's finally realized he may as well give up. I saw him on the afternoon before the murder and he seemed to be going through the motions."

"Could he have hidden in the building after he left you?"

O'Halloran raised bushy eyebrows. "I saw him into the elevator, but he could have stopped off at another floor. You reckon he killed Kantor?"

"What do you think?" Peter felt he was getting the hang of interviewing.

"Aye, it's possible. He's a bitter man."

***

"Kantor was like my father to me."

To Peter's astonishment, the diminutive Chinese man dabbed his eyes with a blue silk handkerchief.

Who said that interviewing was difficult? Weiqing Chang was a treat. He'd readily agreed to an impromptu meeting, and had poured Peter a cup of Chinese tea. A portly man, he wore a flaming red vest, a gold tie with red stripes, and a wide belt. His face was round, topped by receding crew-cut hair. Acne scars dotted his cheeks. Squat black-framed glasses made him seem easygoing, but one look at his brown eyes dispelled the notion.

Born in northern China, Chang had met Kantor in the States whilst training as an economist. Kantor had sponsored him to come to Australia, where he'd worked with Kantor ever since.

If Ross Petrov had a small office, Chang didn't have one at all. He worked in a large partitioned area in the middle of the third-floor trading area. Low, maroon-colored partitions separated a couple of dozen young men and women in perpetual motion, gesticulating on phones, conferring in shouts, clustered in the small meeting rooms by the windows. Here, people ran rather than walked, and the blanket of voices, phones, and printers made Peter feel as welcome as in Draconi's.

"Mr. Gentle, even my mother loved him." Chang blew his nose. His English was accented but precise. "She came from China just two years ago, and still cannot speak much English, but she always made him a special dish when he came to our house."

"Weiqing, please call me Peter. Did everyone at Scientific Money love Kantor like you?" Peter couldn't keep his damaged hand in his pocket any longer. He found a paperclip on the desk and began to bend it backward and forward. Chang looked at the bandage without comment.

"Everyone. I mean, this is his child, this company, his and Rollo's. Yet he never made anyone feel he was the boss. He was so humble."

"Did Kantor get along well with Rollo?"

Chang leaned back, fingers interlaced over his stomach, and surveyed Peter across his desk. "Naturally. They are brothers."

"Even brothers can argue."

"Not Kantor and Rollo. Peter, have you ever been part of building a dream?" A soft smile settled on Chang's face.

Peter sipped the flower-scented tea. Lovely, but it made him long for a macchiato at Draconi's. "I can't say I have."

"Well, that's what Kantor and Rollo were… are doing. And they could only do this, Peter, because they loved each other like, well, like brothers."

"How did Benedict Dancer get on with Kantor?"

"Fine."

"I've heard they quarreled over salary."

"Discussed, maybe. Quarreled, never. Kantor encouraged open debate, but our culture here says that we do not take things personally. It sounds simple, Peter, but we do believe in this dream."

Peter wriggled in his seat, took in the open face. Was Chang lying? He certainly looked honest.

"Was Marcia Brindle close to Kantor?"

"Not close like me, perhaps, but she liked him. Everybody did."

Sure, one huge happy family, Peter thought. The paperclip broke. He dropped the pieces on the carpet.

"I've heard that you did the programming of the invisible passes."

"Yes. When we first established Scientific Money, there were few people aboard, and I taught myself how to modify the security system's software. With help from the security company, of course. But now all of that is outside my responsibility."

"Why the special passes?"

"Rollo wanted them. You have met him, Peter? Then you'll appreciate why."

Peter nodded. He brushed hair off his forehead with the injured hand and winced at the pain. "Will you take over as custodian of Scientific Money's investment theory?"

"Me?" Chang removed his glasses and rubbed red-rimmed eyes. "It's a problem. Only Kantor and Stan Friedman ever understood the theory. I guess Rollo has to hire another genius. But that's not so important short term. The theory has not needed to be revisited for five years, so we have faith in it."

"Stan Friedman. How much of the theory was his, and how much of it Kantor's?"

Chang's face pinched in disgust. "Have you been talking to that crazy brother? Kantor sometimes called the guy his stalker. Just a joke, of course."

"The theory?"

"It was a joint effort. But the basic idea was Kantor's. He was so intelligent. If you had met him, you would know."

Chang shook his head and poured some more tea. Whoops of glee came from a pair of traders bent over a screen.

"What's your job as Research Manager entail?"

Chang's eyes narrowed behind the black frames. "I'm

responsible for all the research into the economy and investment markets. And individual stocks. Of course, we don't have a big research department, so in fact I do a lot of it myself."

Peter drummed his feet. Suddenly he knew what had been bothering him. "Why does Scientific Money need any research at all? Don't the computers do everything? Economic analysis, market analysis, individual stock selection. Human research shouldn't be necessary."

"Very astute, Peter." Chang leaned forward. "I keep track of indices, major companies, economic data, etc. I produce our customer bulletins. Since we are a quant company, the actual research required should not be great, but the firm's stated philosophy is to run a real research center because our customers want that kind of information. Also, we have a couple of non-quant funds that have just been launched. But you are correct, that's why the research function is so small."

Everything Chang said made such good sense.

"Now I think your time is up." Chang beamed. "Did you enjoy the tea?"

But if Chang was correct, Peter's thinking was up the creek. No, I'm right, he thought, gritting his teeth.

"So who smashed Kantor's head in?" he said.

The blue handkerchief appeared again. "I really cannot imagine. The police think it was a drug addict."

Peter snorted.

***

Blue and white plastic tape hung across the door of Kantor Keppel's office. Peter glanced down the empty corridor before slipping in under the tape. The office was enormous, the same size as Rollo's, but whilst Rollo's office was a showcase, Kantor's felt more like a den. Peter walked past couches and a small settee that held a pillow, suggesting it doubled as a bed. A library full of books lined the wall opposite the window. In the middle of the room was a large, unadorned pine table, its surface scarred and scribbled upon. At the far end stood a mammoth desk, buried under papers, flanked by not one but three silent computers. He glanced out the window, across to the Westgate Bridge, the bay a blue-green band on the horizon.

Peter knew immediately that Mick had been correct. This was where Kantor spent most of his hours. His bedroom in The Island had been just a hotel room, a place to rest his head.

He wandered around the room. Already, less than a week after Kantor's death, it smelled of dust and neglect. On the wide bookshelves, Kantor's life was laid out in photographs and awards. A young, tousle-haired Kantor with Robert Merton, the Nobel Prize winner. A Recognition Award from MIT. A framed cover of an award-winning research paper. Kantor center stage in a group photo outside Melbourne University. Framed prospectuses from his days at Coombs Holcomb. The brothers Keppel grinning together at the laying of foundations for Scientific Money House.

Kantor's desk was an unholy mess. Research reports competed with academic journals in piles around the outskirts, and in the middle, chewed pens lay on mounds of correspondence. Computer output sat knee high on the floor. What could be seen of the wooden desktop was scored by Kantor's vandalism. The ancient leather chair sagged when Peter sat in it.

On shelves behind the desk, he found numerous Scientific Money photographs, in all of them Rollo commanding control, Kantor looking rumpled but impressive, his oval face calm with knowledge. But nowhere in the room were there photos with Imogen or Straw. Or Willy, for that matter.

Unsure of what to look for, he sifted through the papers on the desk. Drafts of press releases vied with internal circulars and technical reports. He flicked through a coffee-stained copy of ethicist Peter Singer's *How Are We To Live*—why had Kantor been reading that? The level of correspondence with international economists and local analysts staggered Peter. How on earth did the man keep up with it all? The short answer was that he didn't; Peter spotted mail from 1998 at the bottom of one pile.

Nothing helped Peter understand why a dedicated academic had been bashed to death, nor could he find anything more than superficial about the investment process.

He let his gaze drift across the desk like a searchlight. Nothing of interest. He flicked through a pile of correspondence, and a printed email caught his attention. A simple request from Rollo, asking Kantor to attend an analyst's lunch a few weeks earlier. He was about to put it down when he noticed the caption at the bottom. Rather than ending with "Rollo", the email finished with a solitary "B." What the hell?

Peter sat on the edge of the desk. The room began to spook him. Apart from the vague hum of machinery behind walls, all was funereally quiet. As quiet as *that night.* He shivered, picturing Kantor sweeping papers into his briefcase, rising wearily—the guy had worked till 10:30 PM!—walking to the door, down the corridor... Out of that imagery rose another, a monstrous wave of fear—his own face cradled in water, the reek of his urine, sibilant whispers in his ear. He shuddered, trying to snap back into reality, sending a twitch across his shoulders, and pain shot through his bruised neck muscles. Jesus!

"Big guy, do something," he said, but the leviathan was guarding the fort downstairs.

Alarm welled up in his chest and he ran. Out the door and slap bang into the police tape, which strained when it pulled him up. Strained like a finger bent back to its limit.

***

"Where have you been?"

Peter jumped. Mika sprang out from her cubicle to intercept him. She looked impossibly slim in her canary yellow dress.

"I got lost," he said.

"You met with Weiqing. All meetings are to be organised through me."

"Whoops." He glanced back down the corridor and hoped she hadn't noticed Kantor's open door.

She glowered, hands on hips.

Peter suddenly realized another snippet of data from Kantor's office. Why nothing on the Investment Committee? In his home away from home. Unless secrecy was an issue...

He said, "I saw an email from Rollo to Kantor with B at the bottom. Does Rollo always end emails like that?"

"No. Only with Kantor. It was a joke between Mr. Keppel and his brother. He would sign as Boss, Kantor as Slave."

Peter stared at Rollo's silent office door. So Rollo could have sent the threatening email. The implications were too monstrous to consider.

Mika stared at his bandage. "What did you do to your fingers?"

"Accident. Caught them in a blender."

CHAPTER 21

As soon as Peter emerged from Scientific Money House, he pumped himself up by scanning the sun-drenched city skyline across the river, spotting the buildings he'd once worked in, fixing his eyes on the vicinity of his apartment. Soon, he promised, soon I'll be back there. Especially if I keep acquiring data as well as I have this morning.

Identifying city buildings was a passion of his. He knew virtually every office tower in Collins Street by sight. He'd even done some historical research, knew that two building booms had raised his city. The first and greatest was on the back of gold fever in the 1860s, giving rise to the period splendors lining Collins Street. The 1960s boom sprang up during the golden age of natural resources, sending skyscrapers up along Bourke and Collins Streets.

He was ravenous. Did that signify some of the pervasive fear had left him? He inspected Mick with gratitude. If the lug had moved in the previous two hours, it wasn't apparent.

Mick nodded back. "You sure this traipsing around won't be a waste of fucking time?"

"Trust me."

"Who else would?"

They both smiled.

Peter's mother had loaned him her clunky old mobile. Crossing the footbridge, Peter used it to ring Rollo. Mika answered and gave him Rollo's mobile number.

"I wonder if I could obtain access to the restricted computer area, Mr. Keppel," Peter said, cupping his hands over the mobile as a train rattled past.

"Sorry, Peter," Rollo said. "Too commercially sensitive. But my team will tell you all about what goes on in there."

Ha! None of them seemed to know zip.

"Why don't you come and see me in the apartment tomorrow at 11:00? Tell me what your conclusions are."

"Okay, Mr. Keppel."

When he reached tree-lined Collins, Peter rang Bishop with an update, omitting to mention the beating. The lawyer was as curt as ever. Peter then rang his client, to receive another harangue about slowness.

"Some people are suggesting Kantor and Rollo were rivals," he cut in.

Imogen's voice was chilly. "Nonsense. You have never seen brothers so close. When we lived in America they would ring each other every day. Who is saying these things? Willy?"

What Peter needed now was independent, external data. His logical starting point had to be the Skulk Club. If its dozen members didn't have the inside scoop on Scientific Money, nobody did. And Peter looked forward to showing them that he was back in action, unemployed no longer.

He led the way to Draconi's, where Hector surprised him by drawing him aside.

"You're mixing in strange company, m'boy." Hector's drooping mustache always gave Peter the impression of a beagle. "That big fellow looks like trouble."

Peter chuckled. "Not at all, Hec. He's an old friend. We've gone into business together. As private eyes, actually."

Leaving an astonished Hector, Peter hurried through the restaurant. He was in luck. Carlo Fonti and Renni Maisel sat hunched over coffees at the bar. Peter hugged them both and introduced Mick. Carlo had been his workmate at Thompson White. Nearly bald at age thirty-five, Carlo was a quiet, brilliant actuary. Renni had gone to Melbourne University with Peter, and now worked for Merriwether Lang, one of the big legal firms. She was a boisterous American who sang Alanis Morissette songs when drunk.

"Nothing untoward about Scientific Money from my angle, Skull." Renni's face and hands were tanned, even in autumn, the by-product of endless cycling. "I should know, we did the legals for the original prospectus. They're one of our biggest clients, and we reckon the sun shines out of their arses. Rollo and Kantor Keppel are... were a brilliant combo. Skull, this company's one of the best things Melbourne has going for it."

Peter swung a full circle on his stool. "What are the skeletons in their closet, Renni? No company's perfect."

"Nothing I know about."

Throughout the discussion, Mick stood silent and unmoving. When he handed Peter a glass of water and some Panadols, Peter saw Carlo's eyebrows lift. God help me, Peter thought, I've not only got a bodyguard, but a nurse as well. But he had to admit his hand had begun to throb.

Peter quizzed Carlo about Kantor's theory. "What about this Stan Friedman?"

Carlo inclined his head, light glinting off his glasses, pondering. "That's right, I remember him. Friedman and Keppel were always together, maybe five, six years ago. I've got a special paper delivered by both of them at a technical conference I went to. I'm sure it was before Scientific Money. Would that help?"

"You bet." Peter began to drum his feet. "Is the theory sound? You must have a view, Carlo."

"Thompson White's official view is that Scientific Money is soundly based and that quantitative—non-human-intervention—investment is a viable alternative strategy for our clients. I haven't delved into the theory myself, but I've got my doubts."

Peter downed his macchiato and waved goodbye to Hector.

"Apologize to Ziggy for me," he called to Carlo. Ziggy was their cooking teacher, another something Peter had taken up to keep sane during unemployment.

***

Outside, he rang Harvey Jopling and sighed with relief when Harvey himself answered. Now was not the time to talk to Mandy.

Harvey spoke in fast, clipped tones. "Scientific Money are winners, Peter. The public likes the concept, the wholesale market is sold on it. It's got the track record to compete, even with BT. Their marketing is brilliant. Rollo Keppel's a genius. I guess the one open question is whether the recipe will work now that the chef's been murdered?"

"Speaking of recipes, anything fishy about the principals? Rollo? Kantor? Or even Benedict Dancer?" Peter grinned. His interviewing skills might need brushing up, but his networking was immaculate.

"Not that I know of. Hold on." Peter heard Harvey give muffled instructions. "I'm back. No, Rollo's got a big rep in town, as you well know. Honest but ruthless. One thing, buddy. Don't mess with him. Incredibly well connected, has mates all the way up to the Premier."

"Thanks, Harvey. Ciao."

Peter watched Mick inspecting the mid-morning crowd in Block Place. He rang Arnold Ng, waited for Arnold's secretary to track him down.

"Skull." Arnold worked as a project manager at IBM, his offices just near Scientific Money's. Peter didn't know him well. At Skulk Club meetings, after a few wines, Arnold's face went red and he became weepy.

Peter described the security system at Scientific Money.

"Pretty standard," Arnold said. "The firm's one of the market leaders, and the system is a good top-line one. Probably state of the art when introduced, still pretty good. A bit unusual not to have security cameras."

"Apparently the boss hates the thought of being watched. What about this facility to program invisible passes?"

"More usual for smaller firms, you know, where there's an owner-operator who goes in and out all the time. But nothing untoward. They're easy to program."

Peter stayed deep in thought as he and Mick rode a tram to

the other end of Collins, to 101, the elegant, towering office block set back behind shops. They walked between its granite Doric columns, through the opulent lobby, and took an elevator to Carlo's office to pick up the conference paper from Carlo's secretary. Back outside, Peter found a bench on the footpath near Spring Street while Mick continued his vigilance. The paper, entitled "A New Approach to Quantitative Investment," appeared at first to be nothing more than a rehash of other papers by Kantor. But wait... he looked at the date: November 1993. That was before all the other papers, indicating that at the very least, Stan Friedman had helped with the original work. And at the front of the paper, Peter found a joint dedication:

> Both of the authors wish to thank their beloved families for their patience during the months spent puzzling over this complex area of modern economics.

The language suggested strongly that Stan Friedman and Kantor Keppel had been equal partners in the exercise. Peter's heart raced. Stan Friedman had drowned six months after the conference.

He rang Giuseppe Marino, got lucky again. Giuseppe was one of the quieter Skulk Club members, but conscientious in keeping in touch. Unlike most of them, he'd married young, and often showed photos of his three daughters. He'd trained as an accountant, but now worked for the Australian Taxation Office, heading a team that investigated companies' tax bills.

"Yes, I know what you want, Skull." Giuseppe's voice was so soft, Peter had to strain to hear it over the whir and clatter of trams. "Our teams know more about what goes on in these big companies than the regulator. The sniff of evasion, the stench of decaying fortunes—we're connoisseurs."

Peter smiled at the lyricism behind Giuseppe's job fervor. "Anything on these guys?"

"Scientific Money isn't in my area. But I can ask. When do you need this by?"

Now, Peter thought, I need data now. "As soon as you can, Giuseppe. It's important."

"I'll try for tomorrow, mate. You'll owe me lunch. At Blakes."

"Done. What do you know about Rollo Keppel's management team?"

"Can't help, Skull. The only one I know is Marcia Brindle, and that's only because we sit on a committee of the Society of Accountants."

Peter jiggled his legs. When would those painkillers kick in? His sore back deserved a glass of red. "What's she like?"

"Highly regarded. Very professional, dedicated to improving the standing of accountants in the community. I admire her, Skull."

"And personally?"

"Our relationship isn't that deep. I've found her very pleasant."

"Grazia, Giuseppe."

"One thing I remember. She mentioned that she's thinking of starting her own accounting practice. I think she said it to get me interested."

"When does she plan this?"

"She didn't say. But she's not young, even in our profession."

Establishing your own practice takes capital, Peter thought. Is there a money connection here?

Tomasina Symons was probably the most highly paid Skulk Club member. Peter crossed Collins to 120, tucked away behind St. Michael's Church, where Macquarie Bank, one of the most successful Australian investment banks in recent years, occupied a number of floors. It focused on acquiring and keeping the best people. Tomasina was one of its rising stars.

Peter had to wait fifteen minutes before being ushered into Tomasina's office, Mick in tow, to find her pacing the room. Her face was lean and intense as a wolf's.

"Skull, it's a bad time to chat. The Renson deal is on the boil, and I stand to lose the plot."

Peter tried to stop thinking about food, about Draconi's food. "Two sec's, Tom. What's the gossip on the guys at Scientific Money? Who's diddling who?"

"Not much goss, they're the good guys. We wish they'd crack up, especially with the professor's death, but that Rollo's too tough." She chewed the inside of her cheek. "He should be at Macquarie, y'know. Now piss off."

When Peter reached the door, Tomasina grabbed his elbow. Her eyes were dry and hot, as they always were during the climax of a deal.

"Hey, one thing," she said in a lowered voice. "That Dancer. I've seen him lots of times at Marchetti's. Drinks a lot." She saw Peter's expression. "Yeah, I know, we all do. But this guy's a serious drinker. Obsessed with money. Used to slag off about Kantor Keppel. I took it as the usual bitch-and-moan, but maybe it's useful to you."

Peter grinned. What had the muscle man said, a waste of time? "Thanks, Tom. Ciao."

"No quoting, understand. Go on, piss off and leave me to my heart attack."

CHAPTER 22

Tusk had figured it out long ago. Money and sex were the number one motivators in his book. But fear, as administered by the likes of Bertoli and Marcantonio, came a close third. Fear disabled, fear crippled. He recalled interviewing one witness who'd recanted vital testimony, watching him literally freeze when terror seized his face.

Fuck, he hated those who traded in fear. And the hatred was knotting his guts.

Time check—1:01. Back at bloody Draconi's. He scanned the crowd. No alarm bells. Hector's mustache, as he delivered plates of pasta, kicked off mental humming. The Beatles, "I am the walrus, coo coo coo choo."

"Peter, m'boy," Hector said. "If you need another mind on this case of yours…"

Tusk expected sarcasm. Instead, Gentle showed kindness. "Yep, Hec, we'll call if you can help."

"Spare me," Tusk said, when Hector moved on.

Gentle chuckled. Chirpy, now that he seemed to have forgotten what those bastards did last night. "Hec misses the courtroom drama."

"Okay, run through who you've talked to."

Gentle's debriefing, in between gobbling pasta and wine, was shambolic. He rocked on the chair, tugged at hair, drummed fingers. Just like in school—funny then, weird in an adult. Half his interviews had been useless crap, others had been botched. Some interesting tidbits, a handful of unverified motives, that was all.

Tusk ate as Gentle summarized his Skulk Club discussions. Superb pasta, but nothing could ease that familiar tension coiled in his muscles. The sensation that every fiber was one eye-blink from action.

What a waste of time, Gentle chatting with all of his yuppie mates, though Tusk had been surprised to find he'd liked most of them. As geeky as Gentle had turned out, Tusk would have bet he'd be a loner, but he seemed to have more friends than you could poke a stick at. Tusk sighed, thought, Where have my mates gone? How many did I ever have?

"Okay, here's my yesterday," he said, flipping notebook pages.

He stepped through his interviews with exaggerated precision—Strasser, Bella Keppel, Friedman, Willy Keppel, the security guard.

"Let me summarize—" he began.

"No, let me."

His partner's chair squeaked as he shunted forward in excitement. The hooded eyes gleamed.

"Dancer," Gentle said. "Bright, has no alibi, didn't get on well with Kantor, maybe a pay dispute, it's not clear how deep the antipathy. Could be the murderer, but I can't see a big enough motive."

"Brindle. Has no alibi, she's intelligent, so if she planned a murder you'd expect to see one. No clear motive, but I think she's nervous about something, maybe it's related to planning her own accountancy practice."

"Friedman. Clear motive, the timing of the anniversary of his brother's death is a pointer. Could have hidden in the building after meeting the lawyer and gone out through the emergency exit."

"Willy Keppel. Sounds real unsavory, hated Kantor, you believe he lied to you. No alibi. Could conceivably have snuck in with another employee and gone out the emergency exit."

"Bella Keppel. Could have got in and out, but has no motive, and would have needed to be alibi'd by Rollo."

"Rollo. Ditto. A couple of people you spoke to claimed he didn't like Kantor, but they hate his guts. Mostly I heard that the two brothers were like peas in a pod."

Boy Wonder was impressive, no doubt about that. Tusk savored Draconi's aromas: garlic, bacon, coffee. Watched Gentle pick up a fork and bang it on the table, twist it in his long fingers.

"That strange email," Gentle continued. "Five of the six could have signed as B, so it's not much help. The murder weapon is no help, it's a common item. In summary, we've got six potential suspects. Right now the field is way open. But I believe we're already doing better than the police." A breath. "And I still think there's something funny about Scientific Money and this fiendishly secret formula, which may or may not be connected with the murder."

Tusk bridled at the smugness pasted across the Mick Jagger face.

"Good job." Tusk paused for effect. "But let's face it. You don't have a clue about human motivation."

"And you do?"

"Don't get sulky. You want to hear about motives? How about this? Dancer—stiffed by his boss on salary, so smashes him. Brindle was blackmailing Kantor to fund a business and needed to cover up."

"What—"

Tusk held up a hand. "Friedman—we agree there's a motive, call it psychotic hatred, although actually my instincts say he's innocent. Willy baby—lifelong hatred. Bella—screwed Kantor and needed to cover up. Rollo—jealousy, boyhood hatred, discovery of infidelity, you name it, there's a dozen possible motives swilling around."

Gentle's voice soared. "People don't murder for reasons like that."

"They bloody well do, Gentle, and for reasons a lot more trivial."

"Crap."

"I had one case where a man got mad because his brother wouldn't let him watch *60 Minutes*. Stabbed him with a kitchen knife. People kill for any reason."

"Bullshit!"

The nearby tables had gone quiet. Just in time, Hector banged cups on the table.

"He's right, you know," Hector said. "There's no motive trivial or base enough."

Tusk didn't know whether to laugh or cry.

"What is this?" Gentle waved his fork, now twisted out of shape, in the air. "A public debate?"

"Sorry," Hector said. "But you were the one making it public."

"Are you suggesting Rollo…" Gentle looked around at the suits watching his performance. As he sighed and shook his head, his mobile rang.

Hector winked at Tusk and was gone.

"Hi," Tusk heard Gentle say softly. "No, I'm all right.… Yes, my finger is better.… No no, I'm fine. Listen, any ideas about—… Oh, no problem. I'll ring."

Christ, the coffee was good. Even the noise of the place no longer grated with Tusk. "Mind if I say something?"

"As if I could stop you." But Gentle's tone was light.

"The key is to push the suspects hard for motives. Probe around their edges. Like you said, the field's wide open. We don't need to argue our personal calls on who the murderer is. Let's get out and about again."

Actually, the quickest route now to Kantor's murderer was through the scumbags hired to frighten Gentle. But Tusk couldn't raise that possibility.

Gentle nodded over the rim of his wine glass.

"Let's start with Dancer," Tusk said. "Can you try to get us in to see him?"

"Sure. Big guy?" For once Gentle's words didn't spill out. "Tell me, am I a coward?"

Probably, Tusk thought. "You've got every right to be scared. Those guys are scary. Even to me. Was that a woman on the phone?"

Gentle's cheeks bloomed red. "Just a girl I'm trying to date."

A girl? A date? What sort of language was that for a thirty-four-year-old? Tusk nearly laughed but he also felt pity. I bet

Gentle's still a virgin, he thought.

"Keen on her?"

Another blush. "Yes. She's lovely. She's from the country."

"So what's the problem?"

What was the word to describe Gentle's face in repose? Tusk had read it in a biography. A naif, that's what Gentle looked like. A boy in a man's skin.

"I guess I'm just not good at… at girls."

"Can I give some advice?" Tusk recalled Dana's eyes in the morning, when she squeezed his arms. He was a charlatan—Christ knows his track record with women was nothing to boast about—but felt compelled to continue. "If you're keen on her, do whatever it takes. You only get one chance. One chance and that's that."

As with Hector, Tusk expected sarcasm. Again, Gentle surprised him by blinking. "Thanks, big guy."

"Two more things. No more farting around with all that theory. Suspects, Gentle, suspects."

"You're just jealous because you're a moron."

Tusk felt the knot in his stomach untie a fraction. "And stop fucking up all the cutlery."

The nerd whooped.

Tusk nearly laughed too. But the thought of Bertoli's eye-slits tightened his gut again. Under the table his fists clenched. Trembled.

CHAPTER 23

"Go away," a muffled voice said behind the burgundy-colored door. Peter spotted a face peering through the adjacent leadlight window.

He looked at Mick standing immobile behind him, wondered whether he knew him at all. The big lug had surprised him twice, once with soft words of advice, on love of all things, and again when Dancer's secretary had said her boss was working from home, Mick had headed straight for the parking garage without a word of consultation.

Not that the trip took long, just fifteen minutes south of the city. Albert Park, with its streets of terrace houses clustered around one edge of Albert Park Lake and spilling down to the sea, had managed to retain a village feel that kept its residents trendy and its property prices high. Palm trees lined the lake, and on the beachfront rollerbladers competed for space with cyclists. Peter knew the suburb well, Carlo Fonti had lived there for years.

Peter moved close to the door. "Mr. Dancer, could I please have a word with you?"

Dancer lived in a freshly painted double-fronted terrace with a green picket fence, in the expensive part of Albert Park, just half a dozen houses from the beach end of Kerferd Road. The terrace stood out, with a false roof frontage and a protruding central arch, the bricks and paintwork an elegant mosaic of colors: oranges, greens, reds, and yellows. Large windows, their blinds drawn, overlooked a crowded garden dominated by a willow tree sighing in the breeze. Sparrows twittered in and out of the shady veranda. A black Porsche gleamed in the parking space out front. Peter marveled at the tang of salt in the air.

Dancer's voice squeaked, "I've said all I'm going to say to you."

"Rollo asked me to speak to you." Peter looked back and was rewarded by Mick raising eyebrows above his sunglasses.

Unexpectedly, the lie worked. Locks clicked. Peter nearly gasped at the figure scowling at them from the dark interior. In twenty-four hours Dancer had lost all composure. He wore a rumpled suit—had he slept in it?—and fluffy white slippers. Stubble covered his chin. Bloodshot eyes darted behind askew glasses.

"Who's he?" Dancer glared at Mick.

"Mick Tusk,"—extending a huge paw—"Mr. Gentle's associate."

Dancer seemed about to argue, then shrugged. He led them down a dark hallway to a large modern extension at the rear. Light streamed in through skylights and floor-to-ceiling windows. The kitchen looked down onto black metal-mesh chairs surrounding a glass coffee table. A spindly metal sculpture stood by the wall. They sat down at a large jarrah dining table, a pile of papers and a laptop at one end. A wind chime tinkled outside.

"Make it snappy." Dancer's shoulders were hunched. "I've got work to do."

"Mr. Dancer," Mick said, removing his sunglasses, "this will only take a couple of minutes. First, your movements on the night of the murder."

The cheeky sod! Peter glanced at his partner to find out why he'd commandeered the interview, but his face was set in its customary mask.

"I've already told the police," Dancer said, "that I had nothing to do with the murder. I just went home like any other day. Apparently around the time of the murder, or so the police say, but that's just a coincidence."

Mick's deep voice soothed. "When did you last see Kantor?"

"A couple of hours before I left." Peter noticed white flecks around Dancer's lips.

"Did you speak to him?"

"No, I just passed his office."

"Anything seem out of the ordinary?"

"Not at all. Kantor was contemplating infinity as usual."

"What was your disagreement with him about?"

Dancer blinked. "What disagreement?"

Peter jumped at a tremendous thunderclap as Mick slapped his hands on the table and rose as if hinged. Dancer skittled backward in his chair.

"Utter crap, Dancer." All civility had disappeared from the voice snapping in the air. "Everyone in the office knows about it. Come clean, mate, or I'll—"

"Okay, okay." Dancer raised his hands and peered through his fingers. "It's so… so minor. I thought he was holding down my salary below where the market had gone. I reckon I should have a 30 percent increase. We quarreled, okay? But it was nothing, nothing."

In the heat of the morning's hunt, the previous night had faded in Peter's mind. Now he tasted acrid fear as he watched a tic throbbing in his partner's neck.

"You were a member of his fan club?" Mick cracked his knuckles, making Dancer twitch. "Come on, mate."

"It's true. Just an office squabble."

Mick pounded the table again. Startled, a seagull flew off the back fence.

"Your face says it all. You hated him."

"No way."

"The truth, Mr. Dancer mate, or I'll really lose my temper."

Peter stared aghast. Mick's arms, planted on the table, strained.

Dancer panted. "Okay, man. Okay."

The wave of rage in the room cooled, slightly.

"Okay, I didn't like the prick." Dancer blew his nose. "Genius this, genius that, that's all I ever heard, but when it came to treating me right, he was a real arsehole. But I didn't kill him."

Mick had been right, Peter thought, Dancer did have a reason to kill.

"Why not?" Mick said. "You'd never have gotten the raise you deserved with him around."

"If I killed everyone who's screwed me out of my just rewards over the years, I'd be a serial killer by now." Dancer pushed his glasses back up his nose. He looked cockier. "Are we all done then, gentlemen?"

The response was instantaneous. With one motion, Mick scooped up his chair like a paperback book and flung it sideways to crash against the wall, bringing down the sculpture with a thud. Peter leapt to his feet, wincing as his neck stabbed with pain.

"You're still hiding something from us," Mick snarled. He looked about to leap over the table.

"No. Nothing."

"What's got you so scared you're about to piss your pants?"

Dancer shrank even further into his chair. "I don't know what you're talking about." His eyes looked like rabbits' eyes in headlights. "Leave me alone."

At last Peter forced himself to act. Trembling, he placed a hand on Mick's forearm. It felt like a taut bow. Mick looked at him, his face suddenly a mystery, teeth bared, fury etched in lines across his forehead.

And then the storm passed as quickly as it began. Mick stood up straight and wiped his hands down his trousers.

"Twenty-four hours," he said, tossing a business card onto the table. "Call before then or we'll take this to Homicide. Believe me, once we tell them how you've lied, they'll be all over you like a rash. Any excuse, they'll have you up on a murder charge. You want that?"

Dancer gave a hoarse cry. "I've done nothing."

The havoc machine strode down the hall.

As Peter stumbled after Mick, he caught a glimpse in a bedroom of a slim woman in a bathrobe, hand raised to her mouth in alarm. He knew Dancer had no children, and she was much too young to be his wife. Fresh loathing for the executive filled him. He rushed outside.

"Call or you're thrown to the cops," Mick shouted just before he slammed the door with a crash.

They stood in the pale sunshine. A faint breeze tickled Peter's sweating face. He gazed down Kerferd Road to the two pubs overlooking Beaconsfield Parade and the pier. The sea was a blue-gray strip.

"Mick?"

His partner's chest rose and fell. "It worked, didn't it?"

Peter didn't know whether to be outraged or sarcastic. "What if he complains to the police? Or to Rollo?"

"You saw him. Is he going to complain to anyone?"

"What if he's the killer? Aren't we letting him loose?"

"Killer?" Mick spat his words, "He's scared, not guilty. Something's got him shit-scared, though."

Peter listened for the Number 12 tram on Victoria Avenue, a block further down, but he could only hear seagulls cawing and the voices of cyclists on the bike path beside them.

"Should have warned you," Mick said.

"You frightened the shit out of me."

Peter thought, Who is this guy? He's as terrifying as those animals last night. Should I be scared of him, or just glad he's on my side?

But Mick was right; the threats had delivered data. He probed his bandaged finger. "I reckon Dancer could be the one. You heard him—"

"Fuck him." Mick was heading down the side street toward the Peugeot. Peter followed, his back groaning. Where to now?

CHAPTER 24

Only one place to go, so Tusk put his foot down, gunned the Peugeot through the autumn leaves blanketing St. Kilda Road. Wound his window all the way down, relished the pummel of air on heated skin. Focused on traction, on catching traffic lights. Time check—4:56. Thought: Move it, arsehole.

"Where are we going?" Gentle slumped in the passenger seat, a scrawny rabbit.

"Fitzroy."

Across the river, under the Flinders Street Station clock dome.

"Why? What's there?"

"Scaffidi."

"But, big guy—"

"Shut the fuck up." Enough of that big guy shit.

A tape from the glove box. The classic chords of The Rolling Stones' "Brown Sugar." Sky clear, sun low. The stream of traffic swung right, alongside the railway line. At the edge of the city, Tusk turned left, headed north past the cream pillars of Parliament House.

Clear as daylight, Dancer wasn't the perp. Pity he'd lost his temper with the man, but at least someone had begun to speak truth. No, Tusk felt sure that super-cool Rollo was behind his brother's death. And Scaffidi was the key.

Past the hip cafes and designer shops of Brunswick Street. During his wild days, he lived in Fitzroy for a year, in a crowded terrace with threadbare carpets. Once one of Melbourne's tawdriest suburbs, now the yuppies had arrived. Even the drug scene had begun to move out, south into the city.

Moran Street was on the western fringe of Fitzroy. A pub, a restaurant, squeezed in between the peeling paint of terraces. Serpico Restaurant: square and unfriendly. Black glass frontage, a torn umbrella over metal chairs and a table, an alley down one side fading into gloom. Its sign was small and never lit at night, but Tusk knew a constant stream of people, mostly Italians but some Anglos, frequented the place.

"Best Italian food in Melbourne," Cap had told him once. "Only thing is, you need a gang frequent flyer card to get in."

Tusk parked down the street, next to an overflowing yellow garbage bin. Bitter metal in his mouth. No one around except a shrunken Italian woman wearing a shawl.

"What happens now?" Boy Wonder's mouth hung open. Tusk felt uncharitable. You wanted to be a private eye, he thought of saying, welcome to the real world.

"This." Tusk whipped out of the car, threw his sunglasses onto the car seat, no need for the gun in the glove box. Half ran to the restaurant.

He pushed the dark wood of the door, stepped in. His hands felt ready. His whole body had been ready all day. Discreetly lit, tables, chairs. Thick fumes: cigarette smoke, coffee, pesto. A waiter leaning against the bar at the end. A handful of men seated at a table.

Tusk saw Con Marcantonio seconds before the one-eared man, holding cards up before his face, noticed him.

Tusk went for the scum, running down the center of the restaurant, thankful for a clear path. Marcantonio reared, cards flying, blonde ponytail swinging. Reached into his jacket pocket. Tusk launched himself and hit the man hard in the chest. They went down, a grunt from Marcantonio when his massive body slammed into the wooden floor. Chairs flew. A red band flared behind Tusk's eyes.

He rose, clutching fabric, startled eyes bulging before him. Marcantonio flailed, Tusk hit him in the nose, hard, heard a squelch. Blood flew. But a chance fist slammed Tusk's chest with staggering force. He stumbled back.

Marcantonio faced him, tiny eyes burning, meaty arms up, fists cocked. He was huge, chest and legs and shoulders bulging. Blood poured out of his button nose. Tusk glanced around. The others had fled. Only the waiter, shouting into a phone behind the bar.

Marcantonio snarled. "You're—"

Tusk's advantage was speed. A keening sound in his head, he attacked. Swung with his right fist, waited till Marcantonio blocked, felt the jar up his whole arm. Pivoted and slammed a foot into his opponent's leg below the knee. A surprised grunt. The thug started to go down. Left fist hard into a cheek. Knee up under the jaw with a crack.

Marcantonio crashed to the floor, yelping. Tusk put a knee

on his chest and smashed down. Pain raced up his arm. His body electric, guitars soaring in his head.

Someone screamed.

Mad glory pulsed through him. He smashed down again. The body thrashed under him. Something landed across his back.

"Mick!"

He heard the reedy plea through cotton wool. His fist toiled: smash, smash. Ineffectual twigs around his neck. Aftershave.

He shook his head, sweat flying. The world seeped back into place. He let the screeching stick figure, his partner and pal, drag him back. A monstrous beat pounded deep in his chest. He flexed his fingers, which roared with pain.

"For God's sake." Gentle's hair akimbo, like a scarecrow. "You've killed him."

As if in answer, Marcantonio groaned. His square face a swollen pumpkin. Blood everywhere. One eye invisible under a massive bruise. The other eye open and fixed on Tusk.

"No more." Marcantonio's words blubbered from battered lips.

No time to waste, Tusk thought. Sweat stung in his eyes. He winked at Gentle. Raised a fist high.

"I'm going to finish it, you fuck."

The body under him twitched. Tusk's mind was blank. What questions?

"What's Sergio Scaffidi got to do with the Keppels?" Gentle asked, bless his soul.

"Ge'—" Marcantonio's retort stopped by a fist into his chest, not hard.

"I can't control him." Gentle again. "He'll hit you again."

"Sister," Marcantonio exhaled in a hiss. "Bella. Boss's sister."

The connection!

"Mercy." Marcantonio's eye flapped shut.

"You've killed him," Gentle said.

Tusk grabbed Marcantonio's wrist. "He's fine."

Tusk stood, pain coursing through him, as if he'd been on the receiving end. Fuck me, he thought, it's happened again. He felt like crying. Or one part of him did. Another part of him exulted.

Tusk asked, "Is he the one?" They were all alone. Except for the body on the floor and some fallen chairs, it looked as if they'd never entered. "The one who beat you up?"

His partner nodded, face as pale as Kantor's corpse.

"Just as well," Tusk said. "Wouldn't want to do that to a stranger."

Gentle shuddered.

Tusk straightened, stretched his back. Breathed in and out, quelling his body. Leaned down, smeared his hand with Marcantonio's blood, then wiped it across his own face and down his shirt.

"What the hell are you doing?" Gentle asked.

"Making it look like a full fight."

He picked up a chair, sent it flying onto tables, scattering cutlery, a shocking noise in the deathly quiet. Took another chair in one hand and walked over to the bar. Scythed bottles, glass flying. Over to a window, punched a jagged hole.

Sirens out front. Gentle's mouth open, like a bloody fish. Time to hurry. Tusk wrapped his handkerchief around his fingers, pulled out a gun from Marcantonio's jacket, and let it clang on the floor. Tugged the stunned nerd by his jacket.

Outside, the fresh air of the waiting, judging world greeted him. Tusk raised his head to the sun, low and pink-flecked. Breathed steadily. A crowd had gathered, mostly old, a few young punks. The waiter from the restaurant stood wringing his hands. Sirens howled close by. He shivered once. An off-the-wall song in his head, Iron Maiden's wailing "Run To The Hills," but he couldn't do that, could he?

If only he could transplant himself to Belgrave. To the smell of grass. The swoop of birds. Bully's pounding tail. How to explain this to Dana?

CHAPTER 25

Peter Gentle threw up, a convulsive splattering onto the buckled footpath outside the restaurant. It was all too much. Numbed, he'd desultorily answered questions from a young policeman, had seen the waiter gesticulating at them, had watched Mick lie. Mick's face in the restaurant came back to him, mouth agape in blind fury, veins popping in his forehead. If Peter hadn't pulled him off the moaning hulk...

He doubled over and retched, head pounding, vomit burning his mouth. Mick placed a hand on his head; he batted the hand away. He heard sirens, screeching tires, more voices.

"Ivory," said a loud, abrasive voice. "What the fuck you doing here?"

Peter stood up, shivering and yawning. He took in the scene, a surreal hell from some TV cop show. The sun had sunk behind buildings, cool shadow lay over the street. Glass shards littered the footpath under the hole in the restaurant's window. A tall man peered into the interior. Three cars blocked traffic, two of them with flashing lights. Two policemen held back a sea of staring, murmuring faces.

The short man radiating energy in front of Mick looked Italian, his olive face pointed and sharp, his wavy, black hair perfectly parted on the left. He wore a dapper dark suit with a red patterned tie. Black eyes blazed.

Mick extended a hand. "Sam."

Somehow the big man had managed to retrieve his sunglasses from the Peugeot, and his blood-smeared face was as unreadable as ever. But his broad back slumped, one arm of his leather jacket was nearly torn off, and his white shirt was smudged red.

The short man ignored Mick's outstretched hand, thrust his jaw at Peter.

"You Gentle? Peter Gentle?" A precise Italian-accented bark.

Peter nodded.

"And who are you?" he surprised himself by asking.

The little man took out a pack of cigarettes, lit one. His upper lip curled. "Detective Inspector Vinci, Homicide."

The man in charge of the Keppel case. Why was he here?

Vinci stepped up to Mick, close enough to stick his head under Mick's chin if he chose. "I get this name Gentle in connection with this homicide I'm working on. And then bugger me, his name's on dispatch. A brawl. So I take a look. And guess who I find at the party?"

Vinci's machine gun words filled Peter with dread. Nothing, but nothing, to do with this case had panned out as expected.

Mick met Vinci's glare calmly. "You're looking good, Sam."

An ambulance eased through the crowd. Two men in white raced into the restaurant. A tall plain-clothes policeman came over. He was in his fifties, on the edge of fat, and wore an ill-fitting cream suit with stains down one side and a floral tie from the '70s. Peter took an instant dislike to his sun-burnished face, with its cold-fish eyes and blue-tinged nose.

"Inspector," the tall man said in a rasping voice, "there's some guy inside, big feller, badly beaten up. Psycho Tusk strikes again, eh?"

Peter glanced at Mick, but the planed face was looking over Vinci's anger, at a plain-clothes policewoman. She was considerably younger than the others, short and mannish in physique. Black hair hung straight down off her head. She had full lips in a slim face. Her dark eyes stared back at Mick, then she busied herself with her notepad.

Mick flicked a glance at Floral Tie. "Good to see you too, Larry."

Peter recognized the name from the case file. Larry Mixton.

"Fuck you, psycho," Mixton said.

Vinci looked at Mixton with ill-disguised contempt. "Who's the man inside?"

Mixton shrugged. His stony brown eyes turned to Peter, and Peter quailed.

"Con Marcantonio, a small-time thug." Mick hawked reddish spit into the gutter. "We were questioning him. He attacked me."

"The fuck's we?"

"My partner and I. Private investigators."

"I want to see your license."

Mick folded arms across his chest. "Pending."

Vinci exhaled in disgust. "Ivory, you're really asking for it."

Peter's mind reeled from all that he'd experienced. The raw closeness of violence, the animal fear that swept him in waves— he refused to assimilate it all. Help, he thought, close to tears.

"Who hired you?" Vinci demanded.

Peter was puzzled. How did Vinci know his name but nothing about their client?

"I can answer that," he said. "Imogen Keppel."

"Fuck!" Vinci threw eyes up to the sky. "Unbelievable." He jabbed a finger into Mick's chest. "What's Marcantonio got to do with it?"

"Don't know."

Vinci looked about to explode again. He turned to the policewoman.

"Constable," he said, "get them out of here before the press screws up my life even more. Back to HQ and question them. Hard. I want to know who the hell they think they are. You—" Rigid finger stabbing the air in front of Mick. "You're in deep shit, mate."

Vinci rushed off, smoke trailing over his shoulder.

The policewoman bustled them to the third car, an unmarked Ford. Peter heard shouting from the crowd, calls of "Inspector!"

"Handcuffs, Dee?" Mick said. Peter couldn't believe his eyes—the brute actually had a faint smile on.

As she held the back door open and Mick slid in, Peter looked at the restaurant flickering in the strobe of police lights. The ambulance orderlies were emerging with a stretcher. The crowd surged, cameras flashed.

Mick removed his jacket and draped it over his head as he slid into the back seat.

"Dana watches the news," he said, seeing Peter's look.

You should have thought of that before, Peter thought. His back pulsed as he eased into the car. The interior smelled of cigarette smoke and mouth freshener.

"What do we tell them?" he hissed to Mick.

"The truth, Gentle, the truth." Mick seemed fully at ease. "These are the good guys, remember?"

***

"You married, Dee?" Mick's voice sounded light. Peter twisted uncomfortably in his seat and stared at his partner.

"Not yet."

The policewoman was driving fast, down into the city. Peter saw her eyes in the rearview mirror, assessing him, then flicking to Mick.

"Dee," Mick said. "Meet Peter Gentle. Partner and mate. Gentle, meet Deirdre Lasker. We worked together, once upon a time."

"How long have you two been at this?" Deirdre asked.

"Two days."

Deirdre shook her head, black hair swaying. "I've never seen Sam so riled."

"He's always mad," Mick said. "That's just Sam."

By now the car stank of their sweat. And something worse. Peter sniffed his bandage and recoiled—he must have spewed on it. He felt sore and tired and dejected. The seat bit into his bruises, and his broken finger had begun to throb.

"I don't know, Mick," Deirdre said. "This one matters for him."

"Promotion time, huh?"

She grunted. Silence took over in the car. Peter tried to collect his thoughts. Did the police have grounds to charge them with anything? He had no idea. How long could they legally question him? Should he ring Bishop? But no, Bishop wasn't their lawyer. What about his Dad?

"How's the case running, Dee?" Mick asked.

They stopped at the Flinders Street lights in Swanston Street. Peter looked up at the rusty green dome of the station. Six o'clock. None of the people rushing across the intersection paid any attention to the men being taken to be locked away.

"You know better than that," Deirdre said. "No champagne on the horizon, but."

"Any good leads? Besides the druggie crap?"

Deirdre drove silently. A heavy weariness settled onto Peter's limbs.

"Come on, Dee," Mick said. "How can it harm the case? I'm just interested—anything major cropped up?"

"Shut up, Mick."

"What's going to happen to us?" Peter blurted. He felt, rather than saw, the sunglasses swivel to look at him. He stared pointedly at the trees overhanging St. Kilda Road.

"You're being taken in for questioning," Deirdre said, "in connection with a homicide."

"Come on, Dee, that's not right," Mick said. "We're not murder suspects, for Christ's sake."

Peter heard Mick's whisper in his ear. "Let me handle this, Gentle."

"No, I won't." Peter's voice roared in the enclosed space. He wished he could be somewhere else. Anywhere else. He felt nothing but revulsion. Mick was crazy, nothing else could be said, Peter's partner was a bloody lunatic.

***

"So how long did you spend at Dancer's place?" Mixton's hands were creased brown.

"Maybe half an hour," Peter said.

He'd told everything, though his background work on Scientific Money hadn't elicited any interest at all. His head swam. The interrogation room was stifling. A table with a tape recorder, two chairs, fluorescent lights, bare wall, the sneering policeman, and himself—that defined his world.

He'd barely had time to speak to Mick, sitting on a bench in the noisy police hall, before they'd been separated.

"Take these." The big man had handed Peter his dose of painkillers. Mick's sunglasses rested on his knees, his baby blue eyes had rings around them.

"What if I hadn't been there?" Peter hissed. "What if you'd killed him? Would you be walking around playing the cool man, cracking jokes? Don't you care about what you've done?"

"What do you know?"

All Peter's confusion had crowded in on him. "We need to talk about this."

Mick had passed a huge hand slowly across his face. The face that emerged looked haggard.

"Yeah. Talk," Mick said, almost a whisper.

Deirdre walked toward them.

Mick had straightened. The sunglasses slid on again. "Take heart, mate. You've done nothing wrong."

An hour had passed since then, an hour locked in this coop with this revolting policeman.

Mixton leaned forward, hot eyes within touching distance. "Did you hit Dancer to help him talk?"

"Of course not."

"Come on, you threatened him."

"No." Not really a lie.

"Tusk did, then."

"No. Look, you don't understand. We're just investigators, violence is not our—"

"The hell it isn't, Gentle," Mixton shouted, baring yellow teeth. "That Marcantonio, he'll be in hospital for a month. Don't come the choirboy with me, sonny."

"I'm not—"

"Come on, come on. Tell me. Which one of you did it?"

Fear rose in Peter's gorge. "Did what?"

"Come on, you think the psycho will protect you?" Mixton roared. "He's singing right now."

"What do you want? I'm just an actuary."

"Is this how you threatened Dancer?" Mixton threw a photograph onto the table.

Peter looked down. Benedict Dancer lay on his back, something dark around his neck, his tongue protruding.

"Oh no," he said. It couldn't be. He lurched to his feet and spewed up coffee from deep in his stomach.

"You don't think I had anything to do with this, do you?" he shouted.

"His girlfriend places you two at his home," Mixton said, his voice flat and hard.

"How could you think I'd have anything to do with this? It's inhuman."

Mixton sneered. "You're telling me."

Peter rested his whamming head on the table. He heard

Mixton terminating the interview into the tape recorder. The door shut.

He slumped in sad silence. And he knew, without verbalizing it, what he was mourning. His innocence, that's what the world had just stripped from him.

**

Two hours later, Peter was led out of the reeking room by Constable Lasker.

"Where are we going?" Peter felt woozy with exhaustion. Dancer's death made no sense—why was he killed?

"To stay the night." Deirdre looked fresher than ever.

"A suite or an ordinary room?"

They went past the now-quiet cubicles, through a side door into a dimly lit area containing a desk and three cells, bars floor to ceiling. Peter's heart fell yet again. The bars looked so strong and cold, a damp odor of bodies and dust assailed him. Deirdre held open a cell door.

Mick sat on one of the beds, sunglasses resting beside him. His bulk seemed to fill the cell and, except for the extreme paleness of his face, he looked untroubled. The cell door clanged shut and Peter heard Deirdre leave.

"Who interviewed you?" Mick asked.

"Detective Mixton."

"Good old Larry." Mick rubbed his eyes. "Sorry you had to endure him. He's… he's…"

"A scumbag?"

A wan smile flickered on Mick's face. "Yeah, good choice of words."

"What about you?" Peter yawned until his cheekbones ached.

"Sam Vinci himself. Is interview the right word? Mainly he yelled at me."

"But we found some useful clues." Springs creaked when Peter sat down on the other bed. He saw a man lying in the adjacent cell.

"Sam doesn't think so. Or at least he won't admit it. Guess they told you about Dancer."

"I can't get over it, we must have been one of the last people to see him alive."

Mick massaged his cheeks, and Peter realized that Mick was also exhausted.

"You see now that this is no intellectual puzzle?" Mick said.

Peter's gut churned with precipitate anger. He was sick of the whole damn thing. The killings, the beatings, the police, and especially Mick bloody Tusk.

"Well, what I can see is why they kicked you out." His voice rang through the cell and the man next door raised bleary eyes. "I'm amazed they didn't do it earlier, if that's how you carried out your work."

"Fuck you."

"Typical response." Peter spat scorn. "And if I keep at you, you'll throttle me, is that it?"

Peter's face burned. He braced for a heated response, but Mick swung his legs up and lay staring at the ceiling. The only sounds were Peter's heaving breath and snores from the man next door. When Mick spoke, his voice was little more than an exhaled whisper.

"I'm sorry."

"Sorry?"

"Yeah." A pause. "I'm sorry you landed here. Sorry to stuff up your work." Mick's chest rose and fell. "I'm sorry about Marcantonio. Sort of. If I could do it over, I would."

Mick rolled over onto his side, his back to Peter.

"But why—?"

"Go to sleep," came the deep voice.

Peter sat stunned, his thoughts awash. I missed the point, he thought. I thought I knew Mick, just because we hung out together fifteen years ago, because he still looks the same robust giant. So the first time he baffles me, I judge him. And judge wrong.

Moods were Peter's specialty. His own moods soared and sagged like ocean waves. He often felt at the whim of them, but he'd assumed Mick to be exempt from such capriciousness. Jesus, the man seemed to be one hundred percent control.

That crazy rage in Fitzroy—Mick hadn't been able to restrain himself.

He looked at the still figure lying just meters away, nearly moved to shake it awake and offer an apology. Instead he lay down himself and let fatigue instantly seize him, like a heavy blanket snuffing out his whirlwind thoughts.

CHAPTER 26

Tighten and lift, exhaling. Loosen and drop, inhaling. Sweat pooled in Tusk's belly button. One hundred, one hundred and one…

He heard stirring from Gentle's cell bed. A creased face rose to watch Tusk.

"Morning," Tusk grunted between sit-ups.

Funny how the mind worked. While he'd lain in bed, body at rest but brain stewing, the accompaniment had been an old song he'd never owned or even liked. A wild track by Humble Pie: "Thirty Days in the Hole." Stevie Marriott, before drunkenly succumbing in a hotel fire, his voice perilously high, lamenting his incarceration. That's what I deserve, Tusk thought, thirty days in the hole. Thirty bloody years, more like it.

The outside door flew open. Mixton scowled. Vinci dragged on a cigarette, suit jacket on, bright white shirt, and of all things a tie with blue elephants. Freshfaced, as if he hadn't spent the night slaving at the case Tusk knew was driving him crazy.

Mixton unlocked the cell door.

Vinci tapped cigarette ash onto the floor. "Come on, arseholes, out of here."

The Brainiac leapt from his bed. "What, you're letting us go?"

"Investigation pending." Vinci shook his head as if at a simpleton. "I'd like to lock the pair of you up till Christmas, but it'd be a waste of cell space."

Tusk closed his eyes. Chest rising rhythmically. Concrete floor pressing into his back. Images of Yolanda and Nelson. Dana… last night their phone conversation had been short.

Tusk: "Won't be home tonight. Guest of the Force. Don't worry."

Silence.

Dana: "Oh Mikey, what—"

Tusk: "Just a turf matter. No problem. Really."

Dana: "You okay?"

Tusk: "Fine. Be home lunchtime tomorrow. Better go. Love you."

Dana: "Mikey, love you."

So much unsaid, left to be said later. Now Vinci swung his hawk's face down toward Tusk. "You're bloody lucky Marcantonio won't talk. He'll be lying in hospital for, what, another fortnight, and he won't let us press. The fuck's going on here?" Prowling the room, smoking, his black eyes never leaving Tusk's. "But I'm onto you, Ivory, and if you interfere with this investigation again, I'll fuck you over so hard you'll never see daylight. So ditch this schmuck. Go home. Play ordinary citizen again. Hear?"

Tusk curled, stood up. "Who killed Dancer then?"

Vinci shook his head again, blew a smoke ring in their

direction, wheeled out of the room.

"Isn't it great, big guy?" Gentle said.

"They've nothing to hold us on. We only spent the night here to intimidate us."

Tusk flexed hands and arms. No time now to complete a full routine, but he felt physically refreshed. In need of a shower, but otherwise nothing that a run wouldn't fix. A run wouldn't be enough for Gentle—the nerd looked rumpled and unhealthy. Tusk recalled last night's hot words, felt a weight settle on his shoulders.

Time check—7:30 on a Friday morning. The cubicles outside were mostly empty. A policewoman looked up from her screen and yawned. Tusk halted, stared toward his old cubicle by the window.

"Nostalgia, eh?" A smile on Mixton's leathery face.

"Fuck off."

Mixton led them to a desk to sign for their belongings.

"Remember, sonny," Mixton said to Gentle. "You haven't got a license. Next time—"

"Larry—" Tusk's words were cut short by the phone.

Mixton's eyes darted while he listened. After the short call his smile widened.

"Before you go," he said, "the boss wants to see you."

Tusk shrugged at Gentle's look of bafflement. Did Sam want to blast them some more? They followed Mixton to the elevators, up to the top floor, and Tusk knew this wasn't Vinci they were going to see.

On the executive floor, quiet offices contrasted with normal copper chaos. The look was shabby, like a run-down corporation.

Mixton opened a door with frosted glass. A tall bony man looked up from his desk.

"Gentlemen," he said, coming to them with extended hand. "Ted Peacock."

In his twelve years in the Force, Tusk had never been in this office, had only met Deputy Commissioner Peacock once, though the face was familiar from a hundred staff magazine shots. In his office, Peacock looked more like a politician than a policeman. Late fifties, not gone to fat like most older cops. Graying black hair combed sideways. Face bumpy and worn, deep vertical furrows in his brow. Brown suit. Blue eyes boring into Gentle from behind wide, awkward-looking glasses.

"So you're Trevor Gentle's boy." Peacock's voice was like honey. "You say hello to him from Big Ted."

Gentle looked like shit. Suit crumpled like a tea towel, shoes scuffed. White flecks crusting his lips. Eyes puffy under hair like tangled briar. Unease percolated in Tusk's stomach—the expression in those eyes was familiar from school days.

Peacock turned to Tusk. "Son, pleased to see you again. Miss the Force?"

"Yes, sir." Reflex deference, but Tusk did feel respect. Big Ted was a legend, a cop's cop. Decorated for bravery, an incredible success rate in Homicide.

When they all sat down, the Deputy Commissioner began to push his glasses up his nose, then down again, like a puppy worrying at a toy.

"I won't beat around the bush, boys," he said. "I support the idea of the private sector keeping us on our toes, don't get me wrong. But this case has its special features."

Tusk wasn't surprised when Gentle leaned forward like a stooped mantis to interrupt. "It's a particularly nasty case. Two people are dead already."

"You boys know how important Scientific Money is to the fabric of this community? I'm on the Melbourne Major Projects Committee. The Mayor has made it clear that Rollo and his band of brilliant people are part of a major push to bring investment capital into this city."

Gentle's voice rose. "So this is a particularly important case to solve?"

"But in a sensitive manner. Now, I've had calls complaining about your probing, boys, and I'd like to ask you to give the police a free run at this case first. Say for the next month. And then if there's no resolution, why then you two can get into it."

"But we can't stop, Mr. Peacock." Tusk caught a whiff of Gentle's rank stench when his partner shifted in his chair. "We have a client."

"That woman." Peacock took off his glasses, examined them as if they were rocks from outer space. "This is important, young man."

"So is our client."

"And what do you say, Tusk?" Peacock's voice had sharpened, almost to a parade ground bark.

"We've already given Sam's team new information," Tusk said.

"Snippets."

"The fact that Rollo's related to Sergio Scaffidi is a snippet?"

"Snippets that Vinci and his fellers would have found anyway. And in the meantime, you're stirring up a storm here."

The second-most powerful policeman in Victoria looked each of them in the eye.

"You've heard me, boys," he said. "I've asked you to cooperate, lay off until the proper authorities solve this. What more can I say?"

"You can say what you mean," Gentle said. "You're pressuring us to walk away from our client and our livelihood. I'm afraid that's not possible. Mick?"

Gentle jerked from his chair, strode to the door, Tusk trailing. Behind them, the Deputy Commissioner's voice remained level. "Boys, do what you have to do."

Mixton was twirling a toothpick in his mouth. His eyes bulged as they swept past. "What's going on?"

The elevator pinged. Tusk had to give the geek credit. Gentle tossed his hair back, lifted his shoulders, as similar to Mick Jagger as he'd ever look. Smiled at slob cop Mixton.

"Time to get back to work."

CHAPTER 27

One breakfast during twelve-year-old Peter's first summer break after entering Mont Albert Grammar, his father handed him a hardcover book without a dust jacket. Its spine was beginning to crack, loose pages stuck out, and it smelled like his grandparents' bookshelf.

He hadn't even been aware that Dad read books. The policeman was the busiest father among all his friends, forever out of the house, on the job.

Peter found the book challenging at first. He'd never heard of the author Emile Zola, but read in the foreword that he was a French writer from the turn of the century, which explained the archaic style. But as he read, something about the book gripped him.

The story itself was exciting, a tale of the anti-Semitic incarceration of Alfred Dreyfus, imprisoned on Devil's Island upon being wrongfully accused of spying. Zola, a distinguished man of letters, took up the case. In the book's rousing finale, his passionate cry, "J'accuse," echoed through the French courts and freed Dreyfus.

Peter read outside, sheltering from the summer sun under their gnarled apple tree. He skipped lunch and read through the afternoon on his bed. His mother insisted he eat dinner, but afterwards he threw himself back on the bed. When he finally snapped the book shut, sending dust up into his nostrils, he felt his mind and heart beating as one.

After his mother tucked him in, he lay awake for hours. When he heard his father's car pull into the driveway, way past midnight, he ran down the hall.

He hugged the tired man. "Thanks, Dad."

"What's it saying, Peter?"

"Justice."

The word rolled across his tongue like a slick marble.

***

On the dappled footpath outside Homicide, the cool air on Peter's cheeks felt like freedom. The leafy boulevard of St. Kilda Road curved in both directions, encasing the passing cars in autumn reds and browns, yellows and greens. He lifted his face to catch the sun pouring through a gap in the clouds. When the memory of his father's face appeared in front of him, vivid as his fatherly memories inevitably were, he closed his eyes.

"It's good to be out. Eh, big guy?"

Beside him, Mick balanced on the balls of his feet. His pale face was smudged, his blond stubble hair looked greasy, and his jacket showed a rip down one arm. But his back was ramrod straight once more.

"You think that was smart, back there?" Mick's voice sounded tired. "You know Big Ted's one of the greatest policemen we've had? And you just walked out on him."

"It surprised me too." Peter grinned. "But I meant it all. We've been hired to do a job."

A green and yellow tram pulled up, its doors thudding open. They sat at the back, away from the few passengers. Peter's broken finger throbbed and he looked with distaste at the filthy bandage. He organised his thoughts.

"Look, I'm sorry," Peter said.

The tram clattered over an intersection. Peter couldn't decipher Mick's eyes staring out the window.

"It was all too much for me, the whole thing. I shouldn't have said… When was the last time you heard me apologize?"

"You reckon they should erect a plaque?" No smile, but.

"Mick, the one thing to discuss," Peter said, trying to ease his way into the question, but failing, "is… what happened there with Marcantonio? I was wrong to slam you about it, but I've got to know more."

Mick took off his sunglasses. The hurt in the depths of his eyes pierced Peter. "No need. I'm not going on."

"What do you mean?"

"I quit."

"You gave me five days. You promised."

Mick grabbed his arm. "Stop shouting. Let's get off."

They sat on the moat wall in the shadow of the long, solemn gray shape of the National Gallery. Later in the day, a constant stream of people would stroll from the city to marvel at the water pouring down the central window, but now the building was still. Away from the sun, the air felt chilled.

Peter restrained himself from yelling. His feet beat a tattoo on the concrete. He was engulfed by a jumble of thoughts: How can I continue without him? What if I'm attacked? The license—the idea was for Mick to "train" me, how can I get a license now? How can he pull out when we're making progress?

"You can't quit."

"The fuck I can't."

"But—"

"Just listen. For once."

Sparrows chattered in the roadside elms. Mick's face sagged, like the loosening of a grip. "You're right to be pissed at me for what I did yesterday." He spread his hands open. "I've always been a fighter, Gentle. You know that. After Mont Albert Grammar, there were years when that's all I was, two fists. Then I became a copper. I saw what I'd been. I reformed, big time. No more violence for its own sake. For years. But a couple of years ago, this... this thing happened to me."

The pain in Mick's voice was so palpable, Peter touched Mick's knee, fleetingly.

"Something changed." Mick's voice quickened. "I got emotional about some of my cases. Felt for the victims. I came to hate some crims, the worst ones, the organized gangs. Christ, I hate the Scaffidis of this world. He's evil, pure and simple, there's nothing he won't do. And scum like Marcantonio... a bag of shit, preying on the innocent."

"Why—"

"No, listen." Mick pressed the heels of his hands into his eyes. "See, I've figured out what happens. It's a cycle, over and over. I come across a Marcantonio, my blood boils. I tell myself to cool it, remember what happened last time? But part of me says bugger it, why play by the rules, give it to the cunt. And this tension builds up, between the control I know I should exercise and this… abandon. It almost feels delicious."

The worn wheels of a tram clanked rhythmically past them.

"And then something triggers me, I can hear the voice, saying fuck it. Like snap. It's frightening, as if I'm berserk. Must be what happens to people in war, blood-crazy. When I come to, I can't bear to see what I've done. Feel like the earth could swallow me. Then I swear it'll never happen again. See? A cycle, over and over."

Mick folded arms across his chest, squeezing. "Only way to beat the cycle, steer clear of the Marcantonios. I thought this case would be different…"

Mick's eyes were wide, like a child's, and Peter felt tears behind his own eyes.

Mick slapped his leg. "Christ, see what you've done? No, not fair. Tell me, Gentle, how can I be a dad to my kids when I just lose it like the worst murderer?"

"Did they try to do anything about it in the Police?"

"Nah. You're just expected to do your job. I'm not the only one, in fact there are worse ones than me. I'm just obvious— Christ, you saw me, how could anyone miss it?"

Peter waited until a white-haired woman walked by. He felt like a fool.

"Look, Mick, we can make sure it won't happen again." Peter heard pleading in his voice. "Together. Got that? I can help. God knows I need your assistance, this is a business I'm no good at. But I can help you too. I mean, we can talk about it. That's something, isn't it?"

Mick nodded. "You know, you're only the second person I've told. Dana knows, she knows the whole sorry shit. And we agreed, she and I, the only way is to try to leave that world behind."

Without warning, Mick put on his sunglasses and stood up to walk toward the city, past the Arts Centre spire, effortlessly overtaking commuters heading to their offices. Peter struggled to catch up.

"No," he said, grabbing Mick's jacket sleeve. Mick didn't even slow down. Peter ran in front, shoved his hands into Mick's chest. It felt like trying to halt a bus, but it worked. They stood on Princes Bridge, overlooking the slow river. Peter saw triangular wakes behind canoes, the ugly disc of the Casino in the distance, Melbourne's humpbacked skyline.

"I won't let you off the hook." Peter's voice caught with desperation. "You promised me five days and you've only given me two. You promised me, big guy."

"I'm breaking that promise." Mick raised his hand, as if to pitch Peter aside.

"You're going to let that monster go free?" Peter threw his arms up in exasperation. "Fine, go ahead. Walk. See if I care. But the police won't catch him."

An elderly couple paused to watch.

"Justice," Peter cried. "That's what we're talking about here. The right of every human being."

He saw hesitation.

"Justice for Kantor Keppel. Mick, he was a good man, one of those innocents you talked about. What about Dancer, that scared man we bullied yesterday?"

He was close enough to hear air hiss in and out of Mick's nostrils.

"And I can't do it on my own!" Peter yelled.

A seagull wheeled overhead. Trams hummed past. He watched Mick stand still as a mannequin, hand raised.

Then the barrel chest sighed.

"Okay."

Nothing more. Just one word that sent a shiver up Peter's spine and a mad smile across his face.

"You crazy bastard," he cried.

Then he flung his arms around a startled Mick and hugged him, for once feeling his solid analytical heart crack and mend, all in one instant. He laughed and shook his tears off the bridge into the Yarra River, fount of all Melbourne's magic and mystery. And lo and behold, Mick was staring down the river also, sunglasses off, tears glistening in the corners of his eyes, a rare and beatific smile gracing his face.

CHAPTER 28

Hector stopped mid-stride, plates in hands, nostrils flared to sniff Peter. "A difficult interview?"

We're back on the job, Peter thought, even if we look and smell like tramps. He gulped down his glass of wine. He savored the odors of buttermilk and bacon steaming off their heaped pancakes, the soft comfort of the booth, the hubbub, but mostly he savored his own jubilant mood.

"First time, Hec," he said, grinning as he turned on an American accent. "In the slammer."

The restaurateur's mustache quivered. Peter was saved from further explanation by his mobile ringing.

Bishop's voice was clipped. "No time for your update call?"

"We were otherwise engaged," Peter said, taking pleasure in the ensuing silence. He summarized the events of the previous day and night.

"Dancer's death is connected?"

"I don't know."

"Surely. Ring again today."

Draconi's was packed with the late breakfast crowd, calling

greetings, rustling newspapers. Peter poured maple syrup until his plate swam in it, noting that Mick skipped syrup altogether. The first mouthful tasted like nectar of the gods.

"Remember going through the suspects?" Peter said. Less than twenty-four hours ago, he thought.

"Sure."

"Well, nothing's changed in our assessments—"

"—except Dancer's eliminated himself by getting strangled."

"Be serious. As you said, we need to do another round of interviews. In addition, we need to check alibis for yesterday afternoon. And this Scaffidi character. How can we find out about him?"

"I've got some feelers out," Mick said. "Let me try something else."

Peter wolfed down his meal while Mick dialed and turned away to speak softly. By the time he'd finished the call, he was smiling. "I've got lunch later with Constable Deirdre Lasker. I'll see what the police have got on Scaffidi."

Peter couldn't help himself. "Lunch where? What's your connection with her?"

"We went out together once upon a time." Mick forked a pancake. "Before Dana, that is. I'm going to meet the constable here."

"Here? At Draconi's? I thought you despised the place."

Mick's face twitched. "It grows on you."

Peter felt better with the meal inside him. In fact he felt great. Sleep on the hard cell bed had proved surprisingly refreshing. He drummed fingers on the table while he rang Marcia Brindle at work. Her secretary informed him that Marcia was at meetings all day.

Though his own mobile was wrecked, messages had queued up on that number. A day-old message from Giuseppe Marino: "Skull, I've managed to exceed all your expectations. A senior manager with APRA is in town for a seminar. Friday 6:45 PM at the Sofitel. We have ignition, my friend. Ciao."

He rang Giuseppe's secretary to confirm and rubbed his hands in triumph—APRA, the Australian Prudential Regulatory Authority, was the regulator of the funds management industry.

His father, who must have forgotten which mobile to ring, had rung an hour ago: "Son, I've had six phone calls about you. Ring your old Dad as soon as you can. And—" Peter listened to the silence, "—take care, Peter."

He rang Mika to confirm the eleven o'clock meeting with Rollo, and to give her his new mobile number. She told him Rollo wanted to meet at home, not in the office, and then proceeded to enumerate Rollo's virtues.

"Please don't believe any rumors," she said.

Peter remembered her attitude. "Miss Hashimoto, data, analysis, conclusions, that's what I believe in."

He rang Weiqing Chang, heard out the Chinaman wailing about Dancer's death.

"I wonder if you can give me a hand," Peter said.

"Anything, Mr. Gentle."

"I'd like to check out the detailed investment system. It would only take—"

Chang had hung up. When Peter rang back, one of the traders answered; Chang was in a meeting.

He rang The Island and was startled to catch Imogen crying.

"Those animals," she said. "Questioning me on the day of my

husband's funeral." Sobs. "I remember this man Dancer. Does his death have anything to do with my husband's?"

"Maybe. Mrs. Keppel, is Straw under treatment?"

Silence. "I don't understand the relevance of this."

"It's just routine, Mrs. Keppel, but I've had a few people talk about Straw and her closeness with your husband. I'm interested."

His words had the right effect.

"Very well, young man. No, Straw is not currently under treatment. She was for many years, but now her condition is at equilibrium." A pause. "Do you know why we named her Straw?"

"Why?"

"When she was born she had a shock of hair the color of a haystack. She was a beautiful baby, Mr. Gentle."

"The marriage episode must have been difficult for you."

Another pause. "Your research is thorough, Mr. Gentle. Yes, I must agree. I think that was the worst day of my life."

Until now, Peter thought. "Have you kept in touch with Straw's fiancé?"

"Good heavens, no. He was the worst kind of ingrate. I only wish he would disappear from the news."

"The news?"

"Don't you read the sports pages? Magnus Jones is a star player in football."

"Of course I know him," Mick said after Peter had fielded another round of Imogen's complaints about progress. "Plays for Essendon."

Peter ordered more coffee for both of them, and another glass of wine—Bin 407, he deserved some good stuff—while Mick rang Bella Keppel, without luck, then Robert Friedman's office. Peter thought of the case's success fee, imagined depositing the check, ground his teeth. They had to keep pushing. His mind whizzed through all the permutations of suspects and clues, again seeking a path through the maze.

"I've made our meeting with Friedman on Sunday." Mick stretched, a lazy, long motion that was infectious. Peter rubbed his eyes and also stretched. They smiled.

Hector delivered Peter's wine and their coffees. To Peter's surprise, Mick summarized the previous twenty-four hours. Hector shook his head.

"Can you handle this?" Hector spoke to Mick, and Peter felt a burst of jealousy.

The big man rubbed his knuckles, looked at Peter. "Yeah, I can handle this."

"And you," Hector said to Peter. "You've done the analysis?"

"Sort of. Hec, what's justice?"

Peter had surprised himself with the question, but the response was immediate. Hector dragged a chair across from a nearby table and straddled it. His voice lost its restaurant bark, took on a mellow softness.

"There are technical definitions, Peter, but I always used a simpler outlook. To me, justice means protection of people's fundamental rights and the punishment of the wicked. Two sides of the coin—one helping those who need it, the other catching up with those who abuse."

"What about the means of obtaining justice, Hec?" It was a strange tableau, Peter reflected. The old judge wearing an apron, the intellectual with his bandaged finger, the ex-cop smeared with blood. "Can you justify, say, killing a very bad person?"

"That's the tricky part," Hector said. "Of course, there's a legal answer to your question—the law defines what you can't do. But at a more fundamental level it's really tough. If that assassination attempt on Hitler had been successful, who wouldn't say that was a fine thing? I've seen some terrible people, as have you, m'boy,"—looking at Mick, who nodded—"and I've sometimes thought if they were gone, the world would be a better place. But if we let the vigilantes have their way, society would be in chaos. I guess where I come from is that everyone, even the worst human specimen, has rights."

Hector stood up, pushing back his shoulders as if his sermon had invigorated him. "Sure appreciate being asked to help."

"I didn't need the morality lesson," Mick said after Hector had gone. But he didn't seem angry. "I know what I did yesterday doesn't stack up."

"Hey," Peter said. "That wasn't for you. It was for me."

The chair squeaked when he stood up.

"Time to go, podner," he said, and was rewarded by a faint smile, just as his mobile rang.

"Gentle?" The sibilant, tender voice turned Peter's bowels to ice. He gestured wildly to Mick, who was listening at his side in one smooth motion.

"Yes," Peter whispered.

"No playing detective, I said."

The phone went dead. Peter swallowed.

"How the hell did he get my mobile number?" he said. People looked up from the bar. He'd yelled. His legs nearly buckled.

"Good question."

The mobile rang again. It shook in Peter's hand. Mick snatched it from him.

"Listen, you sack of…" Mick said, then held the mobile to Peter's ear. It was silent, apart from a wash of gently driving guitars and keyboards. The line went dead.

"The Cure," Mick said.

"Goth?"

Mick nodded.

Straw was the least of Peter's concerns. "Have you heard Bertoli's voice before? Was that him?"

Mick nodded, just once, and Peter saw his eyes tighten. "That was him. But he won't try anything with me around."

God help him if he does, Peter thought, casting his mind back to the Fitzroy carnage, watching Mick's face intensify.

***

"Rambo's not coming in."

Rollo Keppel directed the words from his penthouse door at Peter, but the blue eyes drilled Mick. He wore a black pinstripe with a tartan tie, and seemed to Peter as effortlessly in charge as ever, though his face was somber.

"No problem, Mr. Keppel," Peter said.

Mick folded his arms. "No problem, Mr. Gentle."

Smart-arse, Peter thought.

Inside, he gaped at the vast expanse of room. He considered his own apartment stylish, but it was a cramped attic compared to the Keppels' sweep and grandeur. Kenny G purred from huge speakers.

"Not bad for a migrant's son," Rollo said, pouring two glasses of white wine. "I remember my father waking me in the dark. I did a paper run. We lived in Northcote, felt like the end of the earth then. Kantor would do my homework, even had my handwriting down pat."

Peter recalled the drunken eulogy rehearsal on the phone. The funeral must be later today, he thought. The wine was magnificent. Ease off, he told himself, my third glass before lunchtime.

He sank into a leather chair. He'd attempted to clean himself up in the restroom at Draconi's, but next to Rollo's faint aftershave, redolent of pine, he smelled his own rankness. But if Rollo noticed his odor, or his tangled hair, or his creased suit, the chief executive showed no sign of it. Peter marveled that a man whose staffer had just been garotted, whose brother had been murdered a week ago, whose empire was under the microscope, seemed to have all the time in the world for Peter Gentle.

"Inspector Vinci has only just left." The skin on Rollo's patrician nose was flaking, Peter saw. "Such tragic news about Benedict... I can't believe it. His wife had to be sedated. I worked with Benedict for eight years, you know. A talented, fine man."

"Do you know anyone with a grudge against him, Mr. Keppel?"

"Not at work. Vinci told me they found some strange sex paraphernalia in a closet. He's hypothesizing a sexual motive."

Any respect Peter had for Vinci evaporated. "Surely the two murders are connected?"

"Not according to the police. The Inspector thinks the

methods reveal two different murderers." Rollo offered a shrug. He gestured at Peter's bandage. "And he tells me you've been in the wars."

The soft voice on the phone came back to Peter. "Nothing to worry about, it goes with the job. Tell me about Sergio Scaffidi."

Peter saw Rollo's lips tighten. "He's my brother-in-law." What a recovery, Peter thought. "Why on earth do you ask?"

"His name has come up. Do you know him well?"

"Hardly at all. Bella is actually his half-sister, they've never been close. Can I ask the point?"

"Don't you know what he does, Mr. Keppel?" Peter's fingers began a dance on his knees. "He's a criminal, a gangster."

Rollo's look was quizzical. "Yes, I'm aware there's something unsavory about him. But listen, Peter, I don't know the man. Unless you think this… criminal has begun killing my relatives and colleagues, I can't see where this conversation is leading us."

"Who inherits if you die, Mr. Keppel?"

"For God's sake, cut out the Mr. Keppel. And that's none of your business."

"The restricted computer area—"

"No."

The finality in Rollo's voice jarred Peter. He inhaled the aroma of his wine, resisted sipping. "You signed emails to Kantor with a B."

"So I did." Rollo shook his head. "So what?"

"Did you write the email Kantor received on the day of his death?"

"What email?" Rollo's confusion seemed genuine.

Peter tried another of the questions Mick had drummed into

him. "When did you see Willy last?"

"My God, what the… years and years ago."

"Have the police questioned you about your movements yesterday?"

Rollo smiled for the first time. "Peter, you're really not very good at this, are you? Now you suspect me of strangling poor old Benedict. Yes, young man, the police have done their job. I was verifiably at meetings all afternoon. Now tell me, how is the case going?"

"Fine, fine. We're making progress."

"Do you have any idea who killed my brother?"

"Well, not yet, we're still collecting data."

"So you've got no further than the police."

"I wouldn't say that."

Rollo leaned forward, placed a hand on the coffee table, close to Peter's knee.

"The reason I invited you here today, Peter, was not to chat about your investigation." His voice dropped. "I've been most impressed by your drive and intelligence. I'd like you to come work for me, in Benedict Dancer's department, one of the most visible areas in the company. It's the kind of job young people would give their right arm for, and I'm willing to seal an agreement on it with a shake of the hand. Right here and now."

Peter's mind reeled. For an instant he imagined himself as an executive at Scientific Money. Rollo was correct; it was a job he coveted.

"That's a bit bold, isn't it?" he said.

"I didn't build up Scientific Money by sitting on my backside."

Jesus, Peter thought, what would Mick say about this? He knew he had to remain sensible, needed Rollo's cooperation. He also had a sudden realization—Rollo couldn't afford to just cut him off, he needed to know what Peter was doing. It was a dance of minds.

"It's an attractive offer," he said, pretending to muse. "I'll need time to think."

"The offer's on the table, Peter."

Footsteps sounded near the door. Rollo jumped up, face suddenly intent.

"I'm going out," said the slim woman at the door held open by Shorty, the Chinese manservant.

She had to be Bella. Peter was swept away by her lushness. Red lips and moody green eyes dominated her olive pixie face. Black hair flowed over her shoulders. She wore white—an elegant white suit, white shoes, a white handbag edged with gold.

"When will you be back?" Rollo asked.

Rollo's voice had a tone Peter hadn't heard before. He wrenched his gaze from the woman in white and saw that Rollo's lips were parted, his eyes intense. Rollo wound one hand around the other. He looked like Peter felt with Mandy, hesitant and unsure.

"How would I know?" The woman sneered, took keys from her handbag, and then was gone. The click of the door latch echoed in the huge room.

Rollo closed his eyes for a long moment. When he stood up and walked over to the window, his movements were slow.

"I never tire of this view," he said.

Indeed, Peter thought, when he joined Rollo. He'd never

seen Melbourne from such a stunning viewpoint—the panorama of office towers melding into the river vista of green, in turn sweeping out to the distant mountains.

"There," Rollo said, pointing to a spot past Princes Bridge. "I remember cycling down to those boatsheds with Kantor once. I must have been fifteen. In those days there were no bike paths, so it took us all morning. I remember we sat at the water's edge. I told Kantor, he was only ten then, I told him that a whale lived in the river. His eyes were so serious, he didn't want to leave, he just wanted to watch for the whale. He went to the library that very afternoon, to check if I'd lied to him."

Light reflected off Rollo's bald head as he shook it gravely. Peter played with a forelock of hair to disguise his confusion. Then Rollo turned to him, face dull, eyes distant.

"Think about that offer now, Peter. Grab the here and now." Rollo blinked. "The past never stays." He blinked again. "And the future won't come looking for you."

CHAPTER 29

"Over there, miss." Hector's smooth voice. "He's been waiting for you."

Deirdre sat down. She was in uniform. She raised an eyebrow toward the receding Hector.

"He owns the place." Mick Tusk looked across the restaurant, trying to see Gentle, but the central bar blocked him off. They'd agreed for Tusk to meet Deirdre alone, for him to sit near the door, so he could continue to watch for Bertoli. The din generated by the lunchtime suits enfolded him. For sure, Draconi's was growing on him.

He and Deirdre didn't shake or kiss, simply looked at each other.

Ten years ago, he'd been as hot for her as any woman he'd ever known. She wasn't built like a classic beauty, body too stocky, but her fiery dark eyes had hooked him. He'd ended the intense relationship, couldn't recall why.

A crop-haired waiter took their orders. Vegetarian pasta for him, still regretting the fatty breakfast.

"Sure was strange to see you again in those circumstances,"

Deirdre said. "What's it like to be a PI?"

Tusk shrugged. "Not sure yet. Our first case."

"Our? You intend to stick with that bumbler?"

"Whoa there, Dee. Be polite. He's my partner. A bit green, but he'll outthink Sam any day."

Garlic wafted from a nearby table. Time check—12:11. Tusk massaged his half-sprained right hand, tried to assess his own state. Edgy. Still disturbed, disgusted at the Fitzroy episode. But also buoyant—Tom Petty's bouncy, high-voiced "Learning to Fly" cycling in his head. He thought of Gentle on Princes Bridge. It was true, it did help to talk. Other than Dana, whom had he been able to confide in? Cap? Not much use: "What's the problem? Fucking Marcantonio invited you to join his card game?"

"Sam hates you," Deirdre said.

Tusk remembered why he'd walked out on her. The heat of her ambition. All she cared about was success. He never blamed her for that—only relentless women survived the male-dominated Force—but he'd had a different agenda.

"I'm just muddying his waters. Is he still in line for an Assistant Commissioner's slot?"

She nodded. "You're right. He just can't stand the thought you might steal his thunder."

"You're looking good, Dee." So true. Some lines around her eyes, but otherwise unchanged. He checked—no ring.

"Wish I could say the same about you. Can't you afford a new shirt?"

"No time yet today."

"I'm seeing a lawyer. You know him. Augustus is his name."

She smiled impishly. "Augustus Bishop."

Bishop. So that was how the carrot-headed lawyer obtained the case file. Bugger me, Tusk thought, Augustus. No wonder the man calls himself by his surname.

"A dangerous game you're playing," he said. "If Sam's mad at me, imagine how he'd be if he found out documents were being passed to us. You'd lose your job, Dee."

"I know," she said. "But I've spent so long fighting to make it in the Force, I'm not going to let my heart be crushed on this one."

"What do you mean?"

Deirdre glanced around. Leaned forward.

"I'm putting myself out on a limb even more in telling you this." Her voice almost down to a whisper. "But I know you, Mick Tusk, and you feel same as I do. This case is being… influenced."

No surprise, but it sounded shocking, coming from her.

"What a mess, Dee," Tusk said.

"Hey, I asked for it. No one pretends it doesn't happen here in Melbourne."

"Is Sam in on it?"

"Don't know," she said. "Don't think so. I think he's being leaned on hard, but he's pushing back. He wants so much to get a promotion, you know what he's like, but he hates rolling over. Mixton's the main one. Big Ted has given him a direct liaison role, and Larry is…"

"I always said he was crooked."

"Who knows? But he's only six months from retirement, and there's no doubt in my mind, he's juggling this case. The higher powers don't want Rollo Keppel touched. He's off limits."

"Christ, he shouldn't be." Tusk told Deirdre about Rollo's attempt to hire Gentle.

"You're not suggesting he killed his brother?" she said. "There's no evidence of that at all."

He sighed. Instinct wasn't evidence.

"Why are you telling me all this, Dee?" he asked. "I know I was a grand screw, but that was ten years ago."

She laughed, black hair bouncing.

"It's called mutual assistance. I'll keep you in touch, as much as I can, without tipping my hand. I want you to keep the bastards honest and crack this case. And if you do, maybe I can end up with some glory." Eyes burning. "I know, I know, it's risky. If it backfires, I'll come to you for a PI job."

Their meals arrived, steaming and hot. When he told Deirdre about their meeting with Big Ted, she shook her head in amazement. He filled her in on Dana and the kids.

"What about Dancer?" Mick pictured the photo of the strangled fool. What had Dancer been so frightened about? Maybe if they'd pressured him more, they might have saved him. "What can you tell me?"

"Talk to your lawyer." Deirdre winked.

Over the meal, they exchanged hypotheses about the crimes. It turned out Homicide's analysis was more fractured than genius Gentle's.

"What about Scaffidi?"

"Off limits. Sam says the connection's crap."

Tusk slapped his hand on the table. "Christ. He should at least roust the mongrel up. Scaffidi's the scum of scum."

"I know. I'm pushing that line myself, but so far nix."

"Bertoli?"

"Trying to track him down."

"All-out search?"

"No, just us. Give us a break, we've got nothing to go on but the connection with Bella Keppel."

"I'm convinced that cunt Bertoli's doing the killing."

Mick felt heat suffuse his chest. He saw in Deirdre's eyes that she'd spotted this ambushing rage. He remembered again the smooth floor, Marcantonio's bloody nose. Flashed on his one meeting with Bertoli, the still eyes in that ferrety face. Despair washed his body as he gripped the edge of the table.

Deirdre's hand was on his arm. His knuckles were white.

Her eyes held his. "Mick? You need help, baby."

He shook off her hand. "Stick your advice, Dee."

A tremor pinched at his neck. A good meeting, that's what he'd tell Boy Wonder.

CHAPTER 30

"You stink."

Mandy's hands were cool. She snipped off Peter's dirt-encrusted top bandage and wound a new one on. He looked down on her tanned neck, half-covered by shiny hair.

"You smell great," he blurted.

She lifted her serious eyes. Her lips parted in an almost-smile.

"Harvey says you've been playing the macho. You know the only reason I agreed to go out tonight, I thought you were a New-Age soul?"

Was she serious?

The Merrill Lynch office crackled with activity. Around Peter and Mandy, in the central area bounded by offices, men with rolled-up sleeves rushed in and out of a conference room. Secretaries hunched over keyboards or phones. When Peter and Mick had arrived, everyone had stared for all of fifteen seconds before returning to work. After introductions, no questions asked, Mandy had whisked Mick off to the shower on the floor, the blockhead winking as he left.

Mandy finished taping the bandage. She wore a white blouse

and a black skirt. "So where to tonight?"

"Ah well…" Panic welled in Peter's stomach.

"So you want me to book the restaurant."

He gulped. "Sure." He thought desperately. "The Dumpling King. In Box Hill. It's one of my favorites. How about I pick you up here at seven o'clock? We can grab a cab."

"What, no limo?"

"New-Age guys walk."

Her face lit up in a smile that banished her bony cheeks. "So they do. Sounds marvelous. Elle's staying overnight at a friend's place, so I can relax."

He knew Mandy had a daughter, but nothing about the girl. How old could she be?

"And tomorrow?" he said. "Football?"

He didn't seem to be able to form whole sentences. "What I mean is… Mandy, would you come with me to a football match tomorrow?"

"You told me that footy is for klutzes."

Fancy her remembering that, Peter thought. "It's part work. Mick and his wife are also coming."

"How intriguing."

"Your turn, mate." Secretaries glanced up at Mick's low voice. Jesus, Peter thought, this is one guy who'd never fit into an office environment, though Mandy had given Mick a new shirt—"Harvey has a million of them, just in case he splatters bolognese"—and he looked brand new.

Although Peter knew where the shower was, he let Mandy lead him down the corridor. She handed him a shirt and a plastic bag for his bandaged hand.

"Come in with me?" he said as he opened the door.

"Is that a threat or a boast?"

The hot water seared the aches from his neck, his back, his legs. He scrubbed until he felt like a boiled lobster, blow-dried and combed his hair, and slapped on aftershave he found in a cabinet. Harvey's shirt was short in the arms and his suit still looked second hand, but Peter's step had a new spring when he emerged.

Harvey was talking with Mick in front of Mandy's desk. Sunlight sparkled on the windows of the office behind them. The pace on the floor seemed to have wound up even more. A red-faced man rushed past, clutching a sheaf of papers. Mandy typed furiously.

Mick reeked of the same aftershave Peter was wearing. The big man sniffed. "Twins. Even our mother couldn't smell us apart."

Peter cackled. Even Harvey smiled.

"Skull." Harvey snapped his yellow suspenders, a sure sign of mid-deal stress. "Had two calls about you today."

Peter glanced at Mick. "What did they want?"

"Background, character descriptions, quite intrusive really. One from the police and one from the Attorney-General's office. I told them you're an unrepentant pervert."

"Thanks, Harv."

"And you... you're all right?"

"What do you mean?"

"You know. You're okay?"

Peter looked at the concern on Harvey's face and momentarily felt annoyance. He'd fallen low a few months ago,

Harvey had ministered to him, and ever since had behaved like a fussy brother. Peter grinned, received a relieved smile back.

"You take care of that secretary of mine tonight, buddy." Harvey winked.

Mandy waved. A gear clicked inside Peter.

***

Peter hopped from foot to foot.

"The theory looks okay to me."

"Aha," Carlo Fonti said lazily, peering over his glasses.

Peter grinned. That tone of voice could only mean one thing.

He and Carlo were of the same generation, and people often grouped them together as two young actuaries, but in fact their skills were complementary rather than identical. Peter was more practical, skilled at finding real-world solutions. Carlo was the acclaimed technician. Sometimes Peter wondered if in fact that was the reason he, rather than Carlo, had been laid off.

How strangely life flowed. Just twelve months ago, he would have been busy a hundred meters from this windowless conference room in 101 Collins, conferring with Fonti his colleague. Now the Thompson White receptionist hadn't even recognized him, and Carlo was moonlighting to help him on a murder case.

They stood in front of a photocopying whiteboard, half-covered with Peter's scrawled notes on the theory developed by Kantor Keppel and Stan Friedman. Mick sat behind a table, arms crossed, almost as if he was following the discussion.

"What do you mean, aha?" Peter asked.

"I've done some work since you rang." Carlo drew a large

chart, referring to notes. "This is the All Ords index since the Scientific Money Quant Fund started." He drew the trough at the start of 1995 and the continuous ascent since then. He then drew another line and labeled it "Quant Fund Performance."

"What stands out?" Carlo asked.

"The Quant Fund has done bloody well," Peter said.

"Too well. Notice that it's never taken a large dive. Even at the worst point of the market it stayed almost level. Now, from what we know about Kantor's theory, it's based on broad economic factors and historic stock volatility, so whenever there are major shifts in the economy it should track them. In other words his theory doesn't know enough about the detailed world to skip major market downturns."

Peter's fingers flitted. "You're right, Carlo. The fund might do better than the All Ords on average, it might move more or less quickly, but over a longer period it should show the same general peaks and troughs. So what that means is…"

"Yes." Carlo smiled, a shy upturn of his thin lips. "Manual intervention, Skull. Bet you."

Peter stood back, stunned.

"So what?" Mick said. Peter had forgotten he was there.

"The whole point of the Quant Fund is that it's a product of the formula, that it's mechanical." Carlo rubbed out his chart. "If there are any human decisions made, it might as well be all of them, because one decision can make or break five years' worth of investment performance. In other words, if they knew, investors would be greatly upset."

"But as you showed," Mick said, "the performance has been great. Who the hell would care?"

Peter felt a savage thrill. Hadn't he sensed something all along? "The regulator, for one thing. This would be major misrepresentation, maybe even fraud."

"And investors would be uncertain about future performance," Carlo said. "They trust Kantor's formula, not the Scientific Money investment team."

Peter and Carlo attacked the whiteboard again, Peter carving out symbols as he went through modern portfolio theory and Kantor Keppel's take on it, Carlo parrying with his own observations.

While Carlo popped out to arrange coffee, Peter remembered to ring Imogen. She was in yet another foul mood.

"Oh, what's the use?" she said. "You're useless, all of you. Straw—come down now!" A pause. "What does that witch say about me?"

Peter was mystified. "Who?"

Imogen hung up.

Peter and Carlo kept working. At the end of a frenetic hour, Peter scratched his head in frustration.

"There's just not enough information on Kantor's theory to prove it one way or another," he said.

"Let's confront Rollo with it," Mick said.

"It might not be Rollo," Peter said. "In fact I'm sure it's not."

Mick snorted. "He's got you 'round his fucking finger."

"You think the rich are to blame for everything."

"Next thing, he'll be giving you a blow job."

"Where did you get that concept from? Bella?"

Carlo had an odd smile on his face. "You two are partners?"

***

"Your friend," Giuseppe Marino whispered in Peter's ear. "Can he wait here?"

Cordoned off by velvet ropes, a large crowd milled around tables of coffee and biscuits outside the Hotel Sofitel Grand Ballroom. Peter could smell his friend's tart aftershave. With his vivid black hair, five o'clock shadow, and brisk movements, Giuseppe looked anything but a tax bloodhound.

Peter signaled for Mick to stay put and headed down the floral-carpeted corridor with Giuseppe.

"First things first," Giuseppe said, stopping next to the hedge of plants overlooking the noisy plaza. "My colleague in charge of Scientific Money's tax audit won't be quoted, capiche? His team has found nothing wrong with the company, but he said he wouldn't be surprised to see skeletons in the closet. The management team is very smart and sly. That's my friend's word: sly."

"Anything specific?"

"Afraid not, Skull."

In a small meeting room, Peter shook hands with Helen Chen, a stern woman in her forties with black hair tied in a ponytail. She introduced herself as an APRA department head.

"I'm a private investigator," he told her when they sat down.

"So Giuseppe said." She clasped her hands together. "This can only be an informal meeting."

"I'm looking into the death of Kantor Keppel." Peter's mind was racing so fast, he had to force himself to speak slowly. "It may have something to do with Scientific Money, although I can't be sure yet. What I'd like to know is, how does the firm stack up in APRA's eyes? Is it spotless? Or are there blemishes in their record that would help my understanding?"

"Mr. Gentle, I'm afraid I'm not much help." Her eyes studied him, and he realized this meeting fascinated her. He could imagine her regaling colleagues about the private investigator. "Scientific Money has never infringed any of the applicable regulations."

"What about behind the scenes? What do you really think about the company?"

"As I said, Scientific Money has complied with all applicable regulations."

After all he'd gone through in the last three days… "Applicable regulations? Two of the company's execs are murdered within a week, I'm helping the police solve this, and all you can do is spout the official record? Excuse me, but that's bloody useless."

She stood up, back straight. "I agreed to this meeting because Mr. Marino and I have been colleagues for many years. I didn't come to be insulted. Mr. Gentle, if you know anything about Scientific Money which should be of concern to APRA, it's your duty to divulge it."

Peter sighed. He had nothing. If he laid out what two actuaries postulated, based on some old papers of Kantor Keppel and a rough chart on a whiteboard, she would think him mad.

"No, not yet," he said. "But I will find out the truth."

"In that case, it's been a pleasure to meet you." Helen Chen swept out.

Giuseppe pulled a long face.

Peter yawned, suddenly swept by exhaustion. "Sorry."

"Hey, no problem, my friend." Giuseppe placed his hands on

Peter's shoulders. "Skull, are you serious, I mean, working with that Neanderthal outside?"

***

If Peter could have bottled and sold his nervousness at that moment, he'd have been a rich man.

"You know, I've never met a writer before," he said, draining his wine glass.

"Would-be writer," Mandy said.

Peter couldn't believe she was finally sitting opposite him, staring so intently over her glass. He watched her long, bony fingers play with the chopsticks.

His senses were flooded. Flooded by Mandy, by the aromas of garlic and jasmine tea, by the surrounding cacophony. He rubbed his chopsticks together and gazed at the waiters weaving through a maze of closely packed tables, overflowing with animated people, Asians and Westerners in equal numbers. Dumpling King had built up its reputation the hard way, through years of low profile persistence. The front door and walls were papered with rave reviews, not for high-priced gourmet food, but for tasty meals at modest prices. Peter loved the spicy Sichuan cuisine and the dumplings, a dozen varieties of glorious steamed and fried dumplings using recipes from all over China.

"Writing must be so interesting," he said.

"Interesting, interesting. That's what everyone says. And, when can we read your book? As if publication is a foregone thing. Especially businessmen, they write memos, so they assume they could switch to other writing just like that."

"That's exactly what I thought." Peter smiled to show he was joking.

But Mandy wasn't about to smile, hadn't smiled since he'd picked her up at Merrill Lynch. The taxi ride, Mick in the front with the driver, Peter and Mandy in the back, had been awkward. If Mick hadn't started a conversation about movies, it would have been disastrous.

"In fact it's hard, bloody hard," she said. "I did a half-day adult education seminar with Max Polkovsky last Sunday, you know him? We had to read our pieces out loud. I was terrified."

"How do you fit it all in?"

"What—a job, raise a kid, study, and write? Lots of people do it. Not everyone adopts the Merrill Lynch model, husband always on shift, faithful wife holding the fort in the mortgaged mansion. But it does feel tough sometimes. I only start writing or studying once Elle is in bed, nine o'clock or so."

She was in full flight, waving her hands. Peter saw her breasts shift under her blouse. An erection sprang up.

"Sometimes I think, why not settle down, remarry. But then I remember how lucky I am. Five years ago I was in the country, marriage a living hell, hardly ever saw a movie, let alone imagined writing."

"How old is your daughter?" Peter asked.

"Eleven. I've also got a son, but he's with his father."

She'd left her husband in Ballarat, that much Peter knew from Harvey.

"He must be young."

"Why do you say that?"

He twisted his hands together. "You're too young for kids."

"My God, you're a romantic, Peter. No, I'm three years older than you."

How did Mandy know his age? He wished he could force himself to gaze into her searching eyes more often. And her hair... she had this way of twirling the ends in her fingers when distracted that made him want to reach over.

"Sometimes I can't believe it myself," she said. "Christian will turn nineteen soon. Us country girls tend to marry young."

"That must be tough, being separated from him. Didn't you gain custody from the divorce?"

"I'm not divorced. Yet. Hopefully the papers will come through soon. And Christian? Yes, I miss him. But we haven't got on over the last few years."

"I..."

"Shit happens, Peter." She scowled and tossed her hair. "Marriage is the pits. What about you? Never thought of tying the knot?"

What could he say? That he liked women, but shyness was his curse if he got keen on someone? That anyone he fancied turned out to be completely different to what he imagined? That the one time... he couldn't even bear to think about that.

"I agree," he said. "Marriage is an overrated institution."

Piled bamboo baskets, hot to the touch, arrived full of succulent dumplings. The first one seared his lips. Wolfing them down, he noticed that Mandy only nibbled.

"Not hungry?"

"I'm a light eater." She talked about her exercise program, regular gym sessions, long walks. "You should exercise, I think it would help to reduce the stress."

What stress? Did he look stressed out?

"I don't believe in exercise," Peter said. "All that mumbo

jumbo, it's just zealots and marketers peddling dangerous ideas. The body doesn't like all that strained puffing."

It was the wrong thing to say. Fine for a boozy Skulk Club meeting but simply wrong tonight. He saw amusement in her eyes.

"But I like walking," he lied, trying to recover ground. "Maybe we can go for a walk together some day."

She smiled—at last—that smile that opened up her eyes. A flame bloomed in his chest.

He found out that she read books, though her tastes were more literary than his. They joked about Harvey's idiosyncratic style at Merrill Lynch. Peter admired the way she spoke about her work with grave affection.

The main courses arrived: smoked duck, spicy pork and tofu, shiny Chinese greens, and steaming rice in a plastic tub.

"How is the case going?" she asked.

His least favorite question. "Not well, that's the honest assessment. Mick and I have done so much good work, yet I can't see an elegant solution. It's so complex, Mandy, unbelievably complex."

He hunched forward and breathlessly recapped the events of the last few days. Everything, every last detail, poured from him.

"Should you be telling me all this?" she said after some time. "You hardly know me."

He grinned madly. "Hey, I can trust you."

"Harvey just can't understand why you've gone into this detective business. Yet you make it sound so interesting."

Peter dabbed his forehead with a napkin. The chili really kicked. "Yes, well, it is. Interesting. The intellectual content is surprisingly high. But I'm struggling with the operational side of it."

His thoughts drifted. Carlo's stargazing look came back to him. He was sure his friend was correct—someone at Scientific Money was cheating, augmenting Kantor's secret formula with human judgment. He shook his head. How could that have led to murder? Had Kantor threatened to tell the world about it? Why would he have? His mind began to go over the permutations of the case yet again.

"Peter?"

"Sorry." His chopsticks held a piece of bok choy. How long had it been suspended there? "This case…"

"Actually, I need to go," she said.

Shit, he thought, she hasn't enjoyed herself. I should have listened more, prattled on less.

Maybe she read his expression. "I'd love to stay. This is a great place. But I'm exhausted."

He felt wild desperation. Only once, all night, had she smiled that smile.

"I'll ask Francis to order you a taxi," he said, nearly knocking over the table as he jumped up. Too much wine—his head swam.

While they waited for the cab, they watched a team of waiters frantically whip the tablecloth off a round table as new customers looked on. The conversation turned to travel. Mandy was saving to take Elle to Europe. Her eyes sparkled when she spoke about her preparatory reading on Paris, Berlin, London.

"Travel's okay," Peter said. "But I can't understand why all my friends are obsessed by it. What's wrong with Melbourne?"

"I'll tell you what's wrong with it." Mandy's eyes flashed.

"Why are Melburnians such big travelers? Because Melbourne is the arse end of the universe. Everyone's so parochial."

I don't know about that, Peter wanted to say. But Francis was signaling.

Outside, they stood under the lights, the street alive with people, looking up at the clear black sky. The cool air prickled Peter's sweaty scalp. He longed to hold her, to kiss her.

"Fitzgibbon?" called a taxi driver.

Mandy swung her handbag over her shoulder and startled Peter by grabbing an elbow to draw him close. Her perfume, something summery, turned his thighs to rubber.

"Thanks, Peter. Lovely night."

"Tomorrow?" he stammered.

She hesitated. He tried to read her look, failed miserably.

"Why not?"

And then she was in the taxi, and it was leaving, and he waved and kept waving till its rear lights had long gone. He kicked a lamppost next to an isolated palm tree.

That was when he noticed Mick, standing motionless farther down Station Street.

"How was it?" Mick fell in beside Peter's savage stride.

"Have you been a statue for two hours?"

"No. I actually popped in to chat with your dad."

"You're joking. What about?"

"Ah, copper nostalgia. Your mum even fed me."

"Jesus, sorry about that."

"Better than my memory of my mum's cooking."

They turned into the street of Peter's childhood, the very street he had been ambushed in just two days ago. He looked down the familiar footpath, the pools of yellow under the streetlights, the dark cars on the curbs, the bushes overflowing onto the footpath, and he shuddered. As if in warning, his broken finger began to throb. He couldn't help it, his mind fantasized a lean figure, nose sharp as a stiletto, reaching out for him from behind a lamppost, and his teeth chattered.

"It's clear," Mick said. "How was the date?"

Peter plodded into the middle of the street and strode homeward.

CHAPTER 31

Bella Keppel's handshake was strong and hot. Nothing like Mandy's touch… Peter shied away from the thought.

"Nice to meet you," he said.

Bella's upper lip curled. "The pleasure's mine."

Her voice mail on his mobile last night had been tantalizing, just a snarl: "Tell the wrestler to meet me on the riverbank at nine."

Mick acknowledged Bella with a curt nod. He wore jeans, a plaid shirt, and brown boots. A light jacket hung over a shoulder. With his sunglasses on, his face looked like marble in the early morning sun.

Peter knew it was unprofessional to gawk, but how could he not? His brief glimpse yesterday had only hinted at Bella's beauty. Her fragile face captivated him. She wore skimpy shorts, showcasing slender legs down to trainers and ankle socks. A black and red tracksuit top was partly unzipped to show a black training top. Shiny black hair was pinned back with a gold clasp.

Wan sunlight bathed the banks of the Yarra, although scudding gray smudges of cloud promised rain. Acrid smoke rose from the chimney of a moored cruise boat. The Southbank cafes were full of couples, young and old, reading bulky Saturday morning newspapers. Dismounting cyclists, a riot of color, puffed.

Peter scratched his hair. There was so much on the go today, he could hardly contain himself. Bella, Marcia Brindle, Mandy… even stiffening bruises and heated words from his parents last night couldn't dampen anticipation of the meetings. Mick, too, had been in a fine mood on the drive in, pointing to a photo in *The Age* of Rollo and Bella, radiant last night, attending an arts award sponsored by Scientific Money. The All Ords was down again, a drop of 4% over the week… Peter wondered how Scientific Money had fared. Apparently Mick the fitness freak had been up for hours, running and playing with his children.

Bella swung on her heels and headed toward Princes Bridge. "Follow me."

Peter fancied himself a fast walker, but he struggled to keep up with Bella and Mick as they charged under Swanston Street. Bella's buttocks rippled, and Peter saw a shuffling homeless man leer.

At the other side of the bridge, rowing teams carried boats down to launch from wooden decking. Peter was already puffing and barely had time to take in the city skyline.

Bella stopped on the first sweeping curve of the river. Here there were no pedestrians, just a steady stream of cyclists. The river lapped gently.

Bella's olive skin shone in the low sunlight. Hands on hips, she looked at Mick. "Okay, I've got something to say."

"We're all ears," Mick said.

"You must understand…" She looked out across the slow water. "Rollo and I don't have your regular marriage. I do my bit, he does his, we get along. Understand?"

"No," Mick said.

Bella and Mick stared at each other intently. Peter might as well not have been there.

"Yes you do," she said.

"He's too old for you. That it?" Mick made no attempt to keep contempt from his voice.

Bella's green eyes narrowed, but she half-smiled. "The tact of the professional."

She walked up the grassy slope and sat down, legs gaping immodestly. Peter's back complained when he slumped down next to her. Mick remained standing.

Bella shielded her eyes with a hand and peered up at Mick. "What's really going on, is I love Willy."

Willy who? Peter clamped his mouth shut to prevent a shout. She meant Willy Keppel? The saxophonist bum?

"Love's a big word." Mick's voice was soft, almost dreamy.

"You're right." Bella shook her head. "Willy was there. That night. I snuck him in."

"Willy?" Peter blurted. "That night?"

"Yes. I made him tell Rollo about us. I got him into the building and up the back stairs with my pass, then walked home. Rollo came home maybe thirty minutes later. We quarreled."

"What time did you let Willy in?" Mick said.

"About eight."

"How long have you been in love with Willy?"

Peter's mind clicked through the scenarios this revelation opened up. Bella had been in the office. Had she even gone home? Had Willy stayed behind? Who was covering for whom?

Bella rested her tiny chin on hands across her knees. "We fell in love years ago, before I married Rollo. Then Willy skipped to America and that was the end, okay? But he came back a couple of years ago, and it was like the old love. You ever been in love?"

"Yes," Peter whispered. He saw Mick nod.

"Well, this is love." Bella's voice cracked harshly. "What Rollo and I have is marriage, it's not the same. Fifteen years I've given him, now I'm doing what I should have done then. Sticking with Willy."

"Why not just keep seeing him?" Mick asked. "You've been doing what you like with men right through the marriage."

She didn't respond. Her face had grown darker, and for the first time seemed to Peter to reflect her forty years.

"Why have Willy break the news?" Peter asked. "Why not you?"

She gave a short laugh. "Willy's sweet, but he's no tough guy. I wanted him to show some balls for once."

Mick took off his sunglasses and stared at Bella below him. "What happened that night?"

"Told you."

"I mean what happened when Willy told your husband."

"I wasn't there, understand? But from what Willy told me, he just tells Rollo and walks out, Rollo follows, they talk in the street, Willy walks away, Rollo walks home. To start flying off at me."

"As expected."

"You're right. I can handle him."

"But you're still with Rollo."

She stood up. Long legs planted apart, she scowled at Mick. Peter scrambled up.

"Yeah, well, the murder came up, didn't it," Bella said. "Rollo said we had to appear respectable, otherwise the cops would be all over us. But I've had enough of that. I'm ready to move now."

Peter marveled at how she could look radiant one moment, ugly the next.

"Bella?" Mick's pale eyes were implacable. "Who killed Kantor? Willy? Or was it Rollo?"

"Get stuffed." A snarl. "They left together."

But she's been wondering, Peter thought. She can't know if her husband or her lover is a killer.

He analyzed furiously. What if Willy stayed behind? Then he could have been the mystery person who went out the emergency exit. Why would he kill Kantor? Easy—because he hated him. Maybe he went to crow to Kantor about taking Rollo's wife, maybe they quarreled. But why wait two hours to do that? What about Rollo? Why would he cover for the brother who is stealing his wife?

"Sergio," Peter said. "What's he in all this?" Mick's eyes jerked in his direction and Peter saw a brief nod of appreciation.

Peter fancied he saw color leach from Bella's face. She smiled at Mick, a grimace that showed teeth. "You go ask him, tough guy."

"Do you know Bertoli?" Peter said.

She rolled her shoulders, and Peter watched her breasts move. "Who?"

"For fuck's sake." The merest mention of Bertoli seemed to have angered Mick. "Your brother's helping Rollo, isn't he?"

"Half-brother," Bella said. "And he's got nothing to do with this."

Then she was gone, loping down to the river and away along the bank, turning heads as she went.

Mick looked as if he might give chase. Something had gone on between Mick and Bella, some chemistry that Peter didn't understand.

"You done good, genius," Mick said, his sunglasses back on.

Peter glowed. "What a schemer. She hasn't cleared herself yet in my eyes. I've never met anyone like her."

"I have."

"A bad experience, big guy?"

"The best and worst. Fantastic in bed, a viper out of it."

Peter felt electric heading back toward Southbank. Seagulls glided over water and bicycle bells jangled. A jogger heaved past. The towers across the river glistened.

"Why did she tell us all that?" Peter asked.

"Not sure. Maybe she knows Rollo did it and is cracking his alibi."

"But Rollo's alibi is stronger than ever. Willy saw him leave the building."

Mick shrugged. "Or maybe she just wants us to pursue Rollo. Leave Willy alone."

They walked through the coolness of the tunnel into teeming Southbank.

Mick was hurrying. "Willy's the key. Let's go get him."

"What about breakfast?"

"Stuff breakfast."

Peter laughed. "Stuff you."

By the footbridge he rang their client.

Imogen was drunk. "When we married, Kantor said to me… I remember the river sparkled, he said, 'Imogen you will always be the light of my life.' Why won't you find his killer?"

Peter held the mobile up so Mick could hear the screech of the last part, and the sound of a glass smashing.

CHAPTER 32

Down a gravel driveway, past a carport housing a Mercedes. Mick Tusk pressed the doorbell and heard a chime deep inside. Time check—11:07. A wide, low-slung house. Large, lush garden, the wet grass springy and green. The crystalline calls of bellbirds.

So typical that Marcia Brindle lives in Donvale, Tusk thought. A relatively young suburb northeast of the city, with large land subdivisions, recently infused with Asian business migrants, Tusk liked its prettiness but the residents… ladder crawlers every one of them.

He looked at his partner, Gentle the excited kitten, bouncing on his feet. His hair already wild, a fresh bandage on his left hand. Blue and red wind jacket, ugly cotton shirt, jeans, and new Reeboks. A yuppie going to the footy.

It had drizzled intermittently on the drive out. Tusk had spotted a yellow vehicle hovering four cars back, but it hadn't seemed to follow them off the Eastern Freeway. Even if he was mistaken, some of the high from the success with Bella had worn off.

"Yes? Who is it?" A confident voice.

"Mrs. Brindle?" Gentle said. "It's Peter Gentle, we had a discussion a couple of days ago?"

"It's Saturday, for God's sake. What do you want?"

"It will only take ten minutes."

Tusk hoped they succeeded in getting in. He'd been disappointed when they found no sign of Willy Keppel in his fleabag hotel. At least they'd managed to find out that he was performing tonight. It was Gentle who suggested they interview the accountant again.

A pause, then the sound of keys.

Tusk breathed deep to ease tension. Early in the morning, before any lights came on in Belgrave, he'd eased out of bed and jogged hard with Bully. Three days without exercise, unless he counted the scrap with Marcantonio. His lungs bursting with sweet air, he stood outside his house afterwards. Reflecting on Dana's tears last night, and his sense of guilt when he failed to cross the threshold and tell her the real story about Marcantonio. Only the five-day limit placated her, that and making love with the lights on.

The door opened and Marcia Brindle sized him up. Gentle had said she was a handful and indeed she was. Older, with a worn face and neat snowy hair. Held herself with confidence. Eyes that took no prisoners.

"Mick Tusk," he said.

Her handshake was vigorous. "I guess private detectives come in all shapes and sizes. We'll go out the back."

A reedy voice called out when they stepped into the long corridor. Marcia waved them on and ducked out of view, and

Tusk could hear low voices conferring. He found himself in a large rumpus room next to an open kitchen. Sofas and easy chairs. Large windows that somehow let little light in. Crusted dishes stacked on the kitchen counter. The acrid smell of cigarette smoke.

Tusk had his game plan for the next two days. Work like crazy, get the bulk of the digging done, then walk, leaving the genius to figure it out. He had his own ideas on who'd done what. Gentle's appeal to justice had hit a chord, but he couldn't stay on longer than that. For Dana's sake. For his own sake.

Marcia entered. "Coffee?"

They both shook their heads. They'd agreed to switch roles as soon as possible, so Tusk kicked off.

"We're sorry to bother you and your husband," he said.

Marcia wore a black tracksuit with white stripes. She sat down on a lounge chair and motioned them to a sofa. Tusk perched on the edge, keeping his body straight and relaxed.

"My husband is an invalid," she said, as if that explained something. "You've had one minute of your ten."

"What were you doing the evening before last?" Tusk asked.

"I worked till late. But let me save you the trouble, the alibi isn't tight. The police inform me I could have slipped out of the office and killed Benedict. As if I'd strangle my colleague and then go back to my ledgers."

Tusk watched a cat pad across the huge back yard. "Going back to the night of Kantor's death, did you notice any strangers in the building? A man with scruffy hair?"

"Who, Peter Gentle? No. As I told your actuary friend, I had my head buried in the management accounts."

"Did you notice Rollo's wife?"

"No."

"Sure?"

Marcia gave a slow nod.

"You know about Bella's infidelities?" Tusk asked.

A pause. Marcia chewed on a thumbnail, gnawed to the quick, Tusk noticed. "Rollo loves that woman in a way you and I might find difficult to imagine, even when she abuses his love."

Tusk realized he admired her. "You say you and Kantor argued that afternoon, about a report format. What else? You need plenty of money, Mrs. Brindle, enough to set up your own practice."

Marcia gave a brittle laugh. "You two have been digging. Yes, I may set up my own practice in the not-too-distant future, and yes, I need capital for that. But no, Kantor never threatened my plans, and no, I didn't kill him. Your ten minutes are almost up. Are we done?"

"Does the name Scaffidi mean anything to you?"

No reaction on the strong face. "Sounds like a stonemason."

That was the question that nagged Tusk: How did Scaffidi fit in? Had Bella and he cooked something up? Or Rollo—Gentle reckoned the tycoon hardly knew Scaffidi, but Rollo had Boy Wonder well and truly mesmerized.

Marcia lit up a cigarette. Tusk leaned back, the signal for Gentle to take over.

"Marcia," Gentle said, "are you aware of anyone programming invisible passes since the first three made for Rollo, Bella, and Kantor?"

"I know nothing about security passes. I just use mine."

"Who makes the investment decisions of the Quant Fund?"

Tusk watched the confidence drain from Marcia's face, like air hissing from a punctured balloon.

"What?" she said. "What are you talking about?"

Gentle's eyes gleamed. "I think you know what I'm talking about. The investment performance of the fund can't be accounted for by a computer program. Someone human helps out."

"What nonsense." A firm voice, but Tusk could see she was rattled, badly rattled. "You know as well as I do that there's an array of computers that—"

"Crap." The beanpole's hands waved. "You and I know that's not true. Who are you lying to protect?"

"How dare you?" Marcia's face twisted. She rose and pointed down the corridor. "Out."

Tusk stood up. "Are you crazy, Marcia?" It was time to personalize. "Dancer said the same to us, less than two days ago, and someone twisted his own bathrobe belt around his neck until he died."

"Out." Her neck muscles rigid. Cigarette trembling.

"No." Tusk's innards boiled. "That's what we did last time. What's going on?"

He realized he'd shouted. Bugger, all his precious control was flying away.

"Out!" She ran to the phone on the kitchen counter. Dialed.

Tusk's heart was racing. Gentle put a hand on his arm.

"Okay, Marcia," Gentle said. "We're going. But you're pushing away the only two people who can help you. Won't you reconsider?"

Tusk felt his anger subside. Gentle was right. Who could ever save the stubborn from themselves?

Marcia slammed the phone back down. Her face ghostly in the shadows of the room. Eyes round as marbles.

"No." A croak. "Get out."

"Ring us," Gentle said.

As they walked out, Tusk felt foreboding in the pit of his stomach. A trembling voice called out in another room. The sky outside had turned gray again but it seemed like sunshine after that dark house. Behind them, tumblers clicked into place.

"Well done back there," Tusk said. He meant it. "Christ, what can we do?"

"We can't make her protect herself."

Gravel crunched underfoot. Tusk made his way up to the Peugeot. Nothing suspicious in either direction. He breathed in the cool scent of pine sap, cleared his nostrils of cigarette smoke. A song surfaced—"When the Levee Breaks," Led Zeppelin's lurching metal blues of apocalypse.

He flipped open his notebook. "Give me that bloody phone of yours."

"Sam?" He hadn't expected Vinci himself to answer. "Tusk here."

"The pretend cop." Vinci's voice held equal doses of amusement and contempt.

"We've just visited Marcia Brindle. Sam, she's shit-scared about something. She needs protection."

Surprisingly, Vinci didn't blast him for going on with the case. "Haven't got the manpower."

"You want another body?" Shouting again.

"Be civil, arsehole. See what I can do."

A dead line. Tusk looked at Gentle's grave face, at the house hidden behind whispering pines. He cursed.

CHAPTER 33

The crowd exploded. A red-faced Melbourne supporter cracked knees into Peter's back when he stood to shout, "Carna Daymons." Chip fragments rained from the man's mouth onto Peter's neck.

Come on the Demons, Peter presumed. Essendon versus Melbourne at the Melbourne Cricket Ground on a Saturday afternoon. Two teams who had once dominated Australian football, but now struggled near the middle of the ladder. The players surged up and down the ground in frantic flurries through the mud, punctuated by leaps into the sky. And the crowd—screaming, waving, swearing—living the Melbourne passion with a moronic intensity Peter found bewildering.

Peter loathed football, always had, but he had to admit the MCG was a stirring sight. Huge stands surrounded the green grass oval. The six massive light poles, for all the world like giant, inverted ice hockey sticks, could be seen from the city when ablaze. Melbourne's home for cricket and football, Peter had read, was now a tourist destination, and every week hundreds of Europeans and Asians soaked up tales of test matches and classic Grand Finals.

He glanced at Mandy, lovely in faded jeans and a bright yellow jumper, chatting with Dana. He wished Mandy hadn't come. His mind refused to let go of the case, and the noise left it impossible for him to talk privately with her. And he was nervous, imagining a thin-faced man slipping a knife into his back from out of the heaving crowd.

He could tell Mick felt the same, despite his love of the game. The big man sat at the other end of their foursome, hands loosely clasped, a picture of relaxation, but his head scanned the crowd in regular sweeps.

Rollo Keppel had rung a couple of hours earlier, pressing Peter on the job offer. Strangely, the chief executive hadn't mentioned their walk with Bella—could it be she hadn't told him? Peter had tried to charm Rollo, saying he would decide by Monday, but the smooth voice had sounded annoyed.

"Why do you team up with that ex-policeman hood?" Rollo had said. "My father was like him, a primitive."

Now it was cold, rain threatened, the man behind Peter stank of sweat, lunch had been tasteless meat pies, and their case was going nowhere while he'd sat watching this bloody game for three hours. He tried to spot Magnus Jones amongst the Essendon players, but they all looked the same. He longed to draw Mandy close. At least she seemed to have found a new friend. Peter looked at Dana. Strange, but he'd never imagined Mick with a wife so earthy, so domestic. And why had she been brusque to him?

His mobile rang, its chirrup barely audible.

"Peter Gentle."

Above the clamor of the crowd, he could just distinguish music.

"Straw?" he said.

Ghostly music, then the line went dead. Almost immediately the phone rang again.

"Straw?"

"No, it's me. Marcia Brindle. I'm sorry we quarreled today."

The maniac behind Peter erupted into incoherent cries.

"Hold on." Peter raced up the aisle to the top step, where the din lessened. "Is that better?"

"I just remembered something," Marcia said. "You asked if I saw any strangers that day. Well, I don't know why it didn't come to me before, you said scruffy and that took me down the wrong path, but I did see one man, after I left Kantor's office that last time and went out for a smoko. He was walking down the third floor corridor. Wore a casual jacket."

Peter's mind snapped into focus. "Can you describe him?"

"No, it was just a glimpse, and I was preoccupied."

How useless. "Well, thanks Marcia. Are you okay?"

"Fine. You really don't need to worry about me. One thing…"

Peter looked down to where Mick was watching him. "Yes?"

"The man. He had red hair."

Jesus! Would the data for this case ever be settled? Peter ran down and scrambled across the knees of Mandy and Dana to shout into Mick's ear.

"Friedman! He was still in the building at six o'clock."

The siren blared and the crowd leapt and screamed for the last time. The final score: Melbourne 134, Essendon 113.

"The bastard," Mick said, tightness around his mouth, after Peter's recap. "Okay, let's send the women off and deal with this

Jones character. We need to hurry. Then we'll ring Friedman."

Peter watched the sloped back of the red-faced man disappear toward an exit, and wished him a horrific traffic accident. He saw Dana kiss Mick. A second siren. Children poured onto the field to kick footballs with their fathers. A chugging anthem, no doubt the Melbourne club song, crackled in the air.

"Sorry we have to leave," he said to Mandy.

Mandy smiled. "Don't worry, I can see you're working."

"Was it that obvious?" He was close enough to count the freckles on her cheeks under those liquid brown eyes.

"I had a lovely time, Peter, thanks for inviting me. It was such a thrill to be at the MCG. You know, I've been in the big smoke for nearly two years and have never been here. And Dana's lovely. She's giving me a lift home."

Great, no wheels for us, Peter thought, but he felt relief that at least the experience hadn't been distasteful for her.

"When will I see you again?" he surprised himself by asking. Mick tugged at his elbow.

"Ring me." Her face looked so serious that he couldn't decipher a bloody thing, and then found himself pulled down the steps.

"Shake a leg," Mick said. "Jones played piss-poorly today. You sure it's important to see him?"

"No one will tell me what Straw is really like," Peter said. "It's like there's a wall around her."

"Okay, you call the shots with this one."

He followed Mick down into the concrete exterior circle. A man vomited loudly against the fence.

Peter rang Imogen and updated her on the Friedman discovery. Her response was sullen.

Halfway around the stadium, Peter spotted Bishop's garish hair. The lawyer, in a double-breasted suit, paced in front of an entrance manned by security guards.

"Where have you been?" Bishop said. "We have a narrow window of opportunity here."

Peter smiled. Connections, he thought, that's what drives the world. When he'd rung Bishop with his progress report in the morning, the lawyer had rubbished Peter's plan to try to see Magnus Jones at the match, then said he had done some legal work for the MCG.

"You offered," Peter said.

Bishop introduced them to Dan, a middle-aged man wearing an Essendon Football Club jacket.

"Have to dash," Bishop said. "You guys think life is tough, I've got a week's worth of work to finish by tomorrow."

The flaming hair vanished. Dan led them through the security guards and left them alone in a small room.

"I nearly called him Augustus," Mick said. "Didn't dare."

Peter chuckled.

A man hobbled in, dressed in a tracksuit and trainers with shoelaces undone, a towel draped over his shoulders. His nuggetty body seemed folded over with fatigue. Dried mud streaked his blonde hair and clean-cut features. Peter could see pouches under the narrow eyes that sized them up.

"What the fuck you want?" Magnus Jones said.

"Peter Gentle, Private Detective," Peter said, extending a hand, which the footballer ignored. "We're investigating the murder of Kantor Keppel. Straw Keppel's father."

Jones sat down gingerly. Compared to the sleek strength of

Mick, he looked thuggish. "Holy shit." He cackled. "Straw Keppel. I haven't had one thought about her for years."

The room now reeked of sweat and mud.

"What happened in 1988, Mr. Jones?" Peter said.

"You really want to know? She strung me along with that whammo body of hers, then bang, a day before the wedding, her parents rang, said she'd pulled the plug. Amazing, eh? She still a looker?"

Peter pictured Straw's bloated figure, smelled her perfume again. "She's a recluse now. Have you spoken to her recently?"

"Nah, not once since that day. Her parents never let me near her."

"Tell me about her. Was she ever angry or violent?"

"Who'd have thought anyone would come talk to me about her?" Jones shook his head. "You know, I should have read the signs. She was a weird bitch. Screwed like a cat in heat, but I could never have a proper chat with her, you know? Moody. Liked to run the show. But violent? I never saw that."

"What was her relationship with her father?"

"What do you reckon, only daughter, he spoiled her rotten."

"Did she ever talk about her dead brother?"

"We just pashed and rooted. I'd heard her kid brother died years ago, but she never mentioned it."

Peter glanced at Mick, who nodded. This had been a waste of time.

"Thanks for your help," Peter said.

Jones shouted after them. "Tell the cunt I'm glad her father got killed."

CHAPTER 34

This case, Tusk thought. Baffling as any he'd come across in the Force. Baffling because of its open-endedness. Every fresh piece of information implicated someone new. A bloody avalanche of suspects.

"Isn't the atmosphere great?" Gentle said.

It had been touch and go getting Gentle past the bouncer at the front door. Sauce stains on the geek's shirt. Hair so tangled it should've had twigs poking out of it.

The Mingus Club was small, tucked away in an alley off Flinders Lane next to a posh Japanese restaurant. Seated close to a hundred patrons, spread across a carpeted floor in front of a small stage. Circular metal tables, round chairs with uncomfortable backs. Murky, with recessed lights on the walls. A bar with expensive drinks, "Tips Bring Sexy Karma" written on its blackboard wine list. Intimate acoustics, though the place was nearly full. To one side of them, a fat businessman smoking a cigar, trying to impress a tough-looking brunette. To the other side, two men with short hair talking animatedly.

"Prefer pubs myself," Tusk said.

"Can't you feel the vibe? I started to listen to jazz a year ago." Gentle was on his third glass of wine. "Did I tell you I'm learning jazz piano?"

Smoke swirled up Tusk's nostrils. "No, and I wish you bloody well hadn't."

After the football, they hadn't been able to raise Friedman. Not that it mattered, they were booked to see him tomorrow. With time to spare, they'd headed to—where else?—Draconi's. Gentle had been in a talkative mood. Luckily one of the members of his club—Alex, son of Russian stock—joined them. He and Gentle had crapped on about the Internet while Tusk listened.

Four men came onto the stage, waved to the audience, and launched into a fast, swinging number. Loping double bass plucked with rigid fingers, soft poncy drumming, weird flowing guitar, rhythmic piano. The murmur of voices around them died for an instant, then started up again.

Gentle leaned back with hands behind his head. "Doesn't that swing?"

"Muzak for old peoples' homes," Tusk said.

Gentle shook his head and laughed. Tusk sipped wine. Time check—10 PM on the dot. Dana would be watching a film on television.

"Check your mobile," Tusk said. "Any more threats?"

Bandaged finger sticking up in the air, Gentle listened to his mobile. "Nothing. Do you think he's gone away?"

"Maybe," Tusk lied. No, Bertoli was around somewhere, he could just feel it. And when he got hold of him... His shoulder muscles bunched up and he rolled them to ease out the tension. Control, he thought, that's what I need, just basic bloody control.

He spotted Willy Keppel, smoking at a table on the other side of the room, talking to someone. Willy looked as if he hadn't cleaned himself up at all before work. Threadbare jeans, blue long-sleeved shirt. Hair wilder than Gentle's.

Light glinted off Willy's glasses. He was staring at Tusk. The wreck stubbed out his cigarette, spoke hurriedly to his companion—something familiar about the scrawny figure with brown hair—and rushed off.

The quartet finished to polite applause. Even before they left the stage, the wail of a saxophone seared the air. Willy sat on a stool onstage. He'd taken off his glasses, his eyes dots of black. In the glare of the small spotlight his face was greasy and red.

"My God." Gentle downed more wine. "He'd make a fortune as a busker in Bourke Street Mall. He looks so pitiful."

"Brother to Rollo, can you spot it?"

"No way. But he sure can play."

Tusk found himself agreeing. Cheeks puffed, the derelict blew like a man under a spell. Smooth tones glided and soared, then honked and stabbed, charging every which way. Occasionally the liquid notes would swoop high and become a frantic, bleating mess, then he'd bring the saxophone down and burble around a simple melody. Willy's eyes were closed, sweat poured down his inflamed cheeks. All chatter had stopped. Wherever the bastard was going, he was taking the audience along.

The applause grew louder after each song, and Willy acknowledged it with dreamy shakes of his head. His shirt darkened with sweat. He grew even more possessed, rising off his stool and walking up and down the stage. A flurry of notes, a brief stop, then he was on his knees, wailing like a police siren. Sudden silence, darkness on the stage.

Clapping and cat whistles erupted.

"Come on," Gentle said. "They never do encores here."

They crossed the room and ducked under a low doorway behind the stage. A narrow corridor, dark and deserted. Tusk clicked into alertness. Pushed Gentle back and advanced first. Found a door, twisted it open.

A tiny room, piled with junk at the back. A broken table, stacked chairs, a sagging piano. A swivel chair in front of a mirror. A fluorescent light tube across the top of the mirror, winking on and off. A single globe dangling from the ceiling.

Willy had put on a leather jacket. He was packing away his saxophone into a case teetering on the stool.

"What the hell?" Sweat dripped off Willy's beard and his chest still heaved. His eyes burned with life. Sax is his savior, Tusk thought, that's what keeps him from falling off the deep end.

"Questions, Willy, questions." Tusk walked up close. Shadows oozed over the walls, bringing memories—running down corridors, footsteps on sticky carpets.

"You again. Sylvester fuckin' Stallone." Willy slammed down the lid of his case, scooped it up, and went to pass, his hot body pushing up against Tusk. Tusk held his ground easily, took in the familiar smell of putrid clothes, sweat, and booze. Felt Gentle's hand clutch him.

"Easy, big guy," Gentle said.

"Are you my mother?" Tusk grabbed Willy, all bones and no weight, under his armpits and lifted him, kicking, up onto the stool. He put his face up to Willy's. The black eyes were frenzied.

"Screw you," Willy said.

Tusk had an idea. He wrenched the case out of Willy's hand and tore open the lid. Picked up the body of the saxophone and raised it high.

"May I?" he said.

Willy raised his hands and shook his head. "No. Please."

Tusk dropped the sax into the case. "You've been screwing your brother's wife."

"Rollo's just a husband in name," Willy said. "Bella never loved him. She's tried to leave him a hundred times. She loved me, then he took her away from me. Bastard."

"When?"

Willy stood up and leaned against the mirror. A crack ran diagonally down it and Tusk saw two Willys, one whole, the other fissured. Hard to tell which looked worse.

"It was '82. My first record contract." The youngest Keppel's shoulders sagged. "You know nuthin' about me. My life went crazy early."

Tusk glanced at Gentle. His partner was watching Willy intently, but his gaze kept flicking back to Tusk. He's watching me, Tusk thought, he thinks I'm going to lose it again.

"I spent ten years in hell," Willy said, voice barely above a mumble. "Nearly died from an overdose. Married once, lasted two months. Slept under the Yarra bridges. Then a record contract. A good jazz group too, you heard of the Dusters? Bella came to me after a gig. She was wild. Man, she was wild. We were happy."

"What happened?" Tusk asked.

"Couple years later, she met Rollo, dunno how. Next thing is, she's married, doesn't want to see me. The bottom dropped out for me. I went to the States. Running away, I guess."

Willy licked his lips. "She was long gone from my life when I came back here. Long gone. And on my second gig, I look out while blowing, and there she is. Even better looking. We're in love."

Willy straightened up, his face defying their disbelief.

"What do you mean, in love?" Tusk said.

"Christ." Lick. Lick. "You think 'cos Rollo's rich enough to have a dwarf pick up his snot after him that he'll get the girl? I'm twice the man he is."

Tusk thought of Bella, her breasts and legs and lips, and wondered what on earth she could see in this toe rag. But he knew it wasn't that simple. In his own dark years, when he had his stint as a Willy in this world, when he was bloody repulsive, that was the time he pulled the ladies more than ever.

"Where do you two screw?" he said.

Willy snickered. "My place. That shock you, Rocky?"

"So she made you face up to Rollo."

Willy stopped licking. "What the hell?"

"We know about it, Willy. Bella told us, so it's cool. Bella let you in and pointed you to Rollo's office. You said you hadn't met him in years."

"So I lied." Willy looked confused. Out with the tongue.

"What did it feel like, seeing your brother for the first time in, what, fifteen years?"

Willy looked at them both, then seemed to come to a decision. "Bella told you?"

"It's cool, Willy."

"Well, let me tell you, it felt sweet. Nervous, like, but sweet. He's treated me like shit all my life, and I walk right in and say to him, 'Brother, you took my girl, I'm takin' her back.'"

An evocative scene, Tusk had to admit. "How did he take it?"

"Rollo's ice, man. I've got to hand it to him, I expected a scene, but he just looked at me, like we'd only talked a day ago. 'Hello, Willy,' he says with that molasses voice. 'What do you want?' I feel nervous, so I says, 'Bella and me been fuckin' for two years, and we're in love, and she's coming with me.'"

Willy laughed, a nasty, harsh sound.

"Choice, Willy, choice," Tusk said.

"Rollo's got this mask, you know, you can never tell what he's thinking. But a musician can see better, we're watchers. And for a moment, the look on his face… priceless, just priceless. Anyway, I just walk out and he follows, no jacket or nothing. In the elevator he looks at me, just like I remember when he was the big brother, and says, 'Get out of my life, Willy.' Just like that."

"A threat?"

"I guess. I just laugh. I feel real slick. Hey, I still do. When I think what that fucker's done… So I tell him to stick it. 'You want money, Willy?' he says. 'How much?' And I laugh again. We're on the street and he gives me the meanest look. 'You're pathetic, Willy,' he says. 'Give up and go away. You'll lose. You always do.' So I spit on him."

"You spat on him?"

"Yeah. And then I walk away."

"Anyone else around?"

"Not a soul."

Gentle spoke for the first time. "Did you see anyone else in the building?"

"No. Was real quiet."

"What did you do afterwards?"

"I had me a drink before work. Felt stoked, I can tell you."

"Have you talked to Rollo since?" Gentle asked.

"No way."

Tusk looked at Willy, up against the mirror, a double image of black eyes and tongue dabbing lips. There had to be more than that. Tusk felt a surge of disgust at all the Keppels.

"You're lying," he said.

Willy licked his lips. The air sat charged and still.

"Come on." Gentle, his hand yet again on Tusk's arm.

"Here." Tusk threw down his business card. "Ring. Too many people are getting killed, you don't want to be in line for that."

They left him cradling his saxophone case and walked out to pay their tab at the bar. The club was nearly empty.

"I know he's lying," Tusk said.

"Do you think he's a killer, though?"

Tusk shook his head in frustration. "Could be. That's the trouble, they all could be."

Only twenty-four hours to go, he was thinking when they emerged into dim light over stone paving. Someone slid from behind and jammed a gun hard into his back.

CHAPTER 35

It happened too quickly for Peter to comprehend. One minute he was following Mick's blocky frame out of the smoke-filled club. The next, someone slammed into Mick, and then Mick moved in a blur. Peter saw Mick's arm come down and his foot lash out, the attacker cried out, something clattered on the ground. And then Mick reached into his jacket and pulled out a gun—a gun? Who said Mick could carry a gun?—and pointed it at a moaning figure at his feet. Another gun lay on the cobblestones. Mick's face shone with fury.

An arm slipped around Peter's neck and a hard object burrowed into his back. Sibilance streamed into his ear.

"Drop it or your friend's dead," the sibilance said.

Bertoli! Terror jolted Peter. He cried out. In response the grip tightened so that he had to stagger to keep his balance. His body shook like a rag.

Mick whirled around to face him, the groaning man slumped between them. Mick's bleak eyes flicked like a reptile's between Peter, Bertoli, and the fallen man.

"Let him go." Mick's voice was a blade in the cool air. "Or I kill you and your partner."

Bertoli's hiss caressed Peter's ears. "Then he'll be dead."

Another voice sounded in the alley. A mild, American-accented voice.

"Relax everybody."

A stocky man limped from a doorway across the lane. He wore a long blue overcoat over a suit and held his hands out in front of him.

"No closer," Mick said.

Peter's breath came in snuffling gasps. He watched the man step into the reach of the overhead streetlight, and what Peter saw set him twitching under Bertoli's grip. The man's face was scrunched up, as if someone had taken an unformed face and twisted it to the right. His cheeks, chin, and forehead jutted out, leaving the rest recessed, so that Peter couldn't see the eyes.

The man's mouth was twisted, as if he'd be incapable of coherent speech, but he spoke in a light drawl. "Mr. Tusk, if I desired your death, or that of your friend here, do you think I would have bothered with all this? I just want a conversation, and this is the only way I know how."

Bertoli's tart aftershave clung to Peter's nostrils. Another surge of fear set him struggling again. The response was a savage twist of his neck that sent pain shooting through him.

Through blurred eyes, Peter saw Mick swing his gun up two-handed, his feet wide.

"Tell that fuck to let go, Scaffidi, or I'll kill you." Mick's voice rasped.

Scaffidi! Peter felt his world spin.

"As you command," Scaffidi said.

The crime boss gestured and Bertoli released his grip. Peter stumbled, righting himself with a hand on the ground. His head spun. He slapped with a shaking hand at snot hanging from his nose and lurched toward Mick.

Around them the lane was dark outside the arc of the isolated streetlights. Peter saw Bertoli watching him with a teasing smile on thin, parted lips. The hit man was shorter than Peter's imagination had supplied, slim and perfectly still in that poised manner he often saw in Mick. He had a razor-sharp face, with a piercing nose and jutting cheekbones. Black gelled hair was swept back over his head. He wore what looked like an Italian designer suit with a thin tie. His slender hand pointed a gun.

"Mr. Gentle." Scaffidi walked forward, ignoring the gun in Mick's outstretched arms, and extended his hand to Peter.

Peter scrambled back.

"Go away," he shouted. He felt urine running down his leg.

Scaffidi lowered his hand. He was close enough now for Peter to see the malformed bumps and ridges on the face. Nestled deep within, Scaffidi's eyes shone fiercely. Rather, one eye did; in the other socket Peter could only see a dull sheen.

"Put the gun down, Mr. Tusk," Scaffidi said. "You have me at your advantage now."

"What do you want, you loony fuck?" Mick's face glistened as it had in Fitzroy. He looked ready to explode. Don't, Peter begged mentally.

"It's not you I wish to converse with, Mr. Tusk." Scaffidi's diction reminded Peter of one of his university lecturers. "I know how you feel about me. Mr. Gentle, can we talk?"

Peter blinked and glanced wildly from Scaffidi to Bertoli and back. His body trembled with an almost irresistible urge to flee. He looked at Mick's bulging eyes and despaired; if he tipped the Balt into action, they'd all die. He nodded.

"Good." Scaffidi began to pace with a slow, limping gait. "Mr. Gentle, I can see you're a man of intellect. They say you have wonderful analytical capabilities. You bring order to the world through your mind."

Mad, Peter thought.

Scaffidi's ghastly mouth continued to twist into words of mild reflection. "I too bring order to the world. A different kind of order, one of flesh and bone, and yes, my methods would not appeal to you. But I too exercise intellect. I have plans, I work long-term. Do you know how much planning and effort it has taken to manufacture—" he pointed at Bertoli—"that machine? So long and yet what a fine outcome."

Scaffidi's pacing brought him directly up to Peter. The man's twisted stare had the force of a punch. Peter shuddered.

"I have worked too long and too hard to come undone at the hands of a neophyte." For the first time Scaffidi's voice dripped menace. "Fate cannot be that cruel. So I'm asking you, I am pleading with you, to please find something else to occupy your time."

"Yes," Peter said. It came out as a snuffle.

"Yes," he shouted at Scaffidi, spittle flying. "Yes! Go away!"

Scaffidi took out a cream handkerchief and wiped his face.

"No more prying, Mr. Gentle?" Back to the reasonable-man voice.

"No more," Peter croaked. "Just leave us alone."

"Very well then," said the monstrosity, wheeling around.

Scaffidi kicked the man on the ground, who stood up and staggered off. Without a backward glance, Scaffidi limped up the lane.

Bertoli bowed. Shivers ran down Peter's spine as Bertoli edged backward with the grace of a panther, gun held casually, eyes glued to Mick's.

Alone. A breeze swirled down the silent lane. Peter saw their shadows on the opposite wall, one rectangular and straight, the other a question mark. He collapsed to the ground on his knees. The big stones were cool on his hands. His ears filled with the sound of his own sobs.

"You okay?"

He looked up at Mick framed in the light. At Mick's solid, solid face. He found himself pulled to his feet.

"Let's get out of here," Mick said.

Peter could only think of one thing.

"Home," he mewled.

CHAPTER 36

"Trevor, talk to him."

Seated at the kitchen table, Peter Gentle half-listened to his mother whispering to his father in the living room. His toast, dripping with butter and smeared with Vegemite, usually the only food he enjoyed at home, today had the consistency of tofu and tasted as bland.

"Go away, woman," he heard his father respond.

Breakfast in Box Hill on a Sunday morning. The scarred kitchen table, the weak light through the venetian blinds, the chatter of birds outside, the old clock showing 7:30 as its second hand thudded around the circle, the *Herald Sun* posing its lurid headlines—it should have been reassuringly familiar. Instead, it felt like a prison cell.

Mick had been kind last night, calming Peter as they made their way down to Flinders Street Station, but once in the taxi they had both lapsed into uneasy silence. Peter's sleep had been mercifully deep, but he'd woken early with a gasp, and now every time he closed his eyes he saw Bertoli's razor's-edge nose and Scaffidi's mangled face.

He yawned and sipped his over-milky coffee. In the scuffed bathroom mirror after his shower, his face had looked puffy, but otherwise had simply been him, Peter Gentle. But who was he really?

"More toast, dear?" His mother's perfume rushed past.

"Thanks, Mum."

There was no escaping it. He was an abject coward. The first time—in the factory parking lot—he could justify by saying that in his entire life he'd never even been in a scrape, had always been able to parlay himself out of physical situations with his mouth and quick thinking. When Mick attacked Marcantonio, he'd been terrified, but somehow managed to act. But last night...

It didn't matter anymore. He was a complete failure as a private detective. He'd just been playing at it, he saw now. Assembling data, analyzing... while out there, psychopaths like Scaffidi lived crime day in, day out. That was the real world, not Peter's cozy mental asylum.

Was Mick so wrong to use mindless violence against people like Scaffidi? Which was better, maniacal force or pissing oneself?

"There you are, dear."

He buttered the two fresh slices of toast. At least Mum and Dad will be happy, he thought, when I tell them it's all over.

The phone rang in the hallway.

"For you, Peter." His father's brow was knotted. "Mick Tusk."

He could hear Mick's deep voice over traffic roar. "I'm in a phone booth in Ringwood. Couldn't ring from home, Dana's mad at me. I'll be around in five."

The big lug has recovered completely, Peter thought. How

often has Mick been in situations like last night? Come to think of it, how often has Dad?

"Look, what's the point?" he said.

A pause. Then, as if Peter had never spoken, Mick said, "I remembered the guy I saw with Willy last night."

Despite himself, Peter's pulse quickened.

"Strasser, Imogen's brother," Mick said. "I rang Strasser. Know what he said?"

Peter looked at his mother, rubbing her hands together, and his father, still in his bathrobe, watching him.

"You know what he said?"

"No, I don't know what he said," Peter spat out.

"Strasser often goes to the Mingus Club, a real jazz freak apparently. And get this—two weeks ago Willy told him that Bella was screwing Kantor. Sounds like Willy was making mischief. And Strasser apparently, like a good brother, rang Imogen."

Peter felt momentarily giddy. "Imogen didn't tell us this."

He couldn't believe it. Their client had a motive to murder her husband. He couldn't see Imogen having the strength to smash Kantor, let alone the energy, but his head buzzed.

"Mick, I can't. Last night—"

"Crap. Forget last night."

"No, it's not on. I'm finished."

"You owe me, Gentle." Mick's voice was harsh. "You signed me up at Draconi's, if you're going to pull out, you owe me to do it there."

Peter had to admit that Mick could use logic sometimes. He rubbed his eyes and exhaled. "Okay."

"Great. A detour to Toorak on the way."

Peter trudged down to his room and slipped on jeans and a black jumper. He didn't bother with his teeth or hair. As he walked out the front door, he heard his mother.

"Peter. Your toast…"

***

Peter glared at the white cat on Imogen Keppel's lap.

"All I see is useless delving into my husband's affairs, Mr. Gentle." Imogen spoke at Peter, even though Mick had been the one to summarize, in a measured voice, their recent discoveries.

Just typical, Peter thought, not a gesture of appreciation since we took on your bloody case.

Imogen wore a floral housecoat over a nightgown. Her auburn hair looked greasy. Her face was sallow and pinched, and he'd caught alcohol on her breath when she reluctantly shook his hand.

The three of them sat in Imogen's living room. No cakes or coffee this time, no flowers in the vases. The room smelled stale, of cats and dust and neglect. A fat gray cat—was it the same one?—was sprawled asleep across the bay windowsill. Other cats prowled in and out of the room.

Mick looked like a docile giant, straight-backed on the edge of his seat. "We're one step ahead of the police."

Imogen opened her mouth, no doubt to deliver another salvo, but the white cat lifted its head as if electrified, and Peter turned to see Straw padding into the room. She also wore a housecoat, but a raven-black one that barely came to her knees, revealing a thin red nightgown underneath. She wallowed past Peter and slumped next to her mother. Her toenails were crimson, and red lipstick was smudged down her chin. Her saucer eyes stared at Peter.

"There's one question we need to ask you," Mick said.

"What a waste of time and money." Imogen stood, sending the cat flying.

"Mrs. Keppel." Mick's voice lost its soft cadence and grew insistent. "Your brother told you about Kantor's affair with Bella, didn't he?"

Imogen's neck turned red, and for the first time she turned to Mick. Peter quailed at the fury he saw on her face, but Mick sat like a statue.

Peter took a glance at the other statue. What did Straw think of this revelation?

"How dare you," Imogen said to Mick. "How dare you even intimate that my husband would consort with that whore."

"I wouldn't dare," Mick said. "But Albert did, didn't he?"

Imogen stared at Mick, her face a mask of rage. Peter held his breath. Then Imogen collapsed back into her chair and covered her face with her hands.

"Yes," she whispered.

Jesus, Peter thought.

"Mrs. Keppel," Mick said, ever so gently. "If we can stumble across this allegation, the police will. What will you say?"

When Imogen lifted her face, tears glistened in her eyes. "I never believed a word of what Albert said. Not one word. Albert was always such a malicious boy. And it all came from that drug addict Willy."

"Mrs. Keppel, can you be more precise on your exact movements that night? It's important, for your sake."

Peter had glanced at the case file in the Peugeot. Imogen had been home that night and had referred to long telephone conversations with Albert, but Telstra records showed only one short call at 9:05.

Imogen looked at Mick, then Peter, then Straw.

"How anyone…" she cried and bolted from the room. Cats scattered.

Peter was stunned. A door slammed upstairs. All the cats except one had disappeared as if by magic; only the hairless one remained, prowling back and forth in front of Straw.

Straw sat unmoved. Peter strained to see reaction in her eyes, but could see nothing at all.

"Straw?" he said.

"Mr. Mistoffelees," she droned.

Peter saw Mick's eyes widen with astonishment.

"Straw, tell us more about the quarrel," Peter said. "You know, the quarrel your dad had with Uncle Rollo."

She sat motionless.

"Straw, please," he said, urgency seizing him. "Mistoffelees, yes. But the quarrel…"

It was no use. The green orbs fixed on him blinked steadily. The hairless cat leapt into Straw's lap and purred, its eyes trained on her face.

Another useless trail, Peter thought. Useless, bloody useless.

He stomped down the hall and across the creaking veranda and waited by the fountain for Mick to catch up. In the gloom of the courtyard, he saw a cat—the bloody Siamese?—slink away down the side of the house. They stood on a carpet of decomposing autumn leaves, listening to voices in the garden next door.

There were two messages on his mobile. Rollo's message was brief: "So what's it to be? The strength or the muscle?"

"Yes, I do need to speak to you." Peter recognized Marcia Brindle's voice, the words spilling on top of each other. Mick leaned over to listen in. "Need to speak. Shit! Call me."

He hunted through his pockets. Mick flipped open his notebook to Marcia's neatly printed phone number. Peter dialed and they listened to the other end ringing.

"Poor bastard," Mick said.

And Peter's mind also flipped to Kantor, lying on that steel pallet. From the outside the economist's life had seemed blessed. Peter looked back at the bay window. The huge gray cat had woken and its yellow eyes stared balefully at him. He shuddered.

***

Peter rubbed his hair hard. "Look, it should be obvious. I'm just not cut out for this kind of work, Mick. It's not... it's not me, it's nothing like I thought it would be."

Sunday morning was one of Peter's favorite times at Draconi's, although since moving back home he rarely made the trip. The restaurant was only a quarter full. Customers, and even the waiters, moved languidly. The crinkle of newspapers, the clunk of coffee cups on the bar, the ebbing murmur, Hector's stentorian voice... the sounds should have filled him with joy.

"You did okay last night, Gentle," Mick said. He'd just rung Marcia Brindle again and left a message. "Those were scary fuckers. You reacted the way anybody would."

Once, Mick had been an aberration here. Now either he or Draconi's had altered. To Peter, there was something natural about his concrete bulk sitting erect on a stool at the bar, sipping tea. Mick wore faded jeans and a stiff white shirt with a button-down collar.

"I wet myself!" Peter saw Hector's head lift from a distant table.

"If I counted the number of times I've pissed myself, I'd run out of fingers," Mick said. "And you are bloody well cut out for this work. We agreed from the start, you apply your brain, I do any rough stuff. Last night was my fault, not yours."

"That Scaffidi terrifies me. Look." Peter held up a hand and watched it shake. "I told him I'd quit, and if I keep going, he'll… I just can't stand it."

Mick reached over to force the trembling hand onto the table. "I've told you before—it's natural to be scared."

The mobile trilled on the table and Peter jumped. Mick grabbed the phone and replied curtly.

"Fuck me," Mick said. "That was Willy. Pleading Bella's innocence and good nature. Sounded pissed."

"Natural to be scared," Peter echoed glumly.

"I'm always shit-scared," Mick said. "It's just that I've learned the hard way how to act despite the fear. In fact I've gone too far the other way. Christ, you saw me with Marcantonio. Would you rather be fight-happy like me?"

"No, I guess not. But look, I don't like violence. Maybe I'm even a closet pacifist."

Mick slapped a hand on the table. Coffee sloshed into Peter's saucer.

"Horseshit," Mick said. "Gentle, you were the one to turn me around on Friday and you said it all. Remember? This isn't about war versus pacifism, it's about justice."

"Justice." Peter shivered. "But I just can't. Can't you get it into your skull that I'm scared? S-C-A-R-E-D."

"Be scared. But keep going. And I promise they'll never put you in a position like that again."

Peter looked at the set of Mick's mouth. Something had altered in Mick's demeanor overnight, and Peter thought he recognized it. "You'll kill them, right? For you, it's justice all right, justice from the barrel of a gun."

He knew at once that he'd gone too far. "Look, I didn't mean that."

"Yes, you did." Mick leaned forward. "And you're not way wrong. I hate those scumbags, and I'm not going to let them get away with this. But no more Marcantonios."

"What about your deadline?" Peter said. "You said you'd only work till the end of today."

"Maybe things will crack open today. Friedman might confess."

Peter snorted. "And he might not. The one thing I've learned about this line of work is that nothing goes as planned. I thought we'd be signed, sealed, and delivered by now, and I've got no idea who did what."

The pale blue eyes were intense. "You know we can solve this."

Peter felt like crying. What would his Skulk Club friends say when they heard he'd quit? He inhaled the bitter aroma of the black coffee. "And if we don't miraculously solve it all by the end of today, tomorrow it's bye-bye Peter? Justice is a fine word, I like it too, big guy, but come tomorrow I face those monsters alone?"

Mick hesitated. Around them the din of Draconi's played on. They stared into each other's eyes.

Then Mick nodded. "You've got me." His voice was hoarse. "Forget the five days."

Peter couldn't believe it. "What about Dana?"

"I'll handle that."

Peter slumped back in his seat. Nothing seemed clear, either in his heart or his mind.

"But all this still doesn't get 'round the fact that I'm terrified," he said. "Look, I wish I wasn't. I wish I could just rise to the occasion and say jolly well, let's tally ho. But my body says no."

A man came around the bar toward them. Peter flinched and Mick reached into his jacket.

It was Bishop. Even on Sunday he wore a suit. And behind him, Hector had sidled up to listen.

"Your dad guessed you'd be here, Gentle," the super-lawyer said in his clipped voice.

"Sit down," Peter said, his mind whirling. He noticed how Mick deferred, settling back in his chair.

"No thank you," Bishop said. "I've an unpleasant duty to perform, although perhaps some would question the use of the term unpleasant. Mrs. Keppel just rang me. She instructed me to ensure that all investigations cease."

Peter was speechless. He felt an inexplicable sadness. For Imogen, for Straw, for Kantor.

"Mrs. Keppel asked me to convey her appreciation for all you've done, but she now considers her actions foolish. She's convinced the police can solve her husband's death."

"Bugger me," Mick said.

"She asked me to give you these." Bishop fanned out two envelopes. "Substantial sums of money. Not the original prize, but more than you could rightfully expect."

"What do you think of this, Bishop?" Peter asked.

The lawyer grimaced. "Not my preference, to abandon ship so easily."

"Then persuade her to change her mind."

"I tried, my sweeties. I told her the egghead and the beefcake were making remarkable progress. But she chose to disagree. And she's the client."

Peter stood up, propelled by emotions he couldn't at first decipher. He walked over to the window of the restaurant and gazed out at the strolling passersby. A solitary diner at the window bench eyed him curiously. He pushed hair out of his eyes.

He walked back. "Mick, what do we do?"

He didn't need a verbal response, he divined it all from one look into the seaside blue eyes.

Mick growled. "Tell him to stick it."

Bishop looked from Mick to Peter.

"You heard Mick." Peter trembled. He recognized his emotion: anger.

Bishop's almond eyes glowed. "She's my client. So I'm going to tell her I sacked you. I'll keep this money. Come and get it whenever you want it. You are officially no longer on the payroll."

Then the lawyer cackled. "I knew I'd enjoy this. Unofficially, and I deny any knowledge of this, you're on the same terms and conditions as applied originally, but to me personally.

Understand? The prize is the same, but you have no client."

A bizarre joy flooded Peter. It was Mick he looked at, the infuriating, stuffed-up lump that watched him with what anyone else would have described as a minor twitch on his mouth.

"Bishop," Peter said, squaring his shoulders. "Wait till you see what we can do."

Hector was grinning.

The carrot-top nodded once. "Report daily," Bishop tossed back over his shoulders as he rushed off.

CHAPTER 37

The crunching chords of AC/DC were powering Mick Tusk. Not the new incarnation of the group—the old AC/DC, fronted by Bon Scott screeching like a banshee.

Robert Friedman scowled when he opened his front door.

"You," he said.

"Just a few questions," Tusk said.

Fatigue or plain stress had creased Friedman's sun-tanned forehead even more than Tusk recalled. The developer wore old jeans and a tee-shirt. His slitted eyes regarded Tusk and Gentle with suspicion. He jerked his head, led them down the corridor.

Tusk had parked the Peugeot half up on the nature strip, behind Friedman's Range Rover, in a narrow semi-circular street off the railway line, just a stone's throw from the Camberwell shops and cafes. Friedman lived in a stately old double brick with arches of white filigree over a narrow veranda and painted patterns on the bricks. Proof that property development had its rewards.

In a cramped living room, two teenage boys slouched over a television. While Friedman told them to go for a walk, Tusk checked out the piles of CDs: some good stuff—Bad Company, Mott The Hoople, Springsteen—plus plenty of crap.

Time check—1:05. Tusk glanced at Gentle. Still a bundle of nerves, face pale, hands in motion, but voluble enough on the drive out.

Friedman led them outside to a veranda shaded by a pergola. A large plastic table, strewn with plans and documents. Cricket stumps and ball next to a drooping willow tree.

"I was hoping you wouldn't come." Friedman rubbed the pouches under his eyes. "Let's get this over with, Jenny will be back from church in half an hour."

Tusk's rancor at Friedman's deceit had been replaced with a determination to settle the truth. He sucked in his stomach muscles, breathed in the fresh air. Relished the filtered sunshine on his cheeks, the clacking of a train over the back fence, the distant sound of announcements at Camberwell Station.

"You snuck back in after seeing the company lawyer, didn't you?" Gentle said.

Tusk looked at Gentle. How did he figure that?

Friedman peered at Gentle. "Come again?"

Gentle had clasped his hands behind his back, but Tusk could still see his fingers wriggling with energy. "Someone saw you. Your hair. And you must have left the building, otherwise your guest pass would have only registered going in, not out."

Friedman took a deep breath.

"Let me tell it then," he said. "After I finished with lawyer Morrison, when I left the building, I saw a bunch of young guys heading in. I joined them, got off on the third floor, went into the stairwell. Climbed past the top floor. The stairs go on to a locked door, I guess onto the roof. I sat down there until after the office emptied."

"Why?" Tusk asked.

"Hard to say." Friedman stuck his hands in his pockets, hunched his shoulders down. "Just an impulse. I was pissed off that every time I tried to see Kantor, I was palmed off to someone else. I guess I'd come to realize I'd never pin Stan's murder on him, but I hadn't seen him personally for yonks. Just wanted to tell him what a crook he is... was."

"Why not just barge into his office in daylight?"

"Don't know. I felt mad, know what I mean? I wanted to really tell him my mind, instead of worrying about upsetting people in the office."

Gentle was jiggling his feet. Tusk kicked him.

"I must have fallen asleep," Friedman said. "Woke at ten."

"Exactly?" Tusk said.

"9:57. I remember, I looked at my watch. I headed down one floor. It was bloody quiet. I'd expected to find his office empty—"

"You knew where his office was?"

"Yeah, went there several times last year. I yelled at Kantor. You know, the things you'd expect me to say. Told him he'd gotten away with murder. He called me a lunatic and threatened to ring the police. By then all my anger was flushed and I felt bad about what I was doing. So I left."

"Anyone else hear you two shouting?"

"Not as far as I know."

"What time did you leave?"

"Don't know, maybe 10:15. You know what the bastard's last words to me were?"

"What?"

Friedman's voice quivered. "He said, 'Your brother was a fine man.' The bastard!"

"How did you leave, Mr. Friedman?" Gentle asked.

"This is the terrible bit." Friedman shook his head and shoulders like a dog coming out of the sea. "I took the stairs again. Walked all the way down to the basement. That's when I heard it."

"Heard what?" Tusk said.

"A shout, something like 'no.' Then a scream and a thump." Friedman's eyes grew wide. "I got the fright of my life. Ran out the fire exit. Didn't know what it was then, but when I heard about the murder, I knew."

Friedman hugged himself hard. "I heard it. The killing."

"You heard it," Tusk said, "or did you do it?"

"No."

"You said it yourself, you hated him. The man murders your brother, you're after him for years. So you hide a poker in your jacket, follow him into the stairwell, and thump him."

"No way!" A single sob. "God, I thought of it, I even dreamt it."

Tusk heard a wattle bird gurgling in the wisteria above them. Just like home, he thought.

Gentle was gnawing at a finger in his excitement. "Were you wearing gloves, Mr. Friedman?"

Friedman nodded. "How—?"

"Why gloves?"

"It was a cold night. No heating in the stairwell."

"No fingerprints, you see," Gentle said to Tusk.

Tusk nodded. For the first time since they'd begun this crazy partnership, it was working well. Damn well.

"You see why I told no one?" Friedman shouted. "Who's going to believe me? I wanted the bastard dead. I did!"

Friedman smashed a fist against the pergola. A flash of color as the wattle bird fled.

"You know something?" Friedman said. "I keep hearing that scream. Ironic, eh? I'm sorry for the mongrel!"

Tusk took a decision. "I believe you."

Friedman stared. Gentle's mouth dropped.

"For what it's worth," Tusk said. "But this is fucking murder, Friedman. You're going to have to talk to the police, okay? Go to them now, we'll keep mum about this meeting. It'll look good on your account, volunteering. If you don't go, we'll have to fill them in, you're in even deeper shit. Your wife know?"

Friedman shook his head. "She knows something is up."

"Did you hear anything of the killer?" Gentle asked.

"I've been racking my brain. No. Nothing. Just the shout and the scream."

"Would you say Kantor knew the killer?"

"Maybe. Just the way he shouted."

And then a weird question from Gentle. "Mr. Friedman, did your brother Stan talk much about Kantor's family—Imogen or Straw?"

"Jesus mate, that's stretching the memory." Friedman was breathing hard. "I recall he said the girl was nice but nutty. And the wife stuck-up. Here's a question for you. Either of you checked back on Stan's murder?"

"I have," Gentle said.

"Well?" Friedman's face was intent.

Christ, Tusk thought, I've felt the scorch of the cross of obsession, feel it right now. But nothing like this man.

Gentle sighed. A shrug, meaning yes, maybe Kantor had been a killer.

They left Friedman staring at the back fence, fists bunched. Tusk felt ready for anything. His head teemed with songs, a sure sign he was full on. He checked out the street. Nothing.

"Why did you say you believed him?" Gentle asked as Tusk drove off.

Greenery everywhere in Camberwell. Trees lining the streets, shrubbery exploding from houses. Every few blocks a park. "Because I do."

"But you're always lecturing me about people's capacity to lie, how people never stop lying."

Camberwell even smelled good. The tang of freshly mown grass. Flowers. "Sometimes you just know they've said it all."

"But Mick, he's the only one we can place at the spot, at the right time. He hated Kantor."

"Yep. But you heard him, he couldn't have killed. It's not in him. Like you. You couldn't kill anyone."

Tusk stopped the Peugeot alongside a park full of gums and arranged flowerbeds. How nice to live here, he thought, as they walked to a bench next to a still pond. The most eastward of all the inner, old-money suburbs, yet only ten kilometers from the city. Tradition meets the upwardly mobile professionals moving in toward the big smoke. Great for jogging. Maybe one day…

"I don't agree," Gentle said. "Until we know for sure, we shouldn't eliminate him as a suspect."

Tusk shrugged, kept his eyes busy. No cruising cars. Nothing out of the ordinary, just a father walking his child in a pusher.

He dialed Marcia on the mobile. No answer. An odd message from Rollo, which they both listened to: "You know, Kantor was so bright, sometimes he couldn't make a decision. He'd sit at his desk dreaming for hours. I had to prod him. Many times. That's what brothers do. Ring me—we need to talk. Before six. Bella and I are dining in Southbank."

"Look, here's the logic." Gentle rocked up and down. "Regardless of whether Friedman killed Kantor, we can take it for granted he must have been the one who triggered the fire exit record."

Tusk pondered, nodded. Gentle grinned, lifted his hand up. Their palms slapped.

Gentle rushed on. "We know Yang the security guard was on the front desk at that time, because he spotted Dancer leaving, so that eliminates Willy."

"Unless he borrowed Bella's pass," Tusk said. "Or she went with him. But yeah, he's not on my radar screen."

"And Imogen, though maybe she has a motive, is eliminated. Bella has no real motive—she couldn't care less who knows about her affair with Kantor. And if she killed him, Rollo must know about it."

"She's tricky. Still on my list."

Gentle nodded frantically, inclined his palms to present his conclusion. "So I believe we're left with Friedman, Bella, Rollo, and Brindle."

"Your bet, Gentle?" From here on in, Tusk knew their campaign would need to escalate, they needed to take a punt.

"Friedman. If not him, then Marcia."

Tusk watched a tram sweep down Camberwell Road. "I thought you admired her?"

"I do, but you said it, everyone can have a motive to murder, and there's something at Scientific Money she's trying to hide. And the weight of the evidence is on her. I just don't believe Rollo could kill his brother. And if he was the murderer, why would Bella protect him? She clearly can't stand him."

Tusk picked up a stone, threw it in a curving arc through the blue sky. "Wrong. It's Rollo all right. And Bella's covering for him because she likes his money. That's why she stuck with him so many years. And you're ignoring Dancer's murder. I'm sure that was Bertoli, and the one he connects with is Rollo, through Scaffidi."

In the car Tusk slipped in exactly the right tape. Creedence Clearwater Revival's "Run Through the Jungle." The eerie ancient sounds matched his heartbeat.

"Same data, different conclusions, eh?" Gentle was smiling. "But you see how it works. Data, analysis, conclusions. A bit more data, and our analysis will lead us both to the same conclusion."

The sheer pompousness of the lecture brought a laugh to Tusk's lips. "No wonder you reckon you're so smart."

Gentle was also laughing. "Piss off. I need to spell it out for the remedial class."

CHAPTER 38

The fleeting moment of levity rejuvenated Peter. At last, the minute tremors across his chest subsided. At last he could don his thinking cap.

Mick fell silent in the Peugeot, absorbed in his head-banging music, on the slow crawl northeast through Sunday afternoon traffic, which suited Peter fine. One more time, he thought. Four suspects remaining. One more time through the scenarios…

Crucial data was missing. Where on earth did Scaffidi fit in? Who was playing funny buggers at Scientific Money? Peter pictured Robert Friedman, fists knotted with rage, consumed by anger even after confessing he'd heard his nemesis being murdered. Could Friedman have murdered? How good a liar was he? In the end it all came down to that—whether he had lied well enough to fool them. In fact, Peter's carefully assembled data was only as good as his judgment of its veracity. This insight, logical as it was, shocked him.

"Maybe I should do a psychology course," he mused, while Mick pulled up under the shade of a pine tree.

"Good idea," Mick said. "I started one a year ago. Never kept it up."

"You?"

Mick's sunglasses swung toward Peter. "Anything wrong with that?"

The sunlit verdancy of Donvale dazzled Peter. Everything looked so green. He waited while Mick climbed out and scanned the area.

"She's in," Peter said, nodding toward the Mercedes in the carport. A fresh breeze rustled leaves around them. God, I'm hungry, he thought. He went to press the doorbell but Mick held his arm.

"What's up?" Goosebumps rose on Peter's arms when something in Mick's manner communicated. The house was silent. All Peter could hear was an automatic sprinkler next door, birds, and his own fragile heart yammering again.

Mick removed his sunglasses. His eyes were calm. He pulled out a pair of thin surgical gloves and slipped them on.

"The door," Mick said, and sure enough, Peter could see the slit at its edge, a slit that widened when Mick pushed it with a finger. The door creaked open to show the gloomy corridor and the light from the family room at the end.

A gun was in Mick's right hand, squat and alien. Peter began to hyperventilate in noisy squalls of breath.

"What's going on?" he whispered.

Mick gripped his shoulders hard enough to hurt.

"Listen," the big man said in a hoarse low rumble. "Stay here, don't move. Whatever you do, don't touch anything. Anything happens while I'm in there, drive the hell away and phone for help. Got that?"

Peter's teeth chattered. "Shouldn't we just ring the police?"

"Just obey instructions for once."

And Mick was gone, a wraith gliding through the door.

Peter stood trembling. No sound from inside. He remembered Marcia Brindle's easy laugh when they first met. He remembered what Mick said, that courage was just getting used to the fear. He took a step toward the door, heard the faint scuff of his footstep. He took another step and then he was inside.

Ahead, Mick disappeared from view. Peter heard his own breath sawing in the air. How could a house be so silent? He took step after step. Don't piss yourself, he thought. He smelled something.

By the time he reached the family room, his legs were rubbery. A horrible odor assailed him. He began to gag, checking himself only by clenching his jaws shut.

The low room was suffused with vague light. Mick stood by the main settee, gun hanging limply by his side. Even for a man for whom stillness was a virtue, his frame appeared unnaturally immobile. When Peter entered, he swung around and raised his gun.

"Told you to stay out there." Mick's flat voice reached across the dust dancing on gray light.

Peter edged forward. The smell was sickening. His head screamed.

"No, Gentle, no."

Marcia. On her back, on the settee. A gaping red slash filled her neck and blackish red covered the blouse below. Blood, screamed Peter's mind. He gagged and then Mick was upon him, shoving him through the back door, out onto grass, forcing his head down as he spewed and spewed, all his soul screaming in the sunlit Melbourne peace.

"Is she...?" he spluttered when he finally raised his head, vomit dripping from mouth and nose.

"Been dead a few hours. Don't touch anything."

"Mick?" Peter looked his friend in the eyes and stifled a sob.

"I know, mate." Mick held him close and Peter felt Mick's heart beating, a fast hammering rivaling his own.

"Now don't you move," Mick said. "I'll check out the house. I think the perp's gone, but you never know."

"The husband!" Peter gasped. He never even knew the man's name.

"Yeah." The set of Mick's face was as grim as Peter had ever seen.

Mick slipped off. Peter stood up, raised his head to the sky. My fault, he thought. I persuaded Mick to leave here last time. My fault.

Panting through his mouth like an exhausted dog, he edged his way back into the house, touching nothing. That cloying, raw smell filled his senses again. He hugged himself and inched forward until he could see the body.

Peter knew nothing about the physical signs of death, but Marcia's didn't look in the least peaceful. Her body seemed arched in agony. One hand trailed over the side of the settee, fingers splayed as if in entreaty. He could see her blouse was white, but only from the sleeves; the rest was a thick red. A pool of red stained the blue of the settee around her neck, and he could see splatters up the back. Only her face held some peace, the unseeing eyes staring at the ceiling. Her tartan skirt had been pulled up to her waist. He saw pubic hair over pale skin and gagged again, only just controlling himself.

He tore his gaze from the corpse to scan the room. Nothing seemed out of place. No sign of struggle. On the table where they had talked to her just a day ago stood a coffee cup. He walked over and sniffed the cold liquid. Yes, coffee. He reflected that he was actually investigating, in his own bumbling fashion, even as a dead body, someone he knew, cooled nearby. Mick was right. He could get used to this. Disgusting, he thought.

Something on the table caught his attention. Marcia's confident face stared at him, on her security pass, sitting up on its backing pin. Without thinking he scooped it up.

Mick was back, moving fast.

"Empty," he said. "No husband."

Maybe she'd listened to them, Peter thought, and at least shifted the husband. Why did she let the killer in? No sign of forced entry. Does that mean she knew the killer?

He listened to the refrigerator humming. "We need to ring the police."

Mick shook his head. "I know that's what I've been saying. But no. They'll crucify us. Two murders right after we visit, you think they'll let us walk?"

The smell encircled them. Peter couldn't argue with the analysis or the conclusion. He nodded.

"Remember, no touching." Mick vanished.

Outside, Peter paused to let sunlight bathe his face.

"Come on!" Mick was already in the Peugeot.

Peter sprinted up the drive. His whole body felt tainted. When the car moved away, he fished out a handkerchief and wiped his face. He could feel vomit lodged inside his nostrils.

"It's my fault," he said.

Mick didn't answer. His face was pale and he drove fast. On the outskirts of Donvale, he turned into a quiet street, opened his door, and threw up, a short sharp cough. Peter handed him his handkerchief and Mick dabbed at the corners of his mouth.

"My fault, not yours." Mick's voice was harsh.

"I persuaded you to leave."

"I should've known better. And that bastard's going to get his." The hands gripping the steering wheel were white.

"Who?"

"Bertoli."

"You can't convict him like that," Peter said.

"It was him. Couldn't you feel him back there?"

Peter ran both hands up through his hair. He didn't want to think about Bertoli.

"Christ." Mick had caught sight of the security pass in Peter's hand. "Are you crazy, Gentle? That's theft. Tampering with evidence."

"What about leaving the crime scene?"

Mick sighed. "Fuck, you're right."

Peter's back began to throb. He heard Mick on the mobile: "Won't be home until I get there."

Mick gunned the engine. The sun had disappeared behind a cloud. Mick's face was as implacable as stone. Peter's throat suddenly went dry.

"Where are we going?" he pleaded.

CHAPTER 39

"Hey mate, you got a booking?" the waiter called.

Tusk ignored him. His body felt light, alert. He remembered Marcia Brindle's blood-soaked body…

The Waterfront: a large seafood and sushi restaurant with produce heaped on piles of ice. Tusk scanned the tables, smelled the oysters. Definitely no Rollo.

Needle in a haystack, Gentle had whinged, but as Cap had drilled into Tusk, systematic effort delivered results. And this was vital. No doubt now that Rollo bloody Keppel was the perp, but they had no evidence. Crack him, that's what they had to do.

Gentle was waiting outside the restaurant, pissed off, hair wild with sweat. "Just because he said Southbank doesn't mean he's here."

It amazed Tusk that on a Sunday evening, Southbank and the Casino complex seemed busier than during the week. Groups of young people, swearing and shouting. Older couples strolling. Tourists, cameras hanging from shoulders. Tusk checked the swirling crowd of people as best he could. No way he could protect the useless nerd now against Bertoli.

"Shut up and use those eyes of yours," he instructed Gentle.

Time check—6:54. Christ, over an hour of searching. Tusk felt frustration building. The next restaurant, a cheaper-looking Greek one with red semi-circular booths. Unlikely for a rich wanker like Rollo, but who could tell? Into the hot odor of savory dips. Nix. He gave Gentle a shake of his head. Yet another restaurant, a posh-looking one with the funny name of The Duck. No Rollo. An Italian place. Same result. He headed out to the promenade along the river.

"Fuck," Tusk said.

Gentle had that schoolteacher look. "Honestly, how can we expect—"

A sudden whoosh exploded in the air. Tusk whirled, hand onto the gun in his jacket, then relaxed. Just a tourist attraction. The high columns lining the river flared into the sky, yellow-orange flames briefly blotting out the office skyline. The waterfront glowed. The Kennett government had installed blue reflectors on the other side of the river and in the light of the gas flares the water appeared unnaturally cool and blue.

He felt heat on his cheeks. Heard Gentle gasp. "There."

Tusk followed Gentle's pointing finger. Through a window, illuminated by the flare, into a restaurant with steel furniture. A landing above the main restaurant, a long table. A man gesticulating, shiny bald head. Rollo!

"It's that Asian-sounding place," Tusk said.

"Yes, The Duck," Gentle said. "It's not Asian, I've been there—"

"Didn't look upstairs."

Tusk whipped his sunglasses into his jacket pocket, ran hard toward the entrance to the complex.

"Mick," he heard Gentle calling behind him.

The slim waiter at the front desk remembered him from his recent intrusion.

"You can't come in," he said, hand raised.

Tusk slapped the man aside, lithely threaded through the tables. Behind him he heard Gentle squawking. He ran up the curved staircase he'd previously missed.

A dozen people around a rectangular table that took up the entire landing. Older men in suits, women in svelte dresses with jewelry shining. Murmuring conversation that stopped as they caught sight of him. A shout behind him. He saw Bella push back her chair and rise, leg visible through the slit in her dress.

"Keppel!" Tusk felt rich with that sense of righteousness he'd loved in the Force.

Rollo was sitting at the head of the table, leaning to whisper to a gray-haired suit. The tycoon stiffened, swiveled in his seat. His eyes widened.

Tusk heard scuffling behind him. Too late for a measured attack. Crimson flared across his eyes as he bludgeoned glasses and bottles with a flailing arm. Glass flew. Someone screamed. Rollo stood and stumbled backward.

"Calm down," Gentle squeaked.

"You lunatics!" Rollo shouted.

"A word, Keppel," Tusk said.

He saw a waiter slam into Gentle. A chef, reeking of garlic, pulled at Tusk's arm. He didn't move.

"What is the meaning of this, Rollo?" said the gray-haired man.

Rollo looked at Tusk. Tusk thrust back his shoulders, shook off the cook, put on his sunglasses.

Rollo nodded. "Enough," he commanded. Tusk had to admire him. Back in charge, just like that.

The waiters fell away. Tusk noted with pleasure that Bella was wiping at a massive stain on her dress.

"I'm sorry," Rollo said, his voice directed at the table but his eyes on Tusk. "These people are with me. A little exuberant, perhaps, but I'll sort this out."

"Darling?" Bella at Rollo's side. Tusk fancied he saw something gleeful in her expression.

"Don't worry, love." Rollo brushed past Tusk to stand before Gentle. "Control your partner now, won't you?"

Tusk watched confusion flood Gentle's face. Despite all the evidence, Boy Wonder was still under the man's spell.

A young guy was shouting into a phone by the door. Rollo spoke to him, led the way out to the waterfront. Tusk checked his hand—wet, but no glass damage.

"You said you could control this." Gentle in his ear.

"Need to stir him up." Tusk felt great. Everything in order at last. For some reason the anthemic bass intro to the Clash's "London Burning" started up in his head.

To his surprise Gentle nodded.

They joined the chief executive by the water, away from passersby. Tusk inhaled the smell of the river, damp and earthy.

"Have you two lost your minds?" Rollo shouted. A Japanese couple stopped to look at them. Rollo lowered his voice. "What possessed you to do that?"

Tusk planted his feet. How to tackle this? But Gentle got in first.

"What's going on at Scientific Money, Mr. Keppel?" Gentle said. "It's not the computers, is it, making the investment decisions. Who is it?"

"What are you talking about?" Rollo's eyes were wide. He licked his lips. For the first time Tusk saw a resemblance to Willy.

"It's not really a quantitative fund at all, is it?" Gentle's words spilled out. "Is it you? Or Weiqing? Or Brindle? Who picks the stocks?"

"What nonsense. Are you on drugs?" Rollo strode up to Gentle, jabbed him with a finger. "I'll sue you if you repeat those accusations."

"I can prove it," Gentle said.

Something in Gentle's eyes must have alerted Rollo to the lie, for he stepped back. Smiled without warmth. "No, you can't."

Wrong tactics, Tusk thought. He stepped up close enough to see dried spittle flecks in the corners of Rollo's mouth. "What happened when Willy came to tell you your wife was having an affair with him?"

The mask fell away. "Why you bloody scum..." Rollo's mouth a snarl. "My personal life has nothing to do with you."

"The police won't think so," Tusk said, "when they find you lied about that night."

"I was with Willy. He saw me leave."

"Did he see you return later?"

Rollo shook with fury. Just another angry man now, not someone in power. "I'll ruin you."

"Tell us, Keppel." Tusk made his delivery calm and neutral. The invitation, Cap called the technique. Invite them to confess, the old cop had preached. "Tell us what happened when you went back."

But the moment had passed. Rollo was in control again. A dismissive wave of his hand. "I didn't go back. So I lied about Willy." Tusk could almost see his brain working. "I didn't want the world to know my troubles. But if you check my story against Willy's and Bella's, you'll see it's the truth."

"You trust Bella to stick to her alibi, Keppel?" Tusk watched the patriarch's face flicker for an instant. "After what she's done to you?"

"Nonsense." Rollo straightened his jacket. "Lunatic nonsense. You won't be ringing the police, I will be."

Rollo stared menacingly at Gentle and walked off.

Tusk felt failure on his back. They hadn't even asked about Dancer or Brindle. He shouted, "How did you get involved with a criminal like Scaffidi?"

Rollo faltered. Strode on.

"You're a killer," Mick bellowed into the night. He held himself from chasing the receding figure. "You and that motherfucking scumbag Scaffidi. You're killers. And we're going to get you."

A hand over his mouth.

"Shhh, big guy." Gentle's eyes were sad.

Water lapped below their feet. Tusk's heart pounded with rage.

* * *

"I'm missing something," Gentle said.

8:30 PM at Windows On The Bay in Mordialloc. Tusk felt

buggered. Disappointment had dulled into stupor. Wine helped, not that he'd drunk much, had left that to his disheveled partner. He watched Gentle stick his nose in his glass before downing another mouthful of red. A connoisseur. An empty bottle of white and a near-empty bottle of red on the table.

"Look, I don't think Rollo did it," Gentle said.

The restaurant was a chaotic place. Used to be a lifesaving club, Gentle claimed. All creaking wood, wicker and metal chairs, exuberant staff with studs and earrings. Hardly an empty table. Near them, a family birthday party, noisy as hell. The meal had been Gentle's idea, what he called downtime, and although Tusk had resisted, he had to admit he'd enjoyed himself.

Tusk grunted. "Pig's arse. He did it all right."

"It just doesn't fit. There's something wrong with the logic. You heard him by the river, his story is spot on. Where's the motive? Jealous rage? Is he the type?"

Their table sat flush against a window. Tusk looked out over the furrowed sand, lit by lights along the bike path. The dark of the shimmering flat sea. Two cyclists streaming past. Port Phillip Bay stretching around in an arc of city lights and an occasional flash of car headlights.

The geek sloshed the last of the red into his glass. Hair nearly obscuring those fanatical eyes, feet tapping on the wooden floor. "Look, there are things I should be following up on. Like the security passes."

"What about them? I thought we figured them all out."

"What if someone else had an extra invisible pass?"

Tusk tried to signal a waiter over a red-faced man shouting toasts to "me mate the birthday boy."

"Who'd have made one of those?" he said. "Chang? You said he seemed honest."

"You're the one who said trust no one. And there's the email too."

Tusk sighed. "Christ, Gentle."

"No one owns up to it. Remember how archaic it sounds? 'The natural order is there for the good of all. If you transgress, the fury of the heavens will descend upon you.'"

"You memorized it?"

"Of course."

Tusk shook his head at the wonder of it all. "This is like that theory you had in school, that JFK was assassinated on the orders of LBJ. You were obsessed. Remember?"

"Yes, well." That silenced the bugger. Tusk watched him lurch off to the restroom, colliding with tables on the way.

Tusk laced fingers behind his head, watched a couple kissing on the sand. The meal had been superb: spicy shellfish, even creme caramel for dessert. Interesting—Gentle had identified the gray-haired guy back at the restaurant as the Attorney-General himself. Over dinner Gentle had crapped on and on—about the Skulk Club, about the merits of the restaurant, about what he called the "glories of Melbourne's bay views," about his exploits as a consultant. They'd even reminisced about their schooldays.

"Tell me, Mick," Gentle had asked. "Where did your name come from? You told me back then, but I've forgotten."

Tusk had chuckled. "In Estonian, my old man is really Arne Tuisk. But when he landed after the war, the bloody official missed the 'i'. Me, I was christened Mihkel. So I should be"—exaggerating the pronunciation—"Mihhh-ckell Too-isk, but instead I'm Mick Tusk. My Dad hates the Anglicized name."

When Gentle returned, Tusk asked him about his date with the secretary.

"Disastrous." Gentle's face was slack with alcohol. "I jus' don't have the com... the comfidence."

"You know what your problem is with women?" Tusk said.

"Everythin'."

"I reckon you should be bolder. You're full of hot air normally—listen to you tonight. But when you go out with women I bet you try to be someone else. Just be yourself. Gab on a bit."

"Ha." Embarrassed laughter.

"And you should fix your drinking problem."

Gentle glared. "That's one of my hobbies. Wine appresh... shiation."

"Hobby my arse. Five days we've been on this case, and every day you've been on the piss."

"Hey, now you're my guru on love and healff?"

Maybe, Tusk reflected, women and alcoholism were the only things he knew all about.

Somehow Gentle had paid the bill on his restroom trip. Tusk helped him down the steps to the parking lot off Beach Road. He paused to let a couple walk past, the woman skipping around the laughing man. Tangy salty air. Cool.

He half-lifted his partner into the Peugeot, drove along the beach until Warrigal Road. Headed north while Gentle fell asleep. Turned off a tape of Thin Lizzy and switched on the mobile. Ignored the dozen messages queued up. Checked some phone numbers and rang Detective-Inspector Balthazar Candle.

Another call wrapped in excuses, no more news about Scaffidi. Phoned drug dealer Buckingham and after being berated for not returning messages, heard the same nil result.

"Just one thing, cherie. An address."

"How much will it cost me?"

He rang Cap. Retired now, settled up in Bondi Beach in Sydney. Christ, Tusk thought, hope he hasn't gone hopeless like Rough Gentle, Peter's dad. Tusk smiled at Cap's curt message and left a hello, finished with, "I'm fucking up again. Could do with a chat." Rang sister Liz, another message with little point.

Belgrave. The house welcomed him as always with its quiet peace. He could see the moon through wispy clouds. Exhaustion across his chest. Eucalyptus in the air. He prodded Gentle awake.

"Where 'm I?" slurred Gentle.

"You're staying the night with us," Tusk said. "Bloody piss-pot."

Gentle mumbled as he lurched behind Tusk. Tusk had rehearsed his lines for Dana along Burwood Highway, but when she opened the door, his words dried up. He was struck dumb yet again by her radiance. Those billowing curls.

"Regred any incomvenience—" Gentle began, pushing hair back ineffectually, but Tusk stilled him with a hand.

"Where have you been, Mikey?" Dana said. "I've been ringing Peter's mobile. A policeman, Inspector Vinci, has been chasing you urgently."

Christ, the messages. Bully rushed out the door, his rump swinging. Tusk saw Gentle back away in alarm. Tusk grabbed the dog, felt the sandpaper tongue scrape his hands.

"It's all over the late news," Dana said. "They've found another body."

"Marsssha," said the swaying idiot.

"And they've arrested someone for all three killings."

Friedman—the poor bastard! The news slammed Tusk.

Gentle must have sensed where his thoughts were heading. "Nod yer faul', big ga."

Tusk ignored Gentle. This was the end. Tomorrow they'd have to confront Sam, try to convince him of Friedman's innocence. The case would be out of their hands.

He went to Dana and enfolded her body. Buried his nose in the earthy riches of her hair. Bully whined around their legs.

CHAPTER 40

Peter's hair refused to obey any commands. He hauled it savagely across his head. Once this case is over, he thought, I'm going to shave it all off.

"Is my tie all right?" he asked. They'd called in on his parents' home and he'd chosen an older work suit, a blue pinstripe, slightly frayed at the sleeves.

He and Mick stood on the Southbank waterfront, autumn sun glistening off the windows of Scientific Money House. Mick nodded. He'd donned jeans, a tan jacket, and short brown boots. The skin on his face glowed; no doubt the fitness freak had been exercising in the early hours.

"No heroics now." Mick had volunteered to do the job, but Peter had readily persuaded him he didn't have the skills. "Get what you can. Cut your losses and get out if things go screwy. It's 11:30 now. I'll get worried if you're not out by 12:30."

Peter's head throbbed behind his eyes. He'd slept in, waking to headlines showing Robert Friedman's face dominating the front page of *The Age*, and inside, smaller shots of Kantor Keppel, Dancer, and Brindle. He and Mick had quarreled.

"Go to the police now?" Peter had cried. "After all we've been through?"

"Got no choice, Gentle." Hard-faced, Mick pointed to the picture of Friedman. "Our duty. Besides, what else can we do? Bloody Rollo will just stonewall us now."

Peter gulped down insipid coffee in the Tusk family room. "We can find out what's going on in Scientific Money. Where's yesterday's enthusiasm?"

It had taken Peter another half hour to persuade the lug, and even then Mick had said little on the drive into the city. Dana had also been curt to him. He couldn't recall much of the latter part of last night, but he was certain that as he drifted off, her bludgeoning voice, from another room, had pierced his swirling brain, crying, "You're going on, aren't you? How could you, Mikey?" Peter's last conscious thought had been, Good luck, big guy.

Now, Peter watched Mick's sunglasses sweep their surrounds.

"Nervous?" Mick said.

"Into the den of Chaos agents, facing certain death…" Peter mimicked Maxwell Smart, "…and loving it."

Not a trace of a smile showed on Mick's face. Peter licked his lips and exhaled hard. The truth was, he was trembly down his arms and legs. At least Bertoli won't be inside the building, he thought.

Mick clapped him hard across the shoulders.

Peter sauntered toward the entrance, and when a group of three people went through the automatic doors, he joined them.

"Has the Quant Fund balanced for April yet?" one of them said as he swiped his security card, hanging on a chain around his neck, across a reader on the wall by the lifts. He was young, with gelled spikes in his hair. With him were a chubby Indian woman in a floral dress and an older man with thick glasses. Accountants, he guessed. They were staring at him.

Peter thought quickly. If he used Marcia's pass, and they tagged him as a stranger, he might get reported. He went for Plan B and swiped the visitor's pass Mika had given him. The elevator pinged and he hurried in first, pressing the second floor button and trying to look inconspicuous at the back.

"You're kidding me," Floral Dress said. "Remember last month?"

Another problem loomed. As far as he could tell, the second floor was completely functional; all the managers except Ross Petrov resided on the first or third. If they saw a visitor get off on Two, they'd think it odd. He decided to go up to the third floor if that happened.

But he was in luck. "What is it with those guys?" asked Gel as they rode up one floor and exited. Peter yawned, tried in vain to suppress his trembling hands.

On the second floor, Peter stepped out into an empty elevator lobby. There was only one door. Glancing around, he swiped Marcia's pass across the reader and held his breath. If they'd spotted Marcia's pass as missing, they may have canceled it. A click. He exhaled, pushed the door, and he was in.

A narrow corridor ran in both directions. He headed right. A thin man passed him without even looking up. A hundred meters along, a heavy door signaled the computer operators' department—the engine room of the company, where all the computer hardware sat amidst expensive cooling and alarm systems. Peter was interested in software, not hardware, so he kept going. Around a corner and near the end of the corridor was another door: Authorised Personnel Only. An unlabeled reader on the side. He swiped Marcia's pass. Another click.

He stepped in, heart running double time, with an excuse ready, in case anyone greeted him. But the large room was empty and silent. It held a conference table, a whiteboard, several Reuters terminals, a relaxation area with easy chairs, and coffee-making facilities. And over on one wall, four computers, all showing Scientific Money screensavers, next to a huge laser printer.

He stood still, listening to his breathing over the ambient hum of air conditioners and computers. All else seemed unnaturally quiet. The room smelled of cheap coffee and stale food. He wondered how many people had access to it.

The chair squeaked when he sat down in front of one of the computers. He thumbed through a manual on the desk entitled "Quant Investment System (QIS)." Copyright Scientific Money Pty Ltd. No author shown. This was the system, no doubt at all.

He clicked the mouse to clear the screensaver. Despite his anxiety he suddenly felt powerful. This was his element. He savored the tactile spring of the keys under his fingers and the gentle slide of the mouse on the Scientific Money mousepad.

The Windows desktop showed an icon labeled QIS. He launched it.

Voices came through the walls, from the corridor. He leapt up and raced to the wall where he could hide behind the opening door. His pulse boomed.

"How long will the batch job take?" he heard.

"Another hour."

The voices faded and Peter ran trembling fingers through his hair. Somehow the frisson excited as well as frightened him. At least here I'm on my own turf, he thought. If I'm caught I can just bullshit my way out of it, and if that doesn't work, hey what can they do? Charge me with trespassing at most.

It felt a world away from that dark alley and Scaffidi's butchered face.

No password was required for the QIS system. He worked his way through the menus—programs to print reports, to enter economic data, to run queries, to print tables of stock-buying instructions. But no decision-making or input programs. Of course not—according to the official story this funds-management system was run by the computer.

Maybe Peter was plain wrong. Maybe he and Carlo just hadn't grasped Kantor's eleven-secret-herbs-and-spices formula. He almost felt relieved—the null hypothesis, that everything was above board at the company, guaranteed Rollo's innocence. But no, everyone seemed to be hiding something. What could it be?

He exited the program and stared at the desktop. A handful of program icons sat side by side with the standard Microsoft Office icons. Sweat running down his sides, he launched the first one. Finding an off-the-shelf statistical program, he exited. Another one—a database of economic indicators. The room felt close. Chest heaving, he tried another icon. And yet another. All useless.

A drop of sweat splashed from his brow onto the keyboard. When he leaned over to wipe it away, a nondescript icon, labeled "Maintenance," in the bottom left hand corner of the screen, caught his eye. He double-clicked it.

"Please Enter Password"

He nearly shouted with joy. He was panting as loudly as Mick's daunting dog. Without conscious thought a number popped into his mind from their case file—Marcia's date of birth: 190344. He tried it.

"Invalid Password. Please Re-enter"

Damn. Excitement turned to despondency. He cast his mind back to a conversation with Arnold Yang, his infotech friend, at a Skulk Club meeting. Security was only as good as users' behaviors, Arnold had said.

"If everyone did as instructed," Arnold complained, "and used a mix of letters and numbers, security would improve many-fold. But no, most people still prefer the passwords they can remember."

Peter thought hard. If the Investment Committee met in this room, who would input any investment decisions? Probably not Marcia. Maybe Chang. He could remember the Chinaman's birth date as well: 111154.

"Invalid Password. Please Re-enter"

He tried Dancer's date of birth. Nothing.

Of course! This was Kantor's baby. He typed in 120744. The reply mocked him.

Rollo was born on New Year's Day—010139.

"Invalid Password. Please Re-enter"

Bloody hell. His head ached.

Voices again in the distance. What else had Arnold said? "Believe me, even the most careful just use key dates backward." Peter hammered out Marcia's date of birth backward. No no no.

The voices grew louder. Very loud. He recognized Weiqing

Chang's high voice and looked around desperately.

One last shot. Which one? Kantor's body on the gurney flooded his mind. The voices looming, his fingers flew: 447021.

He heard the door handle turning, but couldn't pull his eyes from the screen.

Bingo!

CHAPTER 41

"Piss off!"

Tusk faced the huge door.

"Bella," he growled, "open up or I'll break the door down."

As soon as Gentle had emerged from Scientific Money House with a thumb up in the air and a goofy grin plastered across his face, Tusk had known he was right. Rollo was crooked. A murderer in bed with the scum of the earth.

Immediately they'd rung Rollo's office. Mika had told Gentle that Rollo hadn't come in to work, unheard of on a Monday morning. Gentle had thought she sounded scared.

Now Tusk glanced back at Gentle. Hair wild. Puffing. Still beaming like a Tattslotto host.

"Piss off." Bella exercising her vocab.

Tusk bunched his shoulder muscles. Slammed into the door. It met him hard. A faint splintering sound.

"I'll call the police!"

"You do that, Bella." He felt at ease now. Knew what had to be done. Knew he was the one to do it.

The door opened. Bella in a Japanese yukata over a nightie.

Christ, in bed at noon, Tusk thought. No lipstick. Perfume and some other odor in the air.

"Where's Rollo?" he said.

"He went down to the beach last night." Bella's green eyes burned with anger. And something else. Tusk saw nail polish on her toenails.

"Don't give me that."

"It's true." Strain lines around her mouth.

"Let's look around," he said to Gentle.

"No." Bella grabbed his arm.

"Why should we believe you?" Tusk took off his sunglasses, looked into her portrait-perfect face, centimeters from his. Something different about her. Some intensity.

"Willy's here." A half-formed smile.

He realized what the smell was. Cum. She'd just been screwing her husband's brother in her own home.

"The address?"

She hesitated. Tusk knew and she knew that her loyalty stood on the line at that very instant.

"Portsea. Shelley Way. Number Eight."

Her eyes said it all. Treachery. And a good dose of fear.

"Thanks, Bella," he said.

Tusk was still reflecting on the enigma of Bella Keppel as they raced for the Peugeot. Bullied his way into a lane heading for Monash Freeway, sun warming his hands through the windscreen. Suppressed adrenaline bubbled in his gut. Time check—1:31 on the dashboard clock.

Gentle still hadn't come down from his adventure. "You wouldn't believe what I got up to back there." Voice squeaky high, fingers drumming on his knee. "Chang came into the high security room just as I cracked the system. I hid behind a chair. Imagine it, me crouching like a cat burglar. And he didn't spot me!"

"How'd he miss your bloody hair?"

"He was only in the room for a minute."

"You done great." Tusk watched his partner's cheeks color. He headed off Monash at Springvale Road, handed Gentle the mobile. "More messages from Sam—come in for a chat. Also Mandy—sounds upset but don't ring her yet." No need to mention the call from Cap, a long confessional while he'd stood around waiting in Southbank.

Tires squealed as Tusk swept onto the Mornington Peninsula Freeway. This was their last chance to have a crack at Rollo Keppel without the cops. Maybe, he thought, Vinci has already issued a bulletin to pick us up. A twinge of guilt—this wasn't helping Friedman.

Mornington Peninsula: Melbourne's seaside playground. A narrowing strip of promontory with peaceful bay beaches on one side for kids and dog-walking retirees. Cliffs and pounding surf on the ocean side. Tusk viewed the area as part of the egalitarian face of Melbourne, the great leveler during summer. Bricklayers mingled with stockbrokers, teenagers from the rough western suburbs surfed with private-school kids. Strangely enough from his point of view, the rich had to travel further. The closer beach towns such as Rosebud were full of working class families. Further on, enclaves of the wealthy sprang up, in chic Sorrento, and in secluded, upper-class Portsea at the Peninsula's very tip.

Twenty-five years ago, the road to Portsea had wended along

the coast line. Now a freeway pushed through the center of the Peninsula for most of the journey. An hour and a half of controlled driving before he finally swung onto the old beach highway at Tootgarook. Sick of Gentle's nonstop prattling, he found a Powderfinger tape, turned it up loud, the crashing guitars and yearning vocals filling the car.

He kept driving fast when they came off the highway. Gentle navigated, lost them twice. Out of season, Portsea was sedate, a handful of cars parked under the gum trees lining the shopping area.

Finally Tusk cruised down the curve of Shelley Way, switched off the music. High houses behind fences. Blue water through gaps.

The most impressive residence was Number Eight, the last house on the street. Definitely architect-designed, it looked like three adjoining cottages built of gleaming white wood. Tusk stopped the Peugeot at the top of a red gravel driveway.

"Look." Gentle pointed at a gray Lexus at the bottom of the drive.

Tusk flexed his fingers. The end of the road, in all ways. Even the big shots can't escape from justice, he thought, as he led the way down the drive. Behind him Gentle clutched a sheaf of papers.

Sun on his face, a tugging breeze. He pressed the front doorbell, heard a chime deep in the bowels of the house. They listened. Nothing but seagulls and sighing trees.

He trotted around the back. Christ, the rich sure can buy themselves a view, he thought. A pristine lawn stretched down to a cliff protected by a fence. The mouth of Port Phillip Bay gaped before them. A ship steamed for the treacherous Heads, waves rolling around it. Gulls wheeled over the beach fronting white-capped blue water under banks of cotton-wool clouds.

From the back, the house looked even more impressive. Grandiose, pristine white, rimmed by a wide veranda. Wisps of smoke rising from a chimney.

And the back door was ajar.

"Okay." Tusk touched his gun in its shoulder holster but didn't draw it. Glanced at his partner's pale face.

Up the steps and through the cane chairs littering the veranda. His boots loud on the floorboards. The door swung back without a sound. A high-roofed entrance area bathed in light. Hats and raincoats on wall pegs.

"Rollo," he called. Raised a hand and they both stood stock-still. Not a sound over the faint cawing of seagulls.

Around a corner, into a near-circular living room, drenched with light pouring through huge windows. A massive wooden coffee table in the center, strewn with magazines, surrounded by large striped settees and lounge chairs. A model ship hanging above a fireplace in which logs fitfully glowed red. Photos on the mantelpiece. Leaning against a speaker, a large studio photo: Rollo and Bella beaming.

"Well well well," Rollo Keppel said. "If it isn't Dick Tracy the actuary. And his faithful hound dog."

The chief executive sat slumped in a lounge chair. Immobile.

Tusk was staggered at the transformation. Rollo's patriarchal aura had vanished as if it had never existed. He wore the shirt and suit pants Tusk recollected from last night, the shirt spilling out over a paunch no longer held in. His bare feet rested on the suit jacket strewn on the floor. The bald head was greasy and the tan of his face had turned gray. Puffy, dull eyes stared out the window toward the dark blue horizon.

Tusk's boots clomped across the wooden floorboards. Three wine bottles on the coffee table, two of them empty. Red stains on the wall by the fireplace, a shattered glass on the floor.

Gentle slapped his bundle of papers on the coffee table.

"You asked for proof, Rollo." Gentle's words tumbled out shrilly. "There's a special program for overriding the computer's decisions, isn't there?" That nasty nerd's smirk Tusk had hated in school, but now relished seeing. "It even contains a database of manual decisions made. I printed out the entry screens and some of the database. Fraud, Rollo, fraud."

"She left me." Rollo let out a long sigh. "God help me."

Tusk could feel no pity at all. Indeed, an inner voice crowed.

"Fraud," Gentle said.

"Why?" Rollo intoned, shaking his head slowly, as if it was weighed down. "And Willy…"

Rollo looked up at Gentle. The bastard actually wants an answer, Tusk thought. Out of the magnate's world of networks and contacts, why seek the answer to the question of his life from a private detective? What's the chemistry here?

Tusk remembered Bella, hard and sly, back at the Keppel apartment. And Willy, the victor in the possession game, lurking, hidden. He decided to pressure the murderer.

"Why?" he said. "Because she's a rotten bitch who's sucked your money and life from you."

"Bugger you." Rollo heaved out of his seat. He swayed as he glared at Tusk, but his eyes were alive once more. Tusk smelled vomit.

"What the hell do you know?" Rollo turned once more to Gentle. "When I saw Bella for the first time, I could have died and been happy. God, she was beautiful." His face softened, jowls forming on his chin. "Still is. So beautiful every man wants her. And me the lucky one. You know, I thought she'd stay forever. Gave her everything. Even her freedom, as long as she came back."

"Is that why you killed Kantor?" Tusk asked.

Rollo refused to look at him. "I've made some mistakes but my conscience is clear."

"And Dancer? What about Brindle?"

The tycoon stared at Gentle, waiting for something.

"What I don't understand," Gentle said, "is why you need to make investment decisions manually. Why stuff around with Kantor's formula?"

That seemed to be the key. "Because it doesn't work." Rollo spoke matter-of-factly. "Kantor came to me a year after the launch, when it was already a big success, and told me Benedict had spotted crazy decisions. Under certain conditions, not often but often enough, the formula just fails. Produces gibberish. Kantor told me he had concerns even before the launch. What a time to tell me."

Confession time, Tusk thought as he pulled out his notebook, the moment all detectives dream about.

"Stan Friedman had major concerns," Gentle said.

Rollo took a deep breath. "I was bereft. Peter, can you imagine? My whole life in tatters. God, even now I can picture Kantor's hangdog face. And then I had a bright idea. That's how it was—me with the ideas. If Kantor had run the company, we'd be an economic think tank with two employees. My idea? Let the formula run and watch daily for aberrant decisions. I formed a committee. Occasionally, just occasionally, we had to make manual choices. That's why Weiqing set up the research department, we needed to have information for sound decisions."

Gentle began tapping a foot, visibly stilled himself. "How often?"

Tusk heard something and wheeled. A creak? He strained his ears. Seagulls and in the distance, maybe the sound of the sea. He relaxed.

"Five times a year on average," Rollo said. "But once we were forced to act twice in one week. Don't look so shocked, Peter. Our investors have done well. How could anyone complain, with the returns we've given them?"

The chief executive walked to a compact stereo unit in the corner. A familiar saxophone sound filled the room.

"I never hated Willy," Rollo said. "It was the other way around. Look, I even collected his records."

Tusk wondered if the song was the one Willy had spoken of, "Devil's Brethren."

"When did Sergio Scaffidi begin to blackmail you?" Gentle asked. Tusk stared at his partner in amazement.

"Ha!" A sardonic grimace from Rollo. "I knew you were trouble the first time I laid eyes on you, Peter. Brains, that's what makes the difference in this world." A glance of contempt at Tusk. "That's how I got here, could always outthink anyone."

Rollo took a swig from the third wine bottle, suddenly pivoted and hurled it onto the model ship. Glass and plastic and wine showered the floor. Gentle cried out, but Rollo wasn't done yet. He ran past Gentle's open mouth and kicked the portrait photo with a bare foot. A jagged crack skewered his face in the photo; Bella's cool smile stayed intact.

"I don't need to tell you anything." Rollo panted. "What you've got is enough to cause me embarrassment. But God, think what I've survived already."

"But Bella's gone," Gentle said.

A stroke of genius, Tusk thought.

Rollo glowered at Gentle, snorted with self-contempt. "Quite right. What's the point? Yes, I knew Scaffidi years before I met Bella. He fascinated me, that ugly face, but a brain to match mine. In those days I thought he was just a minor wheeler-dealer. He liked me. I had a gambling problem and he persuaded me to quit. Just by using logic. Extraordinary mind really."

Tusk tried to imagine a younger Rollo Keppel and a younger Sergio Scaffidi, talking on an equal footing, all those years ago.

Rollo paced the floor. "When the problem with the formula came up, I had to put some more capital in, to cover the losses. You probably guessed why Marcia had to become involved, as auditor she'd have spotted something the minute I did that." His voice was harsh through bloodless lips. "Scaffidi found out, somehow, a couple of years later. He offered me what he called protection, but it was just blackmail. I was disgusted. He was my brother-in-law, for God's sake. But he just laughed. I paid up. And then he put the screws on Kantor as well."

Tusk scribbled in his notebook. He longed to ask about Bertoli, but elected to keep quiet, with Gentle doing such a fine job.

ANDRES KABEL

"Why not go to the police?" Gentle asked.

Tusk watched them, two brilliant men communing. Deep satisfaction took hold of him. He imagined Vinci congratulating him, Dana's face when he brought home the check. The newspapers: Gentle & Tusk. His head rang with the fiery end of Led Zeppelin's "Stairway to Heaven," drowning out the jazz crap.

"And lose it all?" Rollo sucked in his gut. "Peter, you don't know what it's like to fight as hard as I have all my life. Just throw it all away? No chance."

The tycoon's face had hardened. "You know, if you hadn't stirred Dancer up..."

Rollo seemed to have yet again transformed himself, back to being the executive in charge. He walked up to Gentle, his long nose inches from Gentle's chin.

To Tusk's astonishment Gentle's eyes blazed and he jabbed a finger into Rollo's chest. "And Kantor? Eh, Rollo?"

Rollo snarled. "What do you know, Peter? What the hell could you know? Of course Kantor didn't like any of it. It was always like that, since we were kids. He'd take the moral high ground and it was me who'd make things happen." The blue eyes glowed. "He'd been hard to handle for months. The day before, he was highly agitated. Gave me the strangest look, like we were boys again, told me his conscience was acting up. I persuaded him, like always."

"Is that when you decided to kill him?" Gentle shouted.

A crack resounded through the room. A shot!

"Down! Down!" Tusk shouted.

He drew his gun, returned fire toward the door. Cursed

332

himself for getting distracted. Switched into the combat zone—mind icy cool, body liquid. Dived behind a chair and fired again, ears ringing.

No more shots. Tusk peered around the edge of the chair. Nothing. The sound of footsteps out on the veranda. He ran thundering in a zigzag hunch, crouched behind the door.

"Stay down!" he ordered.

He looked back. Gentle was flat on his stomach, eyes staring in bewilderment. Rollo was crouched down by the window. Both fully exposed. Christ, another disaster, Tusk thought.

Gun extended, he stood beside the doorway. Spun out, gun sweeping, finger calm on the trigger. Nothing. The back door stood open. Raced out and rolled out onto the veranda. No footsteps on the front gravel, so the shooter had to be on grass. Peered out, saw nothing, sprinted down the steps and threw down a lawn table in front of him. Heard his breath heaving. Sunshine on his cheek.

Crackling far below. Shit—the gunman must have vaulted the fence and made his way down the slope. Tusk raced to the edge and peered down. Nothing disturbed the steep incline of brush and stunted trees. Wind whipped the sweat on his face.

Fuck! Someone had shot at them and escaped, right under his nose. Bertoli!

He sprinted back into the house. Rollo lay on his back. A pool of blood glistened in the dazzling light. Gentle sat nearby, against the window, eyes blinking through hanging hair.

CHAPTER 42

Peter Gentle quivered on the floor. He couldn't remember diving down when the shot sounded, all he knew was that the terror was back. The floorboards smelled of varnish. He pressed down, willing the ground to swallow him up.

"Stay down!" Mick shouted.

Chin on the warm wood, Peter saw Mick spring behind the door, holding a gun. Mick looked back for an instant. The eyes that met Peter's were blue frost. Then the big man was gone.

Peter shut his eyes and regretted every decision he'd taken since Bishop rang. His entire body was clenched in a tremble. Please, no bloody more, he thought.

A gurgling moan brought his eyes open. Rollo sat against a window, legs spread, head jammed down on his chest. Peter heard footsteps far away. Otherwise all was quiet except for plaintive gull cries, his own hissing breath, and that continuous call of pain. He wriggled over.

"Rollo."

The moan filled his ears like a dirge as he approached.

"Are you okay?"

Rollo's head rose from his chest. A dull eye lifted to Peter's and then closed. The moaning ceased. Something sticky touched the fingers of Peter's right hand. He recoiled, lifting his hand up to see blood dripping, dripping off a finger.

"No," he said, declaring it a logical impossibility.

Blood seeped from under Rollo's body, and now Peter could see where it came from, a gaping hole in Rollo's shirt. He leaned closer and saw the entrance wound, ragged and pulsing. He felt ill and afraid and somehow in awe.

It can't be. That was the thought that came to him, the thought he recalled later with the clarity of a midnight dream. It can't be. So many deaths.

He tugged the man's leaden body away from the window and rested the bald head on the floor. Horrific red covered his hands. He slumped against the window, heat on his back. Stickiness invaded his left leg.

Rollo's face was slack and elastic, as if all the lifeforce that made it shine with such authority had deserted it. An image came to Peter, the one of Rollo preaching his message to the crowd. Rollo moaned again, a deep, burbling sound that brought hairs up on Peter's neck.

Peter was no doctor, but he sensed death. In his travails with Mick over the last week, he'd encountered many unfamiliar, grim sights. But on the 10th of May, he watched himself watching a man die. And it seemed to him unlike anything he ever expected, this body fading in wretched finality, just an oozing husk in the hush of the sun-soaked room.

He heard footsteps and registered Mick's chunky frame.

"Christ," Mick said. "My fault."

Fault didn't strike Peter as the issue.

"I'll check the house." Mick disappeared.

"Tell."

Peter twitched in fright at the ghostly voice, at Rollo's eyes staring at him, blue and burning.

"Take it easy," Peter said. Hope sparked and he sat up straight. "We're getting an ambulance."

"Tell." Rollo's voice was a hushed breath, so quiet it seemed to issue from his body rather than his mouth. "Bella… love…"

Peter felt helpless tears well up.

"Yes," he said.

Rollo's eyes stayed open but their light vanished as if a switch had been thrown. Peter smelled the stench of blood and shit, and heard himself keen quietly, and knew he could never be the same again.

***

Mick returned and pulled him to his feet. His partner had retreated into the efficient mode Peter had observed after the Marcantonio episode, and Peter dully took in his clipped instructions. Then sirens announced the police, dozens of them. He heard Inspector Vinci shout at Mick but little else seemed to penetrate.

The burly policeman with the pig's eyes took him aside to question him. As Peter recounted the day's events, sitting on a chair in the kitchen, a sense of reality returned. The assassinated man could easily have been him, he thought.

Vinci raced past, issuing instructions.

"He confessed then?" Mixton said.

"I've told you what he said." Peter sighed exaggeratedly. "I think I got the sequence right. You can check with Mick's notes."

"I want to hear it from you, arsehole."

Peter looked at the reddish face across the kitchen table. "What makes you think you can talk to me like that?"

His body ached with a deep chill, but his mind was definitely in control. Mick's right, he thought, it's a matter of practice. The second time you're questioned by the police, it's so much easier. He felt an obscure pride and smiled.

Mixton glared. "What are you smirking at?"

"Look, I've told you everything, absolutely everything I know. Can I go home now?"

No, not home, Peter thought. I need a huge plate of pasta and Hector's easygoing patter. And wine—lots of it.

"You can go when I let you," Mixton said. "Now tell me. Rollo Keppel killed his brother and Dancer and Brindle. Right? He told you that, didn't he?"

"Do you have ears?"

Mixton gave him a look of blatant hatred and thumped off. It came to Peter that he'd done it—he'd broken this case.

An hour passed. He found a glass in a cupboard and drank water, staring out of the kitchen window into fading light, at policemen cordoning off the driveway with plastic tape. He watched the uproar. A couple of helicopters flew overhead, television news he guessed. What a field day for the press.

Mixton returned with Vinci.

"You're in deep trouble, Gentle," Vinci said. For the first time the short policeman appeared flustered. "Deep."

Peter stared him down.

"Take him to HQ," Vinci ordered.

Outside, Peter met up with Mick, also under escort. Mick looked eerily calm.

"Yo, pardner," Mick quipped softly.

Peter smiled despite himself. "Yo."

They crouched down in the back seat of a police car. Mixton honked his horn to clear the rows of press and spectators massed on Shelley Way, and cameras flashed as they sped off. No one said anything during the long drive in, the baleful silence punctuated by crackling radio messages. Occasionally Peter spotted Mixton's eyes staring at him in the rearview mirror. He felt exhausted but his mind refused to rest, and as the sun sank, he reviewed the entire case, from the examination of the body to the confession.

At the St. Kilda Road complex, they were locked up in the interrogation room he'd suffered in before.

"Well, big guy, the logic worked," Peter said when the door shut.

Mick removed his sunglasses. He spoke so softly Peter almost missed the words. "You leave out the bits about seeing Marcia's body and quizzing Friedman and the break-in?"

Peter understood. The police could be listening in even now. He nodded. Did the lug think he couldn't follow instructions?

"How long will it take for them to catch Bertoli?" he asked.

Mick shrugged.

Someone brought in a couple of meat pies and some milky coffee. Peter wolfed his pie down and was drinking his coffee when Vinci burst in, followed by Senior Constable Lasker. Vinci's shirt was rumpled and he bounced on his feet with angry energy.

"You guys fucked up right royally," Vinci said. "I've got you with obstructing the course of justice at the very least. Where'd you get the documents, Gentle?"

"Client confidentiality."

"You've gotta be joking. I'll—"

"Stop focusing on your bloody ego," Mick cut in. "We don't want any of your glory, Sam. In fact we'd just as well stay out of the picture altogether. Right, Gentle?"

Peter nodded.

"You've got Kantor Keppel's killer," Mick said. "You've solved a major fraud. What more do you want? Caught Bertoli yet?"

"We'll get him," Vinci said.

"You pulled Scaffidi in?"

"We've got nothing on Scaffidi. Not till we've questioned Bertoli."

Peter's jaw dropped. Vinci had to be kidding! He looked wildly at Mick, but Mick just nodded at Vinci, his mouth a bitter slash. What was going on?

"Just take what you've got," Mick said, "and you'll get that promotion you wear across your face when you sleep. Stuff us up, Sam, and I'll make sure every newspaper in town hears that you were the prick stumbling behind two private eyes."

"Bastard." Vinci glared at Mick but Peter could tell he was thinking.

"Lock them up," Vinci commanded the policewoman. He slammed the door on the way out.

"What did he mean?" Peter shouted, grabbing Mick. "What's that about Scaffidi?"

"Tell him, Dee," Mick said. "Tell him. Scaffidi's the one with the connections, right? Not Keppel. Scaffidi."

CHAPTER 43

Mick Tusk longed to shove Hector's walrus face through a window.

"Such a shame you boys didn't make the papers," Hector was saying.

Time check—9:55, brooding in Draconi's. Tusk soaked in the bitter bite of his short black—no tea for him this morning—and pondered why he didn't feel at all triumphant.

He'd rung Dana outside the Police Complex. Her voice had been relieved rather than overjoyed.

"Mikey, Mikey," she said, Nelson piping for attention in the background. "Come home, sweetie."

"We're rich," he said. "Dinner out tonight?"

Silence. "On one condition, Mikey. That we talk about... this case. Really talk."

"Sure, Dana. I know a great place."

But even as he'd hung up, he had wondered, would Dana like Draconi's? Not if she had to listen to the scarecrow king and his court. What an audience around the bar! All rapt before Gentle's tale of justice, but each after something different. Jopling the live wire, snapping his fire-engine-red suspenders, wide-eyed about the action: "Mick flattened the goon?" The boffin Carlo, brow furrowed while he chased the details: "Skull, how come the external auditors didn't spot it?" And Hector, literally panting as he kept dashing back from his duties to pursue the most salacious of images. Other members of the Skulk Club—a cheery American woman, the dapper Italian—came and went. It was plain to Tusk that the exploits of Gentle & Tusk, soon to be defunct, would be all over Melbourne by lunchtime.

Tusk ran fingers through his stubble, enjoyed the raspy feel. He was largely ignored. Only Gentle regularly cast alert eyes on him.

"Anonymity is better for business, Hec," Gentle replied to the restaurant owner's question. His suit was scuffed and stained, his hair was greasy, but he beamed. "Isn't that right, Mick?"

Tusk grunted.

They'd spent the night in the same cell as last time. Stunned by Vinci's message that the police were ignoring Scaffidi, he'd fended off Gentle's stream of questions with monosyllabic answers. Waking early, he stretched on the floor and pushed his stiff body through strength exercises. Despite Gentle's indignant demands at the time of their release, they hadn't managed to see any of Vinci's team. Probably just as well—who knows what he or Gentle might have provoked?

"You say Scaffidi had the other two killed," Carlo said. "My question is—why?"

"I think they were about to fold and go to the police." Egg caked Gentle's chin. "Imagine the pressure after years of fooling the public, the regulators… and then a murder. Rollo must have told Scaffidi. Dancer cracked first and then when he was killed, Marcia became afraid."

"How could the press get it so wrong?" Hector asked.

On the way to Draconi's they'd bought all three dailies. It was certainly front-page news. "Investment Chief Killed in Shoot-out," proclaimed *The Age*. *The Australian*: "Scientific Money Murders and Fraud." The *Herald Sun* went furthest out on a limb: "Magnate Murder Suspect Killed." Detective Inspector Sam Vinci was quoted as saying, "We're delighted to have been able to wrap up the Money Murders, as they have been labeled. Our investigations reveal far-reaching fraud and deception." Photographs of Rollo and Kantor festooned all the front pages, and further back, Dancer and Brindle could be found, along with solemn shots of Vinci and one of Deputy Commissioner Peacock.

Bella was mentioned as a mystery woman—*Herald Sun*: "Well-connected sources have identified the sultry Bella Keppel as a possible femme fatale"—but she'd disappeared from press view. More power to her, Tusk thought.

"They got it wrong because that's what was fed to them," he said.

He tried to make light of the whole mess to himself. Kantor's killer had been tracked down, and that was the only assignment Gentle & Tusk had been given. Friedman was back home. Tusk had even managed to trade off their immediate freedom for Vinci's moment in the limelight. Now he could do what he'd threatened for so long. Pack up and go home. Make peace with Dana, if he could.

But logic was the province of the Brainiac; it had deserted

Tusk. The music in his ears should have been Queen's "We Are the Champions." Instead, a song from childhood smoldered in his head, The Who's bitter "Won't Get Fooled Again."

"But they don't even mention Bertoli." Gentle's voice squawked with indignation, but he was grinning. I'm already spending the money in my head, he'd told Tusk.

It was the thought of Bertoli that set Tusk's stomach roiling. The pity was, he knew how things were done in the Force. Rollo's alibi for Dancer's murder had been found to have holes in it, Deirdre had pointed out to him last night.

"Money buys truth," Tusk muttered.

Gentle's eyes probed him. "Maybe they'll catch Bertoli today."

"Maybe," Tusk said.

So, justice for Kantor. Maybe. But what about Dancer? And Brindle? Cap had said on the phone yesterday, "Mick, I know your bloody mind. They're not your fault. God's maybe, Scaffidi's for sure, but not yours." But reflecting on how easily Bertoli—an image, the reptilian eyes under lamplight—had crept up on him and then escaped, Tusk knew Cap was wrong. A complete screw-up, that's all he'd been from day one.

"Mick, I wonder how Imogen is taking the news." When Gentle was in this mood, his mouth was unstoppable. "Hey, what about Willy? Do you think he's happy, now that he's got what he wants? And how about Bella?"

Tusk squeezed his cheeks. Hard. No use pretending. It was happening all over again. Had started last night in the stale-smelling cell. After Gentle had settled into sleep, Tusk's sense of place had wavered. He'd walked down that corridor yet again, under the single naked bulb, to the body of William Bell, the butchered boy from years ago. The semi-dream became confused with Kantor's death. And behind it all he'd sensed the black presence of Bertoli. And Scaffidi.

He realized the feeling that gripped him was more compelling than any obsession. It wasn't that he couldn't exercise control. He could. He knew he could.

He no longer wanted to.

Tusk waited until Gentle began to field Hector's queries about the Bella-Willy affair. He stood up, feeling his strength uncoil. Pulse racing, he said to no one in particular, "Back shortly," and headed toward the entrance.

"Where do you think you're going?"

Tusk looked back at Gentle springing up, glanced into his partner's eyes. A mistake.

"You maniac!" Gentle was plucking at his jacket. "Bloody ox-brain."

Tusk wheeled, shouted into the pale unshaven face. "Rack off."

Gentle shrank back but his eyes were hot. "No way. Come back and talk about it."

"You talk too bloody much."

"And you don't talk enough. Are you going to screw it all up again?"

Tusk thought about hitting the freak.

"Don't try to get rid of me," Gentle said.

Christ! Too much to think about and Hector was heading their way. Tusk plunged out of Draconi's and into the crowd. Cold autumn air, banked clouds. A tram sang as it zoomed past.

His mouth a dried husk. The sound of Gentle panting to keep up with his urgent strides.

The Peugeot bounced out of the parking lot. Tusk wound the window fully down, let the air pummel his face. Quick now, his mind urged, quick.

He commandeered Gentle's phone and dialed as he drove. "Dee, you guys haven't got Scaffidi yet, have you?"

"Hello, I'm fine," Deirdre said. "How are you?"

"No time, Dee. Want some credit as Sam ascends the promo ladder?"

A pause. "You must be mad."

"20 Gully Drive, The Patch. Dee, meet me there."

He hung up and floored the accelerator. Time check—11:10. They wouldn't be there until noon. He headed east, refusing to look at Gentle while the geek prattled on. Along Monash Freeway and then Toorak Road. He'd been startled by the address Buckingham had given him. Who would have thought Scaffidi lived so close to his home?

The road broadened on Burwood Highway. Through the monochrome suburbs. Gentle took a call, quite a long one, and then addressed Tusk. "Guess who? Weiqing Chang, can you believe it? The man actually apologized for lying to me. He was crying. He'll never work again and he's looking at jail."

Tusk's stomach burned. He concentrated on slowing his breathing. Couldn't care less about the bloody Chinaman.

"I asked him about the invisible passes."

Tusk snorted. That nonsense again!

"Do you know what he told me? Kantor was the one who taught him how to do their programming."

Through the familiar meandering shopping strip of Belgrave, only minutes from home. Past pubs nestled amongst ferns and gum trees, and cafes advertising Devonshire teas. The scent of eucalyptus invaded the car.

"And did you read the police file on Stan Friedman's death?" Boy Wonder's voice quavered. He hadn't even dared ask where they were going.

"Pipe down, will you?" Tusk said.

"The investigating officer said there were suspicious circumstances. Bruises on Stan's fingers. But there wasn't enough to go on."

"So Friedman's right, eh?" Tusk snapped. "Kantor, our mild-mannered prof, drowned his protégé? What a crock of shit. Who cares anyway? Now shut up."

He shoved an old Black Sabbath tape into the cassette player and turned it up loud. Let him try to gas on over that.

The Patch. Though it was only ten minutes' drive northeast of his home, Tusk knew little about it, only that it was one of the fancier suburbs in the hills. Near the eastern boundary of the Dandenong Ranges National Park, it was nestled in a valley below the gum forests. He pulled over by a general store to plot his route.

Gully Drive wound up a hill. Some of the houses were typical brick veneer residences, set back behind lush gardens. Others were posh architect-designed affairs. He slowed down. Cool under the blanket of swaying gums, bird cries high above. Foolish to imagine Scaffidi would be here just after noon, but maybe Tusk could find some evidence.

He missed Number 20, realized only when he saw 22 on the

next letterbox that Scaffidi's driveway was artfully hidden under hanging trees. He drove past another two houses and parked.

Gentle had gone pale as paper. His clasped hands shook. A mistake to bring him.

Tusk held up a hand to forestall any pleas. "Don't worry," he whispered. "It's most likely empty. The cops will be here before too long. Any trouble, drive away."

Gentle's eyes were wide. Tusk handed him the car keys. He felt calm and wired at the same time. The way he always felt, as if at a precipice.

"Good luck," Tusk said, as if Gentle needed the luck and not he. The car door latched shut with a quiet click.

He strolled back down Gully Drive. Ducked into Number 22. A timber house. Silent, no cars in sight. A high new fence, over which towered a thick row of pine trees, blocking any view of Number 20. He trotted past the house. Washing on the line. At the very back of the deep block, he reached up, only just managing to curl his fingers over the top of the fence, and lifted himself until he could see over.

Scaffidi's house was nothing like his neighbors' abodes. A two-story squat brick place with a white back porch. Very Italian; no doubt a staircase at the front with columns on either side, maybe a lion statue or two. Two cars nestled out of sight of the street, a yellow Toyota and a gray Commodore station wagon. Smoke from a chimney. Someone was home.

A feeling like relief when he swung himself over, landing with a soft thud in pine needles. He drew out his gun, caressed its solid physicality. Ran along the fence from tree to tree. Pine sap enveloped him, needles scraped his head.

All quiet out back. His body light as cloud. Taking a breath, he scuttled out of the pines and squatted behind the station wagon. Unabated bird chatter. Dim voices inside, no way to tell if one was Scaffidi's. Ran to the back door and tried the doorknob. It turned.

He gritted his teeth, bracing for a squeak, but the door swung inwards without a sound. Peered into a large kitchen, gloomy behind drawn blinds. Odor of dust. The voices came from the front of the house. Tiptoed across the linoleum and stood breathing silently by a door. Heart clamoring. Smell of smoke. Gun clasped high in front with both hands, he stepped into the doorway. An empty corridor. Light at the other end. Louder voices. Laughter.

Feet silent, nimble. Inched forward until he was flat against the wall next to the door.

"How will you get your women when you're retired?"

Chuckles. Tusk stiffened at the high sibilance. Bertoli! Licked perspiration beading his lip. Shut his eyes for an instant, then peered around the doorframe.

After the shuttered back rooms, the open living room dazzled him, sunlight cascading through wide windows. Bertoli's thin form, feeding sheets of paper into a roaring fire. Laughter from the other man, his back to Tusk.

Whether Bertoli heard his breathing or just sensed him, Tusk had no time to ponder. The snake-eyes swung around and papers fell from Bertoli's hands.

"Freeze!"

Tusk roared as he stepped out, legs apart, gun in both hands, covering them in a short arc. Blood pumping in his head. Fire, hot fire, coursing through his body.

Bertoli stopped in mid-motion, gun already in his left hand, breathing through open mouth, his eyes fastened on Tusk. The other man turned and raised his hands. Mixton, face rough as baked earth, eyes startled.

"End of the road," Tusk said.

He moved closer, gun oscillating between the two of them.

"Drop it!"

Bertoli's gun fell to the floor.

A voice told Tusk not to celebrate. Then time scrambled. Mixton clutched into his jacket. Tusk fired, a deafening crack. He swung the gun toward Bertoli but something struck his right arm with a crunch, shoving the weapon upward, his next shot blasting the ceiling. Bertoli's foot, horizontal at elbow height, already pivoting down. Too fast!

Tusk swung his gun down again, but Bertoli fell upon him, a fist slamming into his stomach, a hand gripping his gun arm. He brought a knee up and felt it hit hard. But Bertoli's hand twisted and Tusk's gun flew from his numb hand. He tore out of Bertoli's grip and danced back, panting.

Bertoli smiled as they squared off. Over the thin nose and cheeks oily in the light, his eyes never wavered. Tusk smiled back and moved to bring him down. A feint and then a snapping punch, guaranteed to floor the mongrel.

But Bertoli was animal speed and Tusk felt searing pain on his left side. He stumbled and his feet were swept under him. Plummeted down, cheekbone crashing against hardness. Twisted to leap back up, but something smashed his head down again, and then he felt a weight straddling him and inhumanly strong hands gripping his head. He heard something crack and white light seared his vision.

An overpowering odor. Aftershave.

CHAPTER 44

A car backfired. Peter jerked in the front passenger seat of the Peugeot. The same crack again. Shots! He sat up, trembling.

"Shit."

He clambered out of the car and looked down the empty road. The sun had vanished and he felt chill air on his cheeks.

"Jesus. Jesus."

He hugged himself, wished only to lie down. A whimper escaped him.

He thought of Scaffidi, the live eye deep in its socket. He pictured Bertoli, smelled that aftershave. He remembered Mick by lamplight, risking all for him.

Peter ran.

"Mick!" he screamed into the sky.

He sprinted between pine trees. A big house. Up steps to a porch enclosed by a white marble railing.

"Mick!"

He pounded on the door, hands pulsing with pain, peered in the front window. A still body by a fireplace, Mick in the middle of the room.

Mick lay on his front, head arched back. Riding him, cord around his neck, soared the hood of Bertoli. Bunched muscles stood out on Bertoli's arms as he strained the cord back. His lips were parted. And those death-adder eyes dared Peter, glowering at him without moving, removed from the dance of death being enacted below.

Mick's eyes bulged unseeing. Great labored wheezes issued from his gaping mouth. Blue. His face was blue!

"Think!" Peter bellowed.

He picked up a white metal chair and wheeled around.

"Throw!"

He released the chair. The window exploded and the chair crashed onto the wooden floor. Inside, the tableau remained unchanged. Mick's bunched shoulders began to slump.

"Go!"

Tears streaming down his face, Peter plunged through the jagged hole in the window. Sharpness stabbed an elbow.

"Jump!"

Insane energy rampaged his body. He charged and launched himself. For the first time, Bertoli's eyes blinked.

Peter landed on Bertoli, attaching to the thin head, flailing his arms and legs, scratching and kicking at hair and cloth and slick skin. Bertoli reared below him, shaking him off like a rag. A hand grabbed his shirt. Blood trickled down one side of the monster's face, but Bertoli smiled as his other hand came at him.

Savage pain shot through Peter's face and he crashed backward, head smashing into the floor. Waves of agony lashed him. His vision blacked out for an instant, then he looked up to see the face of death itself, lips smiling, hands outstretched, coming toward him. He screamed.

A roar blasted his ears. Bertoli lifted up like a rubber doll and flung himself down. Something acrid filled the air. And, oh my God, that smell of blood. Images of Marcia. Rollo. Kantor. He tried to shout but pain blanketed his face.

A minute later, or it could have been an hour, Peter somehow propped himself up on an elbow. His face hurt. Bertoli lay on his back, limbs twitching. Something was amiss with the hit man's face, it looked moth-eaten. A puddle of blood spread patiently. Peter registered moaning.

Mick stood above him. The fierce light rendered him a heaving colossus. His face was a red mask of rage, thunderous breaths issuing from behind bared teeth. The big man held a gun aimed down at Bertoli. His eyes, blue and beautiful, caught Peter's.

No, it can't be. Peter widened his eyes and poured the message—no more death—toward his savior and burden.

"Fuck it," said the mountain.

Peter had never heard a more welcome sound. The gun clattered on the floor. Peter's head sank toward the ground again and consciousness fled, Mandy's burning brown eyes looming in his head. Sirens wailed far away. I'm all right, Mandy, he thought.

CHAPTER 45

Mick Tusk's body was a foreign country. Even with all the shit the nurses had pumped him full of, every muscle ached, every joint felt bruised. His neck flamed.

He paced the hospital room, watched Gentle's chest rise and fall, adjusted the venetian blinds to let in more of the soft sunlight. Half-encased in bandages, Gentle's unlined, unconscious face reminded Tusk of a child's. Time check—11:49. Wednesday, almost exactly a week since the geek sucked him into this godforsaken escapade.

Tusk had scored a night at Knox, his first stay in a private hospital, through the emergency ward. More like a hotel than a place for sick people, with its pastel wallpaper, large shiny bathrooms, television sets, nurses who actually smiled. Even the claustrophobic smell of antiseptic and decay seemed muted. That didn't stop him from hating it, despising all the useless invalids he spotted while hobbling around the ward to prevent himself dozing off.

After yesterday's police circus and a blessedly long sleep, it had taken most of the morning for Tusk to check himself out, over the protests of the officious Dr. Ritten. Now he could only focus on two things—a walk with Dana and Bully in the lung-clearing air of Belgrave, and the health of his mate.

Gentle stirred. Tusk leaned over to take his hand. The eyes opened, blinked.

"I'm alive." Gentle's voice was furry.

"Sure are." Tusk smiled to dampen an unexpected surge in his chest. "The Devil sent you back. Said he couldn't stand the yakety-yak."

Gentle made an attempt to sit up, fell back with a groan. "Jesus, my face."

"Hairline fracture of your jaw. They've immobilized it. The doc says it's not too bad. You'll be sore for a few days, and your diet right now is liquids."

"Cappuccino through a straw, eh? Where am I?"

"Knox," Tusk said. "You yuppies with your bloody private health insurance. Careful moving, you cracked a rib as well. And there's a nasty gash on that arm."

"God, you look terrible," Gentle said.

Tusk fingered his cheek, a swollen eggplant that nearly closed his right eye. Lucky not to crack it, according to Dr. Ritten.

When Gentle's gaze moved to the purple ring around Tusk's neck, his eyes widened. "Your neck, Mick. Jesus, your neck."

Tusk saw the thin chest begin to labor. Christ, he knew what it felt like to flash on the horrors of yesterday.

"Looks worse than it feels," he lied.

"Bertoli?"

"Died on the way to the hospital." Tusk recalled his finger on the trigger, how close he'd come. "Thanks for…"

"Forget it."

So much had happened in the twenty-four hours since the "Battle in the Bush," as the press dubbed it. Reporters were having a field day linking Bertoli to Rollo Keppel. Tusk had never seen anyone as grim as Sam Vinci when the cop looked down at the corpse of his man Mixton. Bye-bye promotion for Vinci; Deputy Commissioner Peacock himself had already announced an internal investigation.

Vinci and Deirdre had grilled Tusk in the emergency ward, but he'd had little to add. Deirdre wore a quiet confidence; she'd been first on the scene and had come out of the case smelling of roses. And something had changed in Vinci's attitude toward Tusk. The cop had even rung him this morning to say they'd questioned Scaffidi but couldn't sustain a link. Scaffidi didn't even own the Gully Drive house. Tusk refused to think about it, knew if he dwelled on the scumbag…

"I owe you, Gentle," Tusk said, voice suddenly shaky.

How could he ever forget that moment? Looking up, lungs on fire, a red film across his eyes, to see an apparition outside the window, screaming and dancing as if alight. Then the sound of the shattering window when he could no longer see. Tusk's own courage, or what others called courage, he knew to be merely years of training in violence. What Gentle did merited the true label of valor.

"I'll send you the bill." Gentle winced at an attempt at a chuckle. "Anyway, it's me who owes you, Mick."

"Peter." The lanky figure of Mandy, in a smart gray jacket and skirt, sailed in through the door. She gasped.

"The new look," Gentle said, face reddening. He grunted and sat up.

And then Dana stood in the doorway. Black skirt with shiny black shoes, crimson lipstick, and a red top built for her figure. Tusk gulped. She'd told him she would bring Mandy over. Did she still love him? How could she? His mouth went dry.

"Oh, Mikey," she cried.

She rushed to him, touched the livid halo around his neck.

"Oh, Mikey." Something in Tusk melted when she wrapped her warm body around his bruises. She kissed him, lips sliding.

Incredibly, he felt himself harden.

"Hey," Gentle said. "If that's married life, I want some of it."

Mandy slapped Gentle in mock outrage. Dana pulled away, and Tusk cringed at the look of malevolence she gave Gentle.

Tusk and Mandy sat beside the patient. Dana stood staring out the window. Gentle clutched Mandy's hand like a lifeline while she read out an *Australian Financial Review* article reporting that Scientific Money's Quant Fund #1 had gone downhill ever since Kantor died, losing fifteen percent in value during a week when the All Ords only declined three percent. From being the best-performing investment fund in Australia, its performance was now amongst the worst. Already since the news about Rollo, a panic run on the fund had commenced.

"Listen," Mandy said. "Here's what the editorial says: 'How did this man manage to fool all our regulators?'"

The Age showed a photo of Weiqing Chang coming out of court, his round face grave.

"Harvey told me there's a group of investors mounting a huge class action against Scientific Money and the Keppels," Mandy said. Almost pretty, Tusk thought, when she smiles like that.

"It's all about love," Gentle said. "Kantor did it for Imogen and Straw, Rollo tried to keep Bella."

"Crap," Tusk said. "Money, that's the key."

"Did someone mention money?" Tusk whirled to see Bishop striding in.

The bloodsucking lawyer wore another brand new suit. His eyes twinkled under the curly hair, until he saw the bandages and bruises.

"My God," he said.

Bishop recovered composure quickly, introduced himself to the women, then handed checks to the two partners. Tusk gasped—his check was for $75,000.

"What the hell's going on?" he said. "This is nearly double what you contracted. Too much."

"There's no such thing as too much money," Gentle said.

"Now don't fuss," Bishop said. "That's the partial payment Imogen Keppel made, plus a bonus from me. Call it an incentive bonus—incentive to keep working for me. I always knew the egghead and the beefcake would do me proud, and I've picked up mega business since Sunday."

"What, defending Mrs. Keppel's interests?" Gentle clutched his check like a treasure.

Bishop cackled. "No, she sacked me when she found out from Rollo that you two were still pursuing the case. No, I'm putting together the biggest class action in Australia's history."

"And Mrs. Keppel?" Gentle said.

"In deep trouble." The lawyer seemed to find this almost amusing. "She'll be lucky to escape with any assets, if you ask me."

Tusk thought fleetingly about Straw. Her monastic life would be shattered.

Bishop looked at his watch. "Mustn't dally." He shook hands with Gentle, nodded at Tusk. Strode away.

Dana came over from the window and looked at Tusk's check, then at him. She walked back to the window, her face stony.

"Well, you two are heroes, didn't you know?" Mandy said.

Gentle beamed. "Heroes shmeroes."

Seeing the transparent joy on Gentle's face, for the first time Tusk granted himself permission to measure his success. It's true, he thought, we caught them—Bertoli, Mixton, Rollo Keppel, even Brindle and Dancer and Chang—it was us, no one else.

A crowd bustled into the room. Gentle's parents, followed by a tanned man in his forties and a young guy with dreadlocks, both of them unmistakably Gentle's brothers.

"Oh, Peter, darling." Gentle's mother threw her hands up, rushed to weep over him.

Trevor Gentle stood back. He wore a suit and carried himself erect, like a policeman again, not a drongo retiree.

"Well done, Tusk," he said. "Tell me about it one day. Over a beer."

That's your son's job, Tusk thought.

Back spasms made him wince as he rose. He folded the check once, thought of kissing it, slipped it into a pocket. He went to Dana—honestly, he thought, isn't that much money worth a bit of cheer?—and took her hand.

"Time to scoot," he said.

He looked back from the doorway. Gentle's family and Mandy enveloped the bandaged hero. For a moment, Tusk resisted Dana's tugging hand. Gentle's eyes lifted over the throng and caught his.

An insidious voice whispered to Tusk: Didn't you feel alive, arsehole? For all the heartache, wasn't the last week the stuff of life? He couldn't answer himself.

Gentle nodded.

Tusk nodded back.

CHAPTER 46

Rita, a plump nurse with white hair and a cross on a chain around her neck, trimmed Peter Gentle's hair on Thursday morning, the day after he watched Mandy fall in love with him.

"I've never seen such a mess in all my life," Rita said.

"Ouch! Be careful."

"My cat is better groomed than you."

"Your cat…"

"What's the matter, luvvy? You look like you've left the gas on in the oven."

***

Freshly shorn, Peter managed to tolerate television for fifteen minutes, then rang Mandy and asked her to bring him some mystery novels.

Mostly he slept. The pain came and went, and often he felt so drugged that his mind, now engaged again, refused to function optimally. His mother came just before lunch and announced she would visit every day. He pretended to sleep.

***

Peter half-dozed and reflected on the Keppel brothers. Kantor—an enigma even now. Rollo—battling the fates while the seeds he'd sown bore terrible fruit. And Willy—where was he now? It seemed incomprehensible that such a wreck could hold on to Bella for long, but Peter found himself wishing the sax player luck.

Should he ring Bella and pass on Rollo's final message? She'd curse him. He sat up and drafted a short letter.

> Dear Mrs. Keppel,
>
> Before he died, your husband asked me to tell you that he loved you. My role at this juncture is simply to inform you of his parting words, but I feel I would be remiss if I did not state that I believe his words were most heartfelt.
>
> Yours faithfully,
> Peter Gentle

He asked Rita to mail it.

***

Hector was sitting by the bed when Peter awoke on Thursday afternoon.

"That big friend of yours—Mick," Hector said. "Rang and suggested I bring this."

Iced coffee in a large plastic takeaway cup!

"Am I your best customer, Hec?" Peter asked, slurping the bitter brew through a straw.

Hector stroked his mustache. Peter had never seen him before without his apron. "Either you or Harvey, that's for certain."

After Hector left, Peter rang Arnold Ng at IBM. "Arnold, do you have any software whiz-kids free tomorrow?"

"Skull! That jaw sure makes you sound funny. I can spare someone, sure. But why?"

***

That night, just as visiting hours came to an end, and crowds of noisy relatives filed past his room, three Skulk Club members arrived. Harvey's face was drawn: "This frigging job's killing me." Carlo smiled modestly when Peter praised his role in the case. And Renni Maisel unveiled a bottle of champagne, plastic cups, and one straw.

The pop of the cork seemed to Peter the most joyous sound in the world. He drank and laughed until Rita caught them and sent his friends packing.

***

"A nice, steady office job is what you need, Peter," his mother said on her Friday morning visit. Already Peter's jaw felt much better and he'd begun to eat mush without a straw. When she left, he drew up a To-Do list on the margin of a newspaper.

1. Move out of home into city apartment
2. Buy car
3. New suit
4. Ask M to begin hunting for more work
5. Flowers

***

Late Friday morning, just after Rita removed the bandages on his face, Helen Chen from the Australian Prudential Regulatory Authority rang.

"Mr. Gentle, do you recall the meeting we had about Scientific Money?" she said.

"I most certainly do." Peter flexed his jaw. At last he could speak freely again. "Are you happy with the outcome of your dithering?"

It was an unkind cut. She was just a middle-ranking bureaucrat.

"That's the past, Mr. Gentle. What I'm ringing you about is whether you'd be interested in a consultancy with APRA. The brief would be to help us strengthen the regulatory structure to guard against future occurrences of this kind. A major brief, I can tell you."

Peter's head pounded as he shook it. Nobody would ever devise rules to prevent people of the caliber of Kantor and Rollo Keppel fooling the system.

"Sorry, Ms. Chen. I don't do consulting. I'm a private detective."

***

Rita found him a pad of paper, on which he drew complex, spiraling diagrams, spreading the pages over the bed.

"Trying to puzzle out one of them books?" Rita was changing the dressing on his arm.

He laughed. "No, it's a real puzzle. The one I've just been involved in, actually."

"But that's all finished. I didn't even see anything about it in this morning's *Herald Sun*."

"I just need to understand it fully."

"Certainly keeps you occupied, luvvy."

***

On Friday afternoon an unexpected visitor dropped in. Sam Vinci wore a bright green tie and his hair shone with gel, but Peter saw bags under the restless eyes.

"You intellectuals never stop," Vinci sneered. He bent to look at diagram boxes labeled "Rollo" and "Kantor."

"You can thank your lucky stars we don't." Peter recalled his experiences in custody and decided to needle the policeman. "Have you nabbed Scaffidi yet?"

"As if you'd understand." Vinci twirled a match between his fingers and chewed its end. "You okay?"

"Passable. What do you want?"

"Fuck you too. Just came to apologize for…for things. No, don't start up, just hear me out." Vinci spoke to the window. "It's not often I say this, but you're a smart bastard, and Ivory's a hell of a cop, even now. You guys did this city a service. There, I've said it."

"Give us a medal then," Peter said.

"Smart-arse. You think we're all morons, don't you? Well, I had them print out the security system details for Monday. Marcia Brindle visited the second floor, only she was dead."

Was the policeman going to threaten his Private Investigator's license? Peter stayed silent.

"Don't worry, water under the bridge now." Vinci finally deigned to look at Peter and his voice was filled with bitterness. "And I know Bertoli killed the other two for Scaffidi, not Rollo

Keppel. Only, your trigger-happy mate shot him before we could prove it."

"He didn't have much choice at the time."

Vinci pointed at the sheets of paper covering the bed. "Why you going over that shit again?"

"Something's needling me."

Vinci narrowed his eyes, then smiled. It came out more like a grimace.

"A joke. Right?"

***

Peter dreamt of Sergio Scaffidi perched on the edge of his bed. In the darkness the crime boss's twisted face contained shadows within shadows and his one eye was invisible in its sunken socket.

"How did you get in?" Peter asked. Icy terror gripped his bowels but he couldn't move.

Scaffidi rubbed thumb and first two fingers together.

"So you didn't heed my warnings." The American accent hovered in the air.

Peter lay frozen.

"Ah, but you need not fear, clever one," Scaffidi said. "That entire sorry episode is now behind me. I just wanted to say I admire your mind, my friend. Such speed of analysis. I hope and pray we never meet again. For your sake or mine, who can tell."

As Scaffidi limped away, he turned for a parting whisper.

"Just you tell that muscle man of yours. He ever sees me again, he's dead."

***

Dr. Ritten was thin and intense, with long earlobes that he continually tugged. On Saturday morning, Peter asked to leave.

"I feel perfectly fine," he dissembled.

"No, you don't."

"Look, I can check myself out, can't I?"

Dr. Ritten sighed. "Very well then. Let's make it tomorrow morning."

Later that day, a Skulk Club contingent visited on the way to the football game. Harvey had flown to Singapore and Renni hated Australian Rules, but Carlo came with Giuseppe Marino, Tomasina Symons, and Arnold Ng. Their stay was short but raucous.

Arnold handed Peter a folded sheet of paper before they left.

***

Friedman's hair had grayed noticeably in just a few days. The developer's experience in jail had shaken him.

"Justice? You call what we have justice? I tell the truth and they charge me with three murders!"

Peter watched him rise from the chair next to the bed, then sit down, over and over. For some reason he seemed to regard Peter as his confessor.

"I keep thinking. If I'd told the truth at the start, maybe they'd have caught killer Keppel earlier, before the other two got slaughtered."

The sheet Arnold Ng had given him listed four names. Peter was still recovering.

He fingered the two CDs Friedman had given as a thank-you gift—"Cuban music, from Ry Cooder, brilliant, one for you and one for your ferocious mate"—and imagined Mick's disdain at the soft rhythms.

"Did you bring it?" he asked Friedman.

"But Stan's diaries don't contain any business information." Friedman handed him a pile of slim volumes bound with a rubber band. "Just personal stuff and not much of that. What the hell are you looking for? I've been through them a thousand times, never found anything useful about Kantor."

"I don't know yet," Peter admitted.

The look in Friedman's wet eyes was as intense as any Peter had ever seen. "But you are going to prove the bastard killed Stan, aren't you?"

***

Peter returned to square one. He tore up his chaotic sheets of paper and redid the entire logic chain, this time on one sheet. At the top he printed a heading in capitals: The Data, The Analysis, The Conclusions. Time slipped away, and when the phone rang he spilled tea on the page.

"Is this Peter Gentle?"

He couldn't place the woman's voice. "Yes."

"I got your letter." Bella! He heard a sniffle. "Just rang to say thanks."

Peter didn't know what to say. The silence stretched into embarrassment.

"Anyway," she said, "for what it's worth, I never did screw Kantor."

"But you said…"

"Just to hurt Rollo. I was a mess then. I was amazed people

believed me. Shit, Kantor would never have done it, all he cared about was his family. And Rollo…"

Peter heard sobbing before she hung up.

***

"Your hair!"

Peter jerked out of sleep. Mick and Dana stood over the bed, holding hands.

"What about it?" Peter grinned, barely able to contain his delight. He had so much to talk about with Mick.

"It's neat. It's tidy. It's even presentable."

Mick's bruises had faded to gray-flecked yellow and he looked as mammoth and unbreakable as ever.

"Get stuffed." Peter rubbed sleep out of his eyes and sat up. "It's my last night here, big guy. Boy, have I got something to tell you."

"Had a call from your mate Harvey," Mick said. "He's asked me to join the Skulk Club."

"And you've accepted?"

"I said I'd think about it. Reckon I'd fit in?"

"Of course," Peter lied.

They chatted. Peter filled Mick in about Vinci and Bella, but one look at Dana convinced him to defer relaying Scaffidi's message. From Mick he learned that Deirdre Lasker had been promoted. Mick handed him a gift of a cassette.

"There's only one song on it," Mick said. "Not your style, but I couldn't resist. A guy called Frank Black, used to be with the Pixies. This song is called 'I Love Your Brain.'"

Peter laughed.

"We're leaving for a holiday, tomorrow morning, the whole family, up the coast in Merimbula," Dana said coldly. Peter thought she looked beautiful in her white shirt and jeans and blue jacket. Her hair billowed in black curls. Why did she hate him so? She just needs to get used to me, he thought.

"Too much water in Merimbula," he joked. He hated beaches.

Mick took off his sunglasses and cleared his throat. "And something else." His eyes were round and uncharacteristically vulnerable. "I really enjoyed working with you, but—"

"Shit." Peter couldn't believe his ears. "After all we've gone through. After all I've done for you, you moron."

"Everything okay, luvvy?" Plump Rita.

"Get out!" Peter shrieked at Rita, and when she fled, he turned back to Mick, standing like a stuffed animal by the bed. "What, you're going back to driving taxis? How much money did you earn in a week working with me?"

"Stop being so selfish." Dana threw him a look of revulsion and stormed out.

Mick shrugged. "The fucking cowboy life is no good for me. You saw what it does."

"But…" Peter wanted to say they could work on the anger business together. Instead he took a deep breath and stared at his friend and ex-partner.

"Did you bring your case notes?" he said. He'd rung Mick earlier in the day to request them. Why didn't you bloody tell me then? he thought.

Mick handed him two spiral notebooks. "What the hell do you need those for?"

Peter contemplated explaining. Would it persuade the cretin to change his mind?

"Reminiscing," he muttered.

He opened the first notebook, toward the beginning, marveling at the dense, precise writing, and flicked quickly through the pages. There! As if he'd always known it! His heart beat faster. He snapped the notebook shut.

He saw the blue eyes narrow, just a fraction, and wished he'd waited till Mick left. Luckily Mick had other matters on his mind.

"No hard feelings then?" Mick said.

Bitterness swallowed Peter. How could he contemplate looking for more private investigative work without Mick?

"Hard feelings?" He heard his voice rise. "Do you have any idea how well we did on this case? We were dynamite."

"We got lucky." Mick squared his shoulders, as calm as ever.

"Lucky? You got lucky, when I found you."

"Whatever. Grow up, Gentle." And the poised block of Mick's back headed out the door.

Sudden remorse swept over Peter. He threw off the sheet and plunged into the corridor, almost colliding with a furious Rita.

"Sorry, Mick," he shouted, knowing he'd never catch up, even as he ran on, his pajamas flapping around his ankles. "Sorry!"

CHAPTER 47

A sign—For Sale—hung on the white fence of The Island. After paying the taxi driver, Peter stood outside the front gate and rubbed his jaw, which had inexplicably begun to ache the moment he left the hospital. Mathoura Road dozed on a Sunday morning. Gray scummy clouds hovered above him. The last time it rained, he reflected, Bertoli and Marcantonio came out of the night. He shivered.

Instead of pressing the intercom button, he hooked a foot in the letterbox slit and hoisted himself up onto the top of the gate. He swung his legs over, balanced awkwardly, and then dropped down, grunting upon landing.

The courtyard brooded. He listened for birds, could hear none. A flicker of black flashed in the rose bushes. Quickly he traversed the gloom and tried the front doorknob. It turned in his hand. He stepped into the unlit, dusky hallway.

Straw must have seen or heard him. She stood at the foot of the stairs in full black. The tortoiseshell cat purred around her ankles, and the gray monstrosity dozed on the floor. Straw wore a shapeless black jacket over her goth dress. Giant gold circles hung from her ears. Without make-up, her face looked flaccid. Peter saw bruised hollows below eyes that stared as if they'd never seen him before.

Just like last time, she came to him, dress rustling and jewelry tinkling.

"Magical Mister Mistoffelees." Her whisper was high and mechanical.

Peter flinched at her unwashed odor.

"Straw, where's your mother?" he asked loudly.

She took his hand and led him upstairs, just like last time. In her room, the curtains were drawn and the main lights dimmed, and at first he could hardly see. A jet-black cat lay on the bed, and the ugly hairless one mewed while it wound around its mistress's legs. Cloying incense failed to mask a putrid mix of feline and human reeks. The statuettes over the fireplace shone under spotlights.

Straw pulled at him.

"No, Straw," he said. "Where's your mother?"

She kept tugging.

"You know why I'm here, don't you?" Peter's voice contained a quiver, and when she released his hand, he took a step back. "You killed Stan Friedman."

She stared blankly at him.

"He came here for dinner and said the formula wouldn't work. Have I got it right, Straw? A threat. And how do you deal with threats? I read his diary: 'Had a lovely night at Kantor's. That daughter of his, Straw, especially friendly.' You came onto him, didn't you, like you did with me? So on one of his late night walks, you invited yourself along. Did you have to hit him to prevent him climbing out of the river?"

Not a spark in those moss-green orbs.

"It didn't come to me until I remembered this."

Peter pointed at the central sphinxlike cat statuette on the mantelpiece beside him. "Basket, you called it."

"Bastet." Her fluted voice could have been a recording.

"Goddess of the cats, right? B for Bastet. And then I realized the email must have come from you. The language, the message... You know your way around a computer, don't you?"

She stood perfectly still.

"People make the mistake of thinking you're dumb. All because you don't communicate. But you're not dumb, are you, Straw? You're smarter than the entire police force."

He clasped his hands to check their quivering. Her blank face was pale as alabaster in the dimness. Doubt seized him but he forged on.

"A friend of mine dug into the company software. Kantor made a security pass for you, didn't he? An invisible, special pass for his special girl. Did you visit your dad's office at night sometimes? He adored you, Straw, why kill him?" Something flickered in her eyes. "Let me guess. He was going to pull the plug, wasn't he? And then you'd lose this."

He spread his arms wide to encompass her room and The Island.

Nothing. No reaction. Where had his analysis gone wrong?

"Bad." Her voice was the creak of a rusty door.

A cat began to rub against Peter's legs. He kicked it away. Yes, he thought, logic prevails.

"Bad," Straw intoned, and a shiver coursed down Peter's spine.

The police, he thought.

But Straw drew a gun from her jacket and pointed the squat barrel at him.

No! Peter's legs liquefied, and he found himself on one knee, looking up at the weapon. He felt weightless.

"No," he said, his face crumpling. Mick, help, he thought. "Please."

Wavering through tears: bared teeth. Oval. Green marbles. Gray gun.

"Bad!" she spat.

He saw her glance at the statuette. He heard cats scurrying away. The gun wavered.

Think!

"Walter," he shouted. His entire body tensed for the bullet.

Stillness above him.

"Walter." His words exhaled between pants. "You. Killed. Walter."

"Bad," she hissed.

The gun shook and he knew the end had arrived, but a scream rent the room, and he whirled to see Imogen howling in the doorway. Reflexively he slammed forward. His head struck softness, he heard a grunt, they struck the wall together. A deafening bang.

Pain shot through his back as he landed with Straw on top. And his jaw! He screamed. She must have dropped the gun, for claws raked his face. He looked up at an unbelievable sight. A face taut with livid hatred, green on white, hissing mouth, hot spittle spraying. Grunts as she dug her fingers in, searching for eyes.

His hand felt something on the floor, something small and cold and heavy. Screeching, he grabbed and swung. The tearing at his face stopped. Just like that it stopped, and heaviness fell on him, suffocating. He thrashed and Straw's inert body slid off him onto the carpet.

Peter examined the object in his hand. The cat goddess statuette. Blood on the pointed ears.

He sat up. Shaking. Burning agonies in his jaw. Straw lay still beside him, the tortoiseshell cat sniffing at blood pouring from a wound in the wet dough of Straw's face.

A keening sound penetrated his ringing ears. He raised his heavy head. Imogen rocked on her knees, fingers splayed across her face, eyes transfixed on Straw's prone figure, wailing her symphony of grief.

CHAPTER 48

Once on the trail, Homicide discovered Straw's security pass and tracked down the email on her computer. The murder weapon and Kantor's briefcase were never located, but the clincher proved to be a small stain on a pair of jeans at the back of her closet. The stain matched her father's blood. No evidence could be found to link Straw to her brother Walter's death or the drowning of Stan Friedman.

The trial—fast-tracked because of looming State elections—took Melbourne by the throat. Peter's face on the front page of *The Age*, next to the oval face disfigured by a slash across a cheek, amazed the Skulk Club. His evidence destroyed Straw's legal team's case for mental impairment.

Peter sat with Hector in the packed gallery to hear the sentencing. Someone had dressed Straw in plain cream clothes, rendering her unrecognizable—just a pudgy misfit with expressionless green eyes.

"Fucking brilliant," Mick whispered when he eased into the empty seat next to Peter, his orange-lens sunglasses and tight Metallica T-shirt attracting stares.

"It was your notebook that did the trick." Peter grinned unrestrainedly. "I couldn't figure out how Straw escaped the building. But you'd noted that there was a security pass reader by the emergency exit."

The craggy-faced judge—Hector claimed his nickname was John Wayne—handed down a life sentence.

Imogen Keppel didn't attend the trial. After eleven years of complete silence from her daughter, that Sunday morning she'd heard five staccato words, and evidently wished to hear no more. She need not have worried. Straw uttered not a single word before, during, or after the shortest murder trial in years.

CHAPTER 49

After the trial, Peter led Mick through the city streets to his reclaimed apartment. Mick would stay the night. Once Mick set his suit bag down in the tiny hallway, Peter took him on a tour through the small shiny kitchen, the messy bedroom, and the bathroom. In the open lounge room, he showed Mick the big table he'd bought to hold two PCs and to serve as his work area.

Above the work table hung a sign, the mission statement for his new business: Data, Analysis, Conclusions, Courage. Not that the work had poured in; the last two months had drifted by in a haze of court appearances, moving house, and movie dates with Mandy.

From the narrow balcony Peter pointed out the features of the soaring night skyline. Mick's vigorous physicality made the place feel constricted, and Peter felt nervous as he waited for the big man's reaction.

"Nice," Mick said with a blank face.

Peter changed into a suit and waited for Mick to emerge after a shower before announcing, "I've landed my second assignment."

The legal requirement for a Private Investigator's license was to work for an existing private eye for a year. So he'd registered Mick Tusk, trading under the name of Tusk & Gentle, and persuaded Mick to pretend to train him. A transparent façade, but somehow—perhaps Vinci helped, perhaps even his father—he was getting away with it. But soliciting work... that needed caution.

"Don't tell me," Mick said. His scrubbed face shone with health, and in his new, stern black suit, he could have been a corporate banker. "The genius behind the Human Genome Project has lost his memory."

"Get stuffed, you thug. No, it's a missing person."

They discussed the case as they headed out. It was a cold Monday evening in July, and the Draconi's waiters were taking advantage of the downtime before the dinner rush, some smoking out front, watching the Melbourne sky, others bantering with Hector.

At the bar, Peter studied his ex-partner. The hiss of the coffee machine rose and ebbed. Peter could see that Mick was apprehensive. Perhaps, he reflected, he was the only person in the world, Dana excepted, who could spot the signs. The blue eyes, not hidden because Harvey Jopling had banned sunglasses, blinked too often, and Peter watched with amusement the thick fingers struggling to remain still. And why not be tense? Tonight was a big night: Mick's induction into the Skulk Club.

If only Mick knew the machinations involved in getting an ex-policeman into the Club. Harvey and Peter had organised a special meeting of the Committee and a ring-around of all the members. Some had been openly derisive. Peter had been especially startled when one member protested on the grounds that it would take the number of members to thirteen, provoking bad luck.

"Are you sure you want to join?" Peter had asked Mick over the phone at the bleakest of moments. "You once described them as poncy, frivolous, overpaid yuppies."

"That was before I saw their altruistic sides," came the reply. "No, seriously, I liked them. And bugger it, I can't go on regretting lost copper mateship forever."

The convenient fiction that Mick would form half of city-based Tusk & Gentle certainly helped, for the Skulk Club was nothing if not a city club. But in the end, only Peter's personal pleas had won the day.

Peter inhaled the aroma from his black coffee. Yes, life felt fine. For good luck, he checked out his trophies, using the once-broken little finger to explore his jaw, to trace the scar on his arm, and to find the tiny white scar under his right eye.

"Something's been puzzling me," Mick said. "That day, when you nearly got killed. Why confront Straw alone?"

Peter suspected guilt underpinned the question. If Mick had deferred the partnership break-up, he would have been beside Peter at The Island.

What could he say?

He could say that for once he shelved his logical instincts and simply did what only he could do, explained that bravery isn't an attribute, bravery comes from acting bravely. Indeed, that was a notion he'd played with since the event.

"I don't know, big guy," he chose to say.

He felt Mick's eyes probe his face. Harvey signaled across the restaurant: time for the show to roll. Hector beamed by the door.

But Mick would surely laugh at the more prosaic truth. As the jostling and hand slapping and cursing and hugging commenced, as Draconi's sprang to life with a verve that tapped directly into the vitality of his great city, as Mick blushed, as cries of "Order! Order!" filled the blessed room, Peter fingered his forelock and looked back at that epochal morning.

Peter longed to explain to Mick that he'd traveled to that dark and doom-filled mansion in a kind of stupor. At long last the data was complete, the analysis watertight. And the conclusion, one that nobody would have believed had he suggested it, possessed a logic that sent him forward as if bewitched. He just had to find out. That he might be in danger... it simply never occurred to him.

He grinned. All eyes were focused on his behemoth mate. If only, if only... Peter couldn't avoid bitterness at Dana's vendetta against him. If only Tusk & Gentle was really Mick Tusk and Peter Gentle. An offbeat memory came to him as he began to clap. He recalled Mick catching him while they examined their first piece of data, Kantor Keppel's bludgeoned body. Thanks, Mick, he thought, thanks for being there.

Peter's voice squeaked when it joined the chant.

"Skulk! Skulk! Skulk!"

MEET THE AUTHOR

Hi,

Andres Kabel here, hoping you enjoyed *Deadly Investment*. I live in the wonderful Australian city of Melbourne, the metropolis in which Peter Gentle cogitates and Mick Tusk roams. By all means check out my website bio, but, really, all you need know is that writing this book has been a joy and a privilege, and that I'll scribe more volumes in the series (subject of course to the whims and fates of G & T!).

Now that you're done with my book, consider assisting me, would you please?

Firstly, jump onto your book retailer's website and leave a review. A rating and a few words are all that I need, though of course you can let loose with a torrent of elegant analysis. Do this even if *Deadly Investment* disappointed. Reviews - whether laudatory, indifferent, or caustic - are the lifeblood of the self-published author.

Secondly, stay in touch by visiting my website and leaving your email address for my occasional newsletter. I'll try my utmost not to burden or bore you, and I'll certainly never divulge your address.

There's more to me than Melbourne crime fiction. I write history! I blog! Come see:

AndresKabel.com

Big Decade (bigdecade.com) – my blog of a decade of aspirational obsessing.

Nuclear Power History (nuclearpowerhistory.com) – my blog of offcut snippets from my forthcoming book.

Facebook (also on Facebook – Big Decade and Nuclear Power History).

Lastly, don't hesitate to drop me a line on Andres@AndresKabel.com

MY THANKS

Let's commence with the beginning and end: Pam, my love, you've always walked hand in hand with me through every folly I've ventured into. This book is one such and I've treasured your support and feedback and honest advice.

Our children and their partners have always leapt to my aid when requested and often even when not. So all my heart's gratitude to Ashley, Daniel, Donna, Katie, Meg, and Pete (alphabetical order, right?).

Sven, no brother could have been as tender and stalwart in support as you. I only wish our brother Martin was still here to thank.

Let me beam gratitude to Frank Kennedy, whom I met at a Maui conference nearly two decades ago. Never a truer writing friend has a writer had. He's now ahead of me (two books out) but I shall catch up!

Nowadays we call them beta readers, friends who sacrifice time to read raw writing and offer feedback that results in the final words. You might not recognize that term, friends true and intelligent, but I owe appreciation to: Doug Boynton, Ann

Buchan, Jo Ann Daugherty, Ashley Kabel, Pam Kabel, Jill Kahans, Neil Lahy, Kevin Lewis, Caroline Petit, Andrew Sprague. Special thanks to Margaret Bennett who exhaustively dug into my words, phrases, sentences, and paragraphs - blessed was I.

Stephen Minns let me wander aimlessly around a bustling legal firm's offices. Bernard Lewis at the Victorian Coroner's Office enthused about the philosophy and work of that organization. Roberta Ivers at Random House gave me excellent advice on an early draft.

I experienced the greatest of pleasures in submitting Deadly Investment, chapter by chapter, to the rigors of the Inner City Writers. Because of this book's history, I took on board fewer of your suggestions than I will with future Gentle/Tusk tales but your contributions were massive anyway. Let me thank any ICWer who critiqued this novel but I must name some of the longer-serving writing talents: Siobhan Argent, Eddie Brauer, Jack Cassidy, Alisdair Daws, Marina Dobbyn, Neil Huybregts, Rachel Martin, Jock Read, and Fiona Skepper.

One of the unexpected frissons of jumping into the new age of publishing has been working with consummate, revolutionary professionals. Take a bow: copyeditor Dana Lee, proofreader Dj Hendrickson, cover designer Dane Low of Ebook Launch, and formatters Jason and Marina Anderson of Polgarus Studio. All you self pub'ers out there, snap up their services!